DEATH AND THE DEVIL

THE NOVELLAS

L.J. HAYWARD

Death and the Devil – The Novellas
Copyright © L.J. Hayward

Cover Art: L.C. Chase, lcchase.com
Layout: L.C. Chase, lcchase.com
Bargaining with the Devil Editor: Element Editing Services
When the Devil Drives Editor: Novel Solutions
Devil in the Details Editor: Novel Solutions

ISBN: 978-0-6487846-1-6

First Edition
April 2020

DEATH AND THE DEVIL

THE NOVELLAS

L.J. HAYWARD

WHERE DEATH MEETS THE DEVIL

Where Death Meets the Devil is a stunning debut. It hits all the right marks as a well-plotted, well-paced and well-written romantic suspense novel.
~ **RT Book Reviews**

Hayward ratches up the suspense in this action-packed piece, with constant twists and betrayals on all sides to keep things unpredictable. . . . Fans of tense action and smouldering romance will appreciate the emotional connection between Jack and Ethan; there's plenty of chemistry.
~ **Publishers Weekly**

The masterfully plotted dual-timeline and a swoonworthy assassin with a soft side hooked me from the start.
~ **Cordelia Kingsbridge**, author of *Kill Game*

An addictive, page-turning mix of high-stakes intrigue, edge-of-your-seat suspense, and slow burn romance. I couldn't put it down!
~ **Layla Reyne**, author of the Agents Irish and Whiskey, and Changing Lanes series

WHY THE DEVIL STALKS DEATH

This series gets better with each book! The pacing is great and shifting from one point in time to another is exquisitely done. I was literally hanging on every word and enjoyed each moment!
~ **Gay Book Reviews**

WHY THE DEVIL STALKS DEATH

Hayward is just masterful and these characters are so fascinating, this series is not to be missed.
~ **Joyfully Jay**

L.J. Hayward keeps you on your toes in this fast-paced, danger filled novel; it's a roller coaster ride of a sequel to Where Death Meets the Devil.
~ **The Novel Approach**

WHEN DEATH FREES THE DEVIL

While the suspense is what keeps these books so breathless, the heart of them is really Jack and Ethan. I have loved watching these men grow, both individually and together as a couple.
~ **Joyfully Jay**

Ms. Hayward has really put us through the ringer with twists and turns that kept us guessing at many things throughout this story. Needless to say, this was the perfect ending to an emotional and exciting suspenseful rollercoaster ride that I have never regretted picking up.
~ **Love Bytes Reviews**

I couldn't tear myself from the story. It was brimming with twists and turns causing adrenaline rush. It's ultimate thrill ride!
~ **MM Good Book Reviews**

TABLE OF CONTENTS

WHERE DEATH MEETS THE DEVIL: CODA

When he woke up, it was to the scent of strongly brewed tea...

Jack Reardon snapped upright. Where was Ethan? What was he doing? Why was he here?

Then he heard the shower and let out an explosive breath of relief.

Jack looked around his bedroom. He'd fallen face first on the bed late at night, the room blackened by blinds on the windows. Now, so much later, it was day and soft light filtered in around the blinds, highlighting all the things that hadn't been there when he'd gone to sleep. A pair of leather dress shoes by the door to the bedroom, suit pants and jacket on a hanger hooked to the front of his wardrobe and a weapons harness draped over the corner of his tallboy, two large handguns still in the holsters.

It *was* him. Ethan Blade. Notorious assassin, harbinger of chaos and bane of Jack's stomach lining. Case in point, the queasiness hit right on schedule, burning away the last groggy vestiges of sleep.

"Christ," Jack hissed. Not this again. Not so soon.

Scrambling out of bed, Jack hunted for something other than his underwear to be caught dead in. Because that was it. Despite the tea and the shower and the weapons just *fucking hanging right there*, there was a strong to very fatal chance this wasn't a friendly incursion.

The clothes Jack had discarded on his single-minded drive for the comforts of home weren't where he'd dropped them. They'd made a trail a blind person could have followed from front door to shower. The damp towel pooled on the floor at the foot of the tallboy with its open drawer described how he'd rummaged for a clean pair of boxer-briefs to sleep in. Now, the towel was gone and, yup, those were his dirty clothes neatly folded in the laundry basket.

That was a good sign, right? Ethan wouldn't have tidied up if he was just here to "finish the job," surely. Though, he *was* a bit fastidious about things being not so much tidy as *correct*. He would fiddle with his weapons harness until it lay absolutely perfect across his shoulders. Steeped his tea for an exact six minutes. Made his own ammunition. Planned every job down to the nth degree, even to the point of knowing exactly what would drive Jack crazy with paranoia . . .

On the surface, everything had seemed to end on a positive note. There was the smile and the teasing, not to mention the wink, but it wouldn't be the first time Ethan had plotted mayhem behind a sweet, innocent façade. Jack had, after all, betrayed him, derailed his plan and, potentially been the cause of Ethan spending the rest of his life in a prison cell. It could well be Ethan wasn't here for innocent reasons, but to finally get that revenge Jack had feared so many times in the desert.

Jack scrounged out a t-shit and was in the process of reaching for jeans when the shower shut off. The bathroom was just down the hall from the bedroom. He had maybe twenty, thirty seconds before Ethan emerged.

He considered grabbing one of the Desert Eagles from the harness but dismissed it quickly. Ethan would have planned for that move. There was the window. Jack had scouted an escape route along the outer wall, but again, Ethan had most likely thought of that. He could hide, catch Ethan in an ambush . . .

Who was he kidding? Running or fighting wasn't going to work. Jack may have managed to catch Ethan by surprise once or twice now, but the crazy bastard was on to those tactics. Would have anticipated them and planned accordingly.

The door to the bathroom opened and now he was down to ten seconds.

Going with the only option left, Jack tossed his hastily gathered clothes into the laundry basket and threw himself back onto the bed. He crawled into position, pushing the sheet down in what he hoped was an inviting tangle and leaned back against the headboard, ankles crossed, arms folded over his bare chest. Just in time, too, as Ethan appeared in the bedroom doorway.

With divinely sculpted muscles and smooth, pale skin, Ethan wasn't only ten different types of deadly, but at least that many types of sexy, as well. Not quite as tall as Jack, he had a long, lean perfectly proportioned frame, broad shoulders, narrow hips, sleek thighs and calves Jack could swoon over. His dark hair, damp from the shower, flopped over his forehead and water beaded on his upper arms. One of Jack's fluffiest towels was around his trim waist and a pair of grey socks were on his feet. Unarmed but not vulnerable.

"Ethan." Jack was immensely proud of how unaffected he sounded, as if assassins popping by his bedroom was old hat.

"Jack," he returned, equally cool. His half-lidded gaze skated down Jack's body and back up again, bringing with it a small, almost tentative smile. "You're home."

"Yeah. They finally let me go."

"I'm pleased. I did worry for you."

It sounded sincere and some of the uncertainty eased involuntarily. God. Jack may have decided how he felt about Ethan was okay. That desiring his body and enjoying his humour and intelligence wasn't a bad thing, but it was all part of a double-edged sword. He'd seen Ethan turn from warm and friendly to cold and deadly in an instant in the past. Jack might have missed the death blow, but he knew without a doubt Ethan had killed Samuel Valadian, a man Ethan had been fucking for weeks. And Valadian hadn't even betrayed Ethan. Jack had, and now he wondered if he'd survive it. Fuck, he wanted Ethan to say it was all good, but there was that lingering doubt.

"Thanks," Jack said. "Made Field Leader, as well."

Ethan's smile broadened into a grin. "Congratulations. You deserve it."

Again, it came across as believable and Jack really wanted it to be true. Hoped like crazy Ethan wasn't here for anything more than peaceful reasons. It wasn't so much that Jack didn't want to die, because he fervently didn't, but more that he wanted Ethan to understand why Jack had done what he'd done; that it was for the sake of not only the Office's security, but for Ethan's wellbeing as well. He didn't want Ethan's occasionally precarious grip on morality to be shaken by something Jack had done for all the right reasons.

Ethan brushed a drop of water off the exit-wound scar on his chest. "Field Leader. I presume this means you have more control over your deployments."

Jack blinked, trying to wipe away the image of Ethan's nimble fingers sliding over his firm pec. The thing was, it hadn't been a targeted assault on Jack's libido, but it blew out his carefully shored up foundations all the same. His dick thickened, and his belly warmed.

Damn Ethan for making him horny when he should be wary. And the towel was fluffy enough it hid any sign of Ethan's state of arousal.

"Um, yeah," Jack said. "Some control, not total autonomy. Get to pick my team, which Unit Leaders I work with. That sort of thing."

Ethan nodded and pushed away from the doorframe. One hand on the top of the towel, he came towards the bed. "That's good. It might make it easier."

Easier? What might be easier? But the power to form the words aloud was beyond Jack right then, because Ethan untucked the towel and let it drop to the floor.

The fluff had been hiding a definite interest in something other than a fight. Ethan might be a bit messed up, but he wasn't *that* messed up.

With another uncertain smile, Ethan came to Jack's side, paused, then slung his leg over Jack's thighs and settled down, straddling him. The cotton of his socks rubbed against Jack's bare legs and the feedback response in Jack was as unmistakable as it was in Ethan.

Swallowing the hard lump in his throat, Jack managed, "Make what easier?"

Ethan shifted forwards a little bit. "This." He ran his hands up Jack's arms to his shoulders, his strong fingers flexing as they brushed Jack's black curls.

"This?" Jack had to be sure. He'd been burned too badly in the past. "What, exactly, is this?"

Lips twitching into a smirk, Ethan said, "Exactly? Hmm, I suppose, *exactly*, it would be us, being together, for *this*." He nudged Jack's erection with his own.

This was hooking up? For sex?

It wasn't about revenge?

Clearly taking his stunned relief for overwhelming lust, Ethan pressed against Jack. One arm looped around Jack's neck, the other slipping down between them to tease the waistband of his undies. Christ. He smelt good. Warm skin, soap, musk and the growing scent of sex. Ethan wasn't faking. He was breathing deep and slow, but Jack could feel him shaking ever so slightly. No one was good enough to pretend that level of trembling control.

"For this," Ethan murmured against Jack's skin. "For sex and for everything you make me feel, Jack. For making me laugh and arguing with me. For challenging me and for supporting me." He kissed Jack's temple and added, "For mutual attraction and for losing control. And that is what I want, Jack, that I know I couldn't possibly get with anyone else. You treat me like a man, like a human, and you shag me like you want me to feel everything you feel. It . . . it makes me do the one thing no one else has ever managed to do. You make me forget what I am. Who I am. You make me believe there is something other than the job."

Jack's arms were around him without a conscious decision. Hands pressed to all that smooth, clean skin, he nuzzled his face into Ethan's neck, to get more of that enticing olfactory drug. His dick surged.

It would be so easy to just stop thinking, to let it all go as he had that first time in the cave, to forget there would be consequences and revel in the now, drown in the immediate pleasure and worry about breathing afterward. Ethan was warm, he was desirable, and when he was driven beyond control, amazingly wild and responsive and so fucking beautiful it was all Jack could do to keep from tying him to the bed so he'd never leave.

But there would be consequences. There already *were* consequences and Jack couldn't do this until they were sorted.

Finding a smidge of sense in the turmoil of lust and desperate need, Jack pulled back. He gripped Ethan's shoulders and held him away, needing the few precious inches now between them.

"Jack?" Ethan shook his dark hair out of his eyes and frowned.

Jack was half way certain the Office knew just how close he and Ethan had become. None of his counsellors or evaluators had directly asked if they'd fucked—though they probably would have said, "Did you and Omega Subject engage in any intimate contact?"—and yet Jack had walked away from a couple of debriefs wondering if they'd read between his words and seen what he hadn't said. A worry that may have been confirmed by Tan when he'd suggested Jack do what he could to "keep Ethan happy" in the hopes of luring the world-class assassin-cum-spy to work for the Office.

Even if they didn't already know, they would very quickly. There was nothing ambiguous about a naked man sitting on someone's lap. Not that the Office had cameras in Jack's apartment, but there was an unspoken understanding that working for the Office came with levels of observation. At work and in their private lives. It was passive surveillance—key-stroke monitoring; trigger words in phone and email communications; movement discrepancies—things any half-trained asset could counter, if they wished—which, in turn, was a red flag to their employers.

Even if he and Ethan were discreet, kept the sex to secure locations and didn't go out for romantic dinners, the Office would know. A fact Jack was all too keenly aware of. Which meant Ethan had to be, as well.

Ethan's unfathomable white eyes were half-lidded against the dim light, and the rest of his face was just as blank. But there were other bodily expressions it wasn't so easy to control. His dick, which had been hot and hard against Jack's belly moments before, had lost some firmness but still showed a decent measure of interest in things going in a more pleasurable direction.

It was a sound endorsement of Jack's own capitulating thoughts.

But there was something Jack needed spoken words for. Something more personal than the idea that they'd be watched, however distantly.

He let his hands slide down from Ethan's shoulders, fingers tracing over smooth skin and firm muscles.

Ethan remained still, wary but hopeful. "Jack?"

"Yeah," Jack said, more a confirmation of his presence than an actual answer, but he realised his mistake in the same moment Ethan mistook his meaning. "No," he added hastily, holding Ethan back as he tried to close the space between them again. "I mean, yes, but there's one thing first."

Settling back on his heels, Ethan took a slow, deep breath, then nodded. "Which is?"

Christ. This might have started with Ethan wanting sex, but it could very well end just how Jack had feared it was going to begin—with a deadly fight.

Jack took a fortifying breath of his own. "Are you okay with what I did at the Office? The way I . . . betrayed you."

Ethan's body went tight with tension. Just as Jack was looking for options to get the upper hand before Ethan did, the assassin grinned and relaxed.

"Betrayed . . .? Oh, yes. No, I am fine with it. You're forgiven, as I said in the cell. But honestly, there was nothing to forgive. Everything you did was perfectly understandable. Your plan worked amazingly well. I must apologise for doubting you when you suggested there was an alternative to my frankly unsophisticated plan of a frontal assault. You were right, I was wrong. Now, can we shag?" He punctuated it with a roll of his hips, brushing his dick over Jack's.

Jack blinked. Then blinked again, to give himself another second to parse the preceding babble. A jumble of over the top reassurances ending with a suggestion aimed for distraction.

This had happened once before, in the desert, when Ethan had got side-tracked talking about his cars. A mere twenty-four hours into their strange alliance and the dead-eyed killer had spilled his guts about something very personal to him. Back then, Jack didn't have the knowledge he did now.

Ethan was nervous. Nervous about how Jack would react to his unannounced appearance in his apartment. Nervous about Jack's response to the idea of "seeing" each other beyond the boundaries of their jobs. Nervous about what had happened in the Office. On *that* score, Jack should be—and was—the worried one, not Ethan. Which meant there was something else going on here.

It hit Jack hard. Not as hard as a rubber bullet filled with a tranq and tipped with a needle, but nearly.

"Holy shit! You crazy bastard." Jack shoved at Ethan.

Unprepared, Ethan tumbled back onto his arse on Jack's calves. Before he could do more than steady himself with hands on the mattress, Jack continued.

"You planned it all! You weren't serious about your 'frontal assault.' God, I'm so fucking stupid. I should never have believed you were serious about something that ... that ... obvious. You only made that *plan* so I would argue with you about it. So I would decide to do something different. You *wanted* me to betray you. Why, Ethan? Why the fuck would you put yourself in that much danger?"

Ethan went still, falling into the predator-mien that was his go-to when things went off kilter. A silence filled with his furious thoughts, assessing, countering, working out how to get things back on track. Then, with all the grace of a professional tumbler, he rolled over backwards off the bed and to his feet.

"Perhaps this wasn't a good idea, after all." Ethan turned for the wardrobe and his hanging clothes.

Was this the moment Jack pushed too much and Ethan snapped back? Maybe Ethan was right and this wasn't a good idea. Mind-bending sex out of the equation, his life would be immeasurably easier without Ethan in it. No more doubts about his loyalty to the Office or Meta-State. No shady agreements with Tan. No more moments like this one where Jack couldn't help pushing against an unstable killer but unable to stop himself all the same. No more ...

No. Fuck it. Not giving a shit about consequences was what saved him in the desert, what made Ethan stop looking at him as a target and begin seeing him as a person. What made Jack, in turn, stop thinking of him as nothing more than an assassin and realise there was so much more to Ethan Blade. A man who got nervous and babbled about cars. The scars on his back that told a silent story about violence excused as discipline. How he laughed at Jack's jokes. The way he made Jack smile. The almost innocent man under the hard exterior.

"No," Jack said, firm but calm. He got off the bed, ready to either fight or block Ethan's path to the door. "You're not going anywhere. I'm not putting up with this bullshit. Just tell me, Ethan. I need to know. Why did you do it?"

Already in his underwear, Ethan did stop. His back was to Jack, skin flushed with embarrassment or anger, making the whip scars stand out so much more than they already did. After a tense moment, he re-hung his pants and slowly turned around.

"I did it for you."

Jack nodded. "I gathered. But why?"

Ethan fixed his gaze over Jack's shoulder. "I thought if you were seen to be 'betraying' me to the Office, then it would help them trust you again."

"All right, but that's something we could have planned together, beforehand."

"No, we couldn't have. It had to be real."

"You know, I'm not that bad an actor. I managed to fool Valadian for fifteen months and would have kept it up if you hadn't blown my cover."

"Yes, I know. But . . . it had to be *real*. You had to betray me, Jack."

Maybe this was reason enough to let Ethan walk out for good. These Goddamned convoluted conversations where Ethan must believe he was making perfect sense but confused the hell out of Jack.

"Huh?"

Ethan sighed and some of the stiffness faded from his shoulders. "It's simple, Jack. I betrayed you at the compound. Now, you betrayed me at the Office. We're even."

Shit. Jack turned to the bed and sat, resisting the urge to implore God with raised fits and a plaintive, "Why me?" Instead, he took a few precious, deep, calming breaths.

"Jack?" Ethan took a couple of steps closer.

Jack held up a hand, holding him back. "I get it now. You felt you had to even the score. Okay, fine. But why?"

Frowning, Ethan considered this for a long while. When he spoke, it was soft and resigned, as if once he'd finished speaking, he would be getting dressed and leaving.

"I hurt you, Jack. In the desert. I used you. I've done it dozens of times. Picked a player in whichever game I was sent into, used them, sacrificed them, left them to whatever fate awaited them once I was done. When I was planning the Valadian job, I didn't know you. Not really. I studied your dossier and did a little digging on my own. I knew your strengths and your weaknesses, but I didn't know *you*. I didn't know how I would come to feel about you."

Jack had an insane urge to ask just *how* Ethan's feelings towards him had changed but kept quiet. He wasn't sure he needed to know without a doubt that in those first few days there had been a target on his forehead.

"For the first time, I didn't want to walk away from someone. I understand why you didn't come with me when I asked in the desert. You were angry about how I'd betrayed you. I know what you're like, Jack. I know that if you feel betrayed, you don't forgive easily, if at all. So, I thought if the tables were turned it would even things out and that this time, you wouldn't say no."

Elbows on knees, Jack rested his face in his hands. Pressed the heels of his palms into his eyes and tried not to growl in frustration.

Sure, he and Ethan weren't that different. Soldier and assassin. Both were weapons wielded by others, told where, when, how. Hands roughened by holding guns and knives. Bodies scarred by the enemy. Hearts hardened by too much bloodshed. Lips tightened by too many secrets. Emotions shielded by any means possible. Next to that common history was the present. They could laugh together, had shared some serious thoughts and yeah, there was bucket loads of mutual attraction. But here was a difference.

These crazy-arse *plans*. Ethan's convoluted reasoning. His warped expectations. Like he'd been waiting for Jack to pay him back, to double-cross him, because that was how Ethan's world worked. An eye for an eye, retaliation instead of forgiveness. Show no weakness. That, perhaps, the only way Ethan could imagine Jack wanting to be with him was to prove he was Ethan's equal, or stronger. When Jack didn't take it upon himself to even the playing field it had been up to Ethan to make it happen.

It wasn't that Jack couldn't understand the reasoning. He could, and that was the problem. If they did this mad thing—hooking up now the job was done, outside of any excuses other than *wanting* to—the problems they faced wouldn't just be the Office watching. Jack had his own issues. He'd been through too many psych evals and counselling sessions to be blind to them. But Ethan . . .

Jack was back at that intersection, facing down two different paths.

Beyond the darkness in his hands, Jack heard Ethan sigh and the soft rustle of fabric as he began to dress.

"I understand, Jack," he said. "I won't bother—"

Jack lunged off the bed and grabbed him around the waist. Stunned, Ethan took a moment, then struggled.

"Jack!"

Jack dropped him on the bed. Ethan bounced and clutched at the messy sheets to steady himself.

"Jack?"

"You idiot." Jack quickly clambered on top, straddling his thighs and grabbing his wrists. Holding tight with both knees and hands, Jack pressed Ethan into the mattress, firm but not harmful. "I suppose I shouldn't be surprised you don't do things normally. Have you ever done something the simple way in your entire life? Or is it all convoluted, over-thought plans? Do you wake up in the morning with a detailed itinerary for your day?"

"Yes, but—"

"No buts. Jesus, Ethan. Do you know how I felt about betraying you? I felt like shit. Not once, you dumbarse, did I feel like I was getting back at you. I thought what I did was going to be what drove you over the edge." Jack eased back on his grip a little bit. "It hurts me to admit it, but you're right. You burn me, I don't forgive easily. However, my sister hasn't said a civil word to me in years. She won't let me see, or even talk to, my niece, and I was so angry with her for so long. But not anymore. I know why she did what she did and I forgave her. It does happen." Letting Ethan's wrists go, Jack sat back on his heels and watched him for signs of escape.

Given the chance to break free, Ethan didn't take it. "Your SAS CO?"

"He's got no chance. I'll never forgive him for what he did."

"Director McIntosh?"

Jack shrugged. "I'm working on it."

Ethan hesitated, then gently rested his hands on Jack's thighs. "And me?"

Jack let him stroke his skin for a moment, then took hold of Ethan's hands and removed them from his legs. Ethan closed his eyes and sagged.

"And you?" Jack shook his head, realising now he had to back up his impulsive moves with logic. All he'd known at the time was Ethan was going to leave and he didn't want that. Jack wanted this, whatever it was between them, to keep going. And if that meant dealing with Ethan's twisted thought processes, then that's what he'd have to do. "You are a crazy bastard."

"Half right, Jack."

Jack smirked. "You keep saying that and I keep thinking you're wrong about the half part." To take any sting from the tease, he turned Ethan's hands over in his and ran his thumbs over his palms. "Yeah, I was angry about the shit in the desert. It always hurts to realise you've been lied to. Used. But that doesn't mean I haven't forgiven you. I didn't want to. I wanted to stay angry." Jack pinned Ethan's hands over his head again, then slowly slid down so he was lying over him. "I couldn't, though. You're far too sexy to kick out of bed."

Ethan trembled under Jack. "Is that all it is, Jack? Lust?"

He looked so vulnerable Jack had to tell the truth. "No." Then, because that scared him almost more than the thought of Ethan leaving for good, he added, "There's also mutual attraction." Emphasised with a slow, hard rub of his groin on Ethan's.

Ethan bit his lips, muffling a low moan. His hips pushed back and he wriggled his legs free so he could hook his feet over the back of Jack's thighs. "Yes, there is." Then, a touch warily, he asked, "So, we're even?"

Jack wanted to shake him again, say how they never had to get even in the first place, remind Ethan that two wrongs didn't make a right. But he didn't. Ethan knew all that and yet he still needed reassurance. Damaged innocence at its worst.

"Yeah," Jack whispered. "New slate and everything."

With a neat twist, Ethan had his hands free. He threw his arms around Jack's shoulders and buried his face in his neck, whole body trembling. Except for his dick, which was prodding Jack hard enough to bruise. Jack indulged for a long moment, breathing in the wonderful scent that was Ethan's skin and grinding against him. Then he pulled back, breaking Ethan's hold.

"Jack?"

"Naked, now."

Laughing, Ethan helped but the constant wiggling of his body while Jack hauled down his underwear didn't aid the process much. Stopping every couple of inches to kiss and touch, it took Jack an inordinate amount of time to rip the soft cotton boxer-briefs off over the grey socks. While he was down there, Jack rolled to his back and skimmed off his own undies, tossing them in wild abandon. Ethan laughed harder, but it choked off when Jack swiped his tongue up the length of Ethan's dick on his way back.

"Jack." Soft, breathy, warm.

He caught himself from falling on top of Ethan, holding himself up on his hands. Ethan lay back, sprawled across the mattress. Those eyes Jack thought he'd never get used to were half-lidded, as unreadable as ever. Everything else about him, however, spoke of lust and desire and need. From the flush in his cheeks to the way he caught his lower lip between his teeth; from the heaving of his firm chest to the hardness of his dusky nipples; from the roll of his hips to the feel of his stiff dick rubbing against Jack's stomach; from the clamp of his legs around Jack's hips to the way he dragged his calloused hands from Jack's shoulders, over his chest, across his belly and to the hard V of muscles arrowing downward.

"God," Jack hissed.

Yeah, Ethan was messed up, but so was Jack. Maybe this whole thing would implode in a spectacular eruption of clashing psychoses, or maybe it'd work despite them. The only thing to do was try.

Surrendering, Jack lowered himself slowly, pressing Ethan into the mattress. Ethan watched him as he got closer, his gaze darting from Jack's eyes to his mouth and back again. Jack had to swallow a sudden clot of moans that wanted escape at that very bad idea, but still he ended up nose to nose with Ethan, sharing the same breath, looking into those inestimable eyes. Ethan licked his lips, then gently, cautiously, raised his head. At the last possible moment, he tilted and kissed Jack's jaw under the corner of his mouth.

Such a palpable wave of relief washed over Jack he almost came on the spot. Other partners said they understood his choice not to kiss on the mouth, but still thought it on the table when things got hot and heavy. He shifted to give Ethan more room to play and shivered as the assassin nipped and mouthed his way towards Jack's ear.

Dipping his head, Jack licked a long line from Ethan's shoulder, up his neck and to just behind his earlobe. Ethan shuddered, then gasped as Jack sucked on the sensitive skin. The body under him rocked in response, Ethan's fingers digging into Jack's sides. A soft, pleading "Jack," rolled out of him. Hearing his name spoken so involuntarily, so helplessly, sliced through him like a blood-warm knife and Jack rocked his hips into Ethan's. Dicks collided, and sensation sparked. Both of them groaned, clutching at the other.

It had only been ten days. Jack had had drier spells. Yet this was too much. Too much heat, too much need, too much Ethan fucking Blade. He couldn't wait any longer, didn't want to talk anymore, didn't want to do anything other than fuck.

Jack propped himself up on one elbow, that hand fisted in Ethan's dark hair. The other gripped Ethan's hip, holding him down firmly. Hauling Ethan's head back until the long line of his throat was exposed, Jack attacked it with his mouth. Ethan quivered, his hands grasping at Jack, his whole body shaking with building pressure.

The gentle rocking of their hips shifted into something more insistent, needier, thrusting at the other with almost violent force. The rough catch and pull of dry skin burned but neither seemed to care, too caught up in the sensations of each other's bodies.

Ethan's legs hitched higher on Jack's waist, pushing his groin up harder and Jack's shaft slid into the tight space between Ethan's thigh and groin. The added pressure and heat blazed through Jack's dick and balls, tightening his guts. His thrusts lost their steady rhythm as he strained against Ethan's body, knees digging into the mattress for extra leverage. The tension coiling in his hips increased to almost painful levels.

"Fuck," he moaned into Ethan's shoulder, the impending orgasm building in leaps and bounds but feeling *just out of reach*. "Ethan, fuck...I gotta...*God!*"

Ethan's hands were everywhere. On his back, his arms, his shoulders, sliding down his spine to grasp his arse. He was chanting Jack's name, mouth against his temple. Jack didn't hear the words, but he felt them as if they bypassed his ears and travelled into his brain through skin and bone.

Then Ethan did *something*. Something with his legs, or his hips, or his busy hands . . . or all of them, but Jack didn't care to find out because suddenly he was coming in a blinding, deafening rush.

Gasping for air and sanity, Jack buried his face in Ethan's neck, breathing in deep of the sweat and musk, his body thrumming with the echoes of his orgasm. His hips still rocked, but slower, satiated, just riding the lingering heat and pleasure until he got too sensitive to stay pressed against Ethan.

Under him, Ethan moaned and stroked his hands down Jack's back, ending on his arse. He gripped it tightly. "Jack, don't stop. I'm ..."

Jack moaned, feeling Ethan still hard, still needy. "It's your own fault," he grumbled. "You're the one who did ... that ... thing." Even thinking about it made his head spin with the lingering bliss of his orgasm.

Almost whimpering with frustration, Ethan rolled beneath him. "I didn't think you'd go that quick."

Burrowing deeper into Ethan's skin, Jack mumbled, "Again, all your fault."

"Ah, deflecting blame once more." The attention-seeking buck of his hips belied his wry tone. With a rumbling groan, Ethan resorted to pleading. "Jack, *please.*"

Jack turned his head so Ethan wouldn't feel him smile. *That* was the begging he wanted to hear. He rocked a little harder and Ethan nodded, murmuring encouragement. So Jack pulled back.

"No." Ethan pulled him close with his legs.

"Let me go," Jack said against his throat. "Or I can't get a hand down there."

With gratifying speed Ethan's legs unlocked and dropped. He was wriggling in frustration, panting with the effort of not letting go. Jack shifted enough to expose Ethan's dick. He slid one of his legs over Ethan's, pinning him to the mattress so he couldn't get away. One hand still twined in Ethan's hair, he reached down and stroked his hard dick, watching Ethan arch into the touch. Small, begging noises were escaping him now, his hands fisting against whatever they found—Jack's arm, his back, the sheet, his own mouth to keep the debauched sounds in.

Jack kept his touches light, teasing, drinking down the sight of Ethan losing control. He wasn't sure what he preferred, Ethan wild from the start, bucking and uncoordinated, his voice broken and desperate; or this, the slow eroding of the outer armour, the joy of doing anything and everything he wanted to this man just to get here, to the sweet explosion of innocent wonder at the power of his pleasure.

"Jack, please . . . I need . . . just do it!"

Nearly there. Jack leaned in and kissed his way across Ethan's clavicle, to the hollow at the base of his throat. Christ, he tasted so fucking good. He was already feeling twitches in his dick, expressing its intention to do this again very soon.

Realising he'd lost track of his plan, Jack lifted his head and checked on the progress.

Ethan's eyes were squeezed shut, mouth open as he struggled for air in short, shallow pants. His hips were thrusting against Jack's hand, only Jack's restraining leg keeping him in touch with the bed. But it was still controlled, a deliberate effort to get Jack to do something serious.

If that's want he wanted . . .

Jack closed his hand around Ethan and stroked hard.

Ethan lost it. His eyes flew open, back arching as a broken gasp tore from his throat. As he crashed to the mattress, he clutched at Jack. "Now, now."

Christ. Jack couldn't deny such pure desperation any longer. He tightened his hold and gave Ethan what he needed.

Ethan came with a silent gasp, back arching sharply, fists pulling up acres of sheet. He was so unrestrained, so bloody beautiful in his unfocused release, Jack caught him up and smothered his neck and chest with hot, hard kisses. He stroked the violently trembling body until it gentled against him, every muscle going slack with exhaustion.

When Ethan stopped trembling, Jack loosened his hold and let him roll to his back. Jack lay half on, half off, little ripples of growing desire spreading at the feel of this warm, slick body against his.

They lay in gentle silence, both slowly catching their breath. Finally, Ethan lifted his hand and trailed his fingers down Jack's shoulder and along his arm. At Jack's hand, he brushed the curled fingers, then made the journey back up. Jack shivered at this simple caress.

"So." Ethan's voice was rough and dark and delicious. "Does this mean you won't slam the door in my face if I appeared on your doorstep?"

Jack chuckled into Ethan's chest. "If you appeared on my doorstep, I'd likely have a heart attack. Rather, I'd probably come home one day and find you already inside, naked and waiting with a bow around your dick."

"Hmm." The sound of an idea being sown.

Slapping Ethan's hip lightly, Jack muttered, "That wasn't a request."

No verbal response, just another slow caress.

Another length of pleasant time later, Jack moaned and peeled himself off Ethan. "We should get cleaned up."

"Yes, I suspect we should." Ethan didn't move. Didn't even open his eyes.

"Don't worry." Jack patted his belly. "I'll do it."

"It would be appreciated."

On legs that only shook slightly, Jack stumbled to the bathroom, cleaned himself up, dampened a handtowel and brought it back to the bedroom. Tossing the towel on Ethan, he rummaged through the bedside table drawer. While Ethan lazily wiped himself down, Jack triumphantly held up a box of condoms.

"Still in date, even," he announced, flopping down beside him.

Ethan rolled over, his back to Jack. He reached back and hauled Jack's arm across his shoulders, pulling until Jack was snugged right up behind him.

"How fortuitous," he murmured, voice thickening towards sleep.

"If they hadn't been, I do have latex gloves somewhere."

Ethen snorted a laugh. "I do enjoy creative solutions." He pulled Jack a little closer and all but melted into the mattress.

"Hey," Jack said before Ethan could drop off. "There's something I want to ask you, but I don't want to cause an argument."

With a sleepy little mumble, Ethan said, "I promise not to argue. What did you wish to know?"

Propping himself up on an elbow, Jack looked down at the peaceful, innocent expression and believed it. These were the moments that made all the rest worth it. Not just post-coital, but that helped. More, it was the absence of masks or artifice and no agenda beyond being right here, right now.

He almost didn't want to ruin it by bringing this up, but he had to know.

"When you first came in to the Office, they stripped you down and washed you while you were knocked out."

Ethan's lips pursed. "Something I am very glad I was asleep for the first time. The next time, it was incredibly hard to go along with. Did you know, according to one of the Office assets whose task it was to wash me the second time, I am 'sin waiting for a place to happen'?"

Jack internalised the snicker but couldn't keep from smiling. "No, I didn't know that. I'm sure he or she is rather embarrassed by that now, knowing you were awake the whole time."

"One can only hope. Is that what you wanted to know?"

"No, but now I do, cheers. What I really want to know is this . . ." Jack stroked the naked body pressed to his from shoulder to hip and back again. "Where did you hide the data stick with the spyware you planted in the Office?"

Ethan was quiet for a moment, then turned to look up at Jack with a wink and smirk. "I could give you a hint."

"No, no, no." Jack buried his face in Ethan's shoulder. "Not that again. Just tell me."

Relaxing his whole body, Ethan snuggled into the pillow. "A man must retrain some mystery, Jack. If you want to know, you'll have to work it out for yourself. If you wish to shag again, you'll let me rest."

Shit! Jack really wanted to know, but he didn't want to have to puzzle it out on his own. After a silent battle of wills with himself, he finally accepted that there was something he wanted more than an answer—Ethan in his life.

Jack pushed his groin against his arse. "You get fifteen minutes to rest. Make the most of it."

Ethan laughed, and it was the longest fifteen minutes of Jack's life.

BARGAINING WITH THE DEVIL

DEATH AND THE DEVIL #1.4

BARGAINING WITH THE DEVIL

Meta-State spy Jack Reardon believes it's all been taken care of. He has his verbal agreement with his boss to "keep Blade happy," and Jack is more than willing to do his best in that regard. He also has his bargain with Ethan, to keep seeing each other whenever they cross paths. Small victories, interspersed with exploding bombs, smashed cars, and miffed co-workers, all while consorting with an international assassin.

Contract killer Ethan Blade values his security, and Jack's the first time he's found that with another person. Wiring a warehouse or outback shelter for safety, no problem. Keeping safe a prickly ex-soldier-turned-spy who's a magnet for trouble, not so easy. Instead of faceless, nameless jobs, he's poking his fingers into Jack's cases—a car bomb gone awry, a Hen party gone wild—much to Jack's mounting dismay.

They have a deal; neither one of them can seem to stick to it. It's Jack versus Ethan as the two men learn to navigate their ever-evolving not-a-relationship without losing the benefit of the bargain.

BARGAINING WITH THE DEVIL

(JANUARY)

Jack Reardon stood in the doorway to his bedroom, one hand at his throat and his half-loosened tie forgotten as his brain struggled to comprehend the scene before him.

Barely three weeks before, he'd finally been cleared of any serious breaches of protocol over the whole Blade–Harraway mess. Apparently, working with an international assassin to expose a traitor who'd had access to some of the world's most volatile secrets went a long way to smoothing things over with upper management. Not being fired, or convicted of treason, also went a long way to keeping Jack's career—and life—on track. Even if it was now infinitely more complicated, as evidenced by the scene before him.

After being released from building confinement, he'd come back to his Leichhardt apartment only to have Ethan Blade appear in his home, armed with a proposal Jack had been unable to say no to. Namely, whenever they were in close proximity they'd get together and fuck. Ethan had said he rather enjoyed the way Jack made him feel and wanted more of it. Jack had agreed wholeheartedly—well, *mostly* wholeheartedly—and they'd given the arrangement a practice run for three days before Ethan had vanished as stealthily as he'd arrived.

During the intervening weeks, Jack's doubts about the situation had risen and fallen like the tide. Still, he'd thought he would've had enough time and space to sort out his feelings about it before he saw Ethan again. He certainly hadn't believed the agreement would pay out so soon.

But it had, in the form of a naked man on his bed. A long, lean stretch of pale skin, dark tousled hair, sexy smirk, socks, and a red ribbon tied in a bow around . . . around his . . . his . . . Jack pried his gaze from the bow before his head exploded. He focused on something safer.

"Still with the socks." Damn it. He'd wanted something suave and smooth, something to show he wasn't one swallow away from being a drooling Neanderthal. At least the words were comprehensible and in a logical order. Small victories.

Ethan's smirk morphed into a disarmingly shy smile. "Honestly, Jack. That's what you focus on?"

Attention drawn like a magnet back to that bow, Jack had no fear of drooling now. His mouth was suddenly as dry as the Great Sandy Desert.

It had started as a thoughtless comment—*I'd probably come home one day and find you already inside, naked, and waiting with a bow around your dick*—Jack had blurted in a postorgasmic haze. He'd realised his mistake at the time, and had tried to steer Ethan around it, all the while knowing he may as well let it go. Getting in the way of Ethan's compulsion to finish any job he started never ended well.

Honestly, this wasn't one Jack wanted to derail.

"Well?" Ethan asked.

"Well," Jack mimicked, toeing off his shoes and loosening his tie further, "guess I better unwrap my present."

Tip of his tongue slipping between his lips, Ethan arched his back. The low light of the bedside lamp glided across his smooth chest and slid down over his rippling abs and further, to glance across the satin ribbon in its ridiculous bow.

Jack took the couple of steps required to bring him to the foot of the bed. He paused for a moment, breathing hard at the abrupt surge of need thrumming through his veins. His dick thickened from half hard to fully erect instantly. He warred between undressing or getting his hands on the perfect body before him. It wasn't a difficult choice.

There was something deliciously debauched in being fully dressed while he teased Ethan's naked skin to shivering sensitivity and his muscles to twitchy excitement. From his shoulders down to his hips, across his thighs to the tender, reactive backs of his knees. All the way along his firm, swoon-inspiring calves to his cotton-encased feet. Flipping him over, Jack made his way back up, taking his time to remember proven means and methods and explore new options. Ethan squirmed and moaned, wriggled one way and writhed the other. He pushed into this and pulled from that, then begged for more of both.

When Jack rolled him back over, Ethan was loose and relaxed, eyes half lidded, hands drifting in slow waves over Jack's face and neck, skin to skin.

"I've missed this," Ethan said softly.

The touching, tone, and expression made Jack wonder what Ethan was referring to—his face or the foreplay. Either option had Jack squirming. He had decided how he felt about Ethan was okay. This man wasn't only an assassin, but an animal-loving, fast-car enthusiast whose odd innocence sparked a protective need in Jack. With that in mind, he hoped Ethan was referring to the foreplay. But he also hoped he wasn't.

Jack went with the option he was absolutely certain about.

"Yeah?" He rolled his hips over Ethan's, hard shafts rubbing together, the fabric of Jack's pants hissing over the satin ribbon. "But it's only been three weeks and we haven't even got to the good stuff yet."

Ethan moaned and arched his back, seeking more friction. "I don't care how long it's been, Jack, or what we do. I just need you." He wound his arms around Jack's neck and drew him closer, gaze flicking down to his lips, then back to Jack's eyes. "I don't mind that you won't kiss me on the mouth or that it may be months before we can see each other again. I don't even care that the directors of the Office may know about us. All that matters is that I know *you*, Jack. I know you won't hurt me or betray me." Smirking, he added slyly, "Without good reason, at least."

Jack's heart thumped painfully, as if it were trying to send him a message via Morse code, or about to explode. Christ. The complete trust Ethan put in him never failed to surprise Jack. That level of vulnerability was intoxicating. Far too intoxicating, especially knowing—*hoping*—that Jack was the only one who got to experience

Ethan this way. It almost made Jack forget his belief that kissing mouth to mouth was the most intimate and loving thing a person could do. Almost, but not enough.

Avoiding that dangerous temptation, Jack slid down Ethan's body and off the end of the bed. He tugged Ethan towards him until his arse was on the edge of the mattress, spread thighs to either side of Jack. His present awaited him in its red ribbon, hard and nicely thick.

"Jack?" Ethan propped himself up on his elbows. "Is something wrong?"

Jack ran his hands up and down Ethan's thighs, studying his target. "Just planning."

"Planning what?"

"How I'm going to unwrap my present."

There was a sweetly perplexed smile on Ethan's lips. "It's a simple bow, Jack."

"I know, but it's been a while. I mean, I used to be pretty good at tying cherry stems in knots with my tongue, but I haven't done that for, fuck me, at least fifteen years."

Eyes widening, Ethan said, "Your tongue?"

"Yeah. How else am I supposed to get the damn ribbon off?"

"Like this, perhaps?" Ethan went to grab a trailing end of red.

Jack slapped his hand away. "Where's the fun in that?" He dipped down and licked up the enticing length before him; his tongue bumped over the slick ribbon. "This way is going to be so much better."

"Jack, I didn't do this to make you . . ." Ethan moaned, sounding both resigned and guilty as Jack slid his lips over the wet head of Ethan's dick. He gasped when Jack's tongue flicked over the sweet spot on the underside of his glans. "Jack, I–I– you don't . . . ngh!"

Mouth popping off the end, Jack peppered kisses across Ethan's groin. "Do you want me to stop?"

After a strangled moment, Ethan ground out, "No."

Jack smiled like a cat seeing a mouse. "Right. Time to get serious."

Ethan's groan of despair quickly turned into one of startled pleasure, and Jack aimed to keep it that way.

The alarm went off and Jack grumpily tossed himself onto his belly. It was far too early to get up. Especially when he'd stayed up so late. Why had he . . . ? Oh. Ethan was here. Even as the beeping continued, he snuggled into the mattress, pleasant memories of the night before enriching his awake state. God, Ethan had been amazingly receptive and responsive; wonderfully unhinged. After Jack had got the ribbon undone—orally—he'd claimed his present fully. Just remembering that, and the fun shower after, had Jack aching for more before he had to go back into work.

With a directed thought, Jack silenced the alarm from his neural implant—all the connectivity and applications of a phone without the clunky handset—and pushed up to his elbows. He half expected to be alone in the bed. The first time Ethan had come to his apartment the man had barely slept. Granted, neither had Jack. They'd napped between sessions and Jack had slept deeper for a couple of hours at a time on several occasions over the three days, but Ethan had been restless, prowling around the apartment while Jack slept. He did the dishes from their quick meals, washed clothes, tidied the kitchen cabinets, cleaned the bathroom. He'd said he liked to keep busy.

So it was slightly surprising to find Ethan in bed. He was sprawled on his back, one arm and leg exposed, a small trail of drool from the corner of his slightly parted lips to the pillow. There was even light snoring.

Jack smiled. It was cute. Ethan Blade, wanted assassin, drooled in his sleep. Cute, but Jack didn't want cute right then. He wanted awake and moaning and thrusting.

"Hey, Blade. Rise and shine." He prodded his shoulder.

No response.

Jack leaned in, mouth next to his ear. "Ethan," he said softly. "Eeethaaaan."

Nothing.

After a moment's thought, Jack tried, "Paul. Paaauuul."

The silence was broken only by a couple of snores.

Time to bring out the big guns. Jack stroked his hand from Ethan's shoulder, over his pec and down his abs to rub little circles on his hip. "Ethan, come on. Wake up."

A twitch in one hand, like he might swat at whatever was touching him, but that was all.

For five minutes Jack tried gentle caresses and sexy beseeching, all the while slowly increasing in volume. The biggest response was that Ethan partly rolled over. Then Jack tried overt options. Talking louder, rocking him, picking up his arm and letting it drop like a dead weight. None of it worked. If he hadn't been breathing, Jack would have suspected death from sexual exhaustion. Perhaps it was weariness from whatever job he'd been on before sneaking into Jack's apartment. Jack wasn't sure he wanted to know for sure, though, so he got up, dressed, left a note on the bedside table, and went to work.

Since his promotion to field leader, Jack had been mired in additional training. Most of it consisted of online seminars and instructional videos. He had weekly meetings with a psychologist to learn how to "manage" people. Three years as an SAS lieutenant wasn't experience enough, apparently. He was also being pestered into choosing a second. As a new field leader, Jack's permanent team was limited to him and a second. They'd grab any extra hands they needed on a jobtojob basis. There was a lot more interest in the position than Jack had thought likely. Apparently, people liked the idea of working with the man who'd not only brought in Ethan Blade, but broke him out and then hauled him back in again, all so they could expose a traitor within the Office of Counterterrorism and Intelligence—known simply as the Office.

Then there was the continuing investigation into the network of contacts Samuel Valadian had been part of. Jack still consulted with the team every now and then, as well as with the new investigation into Ethan Blade. After his brief but eventful sojourn with the Office, gathering information on Ethan had increased from a passive interest to a very active one. The team handling it often sought Jack out for his insight or opinion.

At the end of an uneventful day, he'd barely thrown his leg over the seat of his black Kawasaki Ninja when the lingering contemplation of the latest applicant—a guy out of the Auckland branch, recruited from the police force eighteen months ago—dropped away and the thought of getting a return blowjob from Ethan took over. It hadn't happened yet, but perhaps that was because Ethan needed Jack to ask for it. Ethan could still be a bit hesitant about asking for what he wanted, but when he got the courage or was just manic with lust enough to take it—those were some of the most amazing moments ever.

The anticipation only grew and he was half hard when he unlocked the door to his apartment and went in. Only the lamp on the far side of the room was on, enough light for Jack to see well enough, and not so bright Ethan needed his glasses. It felt very promising and as Jack set his helmet on the kitchen counter, he wondered if he would find Ethan as he had last night, naked and seductive.

He didn't.

Before Jack had taken two more steps, Ethan appeared from the hallway leading to the bedrooms and bathroom. He was dressed in a dark suit and straightening his cuffs. As he lifted his arms, his shoulder rig was visible, as were the butts of his Desert Eagles.

Unless Ethan had some sort of kink this was looking less promising.

"Going somewhere?" Jack asked mildly.

"Yes. I have to leave." Ethan came towards the door, the dark panes of his sunglasses aimed at Jack but who knew where he was looking.

"Last night you said you were here for at least two nights."

"I did, but I'm afraid something has come up."

Jack sidled in front of the door. "Really? You're just going to leave?"

Ethan stopped a couple of paces back. Hands at his sides, he appeared nonthreatening. Jack knew better and, honestly, anyone who knew better would move and let the man go, but Jack hadn't got this far by taking the safe path.

"Yes. I did wait long enough to tell you in person, though." There was a slight edge to the words that grated on Jack for some reason.

"Well," he muttered, "that's a change. Last time you just left without a word. No note, no message." Jack hadn't been bothered by it at the time because they'd made their arrangement and he knew he would be seeing Ethan again at some point.

"Hmm." Just how Ethan managed the same bite with a single sound as he had with a whole sentence was beyond Jack. "I thought I owed it to you to tell you in person that I don't think our arrangement is going to work. I'm sorry but I won't be coming to see you again."

Jack gaped. When Ethan had first proposed this mad idea, Jack had had a few moments of doubt, mostly to do with the Office inevitably finding out he and Ethan were still in contact—intimate contact. But he had Director Tan's verbal agreement to "keep Blade happy" to fall back on, and Ethan had said himself that he didn't care about the Office knowing. So why the fuck was it suddenly over? What had happened to make Ethan change his goddamned mind? Had Jack just imagined all his talk about trust and safety?

Christ! Maybe this was for the best . . . No. This wasn't going to happen. At least it wouldn't happen without a decent explanation. Jack just had to stay calm and rational.

"What the hell?" Jack demanded. So much for that decision. "You seemed pretty well entrenched last night." To the point of falling asleep right on top of Jack.

Ethan didn't go as still as he often did when confronted with opposition to his plans. Instead he shoved his hands in the front pockets of his pants. With his shoulders slightly hunched he looked more defensive than hostile.

"That was last night," he said. "I've since changed my mind. I'd like to leave. There's a travel window I can take advantage of if I go now."

Jack realised then what disturbed him about everything Ethan had said so far. The intention to leave for good was aggravating and frustrating, but not exactly disturbing. No, what was bothering Jack was that Ethan hadn't said his name. Not once since Jack had walked in. Right from the start, Ethan had been relentless in using Jack's name. It had been mildly unsettling at first, but when Jack had learned just what Ethan was doing in the desert, it had become clearer. Dehumanising someone by not giving them a name, by referring to them as a number or code, made it easier to do whatever nasty thing needed doing. In order to convince Jack he wasn't a target, Ethan had used his name and somewhere along the way, it had stuck. Its absence now was telling. Ethan was looking for emotional distance, which meant he wasn't totally convinced leaving was the right thing to do.

Jack modulated his next words a bit more successfully than he had before. "I'd prefer it if you stayed. We don't have to fuck or anything.

But you said you could stay two nights, so please stay. We can talk about why you changed your mind."

Ethan did go still then, but only for a moment, breaking it when he took a deep breath and looked away. "And I'd rather just leave."

Retreating to the door, Jack leaned on it, crossed his arms, and settled in for a fight. "Unless you want to smash out through a window, you're not going anywhere." They both knew Ethan could get past Jack without raising a sweat. It wouldn't be the first time Ethan had pulled a gun on Jack, and if he fired . . . well, that wouldn't be a first, either.

"That won't stop me," Ethan said grimly.

Jack grinned. "Slow you down, though. Come on, Ethan. Tell me."

"I don't have to tell—"

"You said you owed me a facetoface goodbye, so I think that means you owe me a facetoface reason. What's changed?"

"I misspoke. I don't owe—"

"Do I need to list the reasons why *you* wanted this? One, mutual attraction, and unless I grew a ginormous wart overnight, I think that's still legit. Two, for making you laugh, which you did in the shower when I made you a shampoo beard. Three, for arguing with you, example this discussion right now. Four, the mind-blowing sex. You're a control freak and need me to drive you out of your head so you can relax, and you were pretty fucking relaxed last—"

"Jack."

It was low and lethal sounding and would make most others duck for cover, but Jack had to stop himself from fist-pumping in victory. His name. At last.

"Yes, Ethan?" he said evenly.

A grinding ten seconds of silence, then Ethan let out a frustrated grunt. It wasn't often he showed even a hint of losing control, outside of bed, and usually it wasn't something to cheer about, yet Jack took it as another little victory. Turning on his heel, Ethan stalked over to the balcony. Back to Jack, he stood to the side of the glass sliding door and looked out over the sparkling Sydney skyline.

Jack took the time to think back on what Ethan had said, how he'd reacted, and came to a disappointing conclusion.

"Is it the sex? Was it something I did?" He bit back a "you didn't say no." No one liked hearing that when they'd changed their mind for whatever reason.

"No." It was a bit too fast for Jack to credit it, but Ethan added, "Not exactly," in a resigned tone.

Stomach swirling uneasily, Jack closed a bit of the distance between them. This would probably go better with lowered voices. "What did I do wrong?"

"Nothing. I mean that, Jack. It's not you."

Fuck. The whole it'snotyouit'sme routine? Jack really wouldn't have thought it a line Ethan ever had to trot out before. According to him, his past sexual experiences had usually ended when his target— not necessarily the person he'd slept with—was eliminated. Ethan wouldn't have needed a convenient excuse to leave. So, perhaps he honestly meant it.

"Tell me," Jack prompted.

Ethan ducked his head and said softly, "I won't fellate you, Jack."

It took a moment to register and Jack had to get confirmation. "Pardon?"

Letting out a sharp breath, Ethan said in a clear voice, "I don't like performing fellatio. It has never been something I was comfortable with. Everything else is fine, but that . . . I'm sorry, Jack, but I won't and as such, I feel you shouldn't fellate me, either. It's unfair."

Jack digested that. "Okay. That's fine. Some men don't like doing it. I'm not going to insist or bother you about it. It's your choice. But is that reason enough to leave?"

"No. It's something I worried about, though. Before I decided to end this."

Crap. They hadn't even got to the big issue yet.

Jack ran a hand over his face. "Just to be clear about this. I love giving blowjobs, and I know you like getting them. So, when we clear up this other thing and get back to the original *arrangement*, I'll keep blowing you, you'll keep going crazy when I do, and neither of us will care that it doesn't happen the other way around. Trust me, you do plenty of other things to make me incredibly happy."

Ethan turned and, surprisingly, slipped off his glasses so he could look at Jack with his pale, unchanging eyes. "Truly?"

It would have been nice to touch him, to pull him close and show him how true it was, but despite the lowering of the shades, Ethan held himself stiff. No touching allowed.

"Stick around and find out for yourself."

The corner of his mouth quirked up and vanished as soon as it had appeared. "It's good to know that, Jack, but it won't change my mind. This isn't going to work. I can't be here with you. I don't feel ..."

It was like pulling hens' teeth. "Don't feel what?"

"Secure." Now it was out, the tension eased from Ethan's shoulders and the dam busted. "When I woke up this morning and you weren't here, I felt vulnerable. This isn't one of my safe places, Jack. You have very rudimentary locks on your doors and windows. It wouldn't even stop a determined novice. Then there's the Office."

"None of that bothered you before." Even as he said it, Jack knew where the difference was.

"I didn't fall asleep last time," Ethan snapped. "I didn't feel so comfortable then, or like I belonged here. Or so happy to simply lie there with you that nothing else mattered." He bit off the last word with a sharp clack of teeth as if realising what he'd said, or how plaintive he sounded.

Jack had never been so thrilled and annoyed at the same time. Despite the delivery, Ethan's words of being comfortable and happy with him sent delighted shivers through his belly. But annoyed because his head reverted to thinking maybe Ethan was right and they should forget about their arrangement. Jack didn't want to. God, he really didn't want to, but reasonably there was a point where a good orgasm wasn't worth the trouble of getting it.

He opened his mouth to say as much but closed it before he could.

It wasn't just the sex. That was part of it, a great part, but a lot of it was the man standing in front of him. This puzzling creature who'd wormed his way past Jack's defences with an odd mix of cold-blooded ruthlessness and innocence; who'd done his best to break Jack down, then done all he could to rescue him. A man with compulsions born of a traumatic childhood, scars from a life of violence and cruelty, with such a soft spot for animals that he was willing to let a wild dingo attack him. Someone who, once he was on a path, wouldn't deviate from it. Someone who broke his own rules because Jack refused to follow them.

Getting to know that man was worth it.

"Stay there." Jack pointed firmly at the spot Ethan stood. "Don't move."

Jack went to the kitchen and put the kettle on. While it boiled, he got out a mug and teabag, and then a beer. Ethan drank beer and wine, but Jack knew when he needed to settle down, it was tea. Once the tea was made, Jack motioned him over to the table. They sat opposite each other, their drinks on coasters which looked like various pistols. They'd been a happygettingintotheSAS gift from his old infantry CO. Jack wondered if Ethan had anything like them. Not coasters, but gifts with enough sentimental meaning they lasted through several moves, a career change, and moments you were so furious with the organisation that chewed you up and spat you out that you could think only of destroying everything it had ever given you.

"Tea okay?" he asked instead.

"It's drinkable."

Jack smiled, which made Ethan's lips curl up just a bit as well.

"Well, what are we going to do about this?"

Ethan sighed. "I don't think there is anything we can do, Jack. Our lives simply aren't compatible."

Jack took a sip of beer. "Our work lives, sure. But we're not working together anymore, so that's a non-issue."

"No. It *is* the issue. Director Tan might want to keep me agreeable to working with the Office for his own reasons, but that isn't going to help me if someone else from *your* work has already killed me because I was here with you, asleep and unable to defend either of us."

Putting aside the argument he could defend himself *and* Ethan, Jack agreed. Nothing he'd done this morning had woken Ethan. He could easily imagine someone getting into his apartment and having no trouble shooting Ethan when he was like that.

"Okay, let's look at the other part of it," Jack offered. "What security measures would you add to this place to help you feel safer?"

Tea halfway to his mouth, Ethan stalled for a moment. Then he lowered it to the table. "You would do that for me?"

"Sure. I never worried before because the only sensitive stuff here is in my head, but it wouldn't hurt to have another lock on the door."

"I'm not talking about another lock, Jack. I mean surveillance on the front door and pressure mats at the windows and balcony. Motionbased sensors in every room. A tap into any electronic security systems this building has."

"The Office will install—"

"Not the Office. If they install it, they'll control it."

"True. So, do you have an associate who can do all that?"

Ethan shook his head. "I can do it. I've done it myself in all of my safe places. But that won't be enough, Jack."

"Yeah, I know." Finishing his beer, Jack thought for a moment. "Look, stay tonight. I won't tire you out in bed. In fact, I'll banish you to the couch. Give me tomorrow to see what I can do about the Office, then we'll see where we are. Yes?"

Ethan swirled his tea around the mug for a moment. "Yes."

"Good." Jack stood and held out his hand for Ethan's mug.

When he held it up, Ethan didn't let go, keeping Jack from moving away. "Jack, thank you for understanding."

"No problem." Safely at the sink, back to Ethan, Jack let out a relieved sigh. Ethan wasn't going anywhere just yet.

A pair of strong arms slid around his waist from behind and Ethan's weight leaned on him. "Jack?"

"Yeah?"

"We could still shag. I'll just be careful not to fall asleep after. If you wished."

Jack smirked. "Do I get to suck your dick again?"

Ethan pressed his face into Jack's shoulder blade, probably to hide his blush. "If you so desire."

Jack desired. Very much. But all he said was, "We'll see."

As promised, Ethan didn't fall into a death-like sleep that night. When Jack awoke in the morning, Ethan watched him prepare his liquid breakfast while outlining the security measures he'd spent the night devising. Leaving Ethan to measure and plan, Jack went to work. A few discreet enquiries and a couple of hours looking through some archives gave Jack what he needed, and he made a time to meet with Tan after lunch.

Alex Tan listened silently while Jack laid out several cases with precedence for what he was proposing and took care to remind the director how they would still have a traitor in their midst without

Ethan Blade; how if someone else in the Office decided to go after him, Tan's word would mean nothing when Blade came looking for revenge.

The not-so-subtle threat slid off Tan like water from a duck's back. He made a show of looking over the printed files Jack had, though it was more a stalling tactic than a need to see the information. Tan had probably known this was coming from the moment Jack had agreed to keep Blade happy.

"This is all very thorough, Mr. Reardon. Well done on presenting your case."

"Thank you," Jack said.

"Of course, any agreement we might come to wouldn't cover any overt criminal actions made by Mr. Blade within the Meta-State."

Nicely ambiguous, leaving Tan the room to decide just what it meant in any given situation. Jack had expected it.

"Of course, sir. I wouldn't want it to, but if you wish to keep him onside, this is necessary. He needs a firm statement he won't be tracked, detained, or targeted by the Office while he's in the country. Otherwise you will have no chance at ever convincing him to work for you."

Tan picked up the rough draft statement Jack had presented him with. It covered everything Jack could think of and a few more outlandish points he was willing to lose to keep the core requirements.

"Give me an hour," Tan eventually said. "Come back then and we'll make this official."

"Yes, sir." Jack gathered up his research and left. The statement would be heavily doctored by the time he got back, but it was promising.

Walking down the hallway towards his apartment that evening, Jack was joined by his elderly neighbour, Rocco Cesare, and his tan dachshund, Short Round, as they came back from their daily walk.

"Good evening, Nishant." Mr. Cesare smiled at him. "Good day at work?"

"Yes, sir." Jack generally went by Nishant, his Hindi middle name, with casual acquaintances. It matched his Indian heritage, satisfied preconceived racial ideals, and stopped most questions about his origins. "Very good day at work." His jacket pocket held the evidence.

Short Round scrambled at Jack's leg and while Mr. Cesare admonished him lightly, Jack crouched and gave the little dog a thorough scratching. "He's a good boy."

"A good watchdog, too. Let me know you had a man at your place today."

Jack didn't hide his sexuality. He didn't advertise it, either, but he wouldn't hide any man he happened to bring home. His surprise came from the fact Ethan had been seen.

"Nice young chap," his neighbour continued. "Installing your security system. He even popped into my place and gave me some advice. I was ready to hire him then and there, but he said he was booked out for the conceivable future."

Concentrating on rubbing Shorty's head so his ears flapped wildly, Jack swallowed a laugh. Trust Ethan.

Mr. Cesare chuckled. "I thought he would steal Shorty at one point. Could barely separate them."

Done with the affection, Shorty broke away from Jack, pelted up the hallway on his stubby legs and sniffed at the bottom of the door to his home. Done, he looked back at his human and barked once.

"All clear," the old man said, and the two men walked the rest of the way together.

Jack made sure Mr. Cesare and Shorty got in okay, then went the last distance to his door. He found a small camera with a fisheye lens mounted over his door, aimed down the hallway. Knowing Ethan wouldn't be that obvious, Jack ran his fingers across the top of the door frame and down the sides. He found a second micro-camera on the left side, at head height.

He was about to unlock the door when it opened for him.

"Come in," Ethan said.

Jack obeyed. The door was shut, and a rather long number chain entered into a newly installed keypad. Ethan began explaining it all immediately, dragging Jack through the entire apartment as he pointed out all the new systems.

"That was fast," Jack said when he could get a word in edgeways.

His flow interrupted, Ethan looked a bit lost, then chuckled. "It doesn't take long to set up, once you know what you're doing and where the vulnerable points are. Most homes are depressingly easy . . . Sorry, I think I'm just excited to be doing something useful for you."

"Yeah?" Jack leered. "I can think of a few other useful things— Hey!" He jumped aside before Ethan could poke his ribs again.

"You're lucky I also wrote down the instructions on how to arm and disarm it all. I suspected you wouldn't listen to me. Promise me you will burn it when you've committed it to memory."

"I listen, and I promise."

Ethan snorted and headed back to the living room.

Jack followed, digging the folded paper from his pocket. "This might make you like me again." He handed it over and went to get a drink.

When Jack returned with his bottle of water, Ethan was standing where he'd left him, the paper unfolded, though he wasn't looking at it anymore. The black lenses of his glasses were fixed on Jack.

"You did this for me?" he asked softly.

"As we discussed, the Office now has no official recourse to pursue you while you're in Australia, so long as you don't do anything overtly illegal. Turns out it isn't a big deal."

Ethan read the statement again and shook his head. "It is. You've agreed to be seconded to External Threat Assessment at Director Tan's request."

"A job's a job."

"Jack, you don't want to work for ETA."

As if Jack hadn't known that, and there was no point in asking how Ethan knew it, either. He wouldn't say, or he would, and his insight would lay Jack open to the bone.

"It's not like I'm transferring from Internal Threat Assessment. He can't just make me work all his jobs. I can say no if I want. He's specified a certain amount of time I can spend on ETA jobs."

Ethan frowned. "It's twenty-five percent of your yearly working hours, Jack. I don't believe Director McIntosh would be very happy with it."

Jack flinched at the memory of her icy regard when he'd gone to her with the statement. "She wasn't over the moon, but asset sharing happens a lot. She can also veto any request if she wants."

Seemingly out of objections, Ethan folded the paper and laid it very carefully on the coffee table. Then he took the water from Jack's hand and put that down as well. Slowly, he moved into Jack's personal space and moulded his body against Jack's, arms winding around his neck. One amazing and excruciating inch at a time, he worked his lips along Jack's jaw until he reached his ear.

"Please do anything you want to me, right now."

Jack's legs almost gave out at the pure sex in Ethan's voice. He clung to him for support. "Anything?"

"Mm hmm. Anything."

"Jesus," Jack moaned, pulling Ethan down to the floor right there. "I wouldn't know where to start."

Ethan laughed, low and deliciously. "I'm certain you will work it out."

DEVIL ON HIS SHOULDER

(FEBRUARY)

When the dust cleared, Jack's ears were still ringing. He couldn't hear what Harry McGill was saying, but even under a coating of grey dust his second's angry expression was apparent.

Ignoring the diatribe, Jack grabbed the younger man and checked him over. His own shoulder ached from impact with the road and something had landed on his leg, then rolled off, leaving him unpinned but hurting. Harry tried to get away from him but didn't get far, fetching up against the remains of the wall that had just fallen all over them.

"What the fuck?"

That one Jack deciphered well enough. "You're bleeding," he shouted back. "Let me check it out."

"Bleeding? Oh, God! What is it? Have I been impaled? Did something burn me? Oh, God." Harry's Kiwi accent got stronger with each panicked question.

Jack caught his hands and held them down. "I don't think it's too bad, but just let me check, okay?"

With his brown eyes wide and bright in his dusty face Harry settled a bit and let Jack tilt his head to see where the trail of gritty blood on his temple and cheek was coming from.

Jack couldn't really blame the younger man for freaking out. He wasn't as calm as he was acting. His guts were still frozen in shock from the explosion, and if he hadn't had something to occupy his hands, they would have been shaking. It wasn't as if he'd set out to make his first job with his new second so—well, explosive, but shit had a habit of happening.

He never started any task for the International Security Office thinking it would all go smoothly. It was, after all, his job to plan for the worst possible scenario and he was fairly good at it. This time it just so happened things hadn't even followed the worst possible scenario. In fact, all things considered—one half-destroyed building, a mildly concussed second and only two fatalities—it was a close runner-up to a smooth job.

"Found it," Jack yelled over the ringing. "You're not bleeding at all. You just caught some debris." He carefully removed the offending object from Harry's hair. It wasn't a large piece, just the ragged edge of the bomber's hand. The little finger was mostly unscathed, but the ring finger was ripped open and hanging on by a few stretched strips of skin.

"What? Show me! What?" Harry gaped at the hunk of blackened flesh. "Is that bone . . . ?"

"Yup. Oh, no it isn't. Looks like metal to me."

As Jack held it up for closer examination, the bit of metal moved and sliced through the last of the skin holding the ring finger on. It dropped into Harry's lap.

"Argh!" Harry jerked frantically, trying to dislodge it without touching it. When it bounced to the ground, he rolled away and threw up.

Tossing the remaining finger aside, Jack slowly tested his leg. His thigh was throbbing and the muscles ached when he straightened it, but it wasn't broken. Using what was left of the wall as a prop he got to his feet, swearing all the way. Once upright and balancing on his good leg, Jack gave himself a quick pat down. A few twinging ribs but no impaling objects, protruding bones, or blood—his or anyone else's. For once God was smiling on him. He sent a salute skyward even as the adrenaline rush ebbed, leaving him feeling lightheaded. And alive. He grinned, a laugh bubbling up his dry throat.

"Glad you're so happy!" Harry yelled, hauling himself up.

"What's to be sad about? We're alive!"

Harry gaped at him. His hand curled into a fist and he seemed to be eyeing up Jack's face for targets. Jack couldn't blame him. If their positions were reversed he would certainly want to punch Harry. So, he stood still, hands at his sides, willing to give Harry his shot.

He didn't though. All Harry did was press his fist to his forehead and then burst out with, "Alive? You realise that wouldn't be an accomplishment if you hadn't tried to blow us up in the first place!"

Relieved he wasn't punched, Jack said, "I wasn't trying to blow us up."

Arms flailing as he gestured to all the rubble, Harry nearly fell over again, but caught himself on a twisted hunk of black metal. "Then what the hell is all this?" After a double take, he realised what he was leaning on. "Our car. You blew up our car!"

"Christ! I didn't blow up our car." Jack peered at the flattened remains of the Humvee. "It was crushed by the falling wall. In fact, that's probably what saved us. And," he added, starting to get a bit pissed that Harry was blaming him for everything, "none of this would have happened if those two nutjobs hadn't decided to load up a shitbox of a car with C4, which then broke down next to this half-ruined building. This is the job, Harry. To make sure people like those two don't murder people like our customer with things like a car bomb."

"No, yeah, I know. That's why I'm here, to keep people safe from things like those terrorists and their car bomb. A bomb, Jack! That you shot at. That you blew up! Next to me!"

"They were about to get away. I was neutralising a threat! It's called getting the job done. And I did tell you to duck."

With a harrumph, Harry stalked off, limping slightly.

It was probably a good idea to get away from the wall. Loosened masonry was still a hazard. Jack hobbled out of the rubble, looking around for anything salvageable as he went. He'd lost his gun when the bomb went off and it was probably pancaked under a brick somewhere. The Humvee, too, was a total write-off. No one would be driving along the road for a while, either. Luckily, Lim Chu Kang was a mostly rural area with a low population density, which was a miracle in itself. There wasn't a lot of rural areas in Singapore. Had they encountered the bombers anywhere else along their route the casualties could have been much, much worse.

On the far side of the road, Harry was leaning against a fence post and poking at the cracked screen of his phone.

The ringing in Jack's ears had dropped down to a dull thud which rumbled through his head, making him not want to think too hard, but they needed to call this in. He connected to the main group through his implant.

"Scout One to Caravan, come in."

"Caravan to Scout One, what's the sitrep?"

"Threat has been neutralised. Both perps are down. The coast is clear. Bring the customer through."

"Got it. Secondary team is on the way, ten minutes out."

"We'll wait here for them. You get the customer squared away. Scout One out."

"Yes, sir. Caravan out."

Jack dragged his leg over to Harry and used the other side of the fence post for support. "Caravan's underway. Backup will be here in ten." He sighed as he took the weight off his leg.

"Good." Harry wasn't shouting. Either his ears had cleared up some or he wasn't as angry anymore. Or both. "You okay, boss?"

"Yeah, it's just a bruise." Hopefully.

They leaned in silence for a while, surveying the damage.

"I like that it's very contained," Harry said. "Very precise."

"We're in a foreign country. It's only polite to not make a big mess."

"Ah, the Tao of Jack."

"The what?"

The Kiwi grinned, his teeth impossibly white against the dust on his skin. "Lewis Tomas told me about it. He said that since we'd be working together I should know all about it."

Jack grunted, part in pain as he shifted weight, part in derision. "You shouldn't listen to anything that man says about me."

"That's funny, he said the same about you."

Jack eyed him speculatively. Maybe this wouldn't be a terrible partnership after all.

The Caravan—four more Humvees and an armoured limo decoy; the customer was in the third Humvee—passed them a couple of minutes later, safely delivering the customer the rest of the way to the highly classified meeting of signees to the Meta-State Agreement. The conflab was set to take about four days, at which point Jack, Harry, and the rest of his team of ISO security officers would have to do this all over again. Hopefully with fewer explosions. In the meantime, security would be handed over to the on-site team, leaving Jack some R & R in exotic Singapore. He was looking forward to it.

After a thorough medical check-up back at base, and a "brief" debrief that nevertheless took several hours, Jack and Harry were finally released for their four days of R & R. Jack was booked into the Park Regis and when Harry realised he'd booked into the Park, across the river and several blocks away, the disappointment was evident on his hastily cleaned face. Grey grit still coloured the creases in his forehead as he muttered about "bonding" and "developing working dynamics." Vaguely agreeing to meet up at some point for drinks, Jack left him at the Park and finally got to the Park Regis. He managed a shower and application of analgesic cream on his bruises. His thigh still ached, though not as bad, and he'd been advised to keep off it as much as possible. Jack had already decided on a regimen of lazy laps in the hotel pool and was happy he had a legitimate excuse for lounging on a poolside chaise while tanned and buffed waiters bought him drinks. But until the pool opened in the morning he was going to sleep, which happened about a second after his head hit the pillow.

When a strong hand closed around his sore shoulder, he didn't wake gracefully.

There was a lot of gasping, punching, rolling, tumbling off the bed and when his knee connected with his attacker's ribs, a startlingly loud cry of pain. Good. Jack had the prick pinned on the floor between the bed and wall, thighs clamped to the intruder's sides to keep him from getting away. About to deliver a crippling punch to the man's throat, he made out a gasped "Jack!"

"Shit." Jack scrambled off Ethan. His blood still hummed with unused adrenaline. The ingrained instinct to fight burned in every muscle and if he didn't put some distance between them, he wasn't sure he could keep himself from punching the crazy bastard.

Ethan, too, needed space. He scrambled into the corner, his back braced between both walls. As Jack's own breathing eased, he heard Ethan's. It was shallow and hitched on every second gasp.

"Fuck. I hurt you?" Jack got to his feet, prepared to help Ethan up, but his thigh throbbed so badly he had to sit on the bed.

"Not precisely, Jack." Ethan's voice was a little strained. "You merely aggravated a prior injury."

Compassion was a bit hard to come by right then, so Jack said, "You did come at me while I was sleeping."

"For which I will be eternally sorry," Ethan assured him, climbing to his feet with the aid of the walls.

"Right." Jack gently rotated his sore shoulder. "What the hell are you doing here, anyway? And how the fuck did you know I was in Singapore?"

"I have my means, Jack." With cautious steps and a slight hitch in his stride, Ethan came around the bed and sat next to him. "I believe it was part of our arrangement. If we found ourselves in the same place at the same time, then we would get together."

"Yeah, I guess, but I had no idea you were here. Jesus, Ethan, whatever possessed you to come in here while I was sleeping?"

There was a short silence, then a sheepish, "Overwhelming desire?"

"You mean you're horny."

"I suppose that would be part of it, yes."

There wasn't enough light in the room to make out much of his expression, so Jack took a stab in the dark. "Are you blushing?"

"No," Ethan snapped.

"Yeah, you are." Jack laughed. "Why can't you just say it? Call me, say you're close by and you want to fuck."

"Jack." A low-level warning.

"Come on, Ethan. Say it."

"Say what?"

"Say 'Fuck me, Jack.' Say 'I'm really horny and I need you to fuck me right now.' "

Jack loved that Ethan blushed when confronted with his physical desires. He also loved that the man refused to swear, or even use "fuck" as a verb. It was just part of the intriguing and intoxicating mix of part-innocent, part-ruthless, all-sexy mess that was Ethan.

"Why do I need to say it?" Ethan asked, hesitant but honestly enquiring. "I'm fairly certain you already know it's true."

Jack slid closer and tipped his head to get close to Ethan's neck. "Yeah, but hearing it is nice."

"It's vulgar," Ethan whispered.

"It's honest."

Head shifting until they were cheek to cheek, Ethan said softly, "Then, Jack, please shag me."

His dick warming, Jack rubbed stubble over stubble. "That's not what I want to hear. You can do better." He blew a gentle breath onto the skin of Ethan's neck.

Ethan shivered, then flinched and bit off a sudden gasp.

Jack pulled back. "What is it?"

"Nothing, just a bruise on my ribs." Belied by the way he pressed his hand to his right side, leaning that way a little to ease the strain.

"Like shit," Jack muttered. "Get your glasses out, I'm turning the light on."

While Ethan put on his sunglasses, Jack turned on the bedside lamp. It was enough light for him to use and wouldn't be too blinding if Ethan lost his glasses.

"All right." Jack limped around the bed to stand in front of him. "Let's see the damage."

Ethan wore black tactical clothes that, with the addition of a hoodie or coat, would pass for casual. Thin gloves peeked out of a pocket and a rolled-up cap, also black, from another. He began to unbutton the top, but Jack sighed at his slow going and took over the job. When it was open, he gently but swiftly pushed it off Ethan's shoulders. Ethan pulled his arms free, wincing as he did.

"Arms up," Jack commanded, taking hold of the hem of the black undershirt.

"Jack."

"Just do it."

After a moment, Ethan slowly raised his arms. Jack peeled the tight shirt up and off, taking care not to jostle him.

"Holy fuck." He sat on Ethan's right and studied the bruise. "Have you had this looked at?"

Jack was horrified. It went from under his right arm down to his hip and wrapped around his lower ribs until it was an inch or so off his navel. It was a rich purple, mottled with red and blue. At his waist was a straight line of distressing purple so dark it looked black. "What the hell was that?"

"Edge of my armour. It protected me from any broken ribs. I'm rather practiced at judging my injuries. It's just bruised, nothing else."

"Christ. You need more than a best guess with something like this."

Ethan sighed. "It's *fine*, Jack. Please, trust me."

Giving Ethan a thorough appraisal, Jack found other, smaller injuries. A long, rough graze on his left forearm, more bruising on his left shoulder, and two short cuts on his left cheek, hidden from a casual glance by his glasses. They'd been cleaned and had skincoloured butterfly strips applied.

"Tell me what happened," Jack ordered as he stood to find the cream the doctor had given him.

"You're limping, Jack. What happened to you?"

"You first."

"I don't think I should. Plausible denia—"

"Just tell me," Jack snapped. He found the analgesic cream on the counter in the bathroom and stalked back out, his leg not liking it but his growing irritation overriding it.

"As you wish. I was sabotaging a car that was to be used in the attack on—"

"What the fuck? You were involved in the attack today?"

"I wouldn't say involved, Jack."

"Then what the fuck would you say?" God. He hadn't had the urge to strangle Ethan like this since the desert when he'd found out he was just a pawn in Ethan's little game.

Calm as you please, Ethan said, "I was in Port Dickson for completely unrelated reasons and I heard there was to be an attack on a dignitary attending the Meta-State gathering in Lim Chu Kang. Of course, I wondered if you were involved so I looked into it."

"Of course," Jack agreed with bitter sarcasm. "Continue."

Ethan ignored his tone. "When I discovered the means of the attack, namely a car bomb, I decided to derail it. I couldn't do anything overt because I didn't want anyone to link me to why the attack didn't work. So, I sabotaged the car."

"Okay. And then?"

"And then I was discovered before I could complete my sabotage. Had I not been interrupted the car would have exploded upon ignition."

Jack crossed his arms, his right shoulder twinging. "But you were interrupted. By what? A wreaking ball?" He nodded to the ugly bruise.

Ethan's lips quirked up at one corner. "No, by another car."

"You got hit by a car?"

"Yes. It wasn't going very fast. I got away but with my injuries I couldn't go back and finish the job." He wouldn't look at Jack and his tone took on a decidedly self-recriminating tone. "It's my own fault. I rushed and didn't plan for all contingencies properly."

"When did you learn of the planned attack?"

"This morning, around six a.m."

"You had under six hours to get from Port Dickson to Singapore and then hunt down a pair of terrorists?"

"Yes. Plenty of time."

The shame in the admission tugged at Jack's heart. The Office had been aware of a potential attack for three days prior and they hadn't been able to get as close as Ethan had in six hours, four of which he probably spent getting there. If Jack had managed what Ethan had in that period of time, he wouldn't be ashamed. He'd be using the story for free drinks for years. Well, maybe not. He'd probably fixate on how he could have done better but seeing Ethan so embarrassed about it ignited Jack's need to protect him. If there was one person in the world who didn't need protecting, it was Ethan, and yet Jack couldn't convince himself of that.

Anger at the nameless, faceless bastards who'd turned Ethan into this deadly, damaged man was pointless. Ethan would never tell him who they were and despite dedicating a team to unearthing his past, the Office probably wouldn't get answers quick enough for Jack to do anything about the bastards. Jack's rage was directionless, and right now it defaulted to the man in front of him.

"Fucking *hell*, Ethan. You had no right to interfere in this. We knew about the attack, okay? I know you think our techniques are slow and mired in red tape, but we do know what we're doing. Sure, we didn't know it was going to be a car bomb, or where it was going to happen, but we had contingencies. *I* had contingences. I'll admit I didn't actually consider we'd find a car bomb broken down on the side of the road, but we dealt with it all the same. Jesus, do you know how badly that could have gone? I nearly blew up Harry, for fuck's sake. Christ!"

Jack paced away from Ethan, growling at his sore leg as he went. He'd made three passes before he realised Ethan hadn't said anything. He stopped and looked at him.

Ethan sat statue still, hands gripping the edge of the mattress, head bowed, shoulders so stiff and straight Jack could have rested a bowl of soup on them.

The expected spark of fear at what that meant didn't arrive. Instead, Jack's guts twisted in guilt. He'd done this. He'd pushed Ethan and now he'd retreated into his cold, hard assassin's shell. Once, Jack would have taken it as a sign to run—which he'd never managed to do. Back in the desert, stressed out and messed up, Jack hadn't run from cold-blooded Ethan Blade. He'd stayed and argued instead, which had had the odd effect of making Ethan start to view him not as a target, but as a human. It had saved his life. So now, seeing Ethan go distant and still, Jack wasn't worried. He was concerned.

"Ethan, look at me."

Jack had no idea if Ethan complied. His sunglasses hid so much. Jack boldly stepped up to him and, finger under his chin, lifted his head so his face was pointed at Jack's. Nothing in Ethan's expression changed but he didn't fight the gesture.

"I'm sorry for getting upset but you get it, don't you? This is my job. What I'm trained to do. Yeah, you can do it too, but we use different methods and they don't mesh. So, unless you want to give up your life of international crime and come work for Tan at the Office, you can't jump into my work like this."

After a long moment when Jack started to doubt his confidence that Ethan wouldn't hurt him, Ethan sighed and nodded.

"Good." Relief eased muscles Jack hadn't realised he'd tensed, and he sank back onto the bed beside Ethan. Into a not-quite uncomfortable quiet, Jack muttered, "I'm not *bad* at my job, you know."

"I know, Jack." Ethan's tone was soft and, not meek, but carefully not disagreeable. "I just . . . worry about you."

"Why?"

Ethan made a sound that wasn't a grunt or a sigh, or even an exasperated growl, but a combination of all three. "Because I like you, Jack."

Ignoring the curl of warmth under his ribs at those words, Jack smirked. "You like the way I give you orgasms."

Another of those mixed noises, more exasperated this time.

"Don't deny it. You told me you did."

A teeth-grinding moment later, Ethan muttered, "I did."

"So say it."

"Say what?"

"You know."

"We've come full circle, I see."

"If you don't say it, I won't do it."

"Whoever said I wanted you to do it?"

"You did. You said you were driven here by 'overwhelming desire.'" Jack put his outrageous British accent on the last two words.

"How strange. That urge seems to have vanished."

Laughing, Jack hauled himself up the bed and settled against the pillows. It always surprised him how quickly he could go from murderous anger to lusty laughter when Ethan was around. He'd never experienced it before. Arguing with Hamish, his last serious boyfriend, had been like an air strike, hot and deadly for a short time, but the damage took much longer to fix. He and Ian, his first lover, hadn't really argued, but then they'd been teenagers in the midst of their first sexual relationship. Too busy screwing to do much else, until Ian started screwing others. Their first argument had been their last. Not that his arrangement with Ethan was like either of his big relationships. It was just semiregular sex. Maybe that was why he could shift from one to the other so swiftly, so completely.

Unscrewing the cap of the tube, Jack said, "Get your arse up here."

Ethan came cautiously. Whether because of his side or general wariness was anyone's guess.

"Lie down. Let me know if I hurt you."

Watching while Jack smeared cream on his side, Ethan said, "Don't fear, I will."

Jack chuckled and gently worked the pain relief in. When he was done, he helped Ethan out of his shoes and pants and, leaving him on the bed, went into the bathroom to wash his hands. Coming back out, he was caught by the sight of a nearly naked Ethan curled up on his uninjured side, glasses off, eyes closed, and body relaxed.

Jesus. His heart tripped over the simple idea of Ethan being in his bed, not for sex but for comfort and care. Jack realised the reason he could get over his anger with Ethan so quickly wasn't because this thing between them was just sex. He didn't know what it was, but their arrangement wasn't it.

Because this wasn't just sex.

Sufficiently disturbed by that thought, Jack lay back down. Ethan moved over and after negotiating with various sore bits, they found a comfortable position with maximum contact.

"In the morning we're going to discuss just how to safely wake up a sleeping man," Jack mumbled.

"As you wish, Jack."

Snorting at the fake contriteness, Jack turned out the lamp and they settled into silence.

"Jack?"

The seriousness of this tone drew Jack back from the edge of sleep. "Hmm?"

"Who's Harry?"

DEATH OF THE PARTY

(MARCH)

Harry was doubled over, laughing so hard it had gone silent. One hand was braced on the tabletop while the other waved helplessly. Tears streamed down his reddening face and each time he managed to pull his shit together and stop, all it took was one look at Jack and he was off again.

"Ignore him." Lewis blocked Jack's escape route from the small operations room he and Harry were using to monitor Delta Subject.

After the near disaster in Singapore, Jack and Harry had been given their next job by Director Tan of the ETA. Not exactly thrilled to have his agreement with Tan brought into play so soon, Jack nevertheless took the responsibility very seriously. Even if watching Delta Subject—a young Indonesian man in Sydney thanks to his uncle, an unusually generous gangster with links to radical religious groups—wasn't a challenge. The worst part about the whole deal was making bland reports about non-suspicious movements to Unit Leader Keri Sing in the Singapore branch.

"I am." Jack was proud of his calm tone. Between Harry and Lewis, he was about an inch from losing his patience. He'd been at work since 3 a.m., woken from a nice sleep by an alert from the tech assigned to Delta Subject overnight. It had turned out to be nothing, just a midnight run for more pot and snacks, but Jack had stuck around anyway, deciding he'd take an early finish over trying to go back to sleep for a couple of hours. It was now very nearly 2 p.m. and Jack was going home. It didn't matter that Lewis was starfished in the doorway. If he didn't move in the next two minutes, Jack had no qualms about moving Lewis himself. "And I will ignore the urge to punch you, too, if you get out of my way right now."

"Come on, Jack," Lewis pleaded, his grip on the door frame going white. "I really, *really* need your help on this one. I promise, it's a simple in-and-out job. Couple of hours, tops. I'll owe you one." At Jack's continuing scowl, he added, "Two. I'll owe you two. All right, three, but that's as high as I go."

Jack rolled his eyes. He'd already made all his objections to Lewis's request—it wasn't Jack's operation, Lewis had his own field team, Jack was too old to pull it off, it was stupid. All of which Lewis had shot down—it was an ITA operation and despite Jack running a job for ETA he was still an ITA asset; none of his field team were appropriate and McIntosh couldn't spare anyone else at the last minute; age was a state of mind; it wasn't stupid, it was a vital part of Lewis's operation. Jack had to grudgingly admit they were all legit, except for the age one, but that didn't mean he *had* to do this.

To gauge the level of desperation, Jack smiled grimly at Lewis's offer. "Three favours, huh? Tempting." Jack pretended to consider it, sighing like he was going to give in. Just as Lewis was starting to relax, Jack shook his head. "I'm not doing it."

Lewis scowled, finally releasing his hold on the door frame so he could cross his arms. "Stop being so stubborn. You know I wouldn't be here if I wasn't desperate."

Waving at the discarded items on the table, Jack said, "Believe me, I know. You'd have to be absolutely *gasping* to go to anyone with that."

Which only sent Harry off into more gales. If Lewis didn't back off and let Jack go soon, they'd probably have to resuscitate Harry.

"And," Jack continued while Lewis's scowl deepened, "if you're that desperate, why not do it yourself? I mean, after all, age is just a state of mind."

Lewis was a year older than Jack but with his blond hair and bright eyes, he could have passed for late twenties. Jack, however, felt he'd lived more than his thirty-six years and knew he looked it, too. Occasionally.

"Yeah, but a six-pack isn't," Lydia said.

Jack and Lewis both turned to her. Lewis's second—a gross understatement of the fact she was the one who not only ran their cases on a day to day basis, but also corralled Lewis's often erratic but generally brilliant mind, at home as well as at work—stood next to Harry, making sure he didn't actually expire from hilarity. Lydia smiled serenely at them.

"What?" Lewis asked, frowning.

"Age might be a state of mind," she said, "but a good body isn't. And *that*, Jack, is why you're more suited to the job."

"Hey!" Jack and Lewis protested at the same time.

"That's objectification," Jack added.

"Not to mention insulting," Lewis muttered.

"It's not objectification," Lydia said to Jack. "It's the truth, and a compliment, so take it. And while you're at it, take this as well"—she shoved the items on the table towards him—"and go home. Sleep for a couple of hours and I'll call when we have the details set."

There were no more arguments. The moment Lydia joined any discussion, things just happened, whether everyone agreed. Jack liked her. She was one person who didn't annoy him on a regular basis, but he did wonder how she got him—and everyone else—to do what she wanted so easily. He and Lewis had tried to work it out and the only conclusion they'd come to was that she was some sort of super-genius.

Thus, a half hour later, Jack walked into his apartment, still puzzling out how, and when, he'd agreed to Lewis's cockamamie plan. Replaying the last moments of the discussion, he put the case Lydia had given him on the kitchen counter and headed for the bedroom, unbuttoning his flannel shirt as he went.

A whisper of sound alerted him, rocketing him out of his thoughts.

Spinning, Jack faced the man coming up behind. Recognising Ethan in a split second, he morphed the start of a punch into grab. Hand on the back of Ethan's neck, he turned them further and pushed with his whole body. Ethan fetched up against the table with a startled gasp, hands on Jack's upper arms for support.

"Hello, Jack." Below his dark sunnies, Ethan's cheeks were flushed and his lips were parted.

"Ethan," Jack managed, his brain still somewhere back in the operations room, mulling over Lydia's particular brand of voodoo. He couldn't think right now, his body was operating on muscle memory. The most prominent memory his muscles were working off was one of moving over Ethan, of driving this desirable, passionate body beyond control. A memory spearheaded by his dick.

"How are you?" Ethan's hands ran up and down his biceps.

Swallowing hard, Jack said, "Good. You?"

Ethan's lips quirked into a smile. "Tolerably well, if a little frustrated."

"Yeah." Jack's gaze raked over Ethan's face, finding no new scars, which pleased him. "It's been a while."

They'd both been injured the last time they'd been together, which had put a stop to anything too physical, making it two months since their last fuck. Neither of them had promised exclusivity, though, so Jack hadn't been entirely celibate since then. Still, several nights with a guy from Melbourne, whom Jack had pretty much forgotten the moment he was out of sight, was next to nothing compared to even this much of Ethan.

"Mm." Ethan wriggled, then made a sharp motion and, suddenly, he was seated on the table. He slid his arms around Jack's chest, legs wrapping around his. "It has." He rolled his hips and his thickening dick rubbed alongside Jack's.

"Christ," Jack hissed and closed his eyes before he did something stupid.

Ethan's lips grazed Jack's cheek, sliding warm and dry up to his temple, where he pressed a lingering kiss. He repeated the move on the other side, then along Jack's jaw, nudging his way in to kiss the soft skin under his chin. Jack angled his head to give him room. Ethan kissed and nibbled, ranging down Jack's throat and as far into the collar of his flannel as he could. His dark curls tickled Jack's nose and lips, brushing against the skin Ethan's lips were sensitising so Jack shivered with each touch. Quite involuntarily, he turned his head and pressed his face into Ethan's hair, pulling in a deep breath of his scent.

"Jack," Ethan moaned against his neck. He was breathing hard, his chest pushing into Jack's, the silk of his button-down sliding with gentle hisses over the cotton of Jack's flannel.

Needing to taste, Jack dragged his face through Ethan's hair to his temple, kissing down his cheek to his jaw. He teased Ethan's earlobe with his tongue, drawing it into his mouth and suckling on it gently. Ethan gasped and squirmed against him. His hands scrabbled at Jack's shirt, pulling it up until Ethan got skin on skin. Fingers spread over Jack's spine, he hauled himself even closer.

"Jack." Ethan whimpered as Jack attacked the sensitive spot just behind his ear, grazing his teeth over the soft skin, then laving it with his tongue.

The sensation of Ethan starting to lose control—the way his body shook and his fingers dug into the muscles of Jack's back, the sound of his name torn by need and lust—ripped through Jack like a bullet. It left him as breathless and stunned as it did every bloody time.

It would be so easy to just do it right here. Grind on Ethan until they both came. Collapse on the table while they caught their breaths, then go at it all over again. Even as he rubbed hard against Ethan's hips, grunting at the heat building between them, Jack knew he needed more. Needed more skin and more horizontal. He also didn't need to hear Ethan bitch about Jack making him come in his expensive suit pants again.

With a moan of displeasure, Jack pulled back. Ethan, still wrapped around him, came off the table. The sudden weight tipped Jack off balance. Lightning fast, Ethan reached back and caught the table with one hand, the other clamped around Jack's waist. Both legs snapped out, his feet bracing against the kitchen counter behind Jack. Wedged between Ethan's legs, Jack realised he was still upright. A couple of seconds of stunned silence, then both of them laughed in relief.

"So," Jack said, "should we take this to the bedroom?"

"Mm, I think we should." Ethan slithered to the ground, keeping his body pressed tight to Jack's. "Before someone suffers a lasting injury."

"Or a tough-to-remove stain."

Ethan laughed, leaning back in Jack's arms, locks of his dark hair tumbling across his forehead.

Jack couldn't help it. He stared, mesmerised. It felt as if a grenade had gone off in his chest; a sudden burst of heat centred under his solar plexus. There wasn't enough air to fill his lungs. Not enough space to let him escape. His hands were in Ethan's hair before he knew what he was doing. Fingers digging into those thick, soft locks, he tilted Ethan's head back. Laughter dying away, Ethan caught his breath, as if he too was suffering his own internal explosion.

God. Jack was on the brink. Like he was standing at the open hatch of an airplane, about to jump with a parachute he hadn't checked himself.

Wish you were here?

The unexpected return of that little issue jerked Jack out of the moment. It had been several months since the memory of the desert, and everything Ethan had done to mess him up had reared its ugly head. And it had to happen right now, leaving him thrown and shaky like a full-blown flashback.

After a silent minute, Ethan asked, "To the bedroom?"

For the first time since they'd made their little agreement about hooking up whenever possible, Jack considered saying no. The only safe option here was retreat. Back off, way off, until he knew he wouldn't completely mess things up by reacting to something Ethan had already apologised for.

"It's all right, Jack," Ethan said after another empty minute. "We don't have to if you don't want to."

"No," Jack grunted. "I do want to. I'm just . . . not ready right now."

Ethan politely didn't remind Jack that he had been more than ready just moments ago. He just nodded and gave his cheek a chaste kiss. "Perhaps something to eat first."

"Yeah. That'd be good."

Jack's pulse settled while he made a couple of sandwiches and Ethan made himself a cup of tea. By the time they sat on the couch, Ethan appeared mostly settled as well. They ate while Ethan brought Jack up to date on his automobile harem. Neither of them expected Jack to contribute to the conversation much more than the occasional grunt or dumb question about tyre size, so it gave Jack time to get himself sorted out. Afterwards, they started watching the next episode of *Strike Back*, a series they had started on Ethan's first visit. Jack had been itching to get back to it but had held off until he could watch it with Ethan.

So, it was a bit surprising when, just before the first big, all-out, explosive fight, he ended up lying half on Ethan, nuzzling into his neck, and stroking his chest between the buttons on his shirt. The guys on the screen went through their I'd-die-for-you, neither-of-us-is-dying-today speeches while Jack pulled Ethan's shirt from the waistband of his pants and shoved it up so he could play with Ethan's nipples. Bullets rained and cars crashed. Ethan tipped them off the couch so he was on top and able to hold Jack's arms over his head while he bit and licked every inch of Jack's exposed skin. This time, there were no distracting thoughts, no worrying moments and the grenades were all on the telly.

However, there was a disturbing *ping* inside Jack's head.

Jack ignored it, rolling them over so he could slide a leg between Ethan's thighs and slowly rub their groins together.

Ethan arched under him, head tossed back. "Jack. Yes, yes. Please, Jack."

Neither of them cared about removing clothes. They didn't worry about stains. Didn't worry about anything except the other.

Until the *ping*s of Jack's implant were joined by a flashing red light across his right eye.

"Shit!" Jack growled and levered himself up to his knees. Angrily, Jack answered the insistent *ping*ing. "What?"

"*Jack? Did I catch you at a bad time?*" Lydia asked innocently.

Jack groaned. He'd actually forgotten all about Lewis's damn job. "No," he grumbled, getting to his feet. "I was asleep."

On the floor, one of Ethan's brows arched over the pane of his sunglasses. Jack waved at the right side of his head, indicating the implant. He held his other hand out and Ethan took it, letting Jack help him to his feet.

"*That explains why I had to send an urgent alert,*" Lydia said. "*I'm glad you got some rest. Everything's organised. We're just waiting on you now.*"

Holding in more swearing, Jack stepped backwards before Ethan could lock his arms around him. He'd committed to this stupid thing and letting Ethan distract him again wouldn't be good. Thankfully, the reminder of the annoying job had sufficiently deflated his dick. Jack ignored Ethan's fleetingly hurt expression and went down the hallway to the bathroom. He asked for the details while he stripped and stepped into the shower. Lydia sent a message with it, told him they were grateful for his help, and hung up.

Jack washed efficiently and when he got out, Ethan was there, holding a towel for him.

"Work?" Ethan asked blandly.

"Yeah. I have to go in."

Ethan nodded understandingly. "Is it an emergency?"

Before Jack could lie and say yes, he muttered, "No. Just a fucking shit assignment I didn't want to take but got conned into." Slinging the towel around his waist he squeezed past Ethan and headed for his bedroom. Ethan, of course, followed him.

Half dressed in a clean pair of jeans, Jack risked a glance at Ethan. He stood in the corner of the bedroom by the old recliner, hands in his pockets, and his button-down still appealingly rumpled. With his hair tousled and a hint of stubble on his jaw, he was damn-near irresistible. Jack almost forgot about the job again, but spun away before he could say "fuck it" and toss Ethan to the bed.

"Is this assignment dangerous?" Ethan asked.

Grabbing up a T-shirt, Jack grunted. "The most dangerous I've ever been on. And that includes being dropped into an active war zone."

"Oh."

That didn't sound too positive and when Jack's head popped out of the top of his shirt, he gave Ethan another look. He'd gone still, lips straight, shoulders stiff, hands free of his pockets, ready to attack. Or rather, to defend Jack from any threat.

"I was joking," Jack said hastily. "It's not that bad. Actually, it's nothing dangerous at all. Just . . . annoying."

Some of the tension eased from Ethan's body, but his voice was low and deadly. "Perhaps you will require backup all the same."

"Oh, fuck no!" It was out without a thought, hard and vehement, and a little bit panicked. The very idea of Ethan showing up at this thing made Jack want to tie him up. Combined with his overall objections to the job at hand, two unresolved erections and his almost-flashback earlier, this new complication dropped Jack off the edge of rationality. "Didn't we already sort this out? I can't have you sticking your nose in my job. Remember what happened last time you 'tried to help'? Harry still bugs me about nearly blowing him up. Besides, I don't want to be seen—" He swerved off that wrong path.

"I can't be seen in public with you . . ." And onto an even worse one, judging by Ethan's reaction.

Oh God. Jack was going to die. Ethan hadn't gone this cold the last time Jack had got up him for interfering in his job. Then, he'd simply accepted the berating, apologised, and let Jack tend his injuries. Right now, though, he was all Ethan Blade, dead-eyed killer, no hint of Ethan, human being.

Jack didn't die, though, Ethan became terse. "As you wish, Jack," he said, and walked out.

Ten, then twenty seconds went by while Jack stood frozen, half convinced he might still die, half mortified he'd actually said that to Ethan. All that happened was the front door opening and shutting. Another thirty seconds passed before Jack let out an explosive breath and sank down on the end of the bed.

"Fuck," he whispered. "Fuck, fuck, fuck."

Well, it probably had to end at some point. Better sooner rather than later, before Jack had a chance to make an even bigger mistake. At least he could go to Tan and call off their agreement. And maybe get taken off the boring Delta Subject job. A bright side to pissing off an international assassin.

Tossing the twisting sense of guilt into the filing cabinet in the back of his head, Jack finished dressing and by the time he got downstairs, carrying the case Lydia had insisted he take home and check—which he hadn't—an unmarked car was waiting for him. The entire drive to the airport he mulled over those last moments with Ethan. It was all too easy to pinpoint the moment Jack fucked it up. Christ. The very idea of him, Ethan and this assignment . . . He couldn't go there. Not when even the threat of it tempted him to toss the case out the window and ask the driver to take him home. But he was professional, if nothing else, and he got on the plane to Melbourne where, an hour and a half later, Lydia herself picked him up and took him to their base of operations.

The Causeway 353 Hotel was on Little Collins Street, a block away from where the job was going down. Lydia took him to a deluxe suite where the rest of the team were setting up a mobile station. Apart from Lewis, there was a strike team, just in case things went completely haywire. Jack grimaced at each of the lightly armoured people as he stalked in. Surely one of them could have done this.

Probably warned off by Lydia, Lewis kept his distance, organising uplinks and outlining several emergency plans with the strike team; Lydia ushered Jack into the separate bedroom.

"Did you try it on?" She hefted a big case to the king-sized bed and opened it. "Does it all fit okay?"

"All?" Jack asked sarcastically. "I didn't get a chance to try *it* on, but I'm sure it'll be fine. Christ, I can't believe I'm doing this."

"We're forever grateful. Now, strip."

Grumbling, Jack got undressed. Lydia politely turned her back until he grunted an all clear. When she turned back, she looked him over and after a deep breath, nodded.

"Yes, it fits fine."

Jack tried not to blush. "It's a bit snug."

"Hmm? Oh, yes, I suppose. Though it did say it came with a cup for enhancements."

"Is that what that thing is?" Jack turned his back this time and fished around in the underwear until he pulled free a padded cup. "Who the fuck came up with that idea?"

"Probably the same person who thought up padded bras. All right, let's get some oil on that chest."

Lydia was incredibly lucky Jack liked her as much as he did. Anyone else would have been told in no uncertain terms just where they could shove the bottle of oil, the glitter, lipstick, and eyeliner. Instead, he quietly followed her instructions to stand, arms up, arms down, legs spread, now sit, lean forwards, head back, look at the ceiling and, lastly, to smack his lips on a presented tissue. His Saint Thomas Cross tattoo was hidden under a thin layer of synthetic skin. It was too specific an image to be seen on an undercover assignment. Lydia ended up tearing the padding out of the cup and insisting Jack re-place it. Even without the cup, the fire-engine-red boxer-briefs were tight enough to outline in near anatomical detail things Jack usually kept private. Suitably tucked away, Jack put on the black boots and the black bat wings. Lydia carefully placed the glittery red horns amongst the black curls she'd spent forever styling.

The sum result was, supposedly, a sexy devil. Jack had to admit that a glistening set of toned chest, abs and legs, even with the sparkle of red glitter, broken up only by a red-hot pair of underwear was pretty alluring—but only if it was on some other bloke.

"I look ridiculous."

"No you don't," Lydia assured him absently, packing away her big make-Jack-look-like-a-piece-of-meat kit. "You look totally hot."

"Really? Then why can't you look at me without laughing?"

Her shoulders shook as she tried, and failed, to keep in a snicker. "I'm sorry. I really am. You *do* look sexy as hell, excuse the pun, but I keep imaging what Lewis is going to say and . . ." Her snicker turned into a snorting laugh.

Jack muttered, "I'm too old for this shit," then decided to get the humiliation over and done with.

It wasn't as bad as he'd thought it would be. Lewis managed to not laugh aloud and only two of the strike team wolf-whistled. They got through the briefing quickly and then Jack was hustled out the back way to a waiting car. Swearing, he took the wings off to get in and after driving around a couple of neighbouring blocks, they ended up at a nightclub on Collins Street. With minimal witnesses, Jack was released at the staff entrance and, wings in hand, buzzed to be let in.

Thankfully there were two other guys already there, standing around in skimpy costumes. Another devil and an angel. Both of them were at least thirteen years younger than Jack and appeared to be so comfortable in next to nothing they were probably underwear models in their day jobs. They welcomed Jack well enough, though the other devil cocked a sceptical eyebrow at him. The angel—blond, blue-eyed and gorgeous—gave him a long, lingering look and a wink.

This job couldn't go fast enough.

When all six sexy angels and devils had congregated, they were given a run down on the event, cautioned about not making trouble—with a list of "troubles" as long as Jack's leg—and sent on their way.

The hen's party was being held in a private room in the nightclub, a kitschy decorated lounge full of neon-plaid and art-deco refugees. The rest of the club was a flashing montage of lasers, smoke machines and loud music, but thankfully the lighting and sound were muted in the lounge. It was brimming with overly excited women who all had a penchant for pinching the white- and red-clad bums of the angels and devils who carried trays of cocktails and chocolate-coated strawberries. Jack decided early on he was going to be Cranky Devil, as opposed to Camp Devil and I'm-going-to-hit-four-seven-and-ten-on-the-trouble-list Devil. His permanent scowl didn't deter the ladies though. As the cocktails flowed and the music got raunchier, he spent more time politely removing his arse from stray hands than he did handing out drinks and treats.

The Hen herself spent half the time getting selfies with the scantily clad waitstaff, giggling about how "Tom better never see this." Despite his attitude towards the whole thing, Jack snuggled in for photos with any of the women who asked. It gave him a good opportunity to get close to the subject of the job, if she ever showed up. Two hours in and Jack hadn't caught sight of the tall brunette from the pictures Lewis had shown him. His ten-minute check-ins got monotonous very quickly.

"I hate hens' parties," the friendly angel moaned. They stood at the bar, waiting for more cocktails and strawberries. "My bum is going to be so red from getting smacked."

Jack had to laugh. "Move before they connect. It's what I do."

"I tried that, but they hunt in packs. They surround me and I can't escape."

Unsurprised that the stunning young man was being so hotly pursued, Jack just said, "I'll try to help you out when I can. Can't promise anything, though. I have my own goods to protect."

Hefting his full tray, Angel gave him another slow once-over. "I'll say." Then, with a sigh, he muttered, "Once more unto the breach," and returned to battle.

The next half hour passed without incident. Jack made his rounds, dodged pinching fingers, growled for the camera and kept an eye out for his subject. If she didn't show, Lewis would owe him more than three favours.

Towards the end of the third hour, Jack was loitering by the entrance to the lounge, hoping to catch sight of the subject in the public areas of the club, without luck. About to head back to the bar for another load, Jack froze. A familiar shape had flashed through his periphery and he turned to follow it.

There, leaning against the public bar, back to the lounge. A lean body in a fitted black suit. Head of dark, tousled hair. The hint of glasses as he turned to nod at the bartender refreshing his drink.

Oh. Shit.

What the fuck was Ethan doing here?

It couldn't be coincidence. Not here in Melbourne. Beyond even that stretch, nothing Ethan did was ever a coincidence. Everything was planned down to the nth degree. He was here on purpose. As backup? Or to check on Jack's reason for not staying with him?

Ethan turned and his sunglasses—which somehow didn't look dorky at night—pointed right at Jack. After a long moment where Jack seriously considered running, the corner of Ethan's mouth turned up in the smallest of smiles. It was gone before Jack could confirm it. Gone before his ribs stopped squeezing his heart and his guts unclenched. Casually, Ethan knocked back the new drink, set the glass on the bar and sauntered towards him.

Jack scanned him for weapons, finding nothing, but that wasn't conclusive with Ethan Blade. He did find a nametag pinned to his lapel, though. As "Brent" approached, Jack braced for impact.

"Please excuse me," was all Ethan said when he reached Jack at the entrance to the lounge.

Stepping aside, Jack watched as Ethan continued in, homing in on the Hen. Jack stalked him, barely stopping to hand out drinks as he went, his distraction opening him up for a few of the butt-smacks he'd otherwise managed to avoid. When he was close enough, he listened to "Brent" making sure everything was to the Hen's expectations and standards.

"And the wait-staff?" Ethan used his British accent and the Hen's closest companions oohed and aahed. "Are they suitable? Behaving themselves?"

"Oh yes, yes," she effused. "They're perfect. A little *too* perfect, maybe. My fiancé would be horrified to see me surrounded by such beautiful men." She smiled and rested her hand on Ethan's arm, clearly including him in the mix.

He smiled, slow and sultry. "We aim to please, Ms. Foster. If you have any questions or issues, please don't hesitate to find me. I'll do everything I can to ensure you have a perfect night."

If Jack wasn't pretty sure Ethan wouldn't go there, he would have put money on the Hen having one last fling before tying the knot. He was still scowling when Ethan turned and looked right at him.

"Back to work," Ethan ordered, and headed for the bar.

"Yes, you wicked devil, back to work," one of the Hen's friends commanded. She pinched Jack's arse as she took a cocktail from his tray.

Ethan left through a Staff Only door behind the bar and Jack spent the next half hour on the lookout for his subject *and* Ethan, catching glimpses of the latter both in the Hen's party and out in the public area. They didn't cross paths again.

Close to midnight, a tall brunette appeared, causing an eruption of cheers from the party. It took Jack some time to work his way over, finally posing for a series of photos with her and the Hen. While the subject draped herself across his mostly naked body, he slipped her phone out of her pocket and palmed it under the tray of drinks. When he was set free again, he told the bartender he was going for a piss and headed for the Staff Only door.

He came into a narrow corridor a short distance down, where he found the men's staff toilets and went in. He'd replaced the original SIM with a cloned card and put the phone back together when the door opened. Pretending to be checking messages, Jack looked up casually.

"Hi." Angel smiled while biting his lower lip. The silver glitter on his chest sparkled like diamonds under the bright white lights.

Jack dragged his gaze off all that bare, tanned skin and met Angel's big, baby blues. "Hey. How's the bum?"

"I don't know. Want to check it out for me?" He turned and offered his tight, rounded rear for perusal. The white boxer-briefs of the angel costume left absolutely nothing to the imagination.

Christ. Jack's dick certainly wanted to check it out and having suffered two false starts already, it didn't seem likely to take no for an answer. Thank God for the cup. Angel peeked sweetly over his white, feathery wings at Jack.

"Fuck," Jack moaned. "I only came in to check my phone."

Angel faced him, doing sexy-sulk like a superstar. "Wherever did you keep a phone in that outfit?"

"Took the padding out of the cup."

Angel laughed and leaned forwards, pressing his chest to Jack's, putting his mouth next to Jack's ear. "Me too. Not enough room, otherwise."

He smelled good. Like vanilla and spice. And his body . . . slender but firm, and already right where Jack wanted . . . not him.

Jack carefully moved them around so he was closest to the exit. "Look, this isn't a great time for me. I'm working." Not to mention the guy he was fucking on a semiregular basis was wandering around the place and he had a fondness for large firearms. "So are you, and I'm pretty sure fraternising with other staff was number three on the trouble list."

The super-pout was back as Angel reached for the phone. "Can I at least give you my number?"

Dodging him, Jack opened the door. "Maybe later. When the party's over."

Leaving the poor bloke with a glimmer of hope, Jack went back to the party and spent the next ten minutes working around to returning the woman's phone to her pocket. Thankfully, she hadn't missed it—a damn near miracle—and didn't notice Jack slipping it home, distracted as she was by the obscenely large chocolate-dipped strawberry he teased her with.

His official job done, Jack couldn't yet relax because Ethan was still hanging around. He kept his distance, except for a brief moment when they brushed past each other at the bar. Jack thought maybe he'd been forgiven for his harsh outburst when Ethan dragged a discrete finger across his chest. That thought vanished when Ethan studied the mix of red and silver glitter on his fingertip.

"It's not what you think," Jack began, but Ethan merely cleaned his finger off on the bar mat and walked away.

He didn't see Ethan again after that. Stuffing a strangely large lump of regret into an already bulging drawer in the mental filing cabinet he imagined as part of his compartmentalisation abilities, Jack finished out the party, neatly avoided Angel, and hurried to meet the car that had come to pick him up.

Lewis kept the debrief very short and, not wanting to hang around any longer than necessary, Jack threw on jeans—after removing the ridiculously large cup—and T-shirt over the stupid costume and stalked down the hall to the suite reserved for him.

Just why he thought his night should have got any better was a mystery, because of course the suite wasn't empty.

"Hello, Ethan," he said wearily, locking the door behind him.

In a chair by the window in the sitting room, Ethan was perfectly still. "Jack. I trust the job is finished successfully." He'd turned on the lamp behind his chair, throwing soft light around the room but leaving himself in shadows.

"Yeah. All done. Listen—"

"I shall take my leave, then. All's well that ends well." He stood and after buttoning his suit jacket, came towards the door.

"Ethan." Jack would have reached for him but Ethan was exuding a sharp, don't-touch vibe. "Stop."

For a wonder, he did. Poised level with Jack, looking past him at the door, ready to make his escape should he change his mind.

"I'm sorry. What I said earlier, it was wrong. I didn't mean it."

"You did mean it, Jack." Ethan's voice had at least warmed even if only to a pained, wry tone.

Jack grimaced. "I did, but not the way it sounded. Can we at least talk? I don't know about you, but I need a drink. And a shower. And possibly a cushion to sit on. Those women had sharp nails."

The corner of Ethan's mouth quirked up. "You should have dodged better."

There were a lot of things Jack should have done better, but if the only lasting damage was a few claw marks on his arse, he'd take it as a win. He just needed Ethan to listen and understand, once he'd worked out what to say and how to say it.

Ethan wandered back to the window, looking out at the night-time city. He stood back and to the side, not silhouetting himself. Jack went into the kitchenette and opened the bar fridge.

"Want anything?" He grabbed himself a beer from the minibar. The long day was catching up to him, dragging at his arms and legs like a sea anchor. A coffee would have been nice, but he didn't want to wait for it.

"No, thank you," Ethan said softly.

Twisting the cap off, Jack took a long drink and after turning out one of the chairs at the table, sat. Ethan didn't move, didn't look at him, and while he wasn't fidgeting, he wasn't in that cold, predator stillness Jack feared. He knew Ethan better now, understood him more than he had three months ago, but there were still pieces of the puzzle missing. His moments of stillness were one of them. Jack didn't know what might send Ethan into one of these moments. Once, Jack had thought it was Ethan trying to rein in homicidal impulses, but he'd learned fairly quickly that Ethan didn't have any. He had few compunctions about killing in general, but he was far from erratically homicidal. It was probably related to his obsessive-compulsive tendencies but Jack wasn't certain. All he knew for sure was that in the grand scheme of things, it didn't alter how Jack felt more than just physical attraction for Ethan.

That sense of precariousness Jack had felt in his living room earlier was back. Like he was close to doing something either incredibly stupid—or right. This time, he let himself fall.

"I'm sorry." It popped out without thought, but it was real. "I mean that, but you're right, too. I did mean what I said earlier."

Ethan moved then, to look over his shoulder, his expression blank. Not because he'd retreated but because he was working hard to not show his thoughts or feelings. "I know. I won't say it didn't hurt, because it did. But when I got away from you and stopped to think, I realised it wasn't really about my offering you backup."

"No, it wasn't," Jack said. He took another drink, and another, then forced himself to put the mostly empty bottle on the table. "But that was part of it. You know I can't have you interfering with my job. We talked about this last time."

"Which is why I offered, rather than just acting on my own."

"And yet you showed up. You followed me, all the way to Melbourne, wormed your way in and then hung around."

Ethan hesitated, turning to look back at the city outside. Even at this angle, Jack saw his lips twitch, as if he had several thoughts fighting to be said. Whatever the other thoughts were, the one that made it out was, "I wasn't trying to interfere with your job, Jack. All I knew was something had you off-centre. Even the most benign of jobs can go bad if your head's not in the right place."

Wondering what hadn't been said, Jack nodded. "Yeah, I know, but give me some credit. I can get my shit together when required. And you saw for yourself just how benign the job was." His cheeks heated at the memory of Ethan seeing him like that.

This time, there was no indecision and the corner-quirk of Ethan's mouth got so big it pulled the other side up as well. "Mm, indeed I did."

Ignoring that, Jack leaned forwards, elbows on knees, hands dangling. "And this is the bit where you get to call me a hypocrite. What I said about not wanting to be seen with you in public, that came out wrong. I mean, I do think it's a risk, to you. You are a wanted criminal, in case you'd forgotten."

"I hadn't."

"The agreement with Tan only goes so far. It protects you up to an arbitrary point only he knows."

Ethan waved dismissively. "I am aware."

"I know, but here's the hypocritical part. I know you've taken care of yourself for a long time before I came along. You sneak in and out of the country and even though I *know* you've been here, I never find any proof of it. You don't need me worrying about it, but I do. What if it all goes tits up? What if something happens and you have to scramble? What if—"

"Jack," Ethan cut in firmly. "I've had to scramble before and it's been fine. I'm rather practiced at it."

"Yeah." He rubbed his hands over his face. "God, this is going all wrong again."

"It's not, actually. I forgave you quite some time ago."

Jack peered at him over his hands. "You did?"

"Mm hmm."

"When?"

"Precisely? I believe it was when I first saw you in the lounge. You were serving drinks to a pair of very intoxicated women, one of whom was trying to pat your behind. The way you kept just out of her reach while never failing to be polite was enthralling."

Jack eyed him suspiciously. "That's what made you forgive me?"

"Oh no. That's just what you were doing when I did." Ethan's smile turned a bit sexy, a bit teasing, and all smirky. "It's the costume that made me forgive you."

"Fuck off," Jack muttered. "That's ridiculous." Ethan had to be making fun of him.

"No, it's true. You looked . . . amazing. The way your skin gleamed like old gold, light and shadow playing over your chest and abdomen . . ." He bit his lower lip, as Angel had done, but this time the action sparked something hot and needy in Jack's belly. "You have spectacular legs. They were perfectly displayed by the red underwear."

"You've seen me in my undies before." He couldn't help but like hearing Ethan say these things, even if they were exaggerated.

"For brief moments. I'll grant you, the wings were a bit overdone, but the rest of the ensemble was delicious. The horns peeking out of your black curls. The boots. The underwear. All the bare skin . . ." He trailed off and when he spoke again, his voice had gone so husky Jack had to strain to make out the words. "Even the eyeliner and the lipstick."

Jack had rubbed the lipstick off but the eyeliner seemed a bit trickier, so he'd left it for later contemplation. Maybe it would get a stay of execution if Ethan liked it that much.

Visibly pulling himself back from some edge, Ethan continued in a more even tone. "Seeing you in the costume, I finally knew why you reacted as you did when I offered to accompany you."

"Yeah? And?"

"And as sexy as you looked I knew you would find it all completely ridiculous and would hate me seeing you like that."

It wasn't the first time Ethan had pinned him with a spot-on insight. If they managed to keep going it probably wouldn't be the last time, either. And maybe next time Ethan would cut a little deeper and see why Jack felt that way.

But that was something Jack could deal with at a later point. Much later.

"So," he said slowly, "I'm forgiven for my thoughtless words?"

"Yes. And am I forgiven?"

Jack frowned. "For what?"

"For following you and being seen near you in public, after you expressly asked me not to."

Letting him stew for a long moment, Jack stood and took off his shirt. Along with the eyeliner, he'd left the glitter and oil alone. "I don't know, Ethan. Maybe I need a little more explanation. I mean, why, once you saw I was okay, did you stick around?"

Slowly, he undid his jeans and pushed them down, revealing the stupid red boxer-briefs. He really should have taken off the boots first, but he managed to toe out of them without looking too ridiculous. Well, no more ridiculous than he already did. Though if Ethan kept biting his lower lip like that while looking at him, then maybe it wasn't so bad.

"I'll be in the bedroom whenever you're ready to explain your actions." Jack turned and walked into the other room.

It was still ridiculous, but he was willing to put up with it, especially when he heard Ethan—normally so graceful—stumble in his haste to follow.

Jack settled on the bed, propped up on the pillows, and watched as Ethan entered. His jacket was already gone, shirt half unbuttoned as he stopped at the foot of the bed to finish undressing. The panes of his sunglasses roved up and down Jack's body, the looseness of his pants doing nothing to hide his excitement.

Not that the stupid red undies were any better. Worse, even, as Jack's erection threatened to rip the seams. The very long day was dragging on the rest of his body, but his dick was awake and extremely energetic.

Jack tugged at the leg of the undies, trying for some relief and just getting the slow burn of cotton rubbing over his dick. "You realise I've been up for nearly twenty-four hours, right?"

Ethan stopped mid-struggle with his cuffs. "Are you saying you don't want to . . . ?"

"Not at all." He stretched, arching his back, and spreading his legs a little. "Just that perhaps you'll have to take charge."

This time, Ethan froze. Jack worried, until Ethan's hand moved to his crotch, making an adjustment that left him biting his lips. Then he dove into a pocket and pulled out a handful of condoms and lube sachets and tossed them onto the bed. Grinning, Jack relaxed into the mattress and watched him strip.

Naked, Ethan kneeled on the end of the bed and carefully peeled Jack out of the stupid costume. Hard dick finally released, it slapped up onto Jack's belly with a firm thump, making Jack groan. Ethan spent a few moments drinking in Jack laid out like a buffet for him. Seemingly coming to some sort of a decision, he removed his glasses, blinking in the low light as he tossed them to the bedside table, then he picked up Jack's foot.

Strong thumbs pressed into his sole and pushed up towards his toes. Jack moaned, toes flexing, then curling in as Ethan rubbed firmly at the area just under them.

"Is that good?" Ethan asked.

"Very," was all Jack managed.

Ethan made a quiet, pleased noise and continued. Done with one foot, he kissed the ankle, set it down and started on the other. Then he had Jack roll over and worked on his calves. He peppered his ministrations with kisses and gently caressing fingers, so that even as Jack melted into the bed, his dick stayed incredibly hard, pressing into his belly insistently. As much as he wanted to give it what it wanted— what *he* ultimately wanted—the current situation was too nice to give up just yet.

It was a close contest when Ethan reached Jack's arse. Between the strong hands digging into his glutes and the occasional brush of thumbs along the crack and lips across the cheeks, Jack was writhing within moments. Before he could forget about leaving Ethan in charge of things, the crazy bastard moved onto his lower back. It was another challenge, however, when Ethan's hands worked up to his shoulders. Partly because Ethan was straddling Jack's arse, rock-solid dick rubbing over his skin, leaving little trails of moisture. Mostly because Ethan stopped the hard massage in favour of gentle, sweeping strokes of his warm palms that slowly removed the synthetic skin over Jack's tattoo.

Jack knew his reactions to others seeing the tattoo were contrary. He'd got it for very private reasons and became annoyed when people asked him about it. It was right there, branded on his skin for any man he got naked with to see and touch and wonder about. But Jack hated them asking. Wouldn't answer them. Waved it aside. If he was particularly cranky about it he said, "It reminds me of my mother," which was usually enough to make them back off.

It was different with Ethan, though. Ethan didn't ask and yet Jack felt as if he almost knew regardless. All he'd said about it was, "I like your tattoo. It's very beautiful." Since then, he silently reiterated his words with fingers and kisses, which he did now.

But after the first kiss, Ethan pulled back, making lip-smacking sounds.

"What's wrong?" Jack twisted his neck, trying to see him.

"Nothing. I simply wasn't expecting to taste the oil, that's all."

Sinking back into the pillow, Jack mumbled, "We could shower." Though he hated the idea of moving right then.

"Hmm, no, not yet. Maybe after." Ethan leaned down and kissed his shoulder again, this time not pulling away. "It's too beautiful in this light."

Jack wanted to snort in derision, but he was already too far gone again in the sensation of lips and fingers and the pleasant weight across his arse.

A minute, or perhaps an hour, later, Ethan finished his communion with the tattoo and got off him. "Roll over." When Jack had managed it, Ethan slung a leg over his hips again and settled down. He idly massaged Jack's chest for a while, then leaned down and applied his lips.

Jack wrapped his arms around him, loose and lazily running his hands up and down his back. The mellow mood of the massage was starting to ripple with waves of excitement as Ethan mouthed across his chest, kissing and licking and scraping his teeth over sensitised skin. He lapped at Jack's nipples, flicking them with his tongue, sending jolts of electricity down through his belly and into his dick, which was already humming at the touch of Ethan's shaft and balls. Jack's name was moaned between kisses and Ethan starting grinding against him with purpose. Hands gliding lower, Jack's fingers slipped into Ethan's crack, grazing his hole.

"Yes," Ethan hissed, spine arching as he threw his head back. "Jack, yes."

Jack pressed harder on him, watching avidly as Ethan moved to push back onto his fingers while rocking his hips so their dicks rubbed together. He was so fucking mesmerising with his lithe body and skin sliding smoothly over perfectly sculpted muscles. Redness spread under his pale colouring. Jack brought one hand around to his chest, splayed his fingers over Ethan's heart and let the intoxicating mix of dark and light sweep him away. The pounding of his heart was drowned out by the grenade exploding under his ribs, heat washing through him, into toes and fingers and head, but burning brightest right in the centre of his chest.

It could have ended like that, in a glorious mess on Jack's chest, and Jack wouldn't have minded. Ethan was there with him. That was all that mattered.

Ethan, however, had other plans. Still moving against Jack's hand and groin, he grabbed up several of the packets he'd thrown on the bed earlier. Finding one of lube, he tore it open and coated Jack's fingers.

"Inside me, Jack, now," he commanded, guiding the slicked digits back to his entrance.

"Yeah." Jack was too far gone to be amused by Ethan's blatant direction.

Both of them groaned as Jack worked a finger into him. Ethan's head dropped forwards, hair falling over his forehead. He rocked back and forth swiftly, then demanded a second finger. Jack complied eagerly and Ethan all but rammed himself onto them, taking charge like he never had before.

"Christ," Jack moaned, so madly turned on he thought he could come like this. A bit of friction on his dick and Ethan above him, fucking himself on Jack's fingers.

"Jack," Ethan returned, his voice just as strangled by passion. Then clearer, "Another!"

Jack did laugh that time, a little hysterical and a lot lustful. The third finger went in with barely a hitch and after half a minute of this, Ethan tore open a condom and rolled it down over Jack's silk and steel shaft. Sliding off Jack's hand, Ethan shifted over his dick and eased onto him. Jack's groan was soundless as the tight heat pressed around him. Ethan sighed an almost plaintive, "Jack," before venting a little grunt when Jack was finally balls deep.

In the quiet, still moment that followed, Jack reached up and ran his thumb over Ethan's bottom lip. "You have glitter on your mouth."

Ethan pressed a kiss to the pad of his thumb, then guided it to Jack's lips, rubbing it across them. "Now you do, as well."

It was Jack's turn to lock up at the mere thought of the other way the glitter could have been transferred. Some of his panic must have shown in his eyes because Ethan's serene smile faded a smidge before returning, this time wicked instead of peaceful.

That was the only warning Jack got. Suddenly, Ethan had both of his wrists in firm holds and his body clamped tight around Jack's dick.

"Hands," Ethan snapped as he jerked Jack's arms over his head, "are to remain on the headboard."

The moment of fear vanished into one of surprise as Ethan made him curl his fingers around the headboard slats.

"Don't let go and don't talk. If you do either"—Ethan lifted and thrust back down hard—"this ends."

Every iota of alarm evaporated in the flames Ethan's words and body sent shooting through Jack. The desperate need to touch and taste, to see their skin tones so sharply defined before they started to blend and blur, went up in a puff of overwhelming lust for this take-charge Ethan. Lydia could have *ping*ed right then, and Jack wouldn't have registered it. Holding the headboard, watching Ethan, feeling him, giving him anything and everything he wanted, was his only concern.

Satisfied with the situation, Ethan began to move. Slow, steady rolls of his hips that gently drove Jack insane. To watch and feel without touching him, or cursing in overpowering hunger, or telling him, showing him, how fucking good it was, how beautiful and amazing he was, was maddening. Frustrating. Painful.

Glorious.

Jack bit his lips to keep in the words and the whimpers and the praise. That, he could manage. Keeping hold of the headboard was relatively simple as well, even if he might have to think of some platonic reason why the Office had to pay the hotel for damages to the bedframe. However, even for the sake of his sanity, he couldn't—*could not*—shut his eyes.

It would have been easier to deal without the touching if he didn't have to see Ethan. See how his body shifted in the pale light of the lamp, the way his abs crunched and flexed with each roll, the way he grabbed his own dick and started stroking it in time. Yet Jack couldn't look away. Had to watch Ethan start to lose control, start to gasp and pant, start to thrust harder and deeper and wank himself faster. Watch as his head dropped back, exposing his throat for the taking, which Jack couldn't. Watch as he began to moan Jack's name, inviting a frantic, lusty answer, which Jack wasn't allowed to give.

It was excruciating yet perfect.

Leaning back, Ethan let go of his shaft so he could brace himself on Jack's thighs. He let out a long, low groan as the new angle worked his prostate over the head of Jack's dick. The new sensations flooded Jack's body with heat and electricity. His dick throbbed and his balls tightened, aching with the need to come. Jack pulled his knees up, planted his feet, and thrust upwards.

Ethan froze, mouth open on a stalled groan, hands gripping harder at Jack's thighs.

Oh shit. Jack had probably just ruined his chances at coming anywhere near Ethan tonight.

Slowly, Ethan released his hold on Jack's legs and shifted forwards, almost pulling all the way off Jack's dick. Jack wanted to chase him, to be buried in his heat again, to apologise and promise to be good but please, *please*, just finish fucking him before he expired from frustration.

Ethan planted his hands on Jack's shoulders, looming over him with a stern expression. Jack bit his lips to keep from making another mistake.

"Jack." His tone was low and growly.

Jack raised his eyebrows in hopeful apology.

"Jack." Still low, still growly, but with a hint of pleading. "Do it."

Oh. God.

Yes.

Holding the headboard even harder, Jack fucked. Ethan gasped with the first hard, deep thrust, his head dropping forwards, spine arching and fingers digging into Jack's skin. "Yes," he moaned on the next, then, "Jack," on the one after, his body starting to vibrate with each driving penetration. It all blurred into a fantastic rhythm of thrust, groan, shake, repeat. Jack's hips and legs worked separate from his mind, which was focused on Ethan. On how close those sparkling lips suddenly were, on how they shaped his name or the inarticulate, involuntary sounds he made when actual words were impossible. His mouth was *right there*, so tempting, so impossible to ignore.

Jack was suddenly back in his apartment, Ethan in his arms, laughing. Beautiful and happy because of something Jack said. Even after, when Jack had needed distance, Ethan had willingly given it to him. Then, even angry with him, Ethan had followed Jack all the way to Melbourne to make sure he was okay and safe. Ethan, who sliced Jack open with his insightful words, and then cut himself to bleed for Jack in return.

Without thought, Jack was touching him. Fingertips over his lips, across his cheeks, digging into his disarrayed hair. Lost in the sensations, Ethan didn't reprimand him, didn't stop. He just pushed his head into Jack's hands, murmuring his name as he lowered his face to Jack's. Jack didn't flinch, didn't try to stop him, trusting him to respect Jack's lines as he trusted Jack to respect his. Ethan stopped shy of touching him, gazes locked, panted breaths mingling. Jack wrapped his arms around Ethan's shoulders and drove them both to orgasm, Ethan spilling hot and untouched over Jack's belly, Jack emptying deep inside him.

Ethan slowly collapsed onto Jack's chest, face buried in the crook of his neck. He was slack and warm and heavy, but Jack held him there, not wanting him to ever move.

It couldn't last, though. Eventually, with a few sheepish apologies, Ethan peeled himself off and staggered into the bathroom to clean up. Returning with a damp handcloth, he held a wad of toilet paper out for Jack to deposit the condom into, which he then flushed while Jack wiped himself down. The handcloth was then thoroughly washed in hot water. It was a little ritual of Ethan's Jack didn't object to. DNA was not something he deliberately left behind. Afterwards, Ethan crawled back into bed, spine pressed to Jack's side, head on the same pillow. Jack curled an arm around him, fingers brushing over his shoulder.

"Jack?" Ethan asked softly.

"Yeah?" Sated and exhausted, Jack was rapidly spiralling into sleep.

"May I ask you something?"

Squeezing his shoulder, Jack murmured, "Make it quick. I'm nearly asleep."

Ethan covered Jack's hand with his own. "If I hadn't followed you here, would you have been with that angel tonight?"

Groggy fog blown away, Jack lifted his head so he could stare at the back of Ethan's. "What?"

"The blond, blue-eyed angel who followed you into the toilets. You were attracted to him and he was incredibly interested in you. I thought, if I hadn't arrived and messed things—"

"You didn't mess anything up." Jack slapped his arm lightly. "Not the job, not anything with the angel."

Ethan was quiet and tense for a long moment. "Truly?"

"Jesus. *Truly*. He was good-looking but he wasn't my type. He wasn't . . . I don't know. He just . . . *wasn't*, all right?"

After another small silence, Ethan nodded.

Apprehension swirling in his belly, Jack added, "He wasn't you, okay?"

"All right." Ethan snuggled a bit closer, held his hand a bit tighter.

Apprehension morphing into something warmer and deeper, but just as worrying, Jack kissed the back of his head. "You're not going to sleep, are you."

"No."

Rolling to his side, Jack moulded himself along Ethan's back. "Wake me up before you leave, okay?"

"You need your sleep, Jack."

"I need to see you for a while, too."

Ethan sighed. "I was planning to return to your place. If you want me there, of course."

Letting the peace of that wash through him and draw him back towards sleep, Jack murmured, "Always want you there."

He was right on the verge of dropping off when Ethan whispered, "As you wish, Jack."

"Crazy bastard," Jack mumbled on the very edge of sleep.

"Half right, Jack."

ACKNOWLEDGEMENTS

Things have been a trifle wild since *Where Death Meets the Devil* was published. Both wildly good and wildly scary. In all honesty I would not have made it to this point, publishing not just this novella, but two more and, eventually, two more novels, without the support and help of some wonderful friends. Layla Reyne, Erin McLellan and Allison Temple, you're the best Mooseketeers ever! I am forever grateful for everything you've done and I can only hope to repay you all one day. Thanks to the wonderous L.C. Chase as well, for the amazing covers and being so good natured when I asked for five covers, not just two, and patiently accommodated all my wishes.

DEATH AND THE DEVIL #1.6

WHEN THE DEVIL DRIVES

Work-life balance for a spy may be an oxymoron, but Jack Reardon likes a good challenge. And he's almost bested this one. He's settled into his Meta-State promotion as a field leader and into his new team with a second he can trust. Shop in order, he can take a day or two off when Ethan blows into town, their bargain finally starting to paying off.

Assassin Ethan Blade has few pleasures in his life—a decent cup of tea, a job well done, racing his fleet of supercars, and Jack. With plans to combine the last two into one thrilling weekend, Ethan's attempt at having a normal, happy life may deliver everything he's ever desired—or backfire spectacularly.

Jack and Ethan made a bargain, but the deal is thrown into jeopardy when the expectations and identities of the dealmakers shift—stoking the fires of doubt and jealously. Not to mention a contract killer out for revenge and an illness that threatens to reveal closely guarded secrets. Rewards are on the table for both men, maybe bigger than they even realize, if only they can renegotiate—and survive.

A NOTE ON AUSSIE SLANG

In this book, a character uses the phrase "No wukkas." This is one of Australia's most bogan slang terms. It's origin and meaning is "no fuckin' worries." How does this then become "no wukkus"? Well, we switch the first letters of the main words, "no wuckin' furries," in order to use it in polite company, and then we do what Aussies are best at and shorten it to "no wukkas." Simple, right? No wukkas!

WHEN THE DEVIL DRIVES

(APRIL)

CHAPTER ONE

"Jack."

Jack Reardon groaned and lifted his head enough to face the shadowy presence beside him. Ethan Blade, the most irritating person in the world, lay on his side, head propped up on one hand, pale eyes eerily visible in the darkened room and fixed on Jack. The bastard sounded annoyingly alert and refreshed.

"Oh, good. You're awake."

Glaring, Jack mumbled, "I wasn't."

Belly down in a soft bed, sleeping off two orgasms, Jack was quite willing to punch Ethan—except he didn't have the energy. And frankly, neither should Ethan. Instead of being nearly comatose, the man was alert and shifting restlessly. Jack didn't know what had caused Ethan's aversion to bare feet, but the feel of his socked feet sliding against Jack's legs was absurdly erotic. Combined with the fingers he drifted up and down Jack's spine, it inspired the possibility of being interested in contemplating what they could do next.

"I'm sorry." Ethan's attempt at a contrite tone failed. "I believe I'm still on Johannesburg time. I'll let you sleep then." He didn't move, just kept watching Jack with obvious intent.

"Jesus," Jack muttered into his pillow. "There's clearly something you want to do. I might not respond much but go ahead. Knock yourself out."

Ethan's low, throaty chuckle went a long way to fanning the spark of interest. It was a sound usually guaranteed to make Jack want to do stupid things. All it got this time was a slight lessening in Jack's annoyance at being woken.

"I only had talking in mind. However, given such carte blanche I might be persuaded to change my mind." His fingers trailed lower and Jack wondered if this was Ethan working his way towards asking to top. Jack had been waiting for it patiently, hoping Ethan wanted it too, but was unwilling to press the subject. Ethan had, after all, never pushed Jack on his no-kissing-on-the-mouth policy.

Ethan's hand reversed direction and travelled back up to Jack's shoulders. The assassin dug his fingers into the curls of hair laying across Jack's neck. "Tomorrow's Saturday." Ethan dropped his head to rest on Jack's pillow, close enough that his breath puffed across Jack's cheek.

"That's great. You can read a calendar." Secretly, Jack was pleased. Given any regular weekend, Jack might or might not be working, depending on whatever job the Office of Counterterrorism and Intelligence had for him. Right now, he and Harry, his second, were still watching Delta Subject for External Threat Assessment.

The Indonesian national was in country on a student visa and financially supported by his mob-associated uncle, but he was an incredibly low-level threat and sitting a Tier Two op on him was like watching paint dry. At a stretch, there were reasons why Delta Subject should be monitored, but Jack considered it a very long stretch and had told the Singaporean unit leader, Keri Sing, as much with every report he gave on the subject. She didn't agree and thus Jack was still wasting his time.

So, he'd told the Office he was taking the weekend for himself. Harry could reach him if something significant happened with Delta Subject. It was all about optimising opportunities because who knew when a seemingly harmless situation might explode into something major. It may have also had something to do with Ethan having hinted he would be back in country this weekend.

Ethan rolled his eyes at the calendar quip. "I have plans this weekend and I was hoping you'd like to join me. I'll understand if you can't due to work, or just don't wish to." Ethan nuzzled Jack's jaw. "I plan to leave around three a.m. and I'd appreciate being able to share the driving."

"Wait a minute." Jack shoved Ethan back far enough that he became mildly less distracting. "Share the driving? What are you talking about?" Christ! The man still couldn't manage a straightforward conversation.

Ethan knew exactly what he'd done to Jack by the smug tone to his British accent. "I'm going to the Gold Coast tomorrow. I've been asked to drive in an invitation-only charity race on Sunday. A man I've known for a while secured me the invitation."

Jack took a moment to digest that on several different levels. One was a memory of Ethan behind the wheel during a police chase through Sydney, looking sublimely content: transported out of his brutal, lonely life as an international assassin and into a place where he was in complete control. A place where he was just Ethan, not Ethan Blade—perhaps the man he could have been but for the shitty life experiences that had put him on the path of being a professional killer. Watching Ethan drive was a sight that had taken Jack's breath and had yet to give it back.

Another was the implication Ethan had, if not "friends" as such, then at least acquaintances outside of his work. Discovering just who he, or they, might be was incredibly tempting.

The final level was the recent change to Ethan's appearance. Jack had already spent most of their earlier foreplay teasing him about it, with classics such as, "So, *do* blonds have more fun?" and calling him "dude" in surfer drawl before heading downwards to see if the carpet matched the drapes.

"That's why you did this." Jack tugged on a lock of blond hair, so different to the usual dark brown.

"Indeed. It's how Brendan and the others have seen me in the past."

The name-drop made Jack really accept the second level. It was ridiculous to think when Ethan wasn't here, or on a job, he was alone in a lair somewhere. He had to know people he wasn't going to kill or screw. Still, Jack had to know for sure.

"Brendan, huh? He a good friend? Casual acquaintance?"

"He is, I suppose, an acquaintance," Ethan replied, tone even. If he read something else in Jack's questions he didn't react to it. "Someone I first met at Kulnura. He races Porsches but he has a 1967 AC Cobra 427 he's reconditioned. It was originally fitted with Ford's 428 engine but he replaced it with the 427."

As Ethan got carried away talking about long strokes and small bores—and not the sort of strokes or bores Jack might have been interested in—his face lit up. He became vibrant and alive, excited, using his hands to help describe the actions of pistons and crankshafts. Or whatever it was he was talking about. Jack tuned out the actual words and basked in the overwhelming enthusiasm. As much as Jack didn't really care about how cars worked, he very much liked that Ethan did.

It surprised Jack as much as it did Ethan when Jack found himself saying "Yes."

Mid-rant about something called continuation cars, Ethan stopped. "Pardon?"

Feeling a bit foolish for his awkward blurting, Jack grumbled, "Yes, okay. I have the weekend off work, Harry will cover anything that might happen, and I'll go with you to the Gold Coast. Though what I'm going to do while you and Brendan get your car-gasms on, I have no idea." And because Ethan was starting to grin, he added, "Probably just head to the beach and ogle the surfers in their wet boardies."

"You could," Ethan said reasonably. "Or . . ."

Ethan sprang on him, wrestling Jack to his back and pinning him to the mattress with his whole body. "Or you could drive with me."

Jack wiggled so his thickening dick aligned with Ethan's. "I don't know. That seems a bit boring, just sitting there while you drive around in circles."

"I can assure you it will be anything other than boring, Jack. The Gold Coast track is one of the most exciting circuits in Australia. It's not just a *circle*." As if to emphasise his point, Ethan rubbed his groin over Jack's in a slow, delicious rotation.

"Well then, that makes all the difference. When were you wanting to leave?"

"Three a.m."

"Right. It's what? Eleven thirty now." Jack did some quick calculations. "Mess around for fifteen, sleep for three hours and then go."

Ethan laughed. "When will you pack, Jack?"

"It's the bloody Gold Coast. Shorts, tees and thongs, done."

"It is also a charity event. Something a little more formal will be required for the dinner tomorrow night."

Growling, Jack rolled them over. "Fine. I'll take some closed-in shoes as well." Sliding downward, he licked Ethan's nipple.

With a part-sensual, part-resigned sigh, Ethan said, "I shall pack while you sleep."

Jack hid a grin in Ethan's belly. "Whatever. Now, I'm getting old, memory's slipping. Did we ever decide if the carpet matched the drapes?"

They left Sydney just after three a.m. Ethan drove Victoria, his black Aston Martin Vanquish S Coupe, while Jack fell asleep. He woke for breakfast in Newcastle, then dozed again until Port Macquarie. After considering him for a long moment while they were stretching their legs in a public park, and in a move that surprised Jack, Ethan handed over the keys. Despite his smirk, Jack was a bit nervous as he sat behind the wheel. He knew just what the car meant to Ethan; and what it meant to let someone else drive her. She was a dream to handle, though, and Jack settled in easily. Ethan managed to drop off to sleep which made Jack happy. If Ethan could relax enough to snooze, then he trusted Jack with his precious Victoria. Jack smiled nearly all the way to Tweed Heads, where Ethan awoke. Peaceful silence filled the car for a while.

"So, what are you driving in the race?" Jack asked. "V8 Supercar? Formula One? Mini Cooper?"

"I'll be driving Victoria."

"You're going to risk your baby on a racetrack?"

"Of course, Jack. It's the purpose she was built for. Wouldn't it be sad if she never realised her destiny?"

Jack wanted to gape but didn't take his gaze off the road. He'd never hear the end of it if *he* got a scratch or dint in the car, even though Ethan was more than willing to slam it around a racetrack with other amateur drivers.

"Okay. It's your car." Jack couldn't help but wonder if there was another unrealised destiny Ethan mourned.

When they reached Tugun, Ethan pulled up directions on a phone. It had been years since Jack had set foot in Queensland, let alone the Gold Coast, so he was grateful for Ethan's instructions guiding him to Main Beach. In between dealing with numerous detours around the racetrack and the crazy antics of the Gold Coast drivers, they found the staging area without Jack losing his cool. At the gate, Ethan handed over some paperwork and they were directed to a carpark. When the car was at a standstill, Ethan sank back into the leather seat and let out a soft sigh.

Jack was about to defend his driving but stopped himself. In the silence, he studied the man, noting the small smile, the relaxed shoulders, the way he eagerly looked at the activity around them.

God. Another vision Jack wouldn't forget any time soon. Not quite as sublime as Ethan driving at top speed, but close. He wasn't relieved Jack had stopped driving, but because *this* was Ethan's Zen place. And he'd bought Jack here to be with him.

With a muffled *thump*, that grenade in Jack's chest went off again.

He wanted to show Ethan how much he valued this and the urge to do something stupid was strong. Jack was leaning in before he realised it.

"Oh," Ethan whispered, lips parting, head tilting invitingly. Then, "Oh!" His hand snapped up and caught Jack by the face, pushing him back. "Brendan is here."

Pulling away from Ethan's hand, Jack scowled. "What the fuck?" His feelings were torn, both upset about his move being rejected so summarily and bloody grateful it had been.

"Brendan, my acquaintance." Ethan unbuckled and, hand on the door handle, paused. "Before you meet him, I should tell you everyone here knows me as Roy Carter."

Still confused, Jack muttered, "Roy Carter?"

"Yes, Jack. An investment banker from Sydney."

"Right." Forcing his mind into the moment, Jack nodded. "Right," he repeated, then asked, "And who am I?"

Presumably, Ethan rolled his eyes behind his glasses, such was his tone. "You are Jack Reardon, also from Sydney. An ex-soldier, now a specialist security advisor with the International Security Office. Though you don't tell me much about your job. A matter of national security, I believe. Oh, and you prefer to go by Nishant in social situations," he added, then opened the door and went to get out.

"Wait." Jack caught his arm. "What about us? Are we friends? Did I just hitch a ride up here to ogle surfers?"

Ethan went still. "You don't wish people to think we're together?"

Did he? Jack had no issues with being gay in public. Though he wasn't particularly demonstrative, he wouldn't hide the fact he was *with* whomever he was with. If an overly opinionated bigot happened to get more than mouthy, he knew he could take control of the situation without too much difficulty. It was, however, different with Ethan. Mostly because of the Office and Ethan's job as a paid killer. The Office had relaxed it's track and catch policy on Ethan since he'd been instrumental in uncovering a traitor, so long as he kept his work outside of the Meta-State, and tucked away in Jack's apartment, neither of their jobs mattered. Outside of the apartment was where it got tricky. Clearly, when Jack had agreed to this expedition, thoughts on logistics and tactics hadn't been part of his in-the-moment decision-making process.

So, he hedged. "You decide," he said, far more calmly than he actually felt. "It's your call."

The stillness remained for a moment longer, then Ethan nodded once. The look on his face was as expressionless as the opaque panes of his sunglasses.

"So," Jack prompted. "What—"

"Roy! I was starting to wonder if you'd make it."

The mysterious Brendan had arrived. He sauntered up to the car, leaning over to peer through the driver's side window. He was late thirties or very early forties, with a neat body kept in good trim, dark hair and brown eyes bracketed by faint laugh lines. He wore a blue and green race suit, the upper half pushed off, arms tied around his waist to keep it from dangling down to the ground. His grey T-shirt was darkened under his arms and down his chest with sweat. When he and Jack locked gazes through the tinted glass, Brendan's eyes went wide, clearly unprepared to see someone other than Ethan—other than *Roy*—in the driver's seat.

Ethan sprang out of the car on the other side. "Brendan, hey. Sorry we're late. A few last-minute details to sort out before we could hit the road."

Jack very carefully didn't do a double take at the pure Australian accent pouring out of Ethan's mouth. For his part, Brendan didn't seem entirely reassured, giving Jack a sceptical side-eye as he straightened and went to meet Ethan at the front of the car. They shook hands, then shared a manly, one-armed, back-slapping hug.

Part worried, part fascinated by the display, Jack got out of the car, taking a few moments to stretch his legs and flex his back, giving Ethan time to lay whatever foundation he needed.

The two men had released each other but remained close, talking in low voices. Brendan had crossed his arms, yet leaned in to Ethan, clearly comfortable being right inside his personal space. And Ethan looked like it didn't bother him, either. He rested his leg against the car's front, one hand in a jeans pocket, the other flying around as he explained something, making Brendan throw his head back and laugh out loud.

It was just an act. This cosy little picture of familiarity and closeness was part of the whole Roy Carter experience. At least that's what Jack told himself. The uneasy sensation in his stomach was just the remains of the doubtful bacon and egg wrap he'd had for breakfast: it had nothing to do with the way Brendan unfolded his arms and ran a hand up Ethan's arm so it came to rest on the side of his neck, thumb brushing over the corner of his jaw. Or the way Ethan didn't stop it.

CHAPTER TWO

"**N**ishant." Ethan waved him over.

Shaking off the moment, Jack went.

At least Brendan stopped touching Ethan to extend a hand to Jack. "Good to meet you," Brendan said, smiling, pleasantly enough. "Brendan South."

"Nishant Reardon." His hand was taken in a strong, firm grip, then let go so Brendan could cross his arms again. "Likewise." Like fuck.

"I have to say this is a surprise." Brendan glanced between them. "I never thought I'd see the day Roy let someone else drive Victoria."

It was part of a cover. Jack just had to keep reminding himself of that. "It's called blackmail," he said as if they were just a couple of guys joking around. "Took me a while, but I finally got something on Roy. Worth every painful moment to get behind the wheel of his baby."

Brendan laughed. Behind him, Ethan cocked his head enough to let Jack know he wasn't entirely amused.

"However you got here, I'm glad you did." Brendan turned back to Ethan. "There's been a little hiccup to the proceedings. Last-minute entry by Calhoun."

Ethan sucked in a sharp breath. "I thought he was retiring."

"We all did, then he announced this morning he's driving one last time. Tomorrow, in our little race."

"Isn't it invitation only?" Jack asked.

Brendan shrugged. "He was given one, as a courtesy. No one expected him to take it, especially not at the last minute. Not coincidently, his announcement came about half an hour after the line-up for the race was published."

"He's doing this because I won our last race."

"You didn't just win, you *trounced* him. Lucky you had to leave the country so quickly, otherwise I think he might have tried to put a hit on you." Brendan snickered.

Jack didn't find it funny. "What's this? Who's Calhoun?" He directed the question to Ethan, but it was Brendan who answered.

"Todd Calhoun. Won several million in a Lotto jackpot a couple of years ago. Decided he was going to get into amateur racing and pretty much lost it all. Not a bad driver, just too cocky."

"He thinks it's all about the car," Ethan interjected, his tone a touch sour. "It's not what you drive—"

"But how you drive it," Brendan finished for him, grinning.

Ethan returned his grin and Jack's breakfast made squirmy motions in his belly again. "Calhoun challenged me about two years ago. Ten laps at Calder Park in Melbourne. He bet pretty much the last of his money on the race."

"Good race, too. Calhoun was convinced he had it in the bag, but our boy here was in charge the entire time." Brendan patted Ethan on the shoulder, like a proud father. "Roy played coy for what? Six laps?"

Shrugging off the praise, Ethan said, "Seven."

"And then *bam*!" Brendan slapped his hands together, one shooting off the other like it was taking flight. "Rampaging Roy appeared and Calhoun got nothing but exhaust for the last three laps. I thought he was going to burst a vein when he finally caught up to you . . . in pit lane." He laughed again.

Jack looked at Ethan with raised eyebrows. "Rampaging Roy?" He wasn't sure if he should be amused or worried.

"Just a nickname," Ethan murmured.

"It's more than a nickname," Brendan assured Jack. "If you've ever seen Roy drive seriously, you know it's not."

"I've seen him drive pretty seriously." Jack recalled the preternatural calm that had come over Ethan behind the wheel during a police chase in Sydney. He nodded to Brendan. "I get it."

Ethan smiled at Jack, small and shy. All trace of the secret look was gone when Brendan turned back to him.

"How did Calhoun afford the entry fee?" Ethan asked his friend.

"Got himself a sponsor, apparently. No one knows who."

"Entry fee?" Jack asked. "I thought this was by invite?"

"The fee is more like a donation," Ethan said. "For the charity."

Brendan gestured all around them. "The Gold Coast doesn't shut down its main drag for nothing, you know. This whole thing is rather expensive. They have to cover costs somehow."

"Right." Jack crossed his arms. "And how much is the buy-in?"

Ethan smirked at him. "The *donation* is twenty thousand."

"Holy shit." Though, he guessed if everyone here was willing to race cars of the same pedigree as Victoria, then they could drop twenty grand without a second thought.

"The upshot of it is that your practice run got bumped up the schedule," Brendan said to Ethan. "You're supposed to be on the track in an hour."

If that worried Ethan, he didn't show it. "Fine. I'll need to check Victoria over first."

"You've got your usual bay. I could move Victoria for you while you go check-in," Brendan offered slyly.

"Nice try." Ethan patted him on the shoulder. "Bay thirteen, Nishant. Brendan can show you where it is. I won't be long." He sauntered off toward a pavilion on the far side of the carpark.

Jack liked the defeated expression on Brendan's face far too much and hid his smile by getting back into the low-slung car. "Which way am I going?"

Scowling, Brendan waved back the way he'd come from, toward a long row of temporary sheds set up behind one of many equally temporary grandstands that faced the track. "Thirteen's at the far end. No racing off the track," he cautioned.

"Got it. See you later."

Brendan stood back as Jack manoeuvred the Vanquish out of the park, looking a little shocked by the dismissal.

Ignoring the tiny spurt of guilt at leaving Ethan's friend behind, Jack swung the car around and, engine purring like a contented panther, eased it down the narrow space between sheds and grandstand. There was activity on both sides. Cars, drivers and pit crews to one and on the other spectators gathered between the grandstand and a fence that was more a polite demarcation line than a truly effective barrier. They snapped photos and pointed excitedly at the exotic cars. As much as

Jack wasn't a big fan, he had to admit the line-up of speed machines was impressive.

Porsche, Maserati, Ferrari. A BMW Roadster and a lone Lamborghini Diablo. Then, a car appeared that Jack had no inkling about. It looked like a Roadster and Carrera got a little tipsy one night and nine months later, this thing had rolled off the production line. This collection of cars was a veritable rainbow of high-powered dick substitutes. That is, except for the hot-pink Ferrari sporting a breast cancer awareness logo. Two women looked up from the Ferrari's engine as Jack eased by. The blonde smiled and waved happily while the redhead crossed her arms and glared. More friends of Ethan's? Behind Victoria's darkly tinted windows, Jack was just an anonymous shadow, but considering Ethan's reluctance to let anyone else drive his car, it was understandable they thought it was him behind the wheel. Jack waved back for the heck of it.

Bay thirteen was second to last in the row, between a sky-blue Carrera and a blood-red Maserati so low a shallow pothole would probably break it in two. Everyone else had backed in, so Jack carefully turned the black car around and reversed into the shade. He was barely out of the car before the friendly blonde appeared.

Her happily shouted "Roy!" was cut off as she skidded to a stop inches from colliding with Jack. Back pedalling, she eyed him warily. "You're not Roy."

"No," he agreed as the redhead strolled in and looked him over, her scowl deepening. "I'm Nishant."

"Are you a friend of Roy's?" the blonde asked.

"Who else would he be?" Red had a surprisingly low voice, laden with sarcasm.

The tone didn't dint her teammate's misgiving. "I'm just making sure. Remember what happened to Kav and Fred last year?"

The reminder of which was apparently enough to convince Red.

"*Are* you Roy's friend?" Red reiterated, arms crossed and eyes narrowed.

"Well?" Blondie prompted firmly, one brow raised sceptically.

Cornered, Jack held his hands up placatingly. "Yes, I'm a friend of Roy's. He's just at the main tent, signing in or whatever. As I said, I'm Nishant. Nish for short, if you want. And you are . . .?"

It was Red who moved first, coming forward with her hand out. "I'm Katie Cross and this is Vicky Stapleton. Nice to meet you."

Jack shook her hand and turned to Vicky.

"Actually," Vicky said, taking his hand, "it's Victoria."

"Victoria?" Jack looked between her and the car. He'd believed it a quirk Ethan had to give his cars female names and had jokingly thought of them as his harem before, but now he wondered if there was more truth to that than he'd like. The idea of Ethan and Victoria—*human* Victoria—doing more than raving about cars together made his stomach react again.

"She wishes." Katie smirked. "Victoria the Vanquish was named long before *Vicky* ever met Roy."

Vicky huffed, but broke into a cute grin. "It's true. Just happy coincidence. Are you a driver, Jack?"

Now that Vicky was convinced Jack wasn't a car thief they hung around and chatted. About two minutes in, Jack knew he was being interrogated, the ladies determined to A, ensure Jack wasn't some bastard taking advantage of their friend, and B, find out just what sort of "friends" he and Roy were.

Jack, too, wondered if perhaps there was more to Vicky's little crush. Ethan had assured him sex wasn't on his agenda outside of the requirements of a job and Jack had believed him. Then, he and Ethan had started having sex outside the requirements of a job. Their arrangement to hook up was just casual, though. Neither of them had asked for exclusivity, so it was entirely reasonable Ethan was seeing other people. Jack hadn't turned down every offer of sex outside of Ethan's visits, either. He had absolutely no right to be jealous if Ethan had slept with Vicky. Yet, the more Vicky revealed herself as an intelligent, fun woman with a love of engines to rival Ethan's, the less Jack found himself smiling and answering.

It didn't help that when Ethan finally showed up, he greeted Katie with a smile but broke into a grin and hugged a giggling Vicky. Jack may as well have stayed in Sydney for all the attention he got while Ethan and Vicky popped the Vanquish's bonnet and began rooting around in the engine side by side.

When he found himself slumped against a bench beside a similarly scowling Katie, he felt a little better, and ashamed as well.

He'd left the reason for his presence up to Ethan and if Ethan chose to play it straight, well that was Jack's issue. Even though it shouldn't be. He and Ethan weren't actually *together*.

So why the hell was he here?

Katie finally dragged Vicky away, assuring her they would all catch up after their practice runs, or failing that, at the function that night.

Finally alone, or at least as alone as they could be in an open-fronted shed with people bustling all around and a crowd of spectators across the road, Jack watched Ethan pull their bags out of the boot.

"Could you hang this up please, Jack?" Ethan held out the garment bag.

Jack grunted and took it, hanging it on a hook at the back of the shed.

"I'm sorry I took so long to register," he continued, oblivious to Jack's cranky mood. "There was more insurance paperwork than usual because the track is actually part of the public roads. Which means, I'm afraid, you won't be able to ride with me during the race."

"Whatever."

"I made sure that during the practice laps it would be fine. You'll have to suit up, as well." From the overnight bag Ethan pulled out two racing suits, one in black and silver, the other plain black which he absently held out for Jack to take. From the boot he also produced a pair of helmets. "I get fifteen minutes for practice then four qualifying laps. Thankfully, they're awarding starting positions on today's time trials, not on finishing places in previous races. I haven't raced in Australia for nearly two years."

"Lucky." Jack resisted the urge to tie the suits in knots.

Going back to the engine, Ethan began tinkering, still prattling about time trails and starting positions. Jack tuned him out. Not because he wasn't interested in hearing it, or because he was focused on how beautiful Ethan got when he was so excited. No, this time it was an attempt to keep his frustration in check.

Really, why the fuck was he here? He wasn't a part of Ethan's life beyond the bedroom. They'd established that fact weeks back, when Jack had had to draw a firm and hard line between his work and Ethan. Jack didn't know Roy-bloody-Carter and his car-crazy friends. Didn't *want* to know them. Or at least, didn't want to know how fucking close Roy might be to any of them. Didn't want to watch Ethan be Roy, the friendly, touchy guy who didn't move away when Brendan got into his personal space, who hugged and kissed cheeks in greeting, who was sensitive to the fact Katie wasn't his biggest fan and yet somehow managed to make her smile anyway. All normal, natural things.

This wasn't the Ethan Jack knew. Or thought he knew. It wasn't Ethan Blade, the calm and steady contract killer who understood and accepted Jack as a soldier and spy. It wasn't Ethan, the sometimes shy, always intoxicating man who happily locked himself away with Jack in his apartment so they could ignore the demands of intrigue and assassination, and be safe and content together.

This was a well-adjusted normal guy surrounded by people who cared for him and whom he shared regular, sociable space with. Someone who seemed so fucking genuine Jack was starting to wonder if Ethan Blade was the construct and Roy Carter the real man.

Which begged the question, just *who* had Jack been spending so much time with?

CHAPTER THREE

No thoughts had been settled and no answers found to his unasked questions before Brendan arrived with a couple of race officials. They all got under the bonnet, making sure everything was aboveboard with the engine. Satisfied the car wasn't illegally modified, they then subjected Ethan to a breath and saliva tests for alcohol and drugs, which he cleared as easily as Victoria had cleared her tests.

After Brendan and the officials left, Ethan toed out of his shoes and, unconcerned by the wolf-whistles from the spectators, undid his jeans and peeled them down right there in the middle of the shed. Normally, Jack would have made some sort of lewd suggestion himself, but things weren't normal today.

"Showing a bit too much leg there, Roy," Jack muttered as Ethan came over in shirt, boxer briefs and socks, jeans over his arm.

"You don't usually complain, Nish." There was a touch of teasing in his tone, but the exchange of jeans for racing suit was very chaste.

Jack glanced at the crowd, some of whom had their phones up, taking pictures. "Usually you don't strip for an audience." Lowering his already quiet voice to little more than a whisper and barely moving his lips, he added, "They're taking photos."

Ethan shrugged and stepped into the legs of the black-and-silver suit. "It's just my back."

Which was true. Ethan had been very careful to keep his face away from the crowd. Even with his blond hair and sunglasses, there was facial recognition software sensitive enough to find the connection between Roy Carter and Ethan Blade. The other distinctive and identifying part of Ethan's anatomy—his scarred back—was covered up.

Dressed in his suit, Ethan held out the plain black suit. "Your turn to change, Nish. Unless you don't wish to ride with me, of course."

Jack wanted to say no. The angry, confused rumbling in his stomach hadn't eased and the urge to push Ethan away, even further than he already seemed to be, was strong. He felt like the odd man out, the one who had no idea what was going on, or even who this person behind the dark shades was. Brendan, Vicky and Katie all seemed very confident about knowing Roy. They knew how to make him laugh and could understand everything he said when he talked engines and torque and fuel to air ratios. They shared his obsessive love of fast cars and knew who his on-track rivals were. And what did Jack know about him? That he used a Desert Eagle to kill people and had an odd fixation on over-the-top action stories.

He shook his head to refuse, but at the same time, started changing. Between the threads of doubt and confusion there was still that intangible magnetism, drawing Jack to Ethan. An allure of not just physical attraction, but a need to know the truth, to find the man beneath the assassin. And if that man turned out to be more Roy Carter than Ethan? More a man with nothing in common with Jack other than a messed-up military past and insane sexual attraction? Well, he'd blow up that bridge when he got to it.

Jack zipped up the suit. "Let's do this."

Ethan's smile made Jack's breath catch in his chest. "Do let's, old bean!" As did his use of the words Jack had said right before they made a two-man, no-camel assault on a paramilitary compound in the desert.

All the doubts of the past minutes fled and Jack laughed. *This* was why he was here. This sense of connection and shared moments. The idea that laughter could be born from one of the most harrowing events in Jack's life all because of the man standing beside him. The man whose unabashed smile could make Jack think dangerous thoughts.

Together, they settled their helmets in place, got into the low-slung car, and headed out to pit lane.

The idea of driving around and around in circles had never appealed to Jack, but then he'd never been in the jump seat of a racing car before. Sure, he'd been in the car when Ethan had performed some fancy moves while avoiding their police pursuit, but that wasn't this.

Ethan took the first couple of laps slow, like he was on a leisurely Sunday drive, commenting as he went about how he would have to take each corner, when and how hard to brake, frowning at the hairpin turn and scowling at the chicanes. The second straight, longer than the first, ran alongside the beach and, through Ethan's window, Jack caught sight of yellow sand and flawless blue water between the grandstands. They slid gracefully around a series of corners Jack wasn't looking forward to at top speed, and then back on the first straight, this time with palm trees and high-rises outside Ethan's window.

Third and fourth laps were faster. The Vanquish responded beautifully, gliding over the road, swishing through the chicanes and hugging the barriers around the corners. Ethan's one-sided discussion dropped away, reduced to a few mutters, as he tested the angles and available space. He seemed to mould into his seat, becoming more and more a part of the car the faster they went, knees pumping rapidly as he shifted through the gears with well-practiced ease.

This was Jack's man—peaceful, perfectly in control, finally at one with the world that was speeding by so fast it was just a blur of light and shade. It didn't even matter that Jack seemed to have disappeared from Ethan's perceptions. Getting the chance to see this again was worth the invisibility.

Two more laps like that and then, coming through the tangle of turns at the far end of the track, Ethan flashed Jack a tight smile, working Victoria back up to top gear.

"Ready, Jack?"

"For what?" he asked, stupidly.

"For a real circuit." Ethan grinned and then, sinking even deeper into his car-trance, added, "Hold on."

The car leaped forward down pit lane straight. Jack was pressed back into his seat and the world outside the car was no longer a blur, it wasn't even there anymore. All that existed was the black ribbon stretching out before them and the sleek machine carrying them along it. Ethan's hands shimmered in his peripheral vision, the left flashing between wheel and gear stick, the right twisting and turning them through the chicane, hitting lots of curb. Hard on the brakes and they took the hairpin turn so tight Jack could have brushed his fingers against the barrier, if the speed wouldn't have snapped his arm right off. Down the beach straight, hitting the next chicanes so quickly they were gone before Jack felt the bumps. Then the rapid-fire corners—left, left, right, curve, hard left—and Ethan opened Victoria back up on the pit lane straight.

Then it all happened again. And again. Each lap time seemed to get shorter. By the fourth one at top speed, Jack was cool with it. Swaying with the car around corners, thrilling at the tight in, wide out on the hairpin, loving the two-wheel bumps on the chicanes, feeling like he needed to cheer whenever they flew down pit lane straight.

Then it was over.

Coming out of the final corner, Ethan didn't increase speed, just coasted Victoria, slower and slower until the world rebuilt itself around them again—tall buildings, swaying palms, concrete barriers, splashy sponsor ads and excited spectators in the grandstands. Rather tamely, Ethan swerved them into pit lane and cruised sedately to where Brendan stood with Vicky and Katie, all of whom gave them an enthusiastic thumbs up.

Only when they were at a complete stop did Jack feel the quivering in his stomach. The rush of the speed, the electrifying sensation of balancing between precise control and wild chaos, the nearly orgasmic sight of Ethan so focused. It hit him all at once. He fumbled with getting his helmet off, and then the harness, letting it snap back over his shoulders so he leaned forwards, breathing hard, trying to decide if he was going to vomit or laugh.

A hot hand landed on his back. "Jack? Are you all right?"

Gone was the Australian accent, back was the British. A familiar touch, rubbing up and down his spine. Ethan had replaced his helmet with the more familiar sunglasses. The world tipped back toward normal.

"Yeah." Jack straightened, taking several deep breaths. "Just haven't felt anything like that since my first parachute jump."

Ethan's smile was hesitant. "Is that a good thing, or bad?"

Christ. It was back. That goddamned grenade in his chest. Mixed in with the lingering effects of the drive, its explosion wasn't as crippling as it had been in the past, but it tugged him toward Ethan, as if the only way to suppress the shock wave was to smother it with this man.

"Yeah." It was about the only sound Jack could make right then.

"Yes?" Ethan leaned in, voice lowering to the husky timbre that rattled Jack so nicely.

"Yeah, good."

Whatever Ethan might have said in response was lost in a sudden rush of people around the car. It was only Brendan, the women and the two officials, but it felt like a veritable horde invading their moment. Still, Jack's irritation was mellowed with relief as he got out of the car. His legs trembled a little but steadied smartly when Brendan made like an arrow for Ethan, laughing and exclaiming about the return of Rampaging Roy. Vicky, too, was bouncing between Ethan and the Vanquish, as if she couldn't decide which she wanted to hug more. It was Katie who came to Jack.

"First time on a track with him?" she asked shrewdly.

Jack scraped together a faint smile. "First time ever."

She glanced toward Ethan, who was demurely denying his prowess to his two fans. "You picked a good one, then. I wish I drove like Roy. He could go professional any day and yet he won't. I don't get it." She shook her head. "And his devotion to the Vanquish . . . With a better car, he could own any track." On that note, she went to offer her compliments to Ethan.

Jack had no chance to talk to Ethan. The officials occupied Ethan with more instructions and details and before long they were motioning him onto the track again. This time, with a closeup audience, Ethan was extra careful when exchanging his sunglasses for helmet so he wouldn't be blinded by the sunlight, or expose his white irises to his fellows. How any of them would react to Ethan being a Sugar Baby—the child of a woman addicted to the drug Sugar, born with tissue over his eyes, the removal of which left his pupils unable to adjust to light grades—Jack had no clue, but it was another feature that could be used to link Roy Carter to Ethan Blade, so best left hidden.

Once again, the Vanquish hit the track. From a standing start this time, Ethan had four laps to get his time as low as possible, to get a good starting position in the race the following day. Katie and Vicky took Jack to the closest grandstand, to better see the track as well as the big outdoor screen hanging from the roof of the stand opposite theirs. Brendan stood not far away, not quite ignoring Jack, but not acknowledging him either.

Nose to the starting line, Victoria the Vanquish looked like a black panther ready to hunt. Jack kind of wished he was back in the car, about to witness Ethan in his element again, but at the same time was glad he wasn't. He didn't want anything to distract Ethan, wanted him to get the best time he could. He needed Ethan to experience that ephemeral rush of control, that sensation of being in command of his life—an escape from the rest of his deadly, dangerous world.

Without fanfare, the starting light went from red to yellow to green. Rubber burned for a second, grey smoke curling up from the Vanquish's tyres, and then she was gone, roaring away so fast Jack lost sight of her momentarily. Surely she was already at top speed when, in the distance, her brake lights came on and seconds later, she vanished around the hairpin.

On the big screen, Jack watched, breathless, as the black car came out wide of the sharp turn, rear end swinging even wider for a second, before straightening up and burning down the beach straight. Katie murmured about overcorrection and pressed her lips together. Vicky assured her Roy's practice laps had been perfect and that he would undoubtedly recover. Sure enough, he navigated the mix of turns at the far end without issue and Victoria roared past them a second later, powering into the second time trial lap. There was no overcorrection this time and when the car roared past again, the entire grandstand cheered.

There was a timer in the lower corner of the big screen, but Jack ignored it, consumed with watching the car, both thrilled and scared. A weird mix of terror and excitement was in his belly, accompanied by a low-level fear. In the car with Ethan he'd felt secure, able to see Ethan in total control, to know implicitly he was okay. Now, watching from outside, he worried with each turn, with every bump over a chicane. He knew Ethan wasn't in any more danger now than he had been during the practice laps, but that didn't quell the anxiety. Part way through the third lap, Vicky put her hand on his arm and gave him a small, understanding smile. She got what he was feeling. For a moment, he wanted to tell her she shouldn't feel that for Ethan, but when her gaze slipped to Katie, he understood.

Victoria flew past, heading into her final lap. Jack's heart climbed into his throat. He still refused to look at the time, willing to count it a win if, *when*, Ethan got out of the car in one piece. A perfect lap and at last, the Vanquish roared over the finish line.

Katie and Vicky dragged Jack back down as Ethan took a slowdown lap, cruising into pit lane as they reached the designated spot for number thirteen. Brendan, of course, sauntered over as well, but everyone held back as Ethan climbed out of the car. Replacing helmet swiftly with sunglasses, he turned toward the big screen. After a moment, the image of the empty track vanished, replaced with a series of numbers.

TOTAL TIME – 4.46.0821

FASTEST LAP TIME – 1.10.6732

AVERAGE LAP TIME – 1.11.5205

CURRENT STARTING POSITION – SECOND

The grandstand whooped wildly. On the screen, a little animation came up, a silver Lamborghini raced past, followed by a black Vanquish, followed by a succession of animated cars Jack missed because suddenly Ethan was right there and throwing his arms around Jack's neck, laughing. Startled, Jack barely got his arms around Ethan before Ethan was pushing him away.

The cheering crowd faded in Jack's perception as Ethan stepped back, no longer laughing. He kept his hands on Jack's chest, a gentle pressure holding him at a distance. Not for the first time, and probably not for the last, Jack wanted to take the glasses off him and see his eyes. He knew they wouldn't tell him anything more than the straight line of his lips and the sudden tension in his shoulders, but it didn't stop him wishing.

In a sudden gesture, Ethan moved one hand to his cheek and leaned in to kiss the other one swiftly. "Thank you," he whispered mysteriously, then turned to greet Vicky, who excitedly dragged him back to the car to gush for about two seconds, before launching into a lecture about what he needed to do to make the car handle better.

Confused, Jack dragged his gaze off Ethan's back, only for it to land on Brendan.

If looks could kill, Brendan's expression was a nine-mil bullet smashing right through Jack's skull. It certainly burned through

Jack's confusion like an incendiary grenade, leaving him upset by Ethan's behaviour, which he redirected at Brendan, giving him his best SAS soldier stare. Neither a glare nor a snarl, it was a flat, cold-eyed expression that promised complete and utter annihilation if so required. It had cowed Taliban fighters in Afghanistan, terrified human traffickers in Cambodia and made a pair of terrorists in Singapore wish their car bomb hadn't broken down where it did. Here, it made Brendan swallow hard and suddenly find something else he had to do right now, somewhere distant.

The guilt wasn't as bad this time. That one look had proven that even if Ethan and Brendan had fucked in the past, it wasn't happening now, and that Brendan really wanted it to.

"Where did Brendan go?" Ethan asked, coming back to Jack. His cheeks were flushed and his smile was wide and unabashed, all signs of his earlier hesitation gone.

"Don't know. Must have had somewhere else to be. What happens now?"

"My part is officially over for today. There are still a few practices and time trials to be done. I'd like to stay here. Katie's driving next hour and I want to watch some of the other drivers as well. I'm only familiar with a couple, so I'd like to get a feel for them on the track before tomorrow . . . and I'm rambling."

Caught up in the sight of a happy Ethan, Jack grinned. "I'm used to it. You do what you have to. I'll occupy myself well enough."

"You're always welcome to stay here. I know it's rather boring for you, but I like having you near." They were standing close, but Ethan shifted a little closer, voice lowering to a husky rumble. "In fact, I'd like to have you much closer right now."

Holy fuck. Jack forgot all about the earlier brushoff and was half-hard in an instant. "Jesus, quit it. There's nowhere private here and you don't have a real backseat in your bloody car."

Ethan shivered and for a moment, Jack thought the lack of privacy might not matter. Shit. They were on the Gold Coast, with a hotel or two on every block. After witnessing Ethan drive, Jack was pretty certain he could get them somewhere secluded within minutes. Even as he was seriously considering it, Ethan moved away from him.

"Later," he said. "I'd really like to be here for Katie and Vicky. And Calhoun is driving last today. I need to see him drive before the race."

The temptation to argue was strong. Jack wanted to try to convince Ethan the women didn't need him as much as he did right then. But it went as quickly as it came, reason reasserting itself before Jack made a total fool of himself.

"Okay. Later. Want me to put Victoria back in the shed?"

Ethan handed over the keys. "Thank you. Are you going to go ogle surfers?"

"Maybe. It seems some crazy bastard got me all fired up then left me hanging. Might need to find someone…" He trailed off as Ethan's sunglasses took on a distinctly disapproving tilt. "To sell me a kabab or something for lunch. What about you? Hungry?"

"I could eat. Could you possibly bring me something?"

"See what I can find. I'll just look for the hot-pink Ferrari, shall I?"

Ethan waved him away and strolled off to find the women. Satisfied with Brendan's current state of not-being-near-Ethan, Jack got in the car and carefully returned it to shed thirteen.

CHAPTER FOUR

Changed back into jeans, Jack closed up the shed and wandered back towards the main pavilion, hoping someone there would be able to give him a direction to head in for food. He noted the pink Ferrari was gone, probably sitting in pit lane awaiting its turn on the track. If he found sustenance in time, he'd head back to watch Katie drive.

He was pulled up short, however, by the sound of a raised, angry voice coming from one of the sheds. Several others had stopped as well, curiously peering into the shadows. Two people stood behind a midnight-blue Porsche, a man in a white racing suit and a woman in jeans and blouse, holding a small tablet. She tapped away on it while the man raged at her about contracts and unfair expectations.

Mid-rant, the driver stopped and said, "You're not even listening to me, are you? Is that him you're constantly messaging? Tell him I'm not driving this piece of shit. I need a *real* car if I have any chance of placing in this stupid race."

Calm as you please, the woman neatly sidestepped the man's swipe at the tablet. "Remember, Calhoun, *you* came to my boss and pleaded for this. Beggars, choosers, blah blah blah." She turned her back on him and walked towards the front of the shed.

This was Todd Calhoun, Ethan's arch nemesis on the track. He didn't look like much physically, a short, wiry man with more attitude than bulk, but the furious way he swung after the woman, fist raised, meant business.

Jack skipped around the bystanders, racing to stop Calhoun. Peripherally, he was aware of another person rushing in as well, a tall streak of blue uniform reaching for his radio as he moved towards Calhoun.

Neither Jack nor the cop should have bothered. Before Calhoun even got close to grabbing the woman, she spun and caught his hand. In a flash, she had his arm up behind his back and chest pressed into the side of the Porsche. All without dropping her tablet or shaking even one strand of hair free of its tidy bun.

"Ow, ow, ow," Calhoun whined, cheek mashed into the top of the car. "That's my gear shift hand."

"And if you want to drive today, keep it to yourself from now on," the woman snapped. After a momentary increase in pressure on his bent wrist, she let him go and stepped back. "Any more questions, Calhoun?"

He slunk off, massaging his hand. "No. I'll drive this heap of junk, but I'm going to call my lawyers. This isn't what your boss promised me."

"You do that." She continued out of the shed, nodding to Jack and the cop as she went past. While not big, she wasn't whip-thin, either. A compact but lean body with sturdy legs and it looked like she spent more time lifting weights in the gym than Jack.

"Ma'am?" The cop turned to follow her. "Is everything okay now?"

Throwing him a big smirk, she said, "Yeah, no wukkas, mate," and kept going.

In the back of the shed, Calhoun was muttering to himself, but nothing in it seemed more threatening than a few half-hearted kicks at the back fender of the Porsche. Jack and the cop backed off.

"Wish all conflicts ended like that." The cop took off his cap and dragged his brown hair away from his sunglasses. "Make my day a lot easier."

Jack snorted. "She had him dead to rights, no worries."

"Yeah." The flashed grin vanished in favour of a serious expression aimed at Jack. "Thanks for coming to help, sir. Not many people would." He was clean shaven with a strong jaw and slightly too thin lips. His utility belt sat on a trim waist, strong, tanned forearms shown off by short sleeves and lean legs not totally disguised by the many-pocketed pants. The name badge on his chest read Constable Stewart.

"Only thing I could do," Jack reasoned as the gathering of onlookers broke up and wandered off in various directions.

Giving him a once over, Stewart smiled. "Look like you can handle yourself, at least."

Jack's dick was still too charged from Ethan to miss the nuance in the look. Or maybe it read too much into it because Stewart gave him a mock salute and stepped away.

"See you round, sir."

"Yeah," Jack said. "Maybe."

Drama over, Jack resumed his own mission. Eventually he found several food stalls, the scent of sizzling lamb drawing him to a kabab place. Two kebabs with everything and two cans of drink in hand, he returned to the grandstand over pit lane. A red Maserati was just coming in, having finished its time trials. When the times came up and then the little cartoon cars whipped past, Jack was proud to see the black Vanquish still in second place. Jack found Ethan and Vicky in pit lane just as the hot-pink Ferrari eased out onto the track to start the practice laps. Ethan was too busy calming Vicky down to pay much attention to the food Jack shoved into his hands. Unwilling to be the third wheel, Jack retreated to the grandstand and found a relatively quiet seat to have his late lunch.

Jack, in his far-from-expert opinion, decided Katie was a good driver. She took the low-profile car through the practice laps without any issues. When she pulled it back into pit lane and got out to talk to Vicky, she looked happy, even smiling at Ethan.

"Who's your pick?"

Jack looked up. Constable Stewart stood a couple of seats away, looking over the row of expensive cars in pit lane. Arms crossed, legs spread, he was a glorious image of man in uniform. Not having a uniform fetish of any sort didn't stop Jack from appreciating the view.

"Aston Martin," Jack said.

Stewart frown-smiled. "Really? It's such an outsider, considering the rest of the cars on the track."

"He's currently in second position."

"Time trials rarely mean anything in the pack." He motioned to the seat next to Jack. "Taken?"

Jack waved him down. "Nope. I'm Nishant, by the way. Nish."

"Aaron."

They shook hands and Jack asked, "So, who's your favourite?"

"The TVR. Like you, I'm sort of going for the underdog."

"TVR?"

Stewart pointed to the chameleon-coloured car Jack hadn't recognised. "British-made sports car. You don't see them over here much."

"Is everyone here a car nut?" Jack said, scrunching up his empty kabab bag.

With a laugh, Stewart nodded. "If you're not, why are you here?"

"Came with the Aston Martin driver."

"That explains it."

"Currently second," Jack reminded him.

Stewart pointed to where Katie was nudging the pink Ferrari up to the line. "Not for long, I reckon."

Jack took a swig of his drink, then said, "We'll see."

Despite his general preference for Ethan, Jack found himself hoping Katie did well, holding his breath each time the Ferrari blurred past them. She had a perfect run and when her times came up, Jack clapped. In the pit, Vicky and Ethan rushed to congratulate the stunned redhead. On the screen, the silver Lamborghini went past, then the black Vanquish, then the pink Ferrari. She'd placed third. Stewart conceded with a nod, then smiled impishly.

"Wait for the TVR results before rubbing it in," he said, standing. "Gotta do a walk around. Will you be here in fifteen?"

"Not sure. I might get bored and go to the beach."

Stewart hesitated. "Do you have a phone?"

"Actually, I don't." Jack wasn't about to admit his telecommunication capacity was hardwired into his brain.

Pulling a pen, Stewart motioned for Jack's hand. He wrote a number on the back of his forearm. "In case you're interested. Hopefully it won't wash off if you go for a swim."

With that, he was away on his rounds again. Jack watched him go. When he looked back at the pit, the familiar dark shades pointed in his direction. The distance was too great to make out if the expression meant Jack should duck for cover or not. Recalling how he had felt wondering about Brendan's and Vicky's intentions for Ethan, Jack made a show of licking his thumb and rubbing it over the inked numbers—but not before he snapped a shot with his implant. He didn't know why he'd taken the photo, and as Ethan turned back to Katie, he considered deleting the image. The hook up back in

February hadn't meant anything beyond immediate gratification, and as nice as it was to know Aaron was attracted to him, it wouldn't go anywhere. Especially when one look at the black-and-silver race suit bending over the engine of the Ferrari was enough to make Jack think "Aaron who?"

Oh God. Jack dropped his head into his hands. This was serious. Somehow he'd ended up in a relationship type *thing* with Ethan-fucking-Blade. He got jealous of people he had no real reason to think Ethan was seeing. The idea of being found attractive was *nice*, but not something that got him excited. When he thought about sex, it was only Ethan who popped into his fantasy.

Shit. He was in trouble.

Even after the pink Ferrari was driven away, Vicky and Ethan trailing along after it, Jack remained where he was, blindly watching another Ferrari go through practice laps and time trial. The beach didn't hold any lure for him now, not when ogling surfers wasn't going to do much more than frustrate him.

He shouldn't have come. Alone at home, he wouldn't have had to confront this new and troubling realisation.

"No beach, huh?"

Jack suppressed a groan. This was all he needed. "No," he said as Aaron sat down beside him again. "How was the patrol?"

"Uneventful, thankfully." He grinned, infectious and cute with dimples appearing in his cheeks. "The TVR's up now and I couldn't miss it."

If he hadn't been in the midst of a crisis, Jack would have enjoyed sitting through the practice laps of the odd little British car. Aaron was fun company, making sly observations about the drivers in the pit, comparing them to the various cars in the event. Jack found himself laughing several times, especially when as the TVR took off for its time trial, Aaron said, "And that's how fast his knickers would drop for the Lambo driver, too."

A strong hand landed on Jack's shoulder and his laugh choked off in surprise. As the fingers squeezed a little tighter than comfortable, Jack looked up and met Ethan's shuttered gaze. Even through the dark panes of his sunglasses, Jack could feel the steeliness of the man's expression.

Before Jack could stutter anything out, the grip turned into something more like a caress, his thumb brushing against the corner of Jack's jaw.

Ethan turned his attention to Aaron. "Hi," Ethan said in his Aussie accent, holding his other hand out. "I'm Roy."

Aaron looked from the proffered hand, to Ethan's face, to the hand on Jack's shoulder, and swiftly modulated his reaction. So, instead of looking like he wanted the earth to open up and spew lava all over him, he managed a thin smile and to shake Ethan's hand. "Aaron."

As Brendan had done, Ethan had shucked the top of his race suit, tying the sleeves around his waist. His dark-blue T-shirt showed off his arms, muscles flexing as he gripped Aaron's hand with unnecessary strength.

"Nice to meet you." Ethan's tone was pleasant but the straight line of his mouth spoke another tune. "I'm glad Nish found someone to keep him company. I was worried he'd be distracted by all the surfers."

Recovering, Jack gave Ethan's wrist a gentle squeeze. "Nothing to worry about. Trust me." He hoped Ethan got the message before Aaron had cause to pull his Glock.

Ethan looked down at him. After a moment, his face relaxed a bit. "I do," he murmured, a touch of his real accent in it. Letting his hold on Jack go, Ethan claimed the seat on Jack's other side. "I've been interested in seeing the TVR. I drove one of the new Sagaras on the Silverstone Circuit in Towcester. Much improved over the older models, though the braking is still troublesome."

The TVR whizzed past them on its second lap, and then on the third, before anyone spoke.

"Yeah," Aaron said, "I had heard that. And no airbags."

Ethan huffed. "I believe the philosophy is 'don't crash.'" He and Aaron chuckled.

In the end, the TVR ended up bumping Katie down to fourth.

A Roadster roared around the track while the men on either side of Jack debated the merits of the various cars and then the last time trial was announced.

"They look familiar," Aaron muttered as Calhoun and his companion got out of the Porsche that had just arrived in pit lane.

"Calhoun." Ethan sat forward, arms on knees, watching intently as Calhoun argued with the officials.

"Is that a GT3?" Aaron asked absently.

"GT2. An old RS model."

"You sure?"

Ethan sat back, lips in a thin line. "Certain. I have a GT3 RS myself."

"Jeez," Aaron hissed. "Why the hell aren't you racing that here?"

"It's in Germany."

"Oh."

Jack sort of hoped Calhoun would get himself disqualified by arguing with the officials, but sadly, he got back into his car and headed out for his practice laps. Also sadly, Ethan and Aaron had nothing scathing to say about the man's driving. He even got a grudging nod from Ethan when he whipped across the finish line at the end of his time trials. Jack's stomach knotted when the animated cars raced past on the screen. Silver Lambo, blue Porsche, black Vanquish, chameleon TVR, pink Ferrari.

"Third's pretty good," Aaron said sympathetically. Then smirked. "Brilliant for a Vanquish, in fact."

Feeling a little protective, Jack said, "It's not what you drive, but how—"

"The defence of all Vanquish drivers." Perhaps there was a bitter tinge to the words, Aaron sore at Jack for various reasons. Or maybe it wasn't there at all, because the smile that followed seemed genuine. "I'm due back at the station. It was good to meet you both. Good luck tomorrow, Roy. Nish."

They shook his hand in parting and when he was gone, Jack braced for impact. Ethan, however, stood and stretched. "The formal dinner starts in a couple of hours. Shall we go to the hotel and get ready?"

"Is it really going to take a couple of hours to shower and put on a jacket?"

Ethan looked down at the track for a long moment, then turned to Jack. Softly, he said, "No, but I need to be alone for a while. Today has been very good, but also trying. Normally, I wouldn't attend any of the social activities associated with these events, but I want to this time. With you."

Anyone else wouldn't have heard the strain in his tone, but Jack had become familiar with Ethan's quirks over the past months. Ethan had been playing the part of a well-adjusted guy all day and now he needed to retreat and recharge before doing it all over again.

"Okay." Jack stood. "We'll go book in and then I'll leave you alone for a while."

Ethan smiled, touching Jack's arm briefly. "When I said 'alone,' I meant us together, alone. I'm sure we can fill at least an hour with something relaxing."

The fact that, however Ethan had meant to play their relationship at the start, it now appeared he wanted them to be here *together*, made Jack grin stupidly wide. "Okay."

They had to leave Victoria locked up in her shed and get a taxi to Q1. Ethan had booked a room on the seventy-fourth floor, three below the SkyPoint Observation Deck where the dinner was taking place. Jack barely got a chance to take in the white kitchenette, dark-grey carpet, red rug and wide windows overlooking the ocean. Rather, he was all but thrown onto the couch, allowed maybe a second to catch his breath, and then Ethan was on him. Straddling his lap, Ethan didn't waste any time, peeling them both out of their shirts, his nails and teeth scoring Jack's skin with light marks that felt suspiciously like brands. Not that Jack cared. He made his own claims on Ethan's body, biting his neck and shoulders, sucking a nipple into aching stiffness, tugging on the strangely blond hair until Ethan whimpered and melted against him. Ethan won the time trials of getting naked, goading Jack to better efforts by tumbling to the red rug and opening his arms and legs in invitation. Jack had rarely been so inspired.

An hour filled up with frantic moments. Ethan's mouth on his neck. Jack's fingers dragging down his arms. Gasping in unison when Ethan wrapped a hand around both their dicks, stroking them to mutual orgasms. Holding on as Ethan rolled against him.

Then Ethan was on his back, one leg hooked around Jack's waist, back arched as Jack drove into him, his fingers digging into Jack's spine. The complete abandonment in Ethan's actions, the utter openness of his expression, the plaintive tone to the way he moaned Jack's name, was as captivating as his fixed concentration at the wheel had been.

"Jack, please." Ethan twisted under him. "I need . . . I, I . . ." He groaned and heaved off the floor. "Please!"

The sight of pale, dishevelled passion caught Jack fast. Dark lashes resting on flushed cheeks, curls of sweaty hair around his face, lips parted, the indelible scent of Ethan winding around them. It was all just so fucking much it swamped Jack. It stole the air from his body, swept his metaphorical feet right out from under him.

Christ. He couldn't help himself, drawn like iron to a magnet. All the manic, driving need to come fell away. His hard thrusts slowed, smoothed. Lowered himself until they were chest to chest, bodies gliding against each other, slicked by the sweat of their wild fucking. He wound his fingers through Ethan's, feeling him grip back, as desperate, as tight. Burying his face in Ethan's neck, he locked his lips on the pulse thrumming under the corner of his jaw so he wouldn't do other, silly, things with his mouth. Ethan clamped his knees to Jack's ribs, ankles crossed over his lower back, breathing out Jack's name, over and over, shuddering with every slow, deep stroke.

This wasn't fucking anymore. It was . . . something else. Something Jack tried to shove away with all the powers of denial he had. Something he threw into the deepest drawer of his mental filing cabinet, where he sent all his most troubling memories. Yet, for the bloody life of him, he couldn't stop. Couldn't get back to the wild, manic pounding of moments earlier. Coming wasn't the most important outcome all of a sudden—the here and now with his Ethan was.

It was inevitable, though, and when it happened, it was simultaneously both the quietest and most powerful of orgasms. The rush of heat through his body from the explosion of his chest grenade, the burst of light behind his eyes, the marrow-deep thrum of connection through release. All of it stole Jack's voice and he pressed his open, silent mouth to Ethan's skin, drawing in everything that was Ethan until he was full to bursting.

CHAPTER FIVE

He came back to himself with the soft touch of a gun-calloused hand resting on the back of his neck, his body cradled within Ethan's.

"Jack." Ethan nuzzled into his cheek. "Are you all right?"

No. No, he wasn't. His carefully ordered world was falling apart around him.

"Yeah." Jack lifted his head enough to breathe something that wasn't Ethan. He had pretty much collapsed on him, his entire weight pinning Ethan to the rucked-up red rug. "Sorry." As he moved, a still hard, insistent dick poked into his belly. "Shit, you didn't come."

"It's fine, Ja . . ." Ethan trailed off into a groan as Jack pulled out of him. A groan that turned into a startled gasp when Jack took his dick into his mouth. "Jack!"

It didn't take much, a few licks across the head, swirls along the pulsing vein under the thick shaft and a couple of swallows while Jack's nose was planted in the springy hair around the base.

Afterwards, Jack settled down with his head on Ethan's belly. Screw the dinner. He was going to spend the rest of the night right here, mesmerised by the contrast between his brown hand stroking across pale skin. Ethan, too, seemed happy with the situation, twining his fingers through Jack's hair, rubbing his cotton-clad foot along his leg.

As with everything, though, it had to end. The filled condom quickly got uncomfortable and Ethan had to dislodge Jack to relieve a cramp in his back. The quiet between them as they collected themselves and headed for the shower was new. Not weird, just different. It stayed with them all through getting clean and grooming side by side before the huge mirror. They moved together and around each other with sure, certain motions, passing razors back and forth, chuckling when they each picked up the wrong toothbrush. Ethan finger combed Jack's usually unruly hair until he was happy with it. Jack styled Ethan's into a mohawk and laughed at his scowl when he saw the results in the mirror. He watched, fascinated, as Ethan inserted blue contacts, not sure if he liked the result of normal eyes on him.

Jack dressed in the suit Ethan had packed for him, a dark-grey Hugo Boss he'd bought with the intention of attending the wedding of an old SAS mate. He hadn't made it. Instead, he'd gone undercover with a paramilitary group in the Great Sandy Desert, where he'd met Ethan Blade. Who looked, unsurprisingly, deadly and sexy in a slim-fitting black suit paired with dark-blue-tinted, wire-rimmed glasses.

It all made Jack even more reluctant to go mingle with other people. He grumbled when Ethan ushered him out of the room but, bolstered by the way the afternoon had ended, Jack reached for Ethan's hand as they walked down the corridor to the lifts. Ethan glanced at him, his strangely blue eyes wide. After a moment, he smiled softly, squeezed Jack's hand, then let it go just as the lift doors opened. Inside, two other couples clearly on their way to the dinner peered out curiously. Close but not touching, Ethan and Jack stepped in. The doors shut and the lift whizzed upwards.

One of the other men scowled at Jack and Ethan, clearly not liking their proximity. Maybe it was just the race rivalry, but Jack wouldn't bet on it. Not the way his date—possibly his wife by the rings on their fingers—shot them apologetic glances.

That, thankfully, proved to be the worst of the homophobia on display at the dinner. Everyone else was more concerned with Roy Carter's stunning time trial being knocked down to third by the scandalous latecomer to the race, to which none of them could get more than a modest "We'll see who crosses the line first tomorrow" from Ethan. Around the fifth repeat of the exact same conversation, Jack excused himself and went for a wander.

What Jack had thought would be a sit-down dinner was a reef and beef themed buffet of tiny portions perfect for carting around on an equally tiny plate while mingling. The bar, at least, was open and

Jack snagged a scotch, sipping the rich, smoky drink as he picked over prawns and rare cuts of filet mignon. With his little plate and drink, he went to see the view.

The observation deck had floor-to-ceiling windows almost all the way around, showing off the glittering Gold Coast to perfect advantage: the long stretch of curving beaches, phosphorescent waves crashing on the wet sand, tall spires of sparkling lights of all colours, flashing spotlights of a concert at the racetrack, and the dark, winding snakes of seawater canals, their banks glowing with the ambient light of homes backed up to the water. It was truly beautiful and Jack found himself looking for Ethan, wanting to share the view.

He found Katie first. She stood in a quiet corner, in a slinky emerald dress that kissed the carpet, her red hair piled on top of her head in an artful tumble of curls. She gulped from a champagne flute, two empty glasses sitting on the narrow ledge in front of her as she gazed out a window. Jack guessed she didn't really see the view.

"Should you be drinking so much?" he asked gently.

Katie scowled at him, then with an effort, smoothed it off her face. "It's non-alcoholic. They're watching us drivers like hawks." She glanced around furtively. "Do you think you could . . .?"

"Afraid not. Roy would clobber me if I got you a real drink."

"Vicky would help him, no doubt." Katie leaned against the window. "Don't mind me, I always get like this before a race. Nerves. I saw Roy before. He's as calm as ever, the prick. I hate him." She scrunched up her face. "Sorry."

Jack laughed. "Don't be. I get it. I wasn't his biggest fan when we first met, either."

"Yeah? What happened?"

She seemed keen for a story, or a distraction, maybe, but there was no way Jack could tell her about Valadian's secret army in the desert, or how within minutes of meeting Jack, Ethan had mowed his way through twenty-odd soldiers with barely a scratch to show for it. Couldn't tell her how Ethan fucked with his head until he was paranoid and confused, then turned around and showed Jack care and compassion, and a startling vulnerability hidden by the outer assassin.

He settled for, "A lot of things neither of us really like to remember now."

Katie studied him for a long moment, then nodded. "But you're good now, right? Happy?"

Jack's guts clenched at the forthright question.

"Oh shit," Katie whispered when he couldn't answer. "It's not great, is it? I'm sorry."

"No, it's .. We're . . ." Jack surrendered his pride. "I don't know what it is, or what we are. This is the first time we've been out like this, around other people. Alone, everything is fine. Great, even. But here, now, I don't know what he expects, or wants. I don't really understand this whole thing and he's off in the middle of it all, being someone I've never seen before and now I feel like I don't know him at all."

Katie snorted. "You're not the only one."

"What do you mean?"

"Well, in the past, Roy's been friendly and he's always happy to talk about the cars or racing, but anything beyond that . . ." She shrugged. "He doesn't socialise. He doesn't talk about anything more personal than preferred tyre brands and he's never mentioned having family or close friends. Then he shows up with you and it's all different. He actually laughs and talks about you almost as much as he talks about Victoria. He put on a suit that's *not* a racing suit. *And*," she added pointedly, "he took off his sunglasses. Who even knew he had eyes?"

Jack chuckled at her part-aghast, part-fascinated tone. He was even amused by her suggestion that he hadn't yet surpassed Victoria in Ethan's affections. He was pretty sure he had, though, since Ethan had let him drive the car.

"Look at it this way," Katie continued gently. "Maybe he's feeling a bit out of sorts, too. This is the first time he's brought someone special to one of these events. Or anyone at all, actually. Maybe you need to get to know each other in this new environment. Or maybe, Nishant, you just need to talk to him about how you're feeling."

Smile dissolving, Jack startled at her use of Nishant. It wasn't that he wasn't used to hearing it, but more that until right then, he'd never associated it with anything to do with Ethan. When he and Ethan were together, they were Jack and Ethan. Not Nishant and Ethan. Much less Nishant and Roy.

Shit.

Jack was such an idiot. The name Roy was a cover, but the man wasn't. Rampaging Roy, race car driver, was as much a part of Ethan as Ethan Blade, paid killer. Just as Nishant was Jack's way to smooth over society's racial expectations. Nishant wasn't separate from Jack, just another shield he used to protect himself.

"Oh, God," he moaned. "I'm such a fucking dickhead."

"No, you're not," Katie said soothingly. Then, in a drier tone, added, "You're just an ordinary dickhead. Also, whatever other issues you two might be having, just know how good you are for Roy. You made him more . . . human."

That pesky, secondary charge on the grenade went off under his ribs, a warm rush from the mini explosion rolling through him. The pleasantness of the heat quickly turned to shame as Jack recalled how pathetically jealous he'd been earlier.

"I don't know how good I've been for him today. Seeing Vicky all over him, I kept getting more and more upset. And Brendan . . . Jesus, Brendan. I pretty much promised to hurt him if he touched E—" he caught himself at the last moment "—even one hair on Roy's head."

"First, don't be worried about Vicky. She's got her crush, sure, but at least seventy percent of that is for his car. He told her nothing would happen a long time ago. I wondered if it was because he was gay, but you're the first proof we've had of that. As for Brendan, he's married with two kids."

"Doesn't guarantee he's not after him."

"No, I guess not. And I do know they've met up when both of them have been—" She stiffened abruptly, her gaze locking on something over Jack's shoulder. "Brendan, how long have you been there?"

Jack spun and found the older man behind him. He looked a little unsteady on his feet, an empty tumbler in one hand.

"Long 'nough," Brendan slurred, raising the hand with the glass in it, one finger extended to point at Jack. "Long *enough* to know you don't deserve him. You don't care about the cars. Don't know anyshing . . . any*thing* about them. It doesn't matter what you do to me, *Nish*. It doesn't matter at all, 'cause in the end, I'm the one who loves what he loves. Who *knows* him."

"Brendan," Katie hissed, but Brendan spoke over her.

"Roy lives for driving. *Lives* for it, and yet, and yet he hasn't been around for nearly two years! He missed the Kulnura meet-up, and Bathurst, two years in a row. And when he does show up, it's with *you*. A . . . a brut who doesn't give a fucking shit about any of this. Or him. I saw you with that cop." He gave Jack a wobblily glare and another jab with the tumbler in his hand.

Jack caught Brendan's arm before he made contact and took the glass from him. Reactions delayed by the alcohol, Brendan jerked away, stumbling so hard he had to catch the wall to stay upright.

"You know, Brendan," Jack said calmly as he set the tumbler down on the ledge next to Katie's empties, "if you'd shown up five minutes earlier, you probably would have gotten the fight you're after."

Katie's eyes went wide and Brendan winced.

"You're right, though. I don't really care about the cars or the racing, but I do care about Roy. I want him to be happy and at peace here, doing what he loves, so I'm not going to argue with you or fight with you. I'm here for him and that's all that matters."

Jack felt the truth of the words as he said them. He might have been swept away by the sight of an enraptured Ethan when he agreed to come to the Gold Coast, and he may have been seriously doubting his place here for most of the day, but right then, he knew this was where he needed to be—with Ethan. Or Roy Carter. Or even Ethan Blade.

Wish you were here?

The words echoed through his head, but this time, they came not just with a pang of dread and pain, but a promise of contentment as well.

"My apologies for being rude to you today," Jack said to Brendan. "I hope we can get past this for Roy's sake."

Brendan squinted, as if suddenly not recognising him. Katie, too, looked at Jack like he'd been replaced by a pod-person.

"Katie, I'm going to find Roy. Do you want to come?" Jack hoped she would take the chance to escape Brendan.

"No. You go." Katie gave the drunken man a sad look. "I'll help Brendan back to his room."

Hesitating, Jack only left when Katie shooed him off. As he went, he heard her mutter, "You really blew it, Brendan. You're not going to race now. Come on, let's go." A moment later there was a startled yelp and a gasp, then the sound of a body hitting the floor.

Jack turned, half expecting to find Brendan faceplanted, but it was Katie who was down. Brendan leaned against the wall, head in his hands, saying "sorry" on repeat. People came from all directions but Jack reached Katie first, crouching beside her. She lay on her side, curled around her stomach, gasping in pain.

"Katie? What's wrong?" Jack checked for blood and exposed bones, finding neither. "Did he hurt you?"

"No," she moaned, unfurling a little. Tears cut across her face. "It was an accident. He stood on my dress and I fell." Gingerly, she held her left arm to her chest as Jack helped her sit up. "Landed on my wrist. I think . . ." She looked like she might puke. "I think it's broken."

"Katie!" Vicky crashed down on her other side. "Oh my God! What happened? Are you okay?" She went to hug her friend, but Jack held her back before she could crush Katie's injured arm.

Then Ethan was there as well, quickly followed by several of the race officials. It all turned into a big production, with Katie and Vicky bundled into a taxi to the hospital while Brendan was discovered vomiting into an ice bucket. After Brendan was disqualified for drinking, he loudly declared it was all Nishant's fault before slinking away, miserable and alone. Amidst speculation about Brendan's accusation and Katie's ability to drive the following day, Jack decided he was over it and told Ethan he was going back to the room. Oddly blue eyes narrowed behind his glasses then Ethan agreed and went with him.

Once alone, Ethan demanded an explanation and Jack told him an edited version of events, leaving out his own personal revelations and focusing on Brendan's slurred admissions. He shouldn't have bothered because he could almost hear the cogs turning in Ethan's nimble brain.

"And so you decided that I've been sleeping with Brendan," Ethan summarised coolly. "I told you, I don't have sex—"

"Outside of jobs," Jack finished for him, also finishing his third helping of minibar scotch. "So you said, but what happened today, and last night, if not sex outside of a job?" His restless pacing took him past Ethan.

Ethan leaned against the kitchenette counter, arms crossed. "That's different, Jack."

"Is it?"

"Of course it is. Besides, he's married."

"Doesn't mean a thing."

"I think it means—"

"You know what I mean." Jack scowled and went for another drink. Where was the acceptance he'd found earlier? Before Brendan went and fucked things up all over again.

"What's wrong, Jack?"

"Nothing." He unscrewed the cap of another tiny bottle. The scotch was gone and he was on to the vodka.

"Don't, Jack." The British accent was back and brooking no argument.

Whether the "don't" was about the denial or the drink, Jack wasn't sure, so he put the little bottle down and sighed. It was like he'd swallowed razorblades and now they had to come out again. "I was jealous, okay? I saw you with him, being all happy and car-gasming and it bugged me that I wasn't a part of it. That he understood that part of you and I don't. And let's not even mention Vicky."

Ethan's lips twitched like he did want to mention Vicky, but all he did was uncross his arms and grip the counter behind him. Gripped it until his knuckles went white. "How do you think I felt seeing you with Aaron? I know I'm not the only person you see, Jack, and it's fine. I understand. I was simply . . . surprised that you would . . . look for someone here."

Jack opened his mouth to explain there hadn't been anyone else for months and that there wasn't going to be anyone else again, but nothing came out. His throat felt too torn up from confessing his jealousy. Nothing with potentially sharp edges was going to come up until it healed. So he sidled closer to Ethan, cautiously, in case he was way off base and got a fist in the throat. Ethan went still. Jack froze, too, wondering if four drinks would slow his reflexes enough for Ethan to pin him without any trouble.

"I wasn't looking—" It was the truth, but it had some potentially dangerous angles, so Jack went with a slightly less hurtful but no less true line. "I'm with you. I'm here for *you*. Aaron was . . . he was just someone *I* could talk to. I mean, you have Brendan and the women, and I was . . . I don't know . . ."

"Being childish?" Ethan cast him a wary side-eye.

"No. Yes." Jack's cheeks heated. "I was lonely. I'm not used to—" *sharing you*, but that was deadly too. "To seeing you like this. I'm sorry."

After a long, terrifying silence, Ethan shifted enough to touch his shoulder to Jack's. "Thank you. I'm sorry, too. I shouldn't have acted as I did this afternoon. I jumped to the wrong conclusions as well."

Jack let out a shaky breath, then nudged Ethan gently. "You know I wouldn't have hurt Brendan, right? I just needed him to not be near you."

"I know." Pushing away from the counter, Ethan stretched and headed for the bathroom.

"And?" Jack prompted.

"And what, Jack?"

"And you wouldn't have hurt Aaron, right?"

Ethan kept walking and just before he stepped into the bathroom, gave a little shrug.

Oh, shit.

Then Ethan's evil chuckle cut through Jack's sudden worry. Biting back a curse, Jack muttered, "Crazy bastard," and went to get changed.

CHAPTER SIX

Race day was overcast but the endless weather checks kept saying there was very little chance of rain. Which meant the pre-race entertainment went ahead. There was a Mini Cooper race, the tiny cars driven around the track by local celebrities, followed by a performance from a band Jack hadn't heard from for at least ten years. The famous, gold-bikini-clad Surfers Paradise Meter Maids made an appearance, putting coins into mock parking meters set up beside the race cars lined up in pit lane.

The turnout for the actual race was spectacular, every seat filled and crowds of people standing five or more thick at the barricades. Thankfully, there was a platinum grandstand reserved for the drivers and their teams. Brendan was absent, as were Vicky and Katie—who wouldn't be driving any time soon with her broken wrist—so Jack found himself rather aimless as Ethan retreated to do a final check on Victoria. Jack spent a while following Todd Calhoun around, just for the fun of it, grimacing as the man schmoozed on anyone who looked like they had spare cash to drop on a new car for him while Calhoun's very capable companion was nowhere to be seen. Just before the main race, Jack went down to pit lane to check on Ethan.

"How's she looking?" Jack asked as Ethan ran a sheepskin glove over the already gleaming paintwork.

"Good. No one tampered with her overnight."

Jack knew better than to ask if Ethan was serious. He hadn't lasted sixteen years as a notorious assassin without developing a few paranoias.

"And you? How are you doing?"

Ethan held up a hand. It was steady enough to rest a brimming champagne flute on.

Satisfied, Jack hung around while Ethan made his final preparations. When it was time for the cars to get on the track, Jack solemnly accepted Ethan's sunglasses in exchange for his helmet.

"You'll stay for the race?" Ethan asked from behind the visor.

Jack startled. "Of course. Why wouldn't I?"

"You haven't ogled any surfers yet."

Pretending to adjust the helmet, Jack leaned in and said just loud enough for Ethan to hear, "Too busy ogling Aston Martin drivers."

For a moment, Ethan's gloved hands touched Jack's chest, then they pushed him back playfully and he got into Victoria. Jack closed the door and thumped the roof of the car twice, stepping back when Ethan started her up.

All around them, the other drivers were powering up their vehicles. The distinctive, throaty whine of the Ferrari, the hoarse growl of the Lambo, the grumble of the Porsche, the deep, smooth purr of the Vanquish. The growing roar made the crowd cheer, notified that the spectacle they had paid to see was about to start. Silver Lamborghini first, the cars rolled out of pit lane in starting order, Victoria nestled in between Calhoun's Porsche and the TVR as they did a slow lap, showing off for the spectators.

Maybe it was his personal connection, but Jack thought the Vanquish stood out from its neighbours. She was elegant and sleek, a vision of style and purpose melded into an appealing whole. Jack had made comparisons between Ethan and his car before, but now he made another one—Ethan in a fitted suit, carrying his twin Desert Eagles—style and purpose in a scarily appealing whole.

Jack made his way back to the platinum grandstand. On the track, the drivers got out of their cars and stood beside them while promotional shots were taken. All but Ethan took off their helmets, to the frustration of the photographer. Overhead, the grey clouds parted briefly and the sunlight cast a sharp shadow over the big screen on the grandstand opposite Jack. He glanced at it, then away, then back again.

The shadow outlined the top of the grandstand Jack was in, a flat roof with a few geometric projections—and a person moving fleet-footed across it, a suspiciously rifle-shaped object in hand.

"Fuck."

Jack raced up the stairs, taking them two at a time, shoving past people without apology. Maybe it was just a tech carrying an aerial, and maybe it wasn't. People joked about "taking out a hit" on someone all the time, but Jack lived in a world where that shit actually happened. He was fucking someone who used it to fund his expensive car obsession. There were some stupidly rich people down there and it was possible one of them had pissed someone off enough to earn a ticket on their head.

The back of the highest row of the stadium was draped with a canvas and Jack tore his way through it, finding a network of scaffolding. Someone was yelling at him to stop but he ignored them and swung out onto the structure of the temporary grandstand. He hauled himself up to the roof, slowing down and carefully peering over the top.

Sure enough, a figure lay at the front edge of the roof, cap on, a high-powered rifle resting on a stand, barrel pointed down at the drivers on the track. The assassin rolled their shoulders, settling into position, adjusting the stock of the rifle and looking through the scope. Jack had no time to hesitate, so he pulled himself all the way up and onto the roof. The roof was on a slight upward angle and he scrambled up it, not caring about making noise.

"Put the weapon down," he called, even as his ascent was noted by the assassin.

Rolling to their back, the person shifted aim from their target and onto Jack. A silencer barely muffled the shot, the cheer of the crowd doing a better job of covering the sound. Jack dropped flat to the roof and the bullet missed. In the seconds it took them to rack the bolt, he was up and moving. He dodged to the side this time, unable to stop his momentum if he didn't want to slide all the way down and off the back end of the roof.

"Aw, fuck," the assassin said and rolled away.

The assassin was a woman.

She came up into a low crouch, dropping the rifle and replacing it with a Glock, also silenced, from a pocket in the front of her hoodie. She fired twice, making Jack dive for what cover he could get behind the support of the big screen hanging just below him. His boots slipped and he had to catch the front edge of the roof to keep from tumbling backwards. It gave the woman time to run. She let the angle of the roof help her, sliding down, arms out for balance like she was surfing a big wave.

Jack glanced down, saw the drivers were once again in their cars, relatively safe. Engines roared, the crowd erupted again and a girl in a tiny skirt pranced across the track, waving a starting flag for show. Everything seemed all good down there, so Jack went after the assassin.

As he scrambled across the roof, then down the scaffolding and back into the grandstand, he called up the image of Aaron's number in his implant. Mentally keying it in, he called the cop.

"Hi, this is Aaron," he answered as Jack took the stairs downward two at a time, scanning the crowd for the compact, muscly body of the woman he'd seen with Calhoun.

"It's Nish," he said aloud, not sparing the concentration for thinking the words into the connection.

"Oh, hey." The words took on a slightly wary tone. *"Didn't think I'd be—"*

"This isn't social. I'm in pursuit of an armed suspect, east side of the racetrack, at the starting line. She's approximately five nine, maybe—" Then he remembered who he was all but yelling at. "The woman from yesterday. With Calhoun, the driver. She's an assassin."

There was a sceptical pause in his head as he hit the bottom of the stadium, having found nothing but stunned bystanders.

"Nish, are you drunk?"

"No," he growled. "I'm ISO. Jack *Nishant* Reardon, specialist security advisor. Check with them if you have to but can you just get me some fucking backup ASAP!"

"Shit shit shit," Aaron muttered. *"Um, okay. Let me call the station. I don't have your number—"*

Jack spun in a complete circle in the relatively clear space at the bottom of the grandstand. "I'll call you. Just get me some help." He cut the connection and turned again.

There! Moving fast but not running, heading for the pedestrian overpass across the track. She had taken off the cap, letting a ponytail of brunette hair free to swish around her shoulders. Hands in the front pocket of her hoodie, she blended into the crowd easily enough. Jack followed her, also not running. If he could just keep her in sight hopefully Aaron would have some of his co-workers here shortly so they could take over. This was their turf, they knew the people and the space.

She was on the overpass, Jack halfway up the stairs behind her, when the race started. With an explosion of sound, the idling engines were kicked into gear and, tyres smoking and exhausts rumbling, the cars burst into action. Silver, blue, black, chameleon. They blurred in Jack's peripheral vision and he felt a pang for not being there for Ethan as he'd promised. Ethan would understand, though. Hopefully.

A sea of people lined the overpass, looking down at the speeding cars. Jack pushed through them, willing to get a few glares in favour of keeping up with the woman. She was at the far end, about to head down, when she turned and caught sight of him. Rather than panic, she grinned, gave him the finger and disappeared downward. Jack stopped being polite and shoved and crashed through the press of people, getting a glimpse of his quarry's ponytail as she hit the ground again and jogged away. A couple of metres off the ground, Jack swung out over the side of the stairs and dropped. Recovering, he sprinted after the woman.

Ahead, she also moved into a dead run in the more open spaces between the grandstands and veered right, towards the sheds. Jack cut through under the stands, where the people had stood to look at the cars the day before. The fence was still in place, but Jack flew over it, barely slowing. The area before the sheds was mostly empty, just a few members of various crews wandering around. Behind Jack, the rolling sound wave of racing cars approached, drowned out everything else, then went again. Except not entirely.

From a shed at the far end of the row, a white Porsche appeared, rear end skidding out wide as the driver swung it around. The car weaved frantically, the driver scrambling to control it even as they tromped on the accelerator. People scattered as the wild Porsche screamed down the road before the sheds. As it whipped past, Jack caught a flash of ponytail flapping in the open window.

"Shit!"

"Nish!" Vicky appeared from her shed, eyes wide as she looked after the Porsche. "That's Brendan's car. What the hell?"

Behind her was the low profile of her Ferrari.

Jack sprinted for Vicky. She held her arms out, as if expecting a hug, but he shot past her and skidded to a stop by the car.

"Keys!" he shouted. "I'm borrowing your car."

"What? You can't—"

"I can," he growled. "And I am. I'll beg your forgiveness later. Keys! Now!"

She gaped at him, pale and shaking.

Jack hated upsetting her, but he didn't have time for this. "Trust me, Vicky. Or I'll hotwire this thing."

"Keys are in it," she said numbly.

These goddamn supercars weren't fucking made for quick getaways. It took Jack precious time to fold himself down into the Ferrari, listening to Vicky apologise to an absent Katie as he turned the key. It did, however, sound very satisfying when he gunned the powerful engine.

Contrary to his needs, he eased the speed machine out of the shed and only when he had it facing the way he wanted, did he really stand on the accelerator.

Holy fucking shit! Being a passenger was one thing. Holding the wheel and feeling it shiver as the car leaped forwards was another thing entirely. What he did like was the paddles on the steering wheel. With a flick of a couple of fingers, he changed gears, smiling at the windup of the engine, then its drop back to a loud purr when he shifted up. The sheds whizzed by, as did the main pavilion, and then he was at the entrance. The rear end of the white Porsche vanished around the corner as Jack slid the Ferrari through the open gates.

Thankfully, a lot of the roads around the track had been closed down and Jack had the space to kick the Ferrari into high speed. He called Aaron again.

"Nish, we have five cars heading for the track. The first should almost be there. Where are you?"

"In pursuit still. Only we're not on track grounds anymore. Suspect stole a car and I'm about four car lengths behind her." He pressed his foot down on the accelerator and the Ferrari ate up the distance between it and the Porsche.

"Shit. Okay, where are you?"

"Dunno the street name, but we're heading south." Ahead, the Porsche made a wild turn down a side street. "Make that east." Jack braked, Ethan's voice in his head, talking his way through the practice laps the day before, helping him now. He downshifted rapidly, feeling the Ferrari respond like a dream, gliding around the corner, tight in, wide out. "Suspect's in a Porsche. I'm following in a Ferrari. Get some fucking cars out here *now!*"

Aaron was talking to someone else at the far end of the line, but came back and said, *"We have a no-chase policy in Queensland."*

Jack grunted. "Lucky I'm not a Queensland cop, then. What can you do?"

"Blockades can be set up and the chopper's taking off now. What colour cars?"

"A Porsche and a Ferrari!" Jack weaved around a couple of parked cars. "How many of them could there be?"

Chuckling, Aaron said, *"You'd be surprised. Colours."*

Teeth grinding, Jack muttered, "White Porsche, pink Ferrari."

Muffled laughter, then Aaron said, dryly, *"I'll pass it on. Stay on the line so we can coordinate."*

Jack left the line open but concentrated on keeping up with the Porsche. Several more corners and they were out of the quiet streets and onto a main road. Traffic filled the narrow lanes of a road obviously adjusted to make way for the racetrack. The lanes were marked by orange cones, flashing signs reducing the speed to forty Ks. It didn't hold the assassin back, though. She bullied her way through the other cars, using the smallest of openings in the oncoming traffic to move past slow drivers. Cones went flying, a couple banging against the front of the Ferrari as Jack clung grimly to her exhaust. He would have loved his bike so he could slice between the cars with greater ease, but the hot-pink supercar was pretty good as well. It certainly got people's attention and had them pulling over to let him past.

All the while, he kept up a commentary for Aaron, telling him in vague terms where they were. It worked, because by the time they were screaming along a six-lane road beside a beach, the police chopper was swinging in overhead. Then, coming in from the north, two cop cars with lights flashing. Behind the cops, barriers had been put up, stopping the traffic coming toward the Porsche and Ferrari. The smaller sports car bumped up over the centre island and down onto the pure, open road. Then it really got going.

"Fuck!" Jack swerved to follow her.

Sparks kicked up from the front of the Ferrari as its low front end hit cement, but he made it up and over. Fingers flicking the right paddle, he got the car up to sixth and it flew.

The cops had stopped, cars angled over the lanes, cutting off escape. The Ferrari slid up beside the Porsche and Jack looked over. The window was down and the Glock was pointed right at him.

CHAPTER SEVEN

Jack pulled his foot off the accelerator just as she fired. The bullet cracked into the wing mirror as the Ferrari dropped back. Plastic and glass shattering, Jack flinched and the car swerved wildly. His automatic reaction was to turn the wheel, making the back end fishtail, spinning the Ferrari into a sideways skid.

When he came to a shuddering stop, Jack panted, hands in white-knuckled grips on the steering wheel. "Now that's overcorrecting."

"Nish? You okay?" Aaron sounded frantic and Jack realised the cop had been yelling in his head all through the near miss.

"Yeah," he answered. "Just a little singed." Looking around, there was no sign of the Porsche. "Fuck! Where is she?"

"Jumped the curb and took another street. They want you to desist. We have cars moving to block her probable route. Your part's done."

Like hell it was done. Jack put the Ferrari back in gear and, even while one of the cops from the parked cars approached, he took off again. Another spray of sparks and he was back on the other side of the road. He took a random side street.

"Which way, Aaron?" he demanded. "I'm not letting her get away."

There was a lot of muttered swearing in his head, then with a sour grunt, Aaron gave him a series of directions. Within moments, Jack was swinging out of the maze of local streets and onto a main road.

Jack found the Porsche on a two-lane stretch riddled with traffic lights hampering its single-minded flight for freedom. The car's white arse was a quickly vanishing blur in the distance, outpacing the civilian cars with a superior engine and far more reckless attitude. When he could Jack passed the commuters, throwing the Ferrari into narrow gaps and slamming his foot to the floor to get through them before they closed. The whole vehicle was humming, skimming across the bitumen like friction was something that happened to lesser evolved machines.

Jack got it now. The fascination with the speed. The glory of being in command of something so fast and dangerous. It didn't mean he wasn't still terrified and that right then, the only option he felt he had was to keep going because anything else seemed too tricky. He was a qualified helicopter pilot and had flown some of the fastest combat birds there were, but this was different. In the air, speed wasn't as immediate as it was on the ground. There was a lot more open space and a lot less things to dodge.

"You're on the Smith Street Motorway," Aaron said. *"We've got blocks on the entrances and cars on the exits. Try to get her to take an exit before you hit the highway. You've got two coming up."*

If he was cranky about Jack not giving up the chase, he didn't show it. Which probably meant they'd confirmed his ISO credentials and decided if it all went pear-shaped, then they could point the finger at ISO.

"Got it." Jack didn't care either way. He was going to get this woman.

A sign for an exit came up and a moment later, the Porsche soared right past it. One chance left. Jack coaxed more speed from the Ferrari, inching it up behind the Porsche. Nose level with the driver's door, Jack eased over, forcing the white car to the left. She was almost off the road when the next exit came up. Then she braked. Jack charged past, startled by the loss of the other car. In his rear vision mirror, he saw her jump forwards again. He slowed and she caught up fast, the smaller car now on his right and cutting in close, trying to drive him off the road.

Jack braked and she shot ahead. He swung in behind her and was on her arse in seconds. With a press of his foot, the Ferrari kissed the Porsche, nudging it into a little quaver, then it pulled ahead again.

"You're almost at the highway," Aaron announced. *"Northbound lanes are clear. We're setting up road blocks at the Helensvale Exit."*

The road arched up and around, then down into an on-ramp for the highway. Sure enough, empty lanes awaited them and the Porsche leaped ahead as soon as it hit the open straight. Seconds behind it,

Jack followed suit, cranking the Ferrari up to nearly 180 kilometres per hour. The police chopper roared in from the east, settling in over them, an ineffectual sentinel.

The roadblock came into view and Jack knew it wasn't going to work. Two cars to cover four lanes just wouldn't cut it. Granted only a maniac would chance the gaps at top speed, but Jack wasn't chasing an entirely rational person. Moments later, the Porsche proved it, slipping to the left and squeezing through the gap on the side of the road. Roaring right up behind it, Jack went right, yelling as he threaded the Ferrari between cop car and the barrier on the edge of the road. Then they were through the barricade and more open road stretched away ahead of them.

"No more blocks, Nish," Aaron informed him. *"We're trying to keep people from entering but some might slip through before we can close all the entrances. There are units on the way south from Coomera. You should be seeing them soon."*

"Right. I'll see what I can do now I don't have to worry about anyone else."

"What does that mean?"

Jack settled into the seat and flexed his fingers around the steering wheel. "Let's see." He planted his foot.

The needle on the speedometer bent further to the right, wavering around the 210 mark. Jack panicked. Fuck, that was wild, but it worked. He shot past the Porsche, the white car shrinking frightfully fast in his rear vision mirror. With a good distance between them, he eased back and when the Porsche caught up, he hogged the road. She tried to swing out left, he was there, weaving side to side. She went right and he cut in front again. It was a deadly game. If she got desperate, then they could both end up in a fiery wreck. Yet it worked. She slowed and he mimicked her, dropping them back to 160, 150, 140. Red and blue lights began registering in the rear vision mirror again, even more coming down from the north. Which was when the assassin got desperate.

She went wide right. Jack moved to block and she ducked back to the left. She misjudged her speed relative to Jack's and the Porsche kicked the Ferrari's left rear corner. Jack's world wobbled. The car pushed one way, then slammed back the other as the Porsche careened into its side.

Oh fuck. This was it. This was how he was going to die. Not in a blazing gun fight or sacrificing himself for his country, but in a hot-pink supercar, spinning wildly out of control. And if he didn't die now . . . Ethan might kill him for hurting a Ferrari.

The car slammed to a sudden, hard stop. Airbags exploded, deflating in an instant. Everything went whiteout—vision, sound, reality—then crashed back with sudden jarring impact.

At least it was all still. It gave him a chance to check things out. Arms attached. Legs where they belonged. Dick shrivelled in sheer terror but present. Then, someone yelling at him, banging on the window of the car. The door was wrenched open and hands were on him, checking all the things he'd already checked. Well, not his dick, but nearly. He managed to answer enough questions to prove he was conscious. When he tried to get out, the cops stopped him. He waited until the fuss had died down and their backs were turned, then hauled himself out of the stupidly low car.

"Hey, mate, you should probably stay put," one of them said.

Jack waved him off. "I'm fine. Where's the other car?"

A sergeant motioned with his chin. "Down there."

That was when Jack realised they were on a bridge. The railing on the outer edge was mangled, pushed outward, scored with white paint. Jack firmed up his balance and went and looked over the side. All he could see of the Porsche was a faded white blob covered by murky water.

"Has she come up?" he asked the sergeant.

"Not that we've seen. Rescue team is on its way. Don't have much hope for the driver, though. The car went over pretty hard." He cut Jack a sidelong frown. "I'm surprised you're on your feet."

Jack grunted knowing he was going to be feeling it in a couple of hours.

Things proceeded with the stately gait of government departments. Ambulances and firetrucks arrived. Jack was checked over, given a list of concussion symptoms and then handed back over to the police. By the time they hauled him away to the Southport Watchhouse to be questioned, they hadn't brought up the Porsche, but a diver had confirmed there was no body inside it. The damage was extensive enough they reasoned she was thrown from the car and now resided in the mud at the bottom of the canal. Jack wanted to believe them, but he held a healthy dose of scepticism.

They put him in an interview room and left him alone, so he took the chance to call Ethan.

"Jack? Are you all right? Where are you?" He sounded concerned rather than pissed, which was good.

"Important things first," Jack thought to him. *"How did you finish?"*

There was a pause, then, *"Second."* There was pride and frustration in his tone.

Jack smiled and be damned anyone who might be watching him, smiling for no apparent reason. *"Congrats. That's brilliant. Who was first? The Lambo?"*

Ethan's laugh warmed Jack's chest. *"No. The TVR of all things. The Lambo blew out on the third lap, at the hairpin."* His voice lowered until it was a husky rumble. *"But the best thing, Jack, was Calhoun. He came fifth. He's busily blaming the car and his sponsor but I doubt they were the real problem."*

Smiling was one thing, laughing another, so Jack held it in. *"I'm really sorry I missed it. Had a good reason, though."* He outlined the events of his own race.

Ethan tsked. *"That was reckless, Jack. You could have been hurt or killed."*

"But I wasn't. Thinking about buying a Ferrari though."

Ethan snorted. *"I don't know about buying one but you'll have to pay Katie and Vicky back for theirs, at least."*

Before Jack could retort, the door opened and the sergeant he'd been talking to at the scene came in, followed by Aaron. The younger cop was in jeans and a T-shirt, obviously off duty when Jack had called him. He leaned against the wall, arms crossed, expression neutral.

"Mr. Reardon," the sergeant said, sitting opposite him. "Just got off the blower with John Axworthy at the International Security Office. He's a pleasant man."

Jack winced at the dryness of the sergeant's tone. Axworthy, Jack's "boss" in his cover job, was a generally disagreeable man. His attitude had some merit seeing as the vast majority of his security personnel weren't his to use. Most of them, like Jack and Harry, actually worked for the Office. In situations like this Director Donna McIntosh, his true boss, would always be appraised of the situation and if she decided it was required, would override Axworthy's authority. Until McIntosh intervened, Jack had to deal with Axworthy's bitterness.

"His weekends are precious to him," Jack said apologetically.

The sergeant snorted. "Mine are too, son, so maybe you don't ask for any more weekends off in the near future, eh?"

Aware that Ethan could actually hear everything, Jack said, "I'll do my best. Have you discovered anything more yet?"

"Actually, the diver brought up a knapsack. Found a couple of handguns, wigs, contacts, three driver's licences with different names. And this . . ." He set a clear plastic bag on the table between them. Inside was a water damaged photo but the image was still clear. "We believe he was her target. Constable Stewart here IDed him as your friend, the Aston Martin driver."

Inside Jack's head, Ethan sucked in a sharp breath.

To confirm it for him, Jack said, "That's him. Roy Carter." To Ethan, he thought, *"Go. Get out of the country. I'll take care of this here."*

"Jack—"

"Do it. Go!"

Meanwhile, the sergeant was asking if Jack knew why Roy would be targeted. Jack played the ISO card to hold him off, saying he would need to confer with his superiors before answering. Against the wall, Aaron was looking more and more confused, trying to reconcile what he'd witnessed of Nish and Roy the day before—a couple—with what he was learning now—an agent protecting his ward.

"Already on my way," Ethan said in the mix. *"Don't worry about the attempt on me. I'll sort out it out, one way or another. Goodbye, Jack."*

Jack didn't even get a chance to say it back, distracted by the sergeant demanding more information. In the end, McIntosh did intervene, backing up Jack's "need to know, and you don't need to know" stance.

Finally, he was released and after another argument, with a detective this time, watched the interview with Todd Calhoun. It was clear right from the outset that he had no clue about who the woman had been. He just knew her as a liaison between him and his sponsor for the race. The sponsor later confirmed that he'd only hired the woman the week before. It also became clear that he had no connection to what had occurred, or knowledge of her ulterior motive for being involved in the race.

With no one to chase, Jack left the locals to continue their investigations—watched closely by the Office—and went back to the Q1. The room was booked for a second night, but all evidence of Ethan ever having been there was gone.

Feeling uncomfortably alone, Jack stayed the night, awake until dawn, in case the female assassin had survived and decided to come after Ethan again. She didn't.

In the morning, Jack fetched Victoria from the racetrack and drove a couple of hours south before stopping. He got a motel room, slept, then drove the rest of the way home in the dark.

Aching from the crash and tired from the long drive, Jack went to a debrief in the Office early Tuesday morning. McIntosh kept quiet during the meeting, leaving all the questions up to Director Alex Tan, who was more fascinated with the idea of a ticket being put on an assassin than with chastising Jack for his actions.

That afternoon, Jack poured over the current John Smith List—a ranking of all known active assassins across the globe—trying to match descriptions with the woman he'd chased. Nothing fitted, which didn't mean much. She might be new enough to have no confirmed hits, or she was good enough she'd never been seen. Jack guessed the former. Jack made a new entry into the auxiliary list under the moniker "Porsche." If she surfaced anywhere else, he would know about it.

Eighteen days later, the Office got word of the assassination of a distant member of the Liechtenstein royal family. She was found shot between the eyes from close range, a note on her body saying, "This is what revenge looks like—EB13." It was not confirmed as an Ethan Blade kill, nor did anyone from the Office find out who could have wanted revenge on the duchess, but Jack knew this was Ethan sorting out the attempt on his life.

What he didn't know was when, or if, he'd see Ethan again.

(MAY)

CHAPTER ONE

"**A**re you sure about this, Jack?" Director Donna McIntosh asked.

In recent times, McIntosh had taken to wearing a pair of tortoiseshell-rimmed glasses when she was reading her screen. Right now, she looked at him over the top of them and her expressive blue eyes were calm, betraying no ulterior motive behind the question.

"Absolutely certain, ma'am." It sounded good. Firm and steady. He made sure he kept eye contact, showing her nothing but seriousness.

After a long moment, McIntosh looked back at the screen in front of her. "There's nothing in the job parameters from ETA that allows for this level of surveillance. Tier Two only."

An External Threat Assessment Tier Two surveillance meant a passive watch—a phone tap fed into a program looking for key words and phrases, scanning for the subject near high-risk targets and no active following or interaction. Delta Subject was strictly hands-off at the moment. It was a low-level job, something a tech could handle in between other, more important tasks.

Jack's irritation at being handed such an unimportant responsibility sharpened. It turned the dull throb in his temples into a definite pounding. For three months he and his small team—Harry and a rotating shift of techs—had been wasting their time on Delta Subject. Jack was going crazy listening to the few phone conversations that had been flagged and running background checks on the young Indonesian national's contacts. He had never been so embarrassed as when he gave the unit leader his report—lists of unremarkable phone calls and a map showing random, scattered points of travel. If Delta Subject was a terrorist, then Jack would eat his shoe.

If McIntosh authorised this small breach of protocol, he could end this farce. He just needed some solid evidence, something to prove he was right about Delta Subject, then he could move on to bigger things.

To that end, he'd used the phone call to an address in Mount Lewis, a problematic suburb adjacent to Bankstown and Punchbowl, places with less than stellar reputations. The phone conversation, confirming the address of a meet-up, was the most suspicious move Delta Subject had made to date and Jack hoped it was enough to warrant McIntosh granting him permission to follow it. There was no chance she didn't see it for what it really was, a desperate plea to do something active, something to prove without a doubt that Delta Subject wasn't a threat.

Finally, McIntosh nodded. "I think I can trust your instincts on this one. You have a go."

That had been seven hours earlier, when Jack's headache had been just a headache.

Over the ensuing ride to Mount Lewis and while monitoring Delta Subject's clandestine meeting, which took place in a surprisingly well cared for old commission house, the headache failed to submit to either paracetamol or ibuprofen. Harry assuring him mixing the two different drugs was what caused the subsequent neck and back pain started a Google war in the back of the surveillance car while their current tech, Scott Lockwood, watched the house.

When Delta Subject left the residence with a bulging bag he definitely *hadn't* arrived with, Jack was croaking out orders through a sore throat and Harry was looking through their cases of equipment for a surgical mask. Scott's assertion that it wouldn't actually stop airborne viruses began another Google search, which ended with a hasty stop at a convenience store for some disinfectant spray, throat lozenges and a big box of tissues.

Waving aside the suggestions he should go home and rest, Jack insisted he had to see this through. It was his hunch, his job, his responsibility—his fault if it all turned out to be nothing. A sore throat and a few sneezes weren't going to get in the way. He was, however, quarantined in the back of the 4WD with his tissues and quickly diminishing supply of medicines while they followed Delta Subject across Sydney to an apartment building in Paddington.

Harry insisted Jack stay in the car while he trailed Delta Subject on foot inside the building. Over the next hour, Jack's second reported more than a dozen people coming and going from the apartment, most of them known associates of their subject and often carrying large bags. From there, with a group of four other men, Delta Subject moved on to his next location.

When Scott pulled the 4WD into a loading zone on Oxford Street, Jack at last felt vindicated. This was where he'd believed they'd always end up with Delta Subject, not that anyone else had ever seemed to trust his judgements. Boyed by the small success, Jack wouldn't let Harry or Scott talk him out of being the one to track their quarry on foot this time. In the end, the only way he could get Harry to let him go was by agreeing to change shirts with him.

"Why?" Jack demanded but already unbuttoning his blue-and-white-checked shirt. Normally, he would have dressed much more casually while trailing a subject, but he'd wanted to impress McIntosh with his professionalism in order to get the go ahead.

"Because you look like a try-hard in that shirt." Harry's smirk disappeared for a moment as he pulled off his old T-shirt. When it reappeared, it was more of a leer. "And this will be ironic."

Borrowed shirt on, Jack left the others in the car to continue monitoring Delta Subject electronically and headed into the nightclub.

His renewed enthusiasm for his hunch was sorely tested when he got inside. The lights bored into his sensitive eyes and the music pounded against his aching head. Overheated bodies pressed against him, hands groping as young and not so young men tried to talk to him, yelling to be heard over everyone else.

Hot and sore and tired beyond all pretence at patience, Jack pushed through the writhing crowd. He wanted to find the dark corners, a secluded place he could watch from: somewhere he could find a wall to rest his aching bones against while he finally got the definitive proof he needed.

He spotted a corner with good angles and headed for it, his body feeling like it might fall apart before he got there. Then the music cut out and a bright spotlight speared the smoky shadows, highlighting a circle of red velvet curtain hanging across a small stage. Jack flinched, the throbbing in his head spiking, the white light cutting through him like a knife.

"Gentlemen and . . . *gentlemen*," a voice purred over the sound system, eliciting a cheer from the masses. "We have a special treat for you all tonight. A newcomer to Slayed, we just know you're going to love her all the same. Please welcome to the stage in her first ever performance . . . *Dixie Normous!*"

The crowd erupted in screams and claps. Shoulders hunching to protect his vulnerable head from the piercing whistles, Jack made another push for the corner. Then the curtains swept back to either side, revealing Dixie Normous. Jack barely got a glimpse of the silver dress that caught the spotlight and shattered it into a rainbow of colours, the coiffed wig of pink hair, the split in the skirt that showed of a length of silky-smooth leg, before a hand landed on his shoulder. It clamped down and spun him around.

"Spot check," a gruff voice rumbled a second before more hands grabbed Jack's arms, holding him in place while the speaker initiated an unnecessarily rough pat down.

Somewhere in his head, Jack knew this was club policy to crack down on drug use, but right then and there, all he knew was *threat, attack, defend.* Even as he went down under two huge bouncers, punching and kicking futilely, Dixie's light-brown face framed in pink, dark eyes circled in glitter and lips painted blood red, caught his eye. Then a meaty fist connected with his jaw and that was all Jack knew until he woke up somewhere quieter, cooler, and still too bright. He was alone in some sort of office, probably still at the club, judging by the faint drone of music coming through the door. Thankfully, he wasn't there for long before Harry and Scott sneaked in and extracted him.

By the time they got him home, Jack was alternating between bone-wracking shivers and take-all-his-clothes-off fevers. He was huddling into his leather jacket, supported by a complaining Harry, when they arrived at his front door. Scott fumbled through Jack's keys, looking for the right ones while Jack tried to help and only succeeded in dropping the keys a total of three times. Finally, the door was opened and, fending off his colleagues' warily offered help in getting into bed, Jack closed the door in their faces and entered his code into the security system.

What a complete train wreck. A routine tail, an unsuspecting subject and a fully trained team. How had it gone so spectacularly wrong? Sure, at the time his brain had felt like it was both contracting and expanding and some bastard had attached weights to his arms and legs, but that wasn't an excuse.

Which left him one option. Now he was home, without Harry nagging him and Scott grumbling about appropriate protocols, Jack would be able to access his implant and use its assistance to analyse the whole operation. The mere thought of performing an in-depth cognitive model while battling some bug made him want to sink to the floor then and there and just sleep until all his problems vanished, but McIntosh had gone out on a limb for him on this one. She'd sidestepped Tan's authority and let Jack follow his wild hunch. If it turned out to be nothing but a monumental fuck-up then it wouldn't just be Jack's neck on the line. He had to salvage something from the whole mess.

His last thought was that he had to lie down and get into a trance state to utilise the broader applications of his implant. The long, soft length of his brown, leather couch was his goal . . .

"Jack?"

Jack pried open his eyes. Well, he tried to. The same prick who'd weighted his limbs had been back, messing with his eyelids this time.

"Come on, Jack," that same, low voice implored. A gentle tap on his cheek accompanied it. "Wake up. Let me know you're in there."

An exhausting effort later got him a narrow crack in the darkness. Fuzzy shapes emerged from the general blurriness, one of which got a little more solid as it came closer.

"Oh, thank heavens," Ethan murmured, breaking into a relieved smile.

The palm on Jack's cheek drifted down the side of his neck, cool and soothing on his tingling skin. Ethan leaned closer, almost as if he was going to kiss Jack, but his lips landed on his jaw in a lingering touch. Jack had no idea where he was or what was going on but it barely mattered.

Ethan was here.

CHAPTER TWO

It had to be a dream. After their time together had ended so abruptly on the Gold Coast, Jack hadn't believed he'd see Ethan again so soon, if at all. Surely Ethan wouldn't risk coming back in country yet. Thus, this was a dream.

Mouth still against Jack's skin, Dream Ethan murmured, "You scared me, Jack."

A very real feeling dream, but just a fanciful, wish-fulfilment dream. So why not make the most of it while he was lost in such a good delirium?

Jack nuzzled into Ethan's cheek. "Boo," he said in his sexiest voice.

Ethan huffed and leaned back. A lock of his dark hair fell over his forehead, caught up on the top of his sunglasses. "Yes, Jack. Boo. Why are you lying on the floor in the entryway?"

"'M not," Jack assured him.

"I'm afraid you are." Ethan's hand settled on Jack's forehead. "You're burning up, Jack. You're sick."

"Nah. Just a headache." Sheer will propped him up on an elbow. "Know what cures a headache, Blade?" His low and sultry tone sounded more raspy and painful, but maybe that was just the effect of the throbbing in his head.

"Plenty of fluid, rest and quiet." Ethan slid his arms under Jack's and hauled him the rest of the way into a sitting position.

"Dun dah," Jack intoned. "Sorry, but that's the wrong answer. The correct answer is . . ." He slung one arm around Ethan's neck and pulled him in until they were chest to chest. "Blowjob. Come on, baby. Suck my brains out through my dick. That way, no headache!"

Even as the words escaped his mouth Jack knew there was something wrong with them: something wrong with the way Ethan

159

went still; how the hands that had been so gentle on his back suddenly became hard and dangerous.

But this was Dream Ethan and Dream Ethan should do all the things Real Ethan didn't. Surely. Unless this wasn't a dream . . .

"Sorry, sorry." Jack clung to him, desperate to take back the pain he'd caused. "Didn't mean it. No blowjob. Never ever. Unless you want one?"

After a tense moment, the rigid body against his relaxed slightly. Enough of a give to tell Jack he hadn't ruined everything.

"No, Jack. I don't want that. Not right now, at least." Ethan adjusted his hold and lifted Jack to his feet. "You need to go to bed and rest."

"Yeah, bed. Sounds good." And not for resting. He had to make up for saying the wrong thing and there was one solid way to do that.

"Did you bring anything home for your symptoms?" Ethan carefully guided Jack onto his bed and swung his legs up.

"Pocket." Jack gave a little hip thrust.

Ethan regarded him blandly for a moment, then sighed and dipped a hand into the front pocket of Jack's jeans. His dextrous fingers found nothing, but it felt nice in the process.

"Jack." It came out on warning tone.

"Other one."

Ethan tried the other pocket and after an equally nice moment, retrieved a half-empty blister pack of throat lozenges.

"Is this it?" Ethan's British accent attained a level of disapproval Jack would have squirmed away from, if he'd been capable.

"'S enough. I'm fine. See?" Jack tried to show off his impressive strength and coordination by attempting to tackle Ethan to the bed and ravish him until he begged for mercy.

Ethan pinned Jack down with one hand. "I'll fetch something stronger when you're settled." He regarded Jack with pursed lips. "First, let's get you undressed."

"Yes," Jack said and helped by unfastening his jeans while Ethan removed his boots and socks.

When it came to removing his jeans, Ethan decided he didn't need Jack's help, commanding him to "just lie still," and "don't wiggle," and "if you keep that up, Jack, something we will both regret might happen." Jack reasoned Ethan was so eager he wanted to do it all himself, so he just lay back and let Ethan have his fun.

"Hmm," Ethan mused when he got to Jack's shirt. "I don't believe I've seen this T-shirt before." He worked the tight-fitting material up Jack's chest and extracted his arms one at a time. "Is it new?"

"Nope."

He cocked an eyebrow at Jack, then completed the job. When it was off, he shook out the sweat-stained shirt. White and so thin it was almost see-through, it featured a faded print of the classic evolution of man progression that ended with a silhouette of a sexy woman.

"Is there something I should know?" Ethan asked wryly.

Jack made a clumsy swipe at the shirt. "It's not mine."

"I should hope not. For one, it's about two sizes too small."

"That's 'cause it's Harry's. He said I looked good in it. Hot." It may have been said sarcastically, but that was information Ethan didn't need. "He also said it would be ironic in a gay nightclub."

Ethan went still. That deadly stillness he tended to fall into when he felt threatened or uncertain. Before Jack's befuddled brain could work out what had caused it this time, Ethan sighed and nodded.

"I assume this was part of some undercover operation." He dangled the offending T-shirt from a very disdainful finger, adding in a dry tone, "In a gay nightclub."

Something about what Ethan's tone implied bugged Jack. "Maybe it was for fun."

"I suppose it could have been." He certainly didn't sound like he believed it. In fact, there was a little too much laughter in the words to not be slightly insulting.

Miffed, Jack scowled at him. Not that Ethan appeared to notice. He gathered up Jack's discarded clothes in preparation to leave. This wasn't going to plan at all.

Looping a finger through a buttonhole on Ethan's suit jacket, Jack tugged him closer. "You're right."

Frown creasing his brows over his glasses, Ethan leaned over him. "About what, Jack?"

Jack tugged again and Ethan gave in, lowering himself until he was all but lying on top of him.

"Jack?"

"It wasn't for fun. It was for work." Jack's nose brushed Ethan's cheek. He breathed in deep of the familiar scent, making things stir. "I don't have fun anymore. Not with anyone but you. Meant to tell you that last time, dream boy."

Ethan pulled in a sharp breath. "Is that true? Or just the fever?" Before Jack even had time to think, let alone answer, he sat up and gently extracted Jack's fingers from his jacket. "Let's not talk about that now, Jack. Not when I can't be sure you know it's me you're talking to."

What the actual fuck? Jack stared at him sitting stiffly on the side of the bed, so close but somehow isolated.

Ethan began folding Jack's clothes, even the T-shirt that had started this weird detour. "I'm going to go out and find you something better than lollies, Jack. You will rest while I'm gone, no arguments."

Maybe Jack hadn't heard right. His ears were aching, admittedly, and since he didn't have the energy for a fight, he decided to go for gold. "Let's fuck."

Ethan let out a startled cough and turned to him, eyebrows arched. "Pardon?"

Jack squirmed to get into position. "Let's screw. It'll be fun. Come on."

Ethan looked at him with such confusion, Jack wondered if he'd forgotten what to do so he went into great detail about how and where and why, which left him horny as hell and Ethan's cheeks blazing with the hottest blush Jack had ever seen.

"—and see, that way you'll be in the perfect position for—"

"Jack!" Ethan stood up so fast he sent the folded clothes flying. "Stop it. We're not doing that. You're ill!" With jerky motions, he picked up the clothes, steadfastly not looking at Jack.

"I'm fine. Just hop on and we'll have some fun," Jack wheedled.

Ethan's mouth opened and closed several times, no sound emerging. Finally, he blurted, "It won't be fun, Jack. Besides, there's nothing to 'hop on,'" and waved in the pertinent direction.

"Of course there's something . . ." Jack trailed off as he looked.

He was sure there had been the Eiffel Tower of erections in his underwear. It had *felt* like there was at least a Leaning Tower of Pisa. What he found, however, was more Nullarbor Plains than Mount Everest.

"Oh."

After a silent moment, Ethan snickered. "Yes, oh." Coming back to the bed, he leaned down and rested his palm on Jack's temple. "As amusing, *and* embarrassing, as you are when you're sick, I'm going to get you some medicine. Now, *please* rest. I would hate it if you got worse."

The earnest words felt soothing in Jack's chest but all that got through the fog in his head was that Ethan was leaving. Again. He didn't want Ethan to go. Not after last time when he wasn't sure he'd ever be back.

"Stay." Jack tried for stern, but it didn't work because Ethan straightened, fixed his jacket and turned for the bedroom door. He needed something more to keep Ethan from going. "Stay and I'll kiss you on the mouth."

Ethan stalled mid-step. Without looking back, he said, "Let me change that from amusing and embarrassing to inappropriate and embarrassing."

Then he left.

The goddamned little shit actually left.

Well. Fuck him. Figuratively.

Jack tried to roll over, but the effort was too much. Everything ached. Unpleasantly. It didn't matter because Jack didn't need to sleep. He had work to do. Something about proving Delta Subject wasn't a danger to anyone. He was going to do something . . . something like a . . . like a cognitive model. Yes. That's what he was supposed to be doing, not dealing with Ethan's issues.

Closing his eyes, Jack tried a few meditative techniques to help him access his implant, but between the ache in his body and the throbbing in his head, nothing worked. He thought he got there at one point, when the overlay in his head flashed past, but when he tried to pull it back up it didn't work.

His last thought before weariness overtook him was that it was all, somehow, Ethan Blade's fault . . .

. . . that he was so hot. The fucking sun was about an inch from the burning ground, broiling Jack alive in his own fluids. Sweat poured from his head, soaking his hat, and down his back, sticking his shirt to his feverish skin. Not to mention his belly, totally wet from where it rubbed against Blade's back with every awkward step the stupid camel took.

Jesus. It would be easier without all the touching. How long had it been since Jack had felt another body against his? So long he couldn't even make a guess. It meant nothing that he had a half-hard dick right now. Certainly didn't mean he fancied Blade. Not at all. It was just all this crazy touching. The way Blade pressed his back into Jack's chest, making him feel all of those strong, smooth plains; feel how his muscles shifted to keep him seated on this ridiculous animal. Making Jack want to groan at how Blade rolled with the camel's gait like they were dancing together, bodies in tune, moving as one. As if they were in a club, grinding on each other, supple hips flowing with the beat of the music.

So loud. The base beat thumping like a second heartbeat in Jack's chest, taking over his limbs so all he could do was hold Ethan close and sway with him, let the music cover up all the thoughts he didn't want to think. Just move. Just hold him. But Ethan left him. Like he always did. There, then gone.

Then Jack was alone in the middle of the club, dizzied by the brightest darkness he'd ever seen. The shadows closed in, enveloping him in hazy occlusions, swamping him in a roiling mess of hot, close bodies. A shifting, undulating prison of beautiful young flesh, tanned and toned, sinuous and sensual. Hands sliding across his chest, tugging at his jeans, imploring him to stay and dance. Lips smiled and tongues teased, but he turned away. None of them were the one he wanted. They weren't Ethan, his beautiful, damaged, deadly man who kept leaving him all alone . . .

CHAPTER THREE

... in his bed. The sheets were soaked with rank sweat, his body curled up tightly, like he was freezing. He was clutching a pillow to his chest, face buried in its damp softness. His throat was dry, tongue glued to the top of his mouth.

Jack whimpered. He was dying. Surely he couldn't come back from this. Even being shot hadn't hurt like this. To add insult to everything else, he had to piss. It was, however, blessedly dark in his room, no lights were on and the blind was drawn, to keep out even the faint glow of Leichhardt at night.

Time passed. No idea how much or if he was entirely conscious for it. All he really knew was that, eventually, he could move. Slow and cautiously, he managed to roll over. Another wiggle got him to the edge. It was mostly falling out of bed, but he ended up on his feet, propped up against the bedside table. Gravity seemed to fill his bladder even more.

He made it in stages. From the bed to the tallboy against the wall, to the old recliner in the corner where his dirty clothes tended to pile up. A short stagger to the door, where he caught the frame in a death grip, convinced another step was impossible. He rested there until his bladder couldn't be ignored anymore. He might be dying but he sure as shit wasn't going to do it in the hallway, pissing himself. Down the hall, using the entrance to the living room as another stop point, then on to the bathroom. It was a victory to find the toilet seat already up. Ethan, he'd learned, preferred a closed commode. Lucky the bastard wasn't here.

Or was he? A few delirious images of Ethan swirled behind his aching eyes as he released his dick and aimed. Memories of the ride across the desert on Sheila the camel, the sound of his terribly British accent as he chided Jack for one thing or another, a sensation of his body pressed close as they danced.

Danced? Jack shook the thought away. He and Ethan had never danced. Especially not at a club. It was just a fever dream. All of it just a crazy product of his flu.

The relief as he peed was glorious. Nothing had ever felt better. His head even started to ease back on the suicidal pounding. A touch steadier, Jack washed his hands, then lifted handfuls of water to his mouth. He gulped down so much water his stomach started to feel queasy and still he felt dry.

His reflection in the mirror scared him so he didn't look and went scrounging through the cabinet for some drugs. Found some paracetamol, so he took four, which exhausted him. Leaving the blister pack on the sink, Jack headed back to bed. During his stop at the entrance to the living room an anomaly caught his attention. It took a good long while before what was odd about the scene registered.

Soft light glowed in the far corner of the living room. The lamp on the end table beside the couch was on. Over the back of the couch was a tumble of colour, a corner of a crocheted blanket. The one Gran had made for her son, Jack's dad. The one Jack had rescued from the box meant for the Salvation Army. A box packed by his sister, Meera, who'd been determined to discard anything that held sentimental value for Jack after they'd had to put their dad into a home. The blanket that lived in the chest beside the TV unit. The blanket Jack only pulled out when he really missed his dad.

Jack charged into the living room. Only his legs didn't support him the entire way. Catching himself on the kitchen counter, he swore, hoarse and low.

"Jack?" Ethan sprang off the couch, casting aside the blanket. He took one look at Jack and rather than go around the couch, flung himself over it and rushed to Jack's side. "I'm sorry. I didn't realise you were awake." One strong arm went around Jack's waist.

Head swirling in surprise and confusion, Jack tried to push him away but only succeeded in nearly falling over.

"Jack, don't be silly. Come on, back to bed."

They were back in Jack's bedroom before he put enough pieces together to form a coherent thought.

"You're here," he croaked out.

"Obviously. Though I did consider not coming back after your performance earlier." Ethan settled Jack back into bed, propped up on his pillows.

That hurt. "I'm a good dancer," Jack insisted.

Ethan sat on the edge of the mattress, smiling slightly. "I'll have to take your word for that. I was however talking about your little seduction attempt."

"Huh?"

A cool hand rested on Jack's brow, then moved to his cheek and finally the side of his neck. "Still running a fever. Don't you recall what you said to me before? About a kiss."

"A kiss?" Jack repeated, to be sure. A significant one, apparently. They kissed. A lot, in fact. Just not on the mouth. Kissing was Jack's issue and one Ethan hadn't pushed him on, thankfully.

"Hmm. You clearly don't remember, so let's leave it alone. I do believe I said once how it was a good thing you couldn't recall much while sick, or I'd have to defend my honour. Best we follow the same route here, as well."

Christ. It must have been bad. "Sorry."

"Thank you, but it's forgotten already. Can I trust you to stay put while I fetch the supplies I picked up for you?"

"Yeah. I'm fucked."

"There's the eloquent Jack Reardon I know so well." Ethan patted his arm in parting.

He returned quickly with a small box, two bottles of electrolyte-replacement drink and a cool cloth. The latter was draped across the back of Jack's neck, making him moan in relief and miss the rest of the preparations.

"How long has it been since the start of your symptoms?" Ethan asked while Jack wallowed in soothing coolness.

"Had a headache all day. Aches started around mid-afternoon."

"Less than twenty-four hours, thankfully. All right, Jack. Roll over."

Eyes flying open, Jack opened his mouth to protest, but suddenly he was on his belly with little idea how he got there. A knee landed on his lower back, holding him down firmly but not painfully. Cool air hit his arse as Ethan pulled down his undies.

"What the fuck?" Jack battled but he was too weak and Ethan too good at restraining struggling victims.

"Just a little prick."

"You fucking—ow!" The sting of the needle was followed by a spreading pressure in his left cheek.

"All done," the smug bastard said, his fingers rubbing the site of the jab.

Peering over his shoulder at what would otherwise be a pleasant view, Jack scowled. "What the hell was that?"

"Antiviral medication. It should help stop you from getting any worse." Ethan gave Jack's bare arse a final, gentle pat before covering it again. "Enough fun for now. You should rest."

Wanting nothing more than to be cranky, Jack had to admit lying still and closing his eyes would be nice.

"I'll be in the living room if you need me, Jack. Just call. Or throw something."

"Throw you out if you hurt my blanket." But he didn't think Ethan heard him, as he was already gone and Jack was sinking back into the waiting embrace of sleep, immersed in images of . . .

. . . Ethan curled up under his blanket with him. Snuggled in tight to Jack's chest, the fringe of blue wool tucked right up under his chin, his head tipped back on Jack's shoulder as he slept. Arms wrapped around his man within the cocooned warmth, Jack rested his cheek on Ethan's head, unable to keep the smile off his face.

"You seem really happy, Jack."

Looking up at the soft words, Jack's neck warmed with a blush at being caught by his dad.

Chris Reardon stood beside the couch Jack and Hamish had claimed, a glass tumbler of scotch in one hand, his ever-present book in the other. Blond and blue-eyed, the only physical traits he'd passed on to his son was his height and a lightening of the Indian-brown skin gained from his mother. Dad had often had to talk fast to convince people Meera and Jack were his kids. Seeing him now, no one would doubt the fatherly pride and love in his expression.

At twenty-five years old and a newly inducted SAS soldier, Jack knew he shouldn't be worried about his dad finding him cuddling another man. Especially not when he'd come out eight years earlier, after Dad had had to break up a fight between Jack and his first boyfriend, Ian, whom Jack had learned had been fucking around behind his back. Dad had never been upset by Jack's sexual orientation.

"Are you happy?" Dad sat in his favourite recliner, putting book and drink down so he could concentrate on Jack.

Against him, Hamish stirred a little, burrowing in deeper. Jack's arms tightened around him automatically.

"Yeah, Dad. I am." Jack whispered so as not to wake Hamish. His boyfriend just got in to Sydney that evening, the last leg of a long-haul flight from Afghanistan, where he'd been deployed while Jack went through SAS training in Australia. Jack had barely got a welcoming kiss before Ham was all but falling asleep in his arms, so Jack had pulled him down to the couch and covered them both with the crocheted blanket Gran had made. He hadn't been thinking about the fact his father was in the house. All he'd wanted was contact with the man he was going to spend the rest of his life with.

Dad smiled. "He's a good bloke. How is he? Apart from tired."

"Good, I think. He didn't say much, just that he doesn't want either of us to go back."

Those intense blue eyes pinned Jack. "You haven't told him."

Uncertainty coiled through Jack's belly, at odds with the secure weight of his lover on his chest. "I couldn't do it over the phone, and he went to sleep so fast now."

"Jacky." A single word filled with all the parental resignation Dad could muster, which was a shit load.

"Dad." Jack felt like he was fifteen, not twenty-five, and defending whatever stupid decision he'd made back then.

"No, Jack." He sat forward, elbows on his knees, shoulders hunched. He didn't like what he was going to say but he met Jack's gaze squarely. "I won't let you do this again. You don't talk to anyone about how you're feeling and instead, you go off and do these stupid things. Uncle Raj's wedding."

Jack shrugged the memory away, jostling Hamish so he grumbled in his sleep.

"When Meera got pregnant."

"Even you had a flip out about that one."

"Yes, but at least I didn't torch her boyfriend's car."

"You wanted to," Jack muttered.

It was Dad's turn to wave it off, then he hit back hard and ruthlessly. "When your mother died. You joined the army, Jack, without talking to us."

A staunch pacifist, Dad had cried when Jack admitted what he'd done. From the moment they'd been told Jack's mum, Usha, had perished in an explosion in her native India, through all the preparations and then the funeral, and after, when they'd come back to Australia without her, Jack had not seen his father cry. But he had cried when Jack said he'd joined the army. In the end, Dad had forgiven him. Meera hadn't and he doubted she ever would.

"And now this," Dad continued, his tone soft, concerned. "You knew Ham didn't like the idea of you trying for the SAS, and yet you did it all the same. You have to tell him now."

Head shaking, Jack squeezed Ham even tighter, knowing somewhere deep inside he'd hurt their relationship by doing this. Yet he hadn't been able to do anything else. Couldn't waste the recommendation Captain Hollingsworth had offered to get him accepted for SAS trials. If he had any chance of doing something about his mother's death, it would be with the elite forces.

"Jacky," Dad tried again. "If you don't, and Ham finds out from someone else, it'll be worse."

"Dad." Jack hated the plaintive whine in his voice. "I can't."

"You *have* to. Either you tell him and let him decide how he feels for himself, or he hears it somewhere else and gets angry."

Jack had often been accused of having a short fuse but Ham left him for dead. The difference was, Ham forgave. Jack didn't. Though he feared this might be the time Hamish wouldn't, or couldn't, forgive.

"Do it," Dad insisted. "Jack, let him . . .

. . . go."

No. He wouldn't let Ham go. Jack loved him, needed him. He held on tighter.

"Jack, you're hurting me. If you don't let go, I'll be forced to make you."

Strange how Ham suddenly sounded British, and not the exaggerated, tosser accent he used when telling jokes. The one Jack found himself falling back on when teasing Ethan.

Ethan.

"Oh, fuck." Jack jerked his arms up and eyes open at the same time.

Ruffled and annoyed, Ethan levered himself up and away from the tangle of Jack's limbs and twisted sheets. He moved quickly but not so fast Jack missed the thin line of his mouth, the narrowed eyes and the hands clenched into fists.

Fucking brilliant. He'd managed, again, somehow, to piss Ethan off without even trying. Jack rolled over and pulled a pillow over his head. This had better be a dream.

"At least you're awake now."

The words were muffled but understandable. Tone, however, was a bit muddled. Jack couldn't tell if Ethan was angry, bored or amused. Either of the latter two would be fine. Still, best to get it over with fast. Like pulling out a knife.

Jack lifted the pillow. "Anything I have to apologise for?"

There was a short silence, and then Ethan sighed. "No. It was my own fault. I heard you tossing about and came to see if you were all right. You were talking in your sleep and despite knowing better, I leaned in to hear if it was anything important. You grabbed me and wouldn't let go."

That didn't sound too bad. "Despite knowing better? I've done this before?"

Ethan had on a pair of Jack's pyjama bottoms, which he adjusted back to a proper height. "Yes. In the desert." He paused, looked away, and added, "You called me Hamish back then as well."

"Oh." Heat rushed through Jack's face. "Sorry. He was—"

"You have no need to tell me, Jack. It's none of my business."

Jack nodded along for the sake of keeping the peace. After the last visit he was starting to wonder if perhaps it *was* Ethan's business.

Ethan came back to the bed and felt Jack's forehead. "I think your temperature's come down."

"I feel better." He didn't really, but he didn't want Ethan to jab him again.

A quick smile curled Ethan's lips. "If you have one of the drinks I got you, I might even believe you."

Grumbling, purely for form, Jack struggled up and took one of the bottles of drink, promising payback if it was raspberry. It was an indeterminably flavoured blue one, which was okay, so Jack drank it down in several goes. Satisfied, Ethan suggested a shower and himself as a crutch. Getting wet and soapy with Ethan was usually one of Jack's preferred hobbies, but this time it was purely functional. Without Ethan's support he wouldn't have made it through washing his hair, let alone the rest of his body.

Clean, dry and dressed, Jack was deposited on the couch while Ethan went to get him something to eat. The couch faced the balcony and the blinds on the sliding door were open, showing off the city as it shone brightly under an autumnal sun. From the shadows he guessed it to be close to midday. Nearly twelve hours since Harry and Scott had grabbed him out of the Slayed office. He could have checked his implant for the exact time, but even though he wasn't feeling quite like a Mack truck had hit him, backed up and got him again, he still wasn't keen on too many mental hurdles.

The exact time didn't matter though, not when Ethan returned with a bowl of soup. The salty warmth pooled in his empty stomach and spread through him pleasantly, making him think he could probably sleep again. Ethan drifted off first, though, stretched out on the couch, his feet pressed against the far armrest, head nestled on Jack's thigh. His sunglasses went wonky so Jack gently removed them and encouraged him to turn so his face was towards Jack's belly, not the sunlit balcony.

It didn't take long for Jack to realise Ethan was honestly asleep. A true, deep, restful sleep. Normally, he only slept like that when they were in bed, sweaty from the battle of driving each other insane with lust. He must have been tired.

There had been plenty of times over the past months when Jack had watched Ethan sleep, naked, sated physically, a small smile on his mouth. Never before, though, had he ever looked as vulnerable as he did now. Dressed in more than socks, peaceful without the satiated sprawl of a body well fucked. Jack watched with half-lidded eyes and fevered bemusement as dark strands curled over his fingers as he carded them through Ethan's hair. He'd worried he wouldn't get the chance to do this again and hoped like hell this wasn't a delusion.

Ethan sighed and shifted against his thigh, burrowing his face into the curve of Jack's abdomen.

In that moment, Jack's fever dream came back to him: sitting on a different couch, with a different man.

For a second, his chest hurt when he thought about Hamish, of how he hadn't been brave enough to tell him about being accepted into the SAS. He saw again, as clear as the sight of Ethan now, Ham's burst of anger when he found out from a mate in the barracks. Watched once more as Ham walked away from him. He never came back, and never did forgive Jack.

Different couch, different man, but the same fear.

They needed to talk before Ethan disappeared, but Jack fell asleep before he could muster the energy to do it.

CHAPTER FOUR

"Jack."

Coming out of it was easier this time, though there was a moment when Jack found himself looking not at Ethan or his apartment, but at the implant overlay. Apart from the usual running applications, there was an extra flashing dot. Ethan shook him again before he could tap the dot to see what it was, making the image vanish as his concentration broke. This time, Ethan shuffled into focus, the concerned frown between his dark brows smoothing out when he realised Jack was fully awake.

"What did I do this time?" Jack resigned himself to another apology.

Ethan smiled. "Nothing. Well, apart from calling me Harry and declaring he looked ridiculous in your shirt."

"Great. And he did look stupid. Way too big on him."

Flashes of his dream came back: the nightclub again, that moment when he'd thought he'd recognised Dixie Normous; the argument with Harry, when Jack announced that as the only gay man in the car he had to be the one who went into the club.

Ethan fed him more paracetamol, refused him a coffee and offered more soup for dinner. Sitting across the table from Ethan, watching him as he ate, Jack poked at his feelings like a tongue testing a sore tooth. That sense of connection, of belonging, was still there. The admission of needing, and *wanting*, more was as strong as it had been on the Gold Coast. The emotional machinegun he'd unloaded on Katie was still riddling him with bullets. Nothing had changed. He wanted Ethan in his life, more than he was already, deeper than he was. And it scared him to death.

Wish you were here?

Sometimes, though, less than he once did.

After dinner, Jack trundled back to bed. He wasn't feeling as exhausted or fuzzy as he had been but thought it best to get in bed before he couldn't do it on his own and Ethan decided to carry him or something equally ludicrous. A couple of minutes later, Ethan joined him, settling onto his usual side with a book. No matter how pretty the person was, watching them read wasn't terribly entertaining, so Jack pestered Ethan until he began to read aloud. It didn't take long before Jack was bored again, despite the outrageous action sequences.

"Ethan?" Jack interrupted a particularly amusing moment where the characters were shocked that going over a cliff should end in them actually *falling*.

"Yes, Jack?"

"Are you okay?"

Ethan frowned at him. "In what sense?"

"I mean, do you feel all right? You're not getting sick?"

Patiently, Ethan marked the page with a bookmark. "I'm fine. Unlike some, I had an anti-flu vaccination. I'm surprised the Office doesn't offer them to the staff."

Jack took the book and threw it across the room. "They do. Had one, even. Guess I'm just that unlucky." Then he made his advance.

"Jack?" Ethan asked warily. "What are you doing?"

"Hoping like fuck I'm distracting you," he answered with his mouth pressed to the strip of Ethan's exposed abdomen between shirt and pants. "If I'm not, I must really be sick."

"Never fear, objective accomplished. I take it you don't wish to be read to anymore." Ethan's skin shivered under the touch of Jack's tongue and teeth. One of his hands landed on the back of Jack's head, fingers twining through his black curls.

"Nope." Jack nuzzled under the hem of Ethan's shirt. "Take it off."

"I don't believe you're ready for sex yet, Jack."

Jack sat up long enough to wrestle the shirt off Ethan, and then his own. "Not planning on sex." He pulled Ethan down so he was on his back and settled over him, kissing his way across Ethan's clavicles. "Just this, for a while."

Ethan made a soft, agreeing noise, then a few more encouraging sounds that, combined with the taste and texture against his lips, made Jack's dick give serious thought to doing something interesting.

Things never got past the "thought" stage, though. For Jack, at least. Ethan quickly developed a significant bulge, which Jack headed for before realising he'd greatly overestimated his stamina. By the time he reached Ethan's belly button, which he teased with his tongue, making Ethan squirm, Jack was so tired he could barely keep his face up enough to not suffocate against Ethan's skin. Not an entirely bad way to go but not exactly dignified, either.

Defeated, Jack rolled off him, landing on his back with a part-weary, part-pained grunt. "Sorry. Guess I couldn't even keep that up for a while."

Ethan moved over and put a soft kiss on Jack's cheek. "It's all right. I liked it all the same. Do you need anything before going to sleep? A drink? Paracetamol?"

Flinging an arm over his face, Jack just nodded. Ethan slipped out of bed and padded away on socked feet, discreetly adjusting his still hard dick as he went.

Jack hated being weak. Couldn't give his man a blowjob and couldn't make it out of bed with any sort of composure to get his own drink. Thankfully, when Ethan returned, sans erection, he put the gear on the table next to Jack and got under the covers on his side. This, at least, Jack could do on his own. Pity about everything else over the last two days.

Jack swallowed some pills, drank half the bottle and then settled down again. Ethan lay close, but not touching. It was hard to tell if he thought Jack needed space, or if he was disappointed about the fooling around not getting far at all. If things had reached their usual, happy ending, Jack was sure Ethan would have been all over him now. Quite literally. Instead, there was space. Space Jack wanted to cross but wasn't sure if he should. Wasn't sure if Ethan if was pissed to be all worked up and then put aside, unsatisfied.

God. Everything had been fucked up by this stupid flu. Two deals gone haywire in as many days. In Jack's absence, McIntosh was probably copping it for authorising the tail. Ethan, too, was undoubtedly regretting showing up this time—not the first time, either, though Jack had usually been able to salvage something good from those previous times. He didn't think he would this time, however.

Sadly, heading back to the Office and sorting out the mess he'd made of his job took priority.

And if McIntosh found out Ethan had been here while Jack was compromised, then it wouldn't just be this op under question.

Jack rolled to his side, his back to Ethan. In the morning, he'd thank Ethan for his help, suggest it was time he went on his way and then go take responsibility for his actions at the Office, so his Director wouldn't have to. It was a completely screwed up situation but Jack would have to deal with it as best he could.

Even though his mind was made up, it took forever for him to fall asleep. It didn't help that Ethan didn't sleep, either, and Jack couldn't tell if the sense of alertness coming from the man was Ethan thinking Jack still needed to be watched over, or disgruntlement at all the ways Jack had disappointed him this time.

When sleep did arrive, it was restless and hectic with nonsensical images, blurring Ethan into a progress report to his directors at work; replacing McIntosh with his father, their disapproving frowns exact replicas. Director Alex Tan angrily informed Jack that not blowing Ethan was a breach of their agreement. An unseen person announced Dixie Normous to a scathing audience, the curtains opening on Sheila chewing cud and spitting.

Startled awake, Jack found himself looking at the implant overlay, watching as it reported the results of the cognitive model. Which shocked him the rest of the way to awareness.

Jack sat up fast, his head spinning only a little bit. Fuck. He'd somehow managed to initiate a model without realising it. How long had it been running? The entire time he'd been sick, or only part of it? A properly conducted model required a deep trance state and usually only lasted several hours while the implant accessed a defined set of memories. During the process, Jack had often experienced flash-back like episodes, coming out of it occasionally rattled. However, thanks to the altered mind-state, he'd not been able to act on those memories, hadn't been able to hurt anyone with them. All bets, however, were off with a model that had somehow managed to run while he was mostly conscious.

Unless . . .

The bed was empty but for him. No Ethan anywhere in the bedroom. Getting up, Jack scouted the rest of his place, feeling strength return to his limbs as he moved without pain for the first time in what felt like forever. Relieved he was better, Jack was nevertheless upset to find no trace of Ethan at all. No mugs sitting in the draining rack from his morning tea. No fastidious tidying of all the small, inconsequential things Jack left wherever. No lingering scent of gun oil at the dining room table from Ethan cleaning his weapons. Nothing to prove he'd been there at all in recent times.

Had Jack dreamed it all? Had his fevered mind and unfocused implant conjured a realistic Ethan Blade out of nothing more than memory and desperate want? It had been nearly five weeks since Jack had seen him last and that hadn't ended on an entirely positive note. All Jack had wanted since Ethan had vanished from the Gold Coast was to see him again, to say all the things he hadn't been brave enough to say then.

A fist pounded on the front door. Casting aside his confused thoughts about whether or not Ethan had been there, about whether or not Jack really wanted something beyond fucking and friendship, he went to the door and keyed on the small screen beside it.

The fisheye camera above his door gave a view of the hallway all the way back to the stairs and lift at the far end. Standing in the middle of the image was Harry, staring at his phone, his other hand raised to thump on the door again.

"Fuck." Jack unlocked the door just as Harry knocked and opened it. "Morning, Harry," he grumbled.

"Morning, Jack." Harry flicked through another page on his phone, then looked up at him. His eyebrows went high and his jaw dropped. "Wow, you look like shit."

"Thanks. I feel like a sparkling rainbow." Jack stepped back and let him in.

Harry snickered and came in. "You do know unicorns shit sparkling rainbows, right?"

Jack glared at the back of his head. "I assume you're here to haul me back in to work."

"Nope. Just a check-in. Make sure you didn't die or anything." Instead of leaving now his mission had been satisfied, he went and parked his arse on a stool at the kitchen counter. "You're mobile and mostly sensible. Guess it can't have been an honest-to-God man flu, huh."

A memory of being forced onto his stomach followed by a sharp sting in his arse made Jack hesitate over his answer. Had he recovered naturally or had Ethan helped? Not quite at the stage where he felt he could grope his own arse in front of Harry, Jack headed for the bathroom.

"Stay there," he told Harry in his best dog-training voice. "I'll shower and then you can drive me in." He might feel better but he wasn't about to risk taking the bike.

"No rush, mate. McIntosh gave you another day off."

Jack locked the bathroom door behind him. Shoving his shorts off, he turned around before the vanity and, up on his toes, tried to get a look at his left cheek. Sure enough, right in the meatiest part, was a small bruise around a tiny red dot.

He sank down and rested his naked butt against the cool marble. Ethan had been here, which meant the vague images of him being exasperated with Jack were real. And the totally embarrassing moment when Jack had had to leave him primed and cocked, and then do absolutely nothing about it. No wonder Ethan had gone before Jack had woken up. Insulted however many times and not even getting what he'd come for.

"Fuck it," Jack muttered, and got into the shower.

If Ethan finally decided it was all too difficult for a few orgasms that he could probably get elsewhere with half the trouble, then it was probably for the best. He wouldn't have to risk getting into the country without being detected, wouldn't have to suffer through Jack's moods and wouldn't have to make dangerously fast exits when it all went pear-shaped. Jack wouldn't have to worry about him or make agreements with a director he didn't respect and end up on dead end assignments like Delta Subject. It was for the best.

So why did Jack want the door to the shower to open so Ethan could slip in and join him?

That fantasy didn't come true and Jack finished showering alone. Dried off alone and pulled on a suit alone. If he had to face down at least one, but more likely two, pissed-off directors, he should probably look like he took the situation seriously.

"Now you look like a sparkly rainbow," Harry announced when Jack stalked past him on the way to the front door. "Storm cloud included. Seriously, you have another sick day owing. Maybe you should take it?"

"Let's go, princess," Jack snapped and regretted it. Harry hadn't done anything wrong.

They may have only been working together for a couple of months, but Harry'd had a crash course in the Tao of Jack, so he just slid off the stool and followed him out. "Any word on when I'll get my T-shirt back?"

Jack frowned, recalling agreeing to swap shirts with Harry before heading into Slayed, but after that . . . "Yeah, probably should just get a new one." That way, even if Jack found it somewhere, he could happily consign it to the nearest incinerator without feeling guilty.

Harry shrugged. "Likewise, mate. Yours didn't last the night, either."

"What happened to it?"

"You don't remember?" Harry hit the down button on the lift, then did a double take at Jack opening the door to the stairwell. Sighing, he dutifully followed his field leader down two flights of stairs. "That's probably for the best."

Refusing to feel the blush creeping up his neck, Jack muttered, "I wish people would stop saying that to me."

On the drive to the Neville Crawley Building, Harry got Jack up to date on the current situation at the Office. Which was, basically, nothing out of the ordinary. Harry and Scott had reported in after dropping Jack off at home, McIntosh had granted Jack his sick leave and that was it. Harry had spent the next day ensuring none of their activities had been noticed by other agencies and submitting the operation details to the unit leader. He hadn't even been called to task about breaking protocol and following Delta Subject.

As Harry drove them down into the underground carpark, Jack suspected McIntosh, Tan and Keri Sing were waiting to explode all over him. Putting the blame where it was due. And the only defence he had was the results of a half-arsed cognitive model done while he'd been wracked with fevers, probably with compromising images of Ethan thrown in for good measure. Until he was able to access the results, he couldn't risk letting anyone know about it.

Not willing to show up at McIntosh's office sweaty and aching, Jack took the lift to the tenth floor, Harry by his side.

As they stepped out into the carpeted hallway, Harry said softly, "I'm with you, boss. All the way."

The support was appreciated and Jack told him so with a grunt. However, Miller informed them Director McIntosh wanted to see only Jack. Leaving Harry sitting dejectedly on a chair in the waiting area, Jack went in to face the consequences.

"Jack, sit." McIntosh didn't have her glasses on and her sky-blue eyes watched him critically as he did as instructed. "How are you feeling?"

"Perfectly fine, ma'am. I'm sorry for the way the operation went down. I'm the only one to blame for it. Both Harry and Scott registered their objection to me going into the club, but I overruled them."

"Thank you for being so candid," she said. "Harry and Scott both submitted reports to that effect as well. However, Harry did insist he was to blame for not realising just how sick you were before you went into the field."

Heartened by his second's support, Jack nevertheless said, "Still not his fault."

McIntosh snorted softly. "I think I've noted in the past how stubborn you can be. No reprimand will go Harry's way over this mess." Her eyes went a little steely as she gave Jack a pointed look. "Consider yourself officially reprimanded, Jack Reardon."

Jack blinked. That had to be the least painful reprimand McIntosh had ever delivered. She was fair, but tough. Granted the whole Blade-Harraway affair had been bigger than this one on the order of magnitudes, but five months later Jack was still treading lightly around McIntosh, even after his actions had been cleared by the director in charge.

"I must inform you that you are no longer working with Keri Sing's unit. However you accomplished it, Jack, you have your wish. Delta Subject is no longer our concern."

Christ. Hearing that should have made Jack's morning, but it felt like a bitter defeat. His first job as a field leader and he failed spectacularly. "Thank you, ma'am. Do you know who's taking it over?"

"Not at this point. It may be they've finally worked out Delta Subject isn't worth the time, or they're keeping it within ETA. Either way, it's not our concern anymore. Everything your team gathered has already been handed over. Once you file a report on the nightclub, that will go to ETA as well."

Nodding, Jack asked, "And Tan? Do I have to face him over this?"

McIntosh gave him a chilly little smile. "No. The moment he declared you off the job, I declared he had no access to you on this matter. Any other agreements you have with him are still yours to deal with, though."

"Yes, ma'am."

His first op as a field leader may have gone tits up and he may have been removed from the job entirely, but at least he'd escaped with his director's backing still in place. He would just have to be extra careful to not piss her off for a while. And when Ethan returned, Jack would do everything he could to make sure he didn't leave again.

ACKNOWLEDGEMENTS

I feel like dittoing the Acknowledgements on the previous novella. All the same people have been just as awesome and supportive, Layla Reyne, Erin McLellan and Allison Temple. Thank you again and forever! This time I also want to give a big shout out to everyone who's stuck with me throughout this process. You are all amazing! We're up to novella two and things are still going forward. Yay us!!

DEATH AND THE DEVIL #1.8

DEVIL IN THE DETAILS

If there's one thing assassin Ethan Blade knows, it's how to plan a job. How to study a target, find the weak spot, and strike. He keeps his guns clean, his knives sharp, and his heart sealed away behind more locks than his precious cars. Alone but safe. Until Jack Reardon burrowed his way into Ethan's life, his car, and his heart. This may just be the deadliest mess he can't plan his way out of.

Jack wasn't sure he'd see Ethan again—not after the less-than-stellar ends to their previous hookups. Even finding the assassin skulking about his apartment isn't as reassuring as it should be, especially when he works out Ethan's motive for being there might not be personal. That said, Jack will take any chance he can to salvage their relationship, assuming he survives whatever plan Ethan is cooking up.

Ethan and Jack had a bargain, but the parameters changed and neither are certain how to move forward—together or apart. But before they can start to renegotiate, lives, trust, and hearts are endangered by ghosts from the past. Even if they dodge their enemies' bullets, there's a risk of friendly fire, and when you let someone get too close, even small knives can cut deep.

LA PETITE MORT

(JUNE)

"**Y**ou came back."

I spun around at the sound of Jack's voice, my free hand reaching into my jacket for a gun. Habit and muscle memory were hard things to counter, despite every instinct assuring me there was no danger. Yet, the relief of seeing Jack standing in the open doorway, hale and apparently happy to find me in his apartment, did not quite mitigate the fact that he had surprised me. It could have been someone else at my back. Someone who announced their presence with a bullet through my spine.

"Jack." It came out on a strained breath as I settled the Desert Eagle back into its holster under my right arm. "I wasn't expecting you so early."

Or, that he would catch me here at all.

Guiltily, I glanced at the distraction in my other hand. The picture frame was plain black, but solid and heavy, and would have made an adequate weapon if required, yet the photo it held meant I would never have used it as such. Since my first visit to Jack's apartment, I had felt drawn to this image but resisted the temptation to pick it up and study it. Those same indelible instincts that protected me from harm kept me from giving in. This time, though, already hurting from Jack's actions over the last couple of visits, all resistance was gone.

"Clearly not." Jack stepped inside and closed and locked the door behind him, dark-brown eyes crinkling and lips curling into a delighted smirk. His pleasure at catching me by surprise tickled in my chest. Being the reason Jack smiled warmed me through and made me want to do nothing else for the rest of my life.

If only Jack wanted the same thing.

Though, the way he was focused on me, so intent and heated, it could be assumed he did. Yet the voice of reason reminded me assumption was a fast way to die. Be certain or be prepared for every possibility. I was failing on so many levels already. I couldn't fail this one.

"There's not a lot going on at work lately." Jack's tone was casual, as was the way he set his helmet on the kitchen counter and started pulling off his riding gloves. His gaze never left me, though. It raked down my body, faltered briefly when it reached the photo frame, then continued on and back up. "I got bored today and since I have quite a bit of leave time owing, they couldn't wait to send me home."

Drat. The plan had been to get in and out unnoticed, a quick ten-minute job. However, as with so many things Jack-centric, it all went haywire the moment I set foot within his home. It had been easy to convince myself I could do this when I'd been securely ensconced within my Kuala Lumpur safe place. Come to Sydney, plant the information Jack needed for his Delta Subject job and leave him to find it on his own. Of course, that had been when I thought I had a two-week window. Khun Sein had stepped up his timeline, and thus here I was, not totally unprepared, but rushed enough I'd been discovered.

"I really didn't think I'd see you again for a good long while." Jack unzipped the front of his leather jacket and tossed it over the back of a chair at the dining table. "If at all," he added ruefully and shoved his hands in his trouser pockets, managing to look like six feet of beautiful contriteness.

Jack had on an off-the-rack, navy business suit, like most of his workwear, but he wore it superbly well all the same. Granted, he didn't look as polished as he had in his Hugo Boss at the Gold Coast, but right now, with his black curls tousled from his helmet and his button-down half untucked from his trousers, he was even more irresistible. Especially since I apparently wasn't the only one who regretted how our last visit had ended. Maybe I'd been too rash in leaving as I had last time. Jack couldn't help being rude and untactful when sick. The hurt was still there, a smouldering coal in my belly ready to be fanned to flames again, but right now it felt small and excusable.

Everything had been so much easier when there were thousands of miles between us. My resolve had been strong. Here, just the warmth of his hopeful gaze wilted my convictions. I had been caught. Perhaps I should make the most of it while I could. A final night of passion and pleasure to keep me warm when I left again.

I set the frame back on the shelf and Jack's gaze followed the picture, a slight frown pinching his brows and his lips parting to speak.

"Don't you have an active case at the moment?" I knew this question would waylay any questions he had about my interest in the photo: Jack had made his thoughts on my meddling in his work abundantly clear.

Jack frowned and shrugged out of his suit jacket, letting it fall over the top of the leather one. The pale blue of his shirt stretched across his chest and arms, defining his pectorals and biceps as they flexed. "Not anymore. We got kicked off the last job."

A little sidetracked, it took a moment for his words to sink in. When they did, I looked at him in surprise. I hadn't known he'd been taken off the watch on Delta Subject, his part of the Salim case being run out of the Singapore branch of the Office. But the smirk on his lips said he didn't mind me asking about his work, at least not as much as he enjoyed distracting me with his body.

"I do believe that I owe you something." Jack's voice lowered into that husky rumble that made my bones ache and my cock hard. He stalked towards me, loosening his tie as he came, eyes narrowing with intent.

Blast it. He'd stolen my tactic and turned it on me. Not that I particularly cared because a moment later he was pressed up against me, his arms around my waist and his forehead against mine.

Defenceless. That was what he made me.

Jack effortlessly stripped me of every survival instinct I had. No one else could have gotten this close to me unless it was what I had expressly planned. No one else ever *wanted* to get this close. It still worried me that Jack did. It was easier to think he used "mutual attraction" as an excuse for wanting my body, not the mind within it. Easier and more painful, because as much as I hoped it was more than just physical, I had to wonder if that's all it had ever been and destined to be nothing more.

"Jesus, Ethan." Eyes closing, Jack rocked his head side to side. His arms tightened, hands pressing into my back with possessive force. "You had me scared you weren't coming back. I've missed you."

Then he said something like that and my dumb heart leaped excitedly. My arms wound around his neck without guidance and I closed the final, miniscule distance between our bodies. "I missed you too." Like my arms, my words appeared to be out of my control. Five weeks ago, I wouldn't have minded. Now it scared me how quickly Jack undid me.

Jack shivered a little, then pulled back just enough so he could slide down to his knees. "Now, about that thing I owe you." His hands went to my belt and began undoing it, the heels of his palms deliberately rubbing over the evidence of my arousal.

Sparks flared in my cock and up into my belly. My heart skipped several beats as my lungs forgot how to work. Jack tipped his head back, curls tumbling away from his face, eyes heated and lips parted as he looked up me. I ran a hand through his hair, loving the feel of his soft locks and how his eyes drifted shut as he smiled. His mouth was perfect, not too wide, nor too narrow, lips well defined but not too thick or thin. They were talented, too. Very talented. I had lost track of the hours I'd spent under their narcotic effect as they roamed across my body. Or wrapped around my cock.

Which he seemed determined to do now, judging by the way he nuzzled into my groin, his fingers slipping the button of my trousers free and finding the pull tab of the zipper.

"Jack, wait." I fisted his curls gently and tugged his head back.

He went with my pull, tilted his head back and rested his chin on the back of his hand that still held the pull tab hopefully. "Problem?"

Oh so many. I sagged back against the bookcase. Sex had been my plan, yes, but the moment Jack went to his knees, I knew I was losing control of the situation. Once his mouth touched my skin, I would be completely useless for anything other than letting him possess me any way he wished.

Jack stood and cupped my cheek in his warm palm. "Ethan? What's wrong?"

He was asking all the wrong questions to get the right answers. Why couldn't it just be simple between us? Why did I have to be such a mess? It had been easier when I was alone and didn't know the reality of what I'd been missing. For years, I might have wished for companionable contact with someone else, something more natural than what I had with my associates, more real than I had with any of my targets. Jack had given me that, and so much more, but I hadn't realised there would be pain as well. Pain in what Jack made me feel. Pain in how he would react if he knew everything about who I was and what I'd done before meeting him.

"Is it me?" he asked.

"No." Right then, it was true. He was happy to find me here, he hadn't mentioned other men, and he wanted me—for sex, at least.

Jack nodded. "Don't you want to fuck?"

He sounded despondent but was trying so hard to be accepting I couldn't help but laugh. I draped an arm around his shoulders and guided his hand back to the still hard mound in my trousers. His fingers wrapped around me and with a single stroke, pulled our bodies back together.

"Yes," I managed around the sudden resurgence of lust. "I do. Just . . . let me take charge."

Jack stared at me for moment, then his mouth curved into a dirty grin. "Okay. Anything you want."

All my convictions trembled under the power of that smile. Anything I wanted? I wanted to let him do whatever he wanted to me. I wanted to crawl into his arms and never leave them. I wanted to tell him everything and still have him desire me afterwards. I wanted to kiss him until he felt the same way.

I settled for grinding against his hand for a moment, then pushed him back. "Excellent. Shall we begin then?"

Jack snickered. "I don't know about you, but I began the moment I saw you."

Pressing my lips together to keep in the laughter, I grabbed his tie and held it over my shoulder as I turned toward the bedroom. Jack pretended a stumble as I dragged him after me, his hands landing on my hips. It reminded me of the night in Melbourne and I suddenly knew exactly how this was going to progress.

Halfway along, Jack pushed up against my back, arms sliding all the way around my waist. He walked in time with me, the hard shaft of his cock rubbing against my buttocks as we went. A couple of steps after that, we did stumble, for real this time. I caught us on the doorframe to the bedroom, both of us laughing as we straightened.

"Tsk tsk, Blade," he said. "I know it can be difficult to walk with an erection, but I kinda expected more from you."

Snorting, I shrugged out of his hold. "It can be difficult, especially when the erection is poking me in the rear."

We realised what I'd said at the same moment. Blood rushed to my cheeks, heating them to the point of steaming. Jack laughed so hard he nearly fell over again. He came at me, leering and hands out to grope. I sidestepped his approach, caught his wrist and twisted, sweeping his feet at the same time. With a startled gasp, Jack landed face first on the bed, arm up behind his back, my knee planted on his bottom, holding him down.

After a silent moment, he turned his head enough to say, "I'm having strange flashbacks. You don't have a needle and syringe, do you?"

I couldn't resist him at the best of times. I was totally lost now.

"Not this time." I let him go and stood back. "On your back, Jack."

Grumbling all the way, he rolled over and scooted up the bed. He scowled at me, but it was the mock one he used when he really wanted to smile or say something tender. It made my heart leap. Maybe . . .

Shaking off my doubts, I stood at the end of the bed and stripped. I had no qualms about my body. It was appealing in form, if not perfect aesthetically. There were too many scars for that, not that Jack seemed to mind. He had his own scars, including the self-inflicted ones. His gaze locked onto my hands, watching avidly as they removed items of clothing and weapons. When I got to my trousers and unzipped them, he bit his lower lip and gripped his cock through layers of material. Which seemed to remind him he was dressed.

"Uh uh." I shook a finger at him as he went to undo his trousers. "That's my job."

"Jesus." He left his clothes alone only to grab himself again and stroke. "Then hurry up. Things are getting pretty tight here."

I smirked and slowed down. Jack tossed his head back and groaned, all but wanking himself.

"Enough of that, Jack," I commanded. "Hands on the headboard. Now."

"Fuck you," he snapped back, but lifted his hands and pressed them to the wood of the headboard. Perhaps this time I wouldn't give in and let him touch me, no matter how much either of us wanted it. "You're killing me here."

Stepping out of my trousers, I folded them neatly and hung them over the arm of the recliner. Then I took off my sunglasses and set them on the tallboy. Turning back, I let my eyelids drop and, in a low voice, said, "If I were killing you, you wouldn't even know it was happening."

Not the most erotic thing I could have said, but sometimes I had to remind Jack just who he was with, to see if this time, he really understood and realised I wasn't good for him.

All he did was suck in a sharp breath and shift his hips as if he was trying to get some pressure on his cock. "Please."

Not this time, then.

Leaving my briefs and socks on, I kneeled on the end of the bed and gestured at one of Jack's feet. He lifted it and I unlaced his shoe painstakingly slowly. Jack growled and his arms flexed as if keeping his hands on the headboard took a great effort. By the time both of his feet were bare, Jack was swearing at me, to which I just smiled as I moved up over him.

"If you take much longer, this could be a solo affair, you realise," he warned, when I very carefully began pulling his shirt the rest of the way out of his trousers.

"Well, that would be disappointing, I suppose." Concentrating on gently sliding buttons through holes was challenging since Jack kept pushing his hips up into my crotch as I straddled him. "However, I'm sure you'll be ready to go again in fifteen minutes."

Jack cackled and started to reach for me. One stern look and he contritely put his hands back on the headboard. Which stymied me when I finished unbuttoning his shirt and realised he'd have to move them if I wanted to strip him completely. Yet, looking at him like this, under me, with his chest bared, blue shirt spread to either side and his arms up like he was surrendering, was incredibly distracting. I pushed the material off his shoulders as much as I could, letting my hands linger on his warm skin. Jack watched as I dragged my palms across his pecs and downwards. His belly trembled and his abs rippled. I drifted my fingers through the thin trail of dark hair that swirled around his navel and ran down into the waistband of his trousers.

I had never been so entranced by a body before. Certainly none of the other men I'd had sex with had ever fascinated me as Jack did. Intercourse with anyone else had always been part of the job and aesthetics hadn't meant as much as the reason why I was there. It had never been like that with Jack, though. Even before we'd had sex, I had felt drawn to this man who didn't flinch from the name Ethan Blade. His voice, his sarcasm, his laughter, his skin, his hands, his—

"Ethan?"

His dark-brown eyes focused on me, the smirking and teasing replaced by an expression of almost pained tension. When he dipped his gaze to where my hand pressed against his abdomen, I understood his problem. Jack hadn't said anything to me, but we'd been together enough for me to pick up on his reaction to how our skin tones looked side by side. He could lose himself for long periods watching his brown hand move over my white skin, or mine over him. If I let him go long enough, the intercourse afterwards was always hard and desperate, and scary at how vulnerable it seemed to make Jack.

Vulnerable wasn't what I needed. Wanted, perhaps, but needed? Not now. Hard and desperate, though . . .

I leaned down, careful to keep our groins apart. Any more stimulation there wouldn't help either of us keep on track, different though those tracks may be. The moment my lips touched the skin of his shoulder a lingering tension in my chest eased. Jack was familiar and warm and the way he turned his head to kiss my temple sent shivers down my spine. I breathed in deep and the scent of his clean skin filled my body. I weakened for a moment, nearly telling him to move his arms, to hold me, touch me. If I did, I'd never be able to leave again. So instead I occupied my mouth with tasting him, replenishing my memory of how smooth his skin was across his pecs, just the lightest smattering of hair and no disfiguring scars. Reminding myself how responsive his nipples were to my tongue, hardening with the slightest of flicks, and how his chest rumbled under my lips when I sucked. I made my way downwards, relishing every sound Jack made, every quiver in his body, every curse he snarled when he remembered he had to keep his hands on the headboard. Smirking, I gave him payback for all the times he'd tortured me with his tongue in my naval.

"Fuck. Jesus. Shit!" Jack bucked, twisting in an effort to dislodge me. "Ethan!"

Sitting back on my heels, I smiled sweetly at him. "Yes, Jack?"

He glared at me. "Stop it, you crazy bastard."

"Hmm. Half right, Jack." I traced a finger across the buckle of his belt. "Does this mean you don't want . . ."

"There's only so long I'm going to keep my hands on this headboard, Blade. Get on with it."

"Since you asked so nicely." Slowly, slowly, I undid his belt.

Jack whimpered. "I won't be responsible for what may happen."

"There you go, shifting blame again." I lowered the zipper, careful of the hard obstruction under it. His response was unintelligible. I took pity on him and got his trousers down and off. The number of wet spots on his boxer-briefs lent credence to his complaints so I divested him of his underwear as well.

Hard cock flopping up onto his belly, Jack let out a relieved whoosh of air. The tension left his thighs and they fell apart slightly, and his abdomen relaxed. A goofy grin spread across his face. "Thank you."

The sight of him so sillily happy broke something inside me, flooding me with heat and anxiety. It didn't matter that he was naked and hard, only that I had made him smile at me like that. And that if I went through with my plan, there was a possibility I'd never see it again.

"I've changed my mind." The words were out of my mouth before I'd even fully realised the thought.

He lost the grin that had set my heart alight. "What?"

I crawled up his body and let myself melt into him. "Touch me. Hold me."

"Always." Jack's arms snapped down and around me, hands pressed to my back, big and hard and comforting. "You know you worry me sometimes."

Snuggling my face into the curve between shoulder and neck, I mumbled, "I do?"

"Yeah. It's just that I never know what you're thinking. I mean, one moment you're all hot and in charge, the next you get this sad look on your face and ask to be held."

I shivered. This was unusual. Jack didn't normally talk so openly about such things. I'd had to dig to get the real story about what happened at the charity race dinner out of him on the Gold Coast. Jack's jaw moved against the side of my head, as if he was about speak again, but he didn't. His arms got even tighter though.

"I'm all right," I assured him, lying.

The only thing holding me together right now was his arms. One look and my plan had been shattered. I could feel the chaos of uncertainty and doubt creeping into me, my body tensing in defence. So much of my life, so much of *me*, was dependant on trained instinct and being at least two and preferably three steps ahead of my targets just to stay alive and finish the job. I had no training, no weapons, no instincts to get me through this.

Well, I had one instinct and I reached for it with every measure of my being.

Jack rolled us over and pulled away so he could look at me properly, concern making him frown. Gently, he ran knuckles down my cheek. "Ethan, what's wrong?"

"Fuck me, Jack." My cheeks flamed, but my cock surged even though it had been flagging. Jack had been right. There was a visceral satisfaction in saying it, and a reciprocal excitement in seeing the effect it had on Jack.

His eyes went wide and his hand stalled half way down my cheek. Then he smiled, that same delightedly stupid one he'd given me moments ago. "You said it." Before I could chide him for narrating the obvious, he lunged down and kissed my nose, my cheek, my chin. "You're blushing so hard. Christ, Blade, do you have any blood left in the lower half of your body to keep you hard?" His hand went questing for answers.

I squirmed, desire starting to push aside the unwanted, terrifying emotions. "Jack." Now, apparently it was my turn to whine, but even that urge fled as his hand dove inside my underwear and found my cock.

"Yes. Yes, you do," Jack answered himself, his fingers closing around me and stroking. "I find, old bean, that I'm of a mind to make you pay for all your teasing."

I chuckled at his atrociously bad British accent.

Between kisses and bites to my neck and shoulders, Jack kept working my cock and said, "Another time, though. Jesus, I'm so fucking primed I might not even get inside you before I blow."

Before I could gather enough faculties to respond, Jack lurched up to his knees, tossed off his shirt and had my boxer-briefs down and cast aside with barely any help from me.

Jack sat still for a long moment, looking up and down my body. He squeezed himself and groaned. "Yup. Another time."

Then he crawled across me, making sure there was a lot of skin contact as he opened the bedside table drawer and foraged for condom and lubricant. Successful, he slithered around until he lay directly on top of me, dropping the gear by the pillow while he kissed my neck and down my chest. Halfway down, he stopped, grabbed the lubricant, and continued.

When I realised his destination, I reminded him, "Jack, I thought you were about to *blow*."

"We covered this earlier. Pay attention." He lubricated his fingers and wormed his way between my legs. "I owe you something first."

His mouth was on me and his fingers were at my entrance before I could even think to protest. As often and strenuously as Jack said otherwise, I still felt it wasn't fair that he fellate me as much as he did. My objections had weakened considerably over time and were reduced now to a few plaintive "Jacks" while my body arched into him and my fingers dug divots in his shoulders. He licked and sucked and the deep pulling sensation threaded from my groin up into my belly and lungs until I couldn't breathe and my heart thudded impossibly loud. Then his finger breached me and I didn't know which way to go, up into his mouth or down onto his hand. Jack solved the issue, as he always did, by synchronising his sucks and thrusts so all I had to do was shake in between them.

When he worked a second, then third finger into me, I couldn't take it anymore. I needed him on me, in me, all around me.

"Jack." I tugged on his arm. "Please, now."

His response was indecipherable around my cock, but his fingers curled inside me and I nearly came down his throat. He kept it up until I was a writhing, whimpering mess, unintelligible and lost to the sensations. Then he stopped right before I reached orgasm.

"I hate you," I moaned as he kneeled between my legs with careless disregard for retaliation. I may have been trembling uncontrollably, but I was sure my aim was still good enough to kick him off the bed.

Jack smirked as he leaned over me, reaching for the condom and diving in to kiss along my jaw, which I willingly gave him access to. "No, you don't." He sat back to open and roll on the condom, stroking my thigh with his free hand as he did so, as if he needed constant contact.

"No, I don't," I said softly and lifted my calves to his shoulders.

"I don't hate you either." Then he shifted forward, pushing my knees to my chest, and entered me.

I was still a little startled whenever Jack penetrated me. There was a slight burn and mildly uncomfortable sensation but it passed quickly as he worked his length into my body. In those first few moments, it was the gentleness of his touch and his attention to me that always took my breath away. The way he focused on my body over his own and made sure he wasn't hurting me, rather than just ramming me in order to get his own gratification. Only when the glide of his cock was smooth did he start to give in to his own wants.

Jack shrugged my legs off his shoulders and pushed them apart so he could get closer. He skimmed his lips over my throat, kissing his way down my shoulder and back across my clavicles. His body moved over me and in me, tender, deep thrusts, making sure I felt every inch of him. Braced on one hand, he reached down with the other to pull at my thigh to let me know where he wanted my legs. Obedient, I wrapped them around him, knees pressed to his ribs, heels against his flexing buttocks. That done, he touched me. My face, my chest, my arm. Soft, wondering caresses that left me dizzy.

It was slow and passionate and beautiful and not at all what I needed. Wanted, yes, but needed? Not if I had any chance of salvaging anything from my botched plan.

Damn Jack and his rules and careless words and his tender touches and his effortless ability to hurt me.

"Jack," I moaned, lips pressed to his cheek.

"Yeah." He rocked into me, harder and deeper.

It felt so good I could nearly fool myself into believing this was all I ever needed. Much more of it, though, and I'd be confessing everything to him, and the plans of a Burmese drug lord were the least of it.

"Jack." There was more pleading in this one, hope that he would hear what I needed without me having to say it again.

Whatever Jack heard, it sent a shudder through his body and he kissed and licked and tasted his way from one nipple to the other, murmuring "Yeah" over and over as he went.

Everything he was doing was wearing me down, kiss by kiss, touch by touch, thrust by thrust. He lifted his head and brought his face to mine, cheek to cheek, and his hand stroked up my ribs, over my pectoral, curved around my neck and his fingers delved into my hair.

I loved it when he touched my head or wound his fingers through my hair. So many memories of being touched like that, from so long ago. It wasn't sexual for me, even when he did it in the middle of intercourse like this. To me it meant caring and comfort and . . . and love. Involuntarily, I titled my head back into his hand, wanting more of it.

"Christ, Ethan," Jack hissed, his fingers digging into my scalp, his hips pushing harder, trying to get closer, deeper. He kissed my jaw, my neck, my ear, then worked his way towards my mouth.

Already on a precipice, I knew that if he kissed me properly, I'd be completely lost.

I bucked, pushing at him with arms and hips. "Jack."

"I know, I know." He shifted sides and sucked my earlobe into his hot mouth.

"No, Jack. I mean . . ." I trailed off as little shots of lightning shot from my ear right down to my aching cock and arse. This wasn't going to plan at all. Gathering my few remaining wits, I got hold of a fistful of his hair and tugged his head up. "Jack, I said *fuck* me."

Jack's hips froze in mid-thrust. Startled, he stared at me for a moment, then asked, "What do you mean?"

Oh dear. I squirmed, feeling my cheeks warm, even more than they had under Jack's attentions. "I mean, like the first time. In the cave, when you drove me crazy." Like when the sex was only hot and amazing, not incendiary and shattering, and I didn't know you like I do now, didn't know just how thoroughly you would destroy my world and recreate it for me in beautiful, painful ways.

"Crazier," Jack corrected absently.

I chuckled because I didn't want him to worry. And nipped at his jaw because I needed him to know I still wanted him. "Please, Jack. Like then."

The shifting of our bodies let his cock slide out of me, so I took advantage of it and wriggled over onto my belly. I lifted my hips for him, knees bent and spread, a silent plea for him to fill me back up.

After a strained moment, Jack moaned, "Fuck," and settled back between my legs. Hands on my hips, he pushed his cock into me, slow like it was the first thrust again. It forced the breath I'd been holding out on a relieved sigh, then a second breath on a gasp as he pulled out and plunged back in, fast and hard.

I didn't know why I thought this position would be easier. The pleasure jolting through me was exactly the same as before, explosive and glorious, just concentrated into sharper, firmer motions. Jack's touches—sweeping caresses up and down my back, hard grips on my hips and shoulders, the bite of his teeth on my shoulder blade—still sent me reeling. The sounds of his panting and grunts, of his flesh slapping against mine, of "Ethan" and his growling blasphemies, riddled me like bullets.

Don't fight them. It's easier if you don't. Just let them do whatever they want . . . It was advice I'd followed since the day it had been given to me. Words that I'd clung to in every sexual encounter with a male target—until Jack. That first time, I'd tried to follow the advice, but Jack had shaken me free of it, relentlessly waking up parts of me, physical and emotional, I hadn't known I possessed. I knew them now and still he was giving them back to me like it was the first time.

I was doomed.

"I'm not going to last long," Jack warned me.

Neither was I at this pace. I got a hand around my cock moments before Jack shoved me down into the mattress. He lay down over my back and wrapped his arms around me, holding me tighter. His weight was oppressive but welcomed, like he could protect me from anything the world fired at me.

"God, Ethan," he moaned, hips going wild.

Every push of his cock into my body was cracking me open. I buried my face in the pillow and clung to the arms around me with one hand, the other around my cock, doing nothing but giving it a channel to move in as Jack pounded my arse.

"Fuck, I'm close." Jack pressed his face into my shoulder.

I let go of his arm and reached back to wind my fingers through his hair, to make sure he didn't pull away yet. I wanted him as close as I could get him right then. My orgasm was building frightfully fast and I clenched my fist around my shaft, hoping it would give me just that little bit of extra—

The orgasm ripped through me, heat and light bursting through the cracks to shatter me into a million pieces that Jack held together with his strong arms and encompassing body. I barely heard him shout "Ethan," but I felt him come, hard and powerfully, his cock pulsing inside me. Several never-ending moments later, the tension eased out of him and his whole weight settled on my back.

It didn't bother me when Jack lingered. I liked the feel of him slowly softening, of the press of his body as he caught his breath, the way his arms stayed tight around me even as the rest of him melted. His nonsensical mumblings as he came back to his senses always made me want to cuddle him.

"Sorry," Jack groaned, sliding out of and off me in one clumsy move. He didn't go far, just snugged down beside me, one arm across my back, hot breath wafting over my shoulder.

"You have no need to be."

I wondered how true that was, though. My plan at distraction had worked—perhaps too well—but the fact remained he'd hurt me several times recently. Though, it was hard to remember just how his words and actions had wounded me right now. Lying here so warm, sated, and aching in the most glorious of ways, I could forget it all.

Eventually, the moment had to pass. Jack grumbled his way off the bed and down the hall to the bathroom. Given a few moments alone, I cleaned myself up as well as I could with tissues and sternly ordered my thoughts. Lust sated, I fixed my plan in my mind, determined to see it through. I'd had my moment of weakness, now it was time to work. Settled, I found two pairs of tracksuit bottoms, pulled one pair on and met Jack with the others. While he dressed, I started making tea and coffee.

"I should leave work early more often." Jack stretched as he came into the kitchen. He didn't lower his arms until he was right behind me and could drape them around my shoulders. He nuzzled into my neck, making silly snuffling sounds.

For a moment, I wished Jack was one of those men who came, then fell asleep. The more hours I had to divert his attention, the more difficulty I was going to encounter.

"Speaking of work, why were you taken off your case?" I poured the boiling water from the kettle into my mug. Jack started to make grumbly noises, so I hastily added, "I'm not prying. I'm simply curious about what could make your directors remove you from a case."

Snorting, Jack leaned against the opposite counter, arms crossed. "If you must know, I fucked up royally. You know how sick I was last time you were here. Well, I tried to break the case while delirious with fever and it didn't work. That's why they kicked me off it. Not that I really care. It was a bloody pointless exercise."

"Hmm. I'm sorry to hear that." I wasn't, honestly. Except that even knowing about it now didn't change anything. It was too late to alter my plan enough to leave Jack out of it.

"How long can you stay this time?" he asked.

"Not long." I stirred his coffee and handed it over, cursing myself for not getting him a beer instead. "Perhaps just the night."

Jack mused for a moment, then took his coffee to the couch. "Perhaps? You don't usually have to guess. Don't you have meticulously planned out travel windows?"

I joined him. "Yes, but I actually have several windows this time." All true. Always plan for the worst possible scenario. Of course, I hadn't planned on being caught here.

"Good. Make it the latest possible one then. I want you here for as long as you can be." He clicked on the telly and flicked to an afternoon news program. Setting down the remote, he let his hand rest on my thigh, natural and non-demanding.

"As you wish," I whispered.

Jack leaned over and kissed my cheek, then settled in to watch the news.

I needn't have worried after that. Content that I had no immediate plans to leave, Jack spent the evening in his usual pursuits. At least, as usual as they were when I was with him. He fed me, laughed at me and with me several times, groped me at nearly every opportunity and, finally, herded me back to bed when I threatened to fall asleep on him on the couch.

It was a ploy, of course. Any other visit, we would have had sex a second and perhaps third time on our first night together. My body wanted him, but I overruled it this time. I couldn't resist everything he offered a second time.

Jack curled around me under the blankets, arm across my waist, head resting on my chest. "You're not going anywhere," he mumbled, thinking I was already asleep and unable to hear him.

I waited until he was firmly asleep, then slid out from under him. Staying awake with him in the bed wouldn't have been impossible, but I didn't want to risk it. Physical desire sated, it was time I got to work.

Though being a Sugar Baby—thanks to my drug addicted mother—had only ever been a curse on my life, the one benefit was increased night vision. It let me move around Jack's apartment without turning on a light that might wake him and let me look at the picture he'd caught me holding. I couldn't quite pick out all the details, but I had studied it enough earlier to know exactly what I couldn't see now.

It was of Jack's parents. His mother, Usha, sat primly for the camera, her white-and-gold sari setting off her brown skin beautifully as she smiled serenely. Gold and gems decorated her fingers and ears, but around her neck was a simple chain with a pendent in the shape of a leaf with a beaded cross on it. I could see so much of Jack in her. Not just the brown of their skin, or the beautiful dark colours of their eyes. There was a strength in her that was more than just the straightness of her spine. She had conviction and determination that her son shared, even if I believed he questioned it in himself at times. They had probably clashed when he was younger and she alive, too similarly stubborn to really compromise for the other. Yet, I also didn't doubt that they'd loved each other greatly. The fierceness with which Jack defended his memories of her spoke loud and clear.

Usha's hand rested on the thigh of the man beside her. Christopher lounged back in his seat, long legs stretched out towards the camera he completely ignored in favour of looking at his wife. The corners of his blue eyes were crinkled, his wide mouth smiling, and his blond hair was highlighted in different colours by the festive lights behind them. His tie was loosened, the top two buttons of his shirt open, the sleeves rolled up to his elbows. There was no suit jacket in sight. I saw more physical similarities between father and son—the height, the legs, the shape of their bodies. Christopher Reardon was a handsome man, like Jack, but it was the humour in his eyes, the shining devotion on his face, the way his body angled towards the woman he loved, that reminded me most of Jack.

In my research for the Valadian job, I'd read very sparsely about Jack's family. Just enough to confirm my course of action with him. I'd found his strengths in his parents, and from there, it was easy to find his weaknesses as well. I should have hated what I did to him back then but couldn't. It had been a job. He'd been the target. I'd hurt him but the job had worked out successfully.

Carefully, I retrieved the small note I'd tucked into the frame. Jack would have been certain to find it there in the morning, had I managed to leave without him finding me here. I had observed over the past months how he always gazed at the photo before heading off to work. At least this way I could be certain he got the note in the morning.

I retrieved my guns from the bedroom and sat down at the dining table to clean them. The chances I'd need them tomorrow had gone from a mild possibility to a near certainty.

Just before Jack was ready to wake up, I got back into bed and pretended to be so deeply asleep he couldn't wake me. After a few attempts, Jack grumbled his way out of bed and into the shower. I waited a bit, got up and made his breakfast—a protein shake he'd guzzle on the way to the garage. When he emerged into the kitchen, he was mostly dressed and fumbling with his tie.

We both knew he could knot his own tie. This was just his strategy at getting close when he thought I wasn't receptive to intimacy. It honestly wasn't needed this morning. I'd set my own trap by leaning against the kitchen counter in a pair of Jack's tracksuit trousers that I'd ensured hung dangerously low on my hips. It clearly worked because even as I ordered him over so I could fix his tie, his gaze locked onto my lower abdomen and didn't move until he was so close he had nowhere else to look but into my eyes.

"Thanks," he said as he pushed in against me, his hands on my hips, thumbs brushing over the skin just above my pubic hair.

Huffing a laugh, I pushed at his shoulders until there was enough room for me to knot and straighten his tie. "Are you certain you have to go to work?"

Jack shrugged while I fixed his collar, then appeared to seriously consider my question when I slid my arms around his waist, under his jacket. I slipped the note into his inner pocket, where he kept his wallet, which he'd need when he went for lunch, or earlier if he decided to spring for a decent coffee. Certain he didn't notice, I let him grind against me for few moments, then pushed him back.

"You really will be late if you don't leave now."

"I guess." He reached around me for his helmet and the protein shake. "You will be here tonight?"

What was one more lie? "I plan to be."

"Good." Jack kissed my cheek. "We're going to talk. No ifs, buts, or I don't want tos."

"Yes, Jack."

He gathered the rest of his riding gear and left. I got dressed, settled my weapons into place and, making sure Jack had definitely left the premises, departed as well. Fifteen minutes later, I'd retrieved Victoria from the storage facility where she stayed when I wasn't in Sydney now that my safe place had been compromised. An hour after that, we were on the open road and heading not to the private airfield where my exfil plan awaited me, but to Canberra, where I'd either waste a day, or much more likely make Jack very angry with me.

DEVIL IN THE DETAILS

(LATER THAT SAME DAY)

CHAPTER ONE

Jack looked at the note. It fitted in the palm of his hand, white paper, folded neatly down the middle, now a little crumpled from spending a couple of hours in a pocket with his wallet. On it was two lines of neat hand writing in Ethan's fastidious penmanship.

Iwan Salim is not your enemy. Followed by a date from a year ago.

Reading it over and over was like sliding a knife between his ribs. Each reread was like another centimetre of cold, sharp steel in his flesh. Any moment now, it was going to reach his heart.

"Whatcha got there?" Harry set a large takeaway coffee on Jack's desk.

Jack resisted the urge to hide the note. Anything else related to Ethan he would have made sure it was kept secret, but this . . . this was too big. From the moment he'd found the note—while taking out his wallet to give Harry money for decent coffee—Jack had tried to deny its existence. The entire time it took Harry to leave the building, walk half a block to the café, get their coffees, and return, Jack had known he couldn't ignore this.

It hurt. Holy Jesus fuck, it hurt and he just wanted to forget all about it, but he couldn't because this was his job. And Ethan knew goddamn well he wasn't supposed to be meddling in it anymore.

It suddenly all made sense. How he'd actually managed to catch Ethan by surprise yesterday, the odd behaviour when they'd fucked, the pretence of being sleepy when the moment he thought Jack was out of it Ethan left the bed and didn't return. Not to mention that display this morning, with the low-riding track pants and the I'm-so-innocently-sexy-come-grope-me ploy. It had all been a fucking lie. A ruse to get this piece of paper into Jack's pocket. Why? Because Jack had asked Ethan not to interfere in his job anymore? Or because Jack had interrupted Ethan from planting the note in the apartment and then disappearing?

The knife hit Jack's heart as he handed the note over to his partner.

Harry perched his arse on the edge of Jack's desk, sipped his own coffee, and read the note several times. His brow furrowed deeper and deeper. "What's significant about the date?"

Jack had already wracked his memory, trying to work out what Ethan meant and come up skint. "No clue."

"So where did you get this?"

"From a source."

"What source?"

"Just a source."

Frowning, Harry said pointedly, "But we got taken off the Delta Subject and Salim job last month. Why are you going to your *mysterious* source now?"

Jack rolled his eyes at Harry's tone. "I'm not. That note just . . . happened to fall into my lap right now."

Harry slurped more coffee. "Are you going to pass it on to Keri?"

Keri Sing was the Singaporean unit leader running the job on Iwan Salim, the leader of a large preman organisation in Jakarta. The Indonesian gangster had ties to terrorist groups throughout South-East Asia and had been on the Office of Counterterrorism and Intelligence's watchlist for years. Jack and Harry had been brought in on the job at the start of the year to keep tabs on Delta Subject, the nephew Salim had sponsored to move to Australia for university. The young man had the right history to be a strong candidate to become a lone-wolf terrorist, but over the months they'd watched the kid, Jack and Harry had realised that was an incredibly unlikely scenario. Not that Keri had believed them, insisting they keep watching the youth as he went about his non-threatening ways. It had taken a nearly disastrous visit to an Oxford Street nightclub for Jack and Harry to be taken off the job. Jack didn't even know if Keri had got someone else to take over the watch on Delta Subject or not. He'd just been glad to be rid of the pointless waste of time.

And now this.

Goddamn that crazy bastard.

"Yeah, I'll give her a call." Jack wasn't quite able to keep the sting out of his words.

Singapore was two hours behind Sydney, which meant it was early there, but not so early Keri could get cranky about him contacting her. Jack could simply pass the information on to one of her team, but this was big enough to go straight to the unit leader.

Harry pulled out his phone and snapped a picture of the note. "I'll see if I can find something about the date while you do that."

The words to stop him bubbled up Jack's tight throat, but he didn't let them out. Amongst the simmering anger at Ethan for doing this, Jack was curious. It had to be something serious to make Ethan go to all the trouble of passing the information on in this manner.

So while Harry sat at his desk next to Jack's and started researching the date, Jack called Keri Sing. Her phone went straight to message. Jack left a terse one asking her to call him ASAP. He then shot off another one through the Office's internal system and one more to Keri's second.

"Anything?" he asked Harry.

"Nothing interesting yet." His second poked at his keyboard with two fingers. "There is a restricted file in Intelligence. I don't have clearance to open it."

"Probably nothing to do with this, then." Jack checked his computer for return messages from Singapore and found nothing.

"Normally I would agree, but the file's original author was an ITA asset, not an Intelligence one." The tip of Harry's tongue appeared out of the side of his mouth as he concentrated.

It wasn't an unusual occurrence. Intelligence often took over files started by either Internal or External Threat Assessment, but something about this one caught Jack's attention. Scooting his chair next to Harry's, he peered at the screen.

Each Office asset had a personal code that consisted of three numbers to indicate their department, three to show their position and four to identify them individually. The code attached as the original author of the file was one Jack had spent a year looking at regularly.

"Fuck." He shot to his feet and stalked towards the stairwell.

"Jack?" Harry called after him. "Where are you going?"

"We're going down to Intelligence," he snapped. "Hurry up."

Harry caught up as they reached the sixth floor where Jesse Feitt, an Intelligence special investigator, worked.

After Ethan Blade had infiltrated the Sydney branch of the Office at the end of the previous year, it had been decided they would ramp up the search for information about him. Since Maria Dioli, the ITA asset assigned to the task, had been murdered, they'd handed the job over to Feitt. Jack liked Feitt and didn't mind helping him out whenever the special investigator asked for his opinion on information they dug up about Ethan, even if it made Jack feel a bit uncomfortable when it coincided with one of Ethan's visits.

Feitt worked out of a small operations room with a team of two techs. All three of them looked up when Jack knocked and entered all in the same move.

"Reardon," Feitt greeted him dryly. Nothing much phased the man, which was needed when your job sent you trawling through some of the worst parts of human society. He nodded to Harry, then asked Jack, "Have you brought me something new about Blade?"

"Not exactly." Jack showed him the note. "You have a file with this date on it. I need to see it."

Feitt regarded him for a long moment, calmly assessing Jack's demeanour. Seemingly satisfied, he nodded again and called up the file in question. "What's it in relation to?"

"Another job that's not related to Blade. At least not directly I don't think."

"Right. The file is one we inherited from Dioli's investigation. What do you need to know?"

"Anything about this date. I'll know it when I see it."

With Harry leaning over his other shoulder, the Intelligence asset opened the file and slowly scrolled through it. Almost immediately Jack saw what he needed, but he let Feitt go further, just in case there was something else. After half the file went past with no other significant information, Jack thanked him and hurried out.

"Jack?" Harry galloped along behind him. "Where are we going now? And what did you see in the file? I didn't see anything important. Just a bunch of stuff about Blade shadowing some Myanmar drug lord."

"Exactly," Jack snapped as they came out of the stairs back on the eighth floor. "Find out everything you can about Khun Sein. See if he has any connection to Iwan Salim."

"And what are you going to do?"

"Check on something else." He skidded to a stop by his desk and looked for messages from Singapore. Nothing.

Harry hesitated at his own desk. "Come on, just tell me what's going on."

Jack pushed gently on his shoulder, encouraging him to sit. "Just look up Sein. I'll be back soon, hopefully with more information."

"But Jack—"

"Harry, just do what I said."

Harry's brown eyes narrowed at him. "We're supposed to be partners."

Jack's hasty departure stalled. Harry was right. Technically, Harry was his second and subordinate, but that was a thin distinction. In reality they had to work like equals to be effective. Jack may have had the power to veto any of Harry's decisions, but over the past six months, he hadn't found any reason to. Harry was smart, capable and after a few rough patches at the start, had settled into Jack's work groove perfectly well, without losing his own means and methods.

"We are," Jack assured him. "Trust me for a bit longer. I'll fill you in when I know more."

Harry nodded, sat and started work. Jack retreated to one of the break rooms. He locked the door behind him, shrugged out of his jacket and then lay down on the bottom bunk bed. His thoughts were racing a bit too fast to find the calm needed for even a light trance and the longer it took, the more frustrated he got. Especially when his circling thoughts kept going back to Ethan.

God, could Jack have been a bigger dickhead? After Ethan had disappeared without a word during his last visit, Jack's hope that he would be back had slowly atrophied over the next several weeks. He didn't have many clear memories of that visit, thanks to suffering a flu, but knowing what he was like while feverish, Jack could assume he hadn't exactly behaved himself. Surely Ethan would have understood, though? He'd been relieved enough to find Ethan at home yesterday that he let himself be distracted by the sex, and desperate enough to keep Ethan close by that he hadn't called him out on the fake sleepiness. It was easy to see it all for what it had been now. A distraction. Ethan hadn't meant to be caught. Which hurt, deeply.

Jack forced Ethan into the filing cabinet in the back of his head. The man wouldn't stay there long, but hopefully it would give Jack the chance to settle enough to access the deeper applications of his neural implant. It worked, and the moment the implant overlay appeared before his inner eyes, Jack found the file holding the bungled cognitive model he'd performed during that last visit. Normally, he needed to be in a deep meditative state to run a cognitive model, letting the implant access memories that could spark physical reactions close to a full-fledged flashback. Being mostly immobile during those times was the best for everyone. Yet somehow this one had run while Jack was delirious with fever, which meant the results couldn't exactly be trusted, tangled up as they were with images of Ethan in compromising—for them both—situations. Thus Jack had been very reluctant to look at them. Thankfully, being kicked off the job meant he had even less reason to.

Jack had initially thought of running the model to prove his theory that Delta Subject wasn't a threat, and as he scanned the results— internally wincing at the threads of Ethan woven throughout—he realised it had worked. He had all the information he needed to prove Delta Subject was innocent. Carefully, he dissected out the more salacious moments around Ethan and collated the pertinent data into a file he could export. It was messy but hopefully enough to convince Keri Sing and her director.

Coming back to full wakefulness, Jack returned to their desks and found Harry slouched over, head in one hand as he desultorily paged down and down on his screen.

"Hey," Jack announced himself. "Find anything?"

Harry blinked and pulled a face. "Nothing. I mean, it looks like Sein's organisation probably supplies opium to Salim for distribution but there's nothing personal between them. How'd you go?"

"Better." Jack sat and, closing his eyes, called up the overlay of the implant and sent the model file to his computer.

Harry stretched and leaned over. "What did you get?"

"Proof Delta Subject isn't a lone-wolf candidate."

"Great. What does that have to do with Sein?"

"Nothing, and everything, I think. Sein had connections to local terrorist-wannabe Samuel Valadian. He was part of Valadian's network, or they were both part of some other entity's network. The more we found out about Valadian, the more it looked like he was just a cog in a larger machine. What set Valadian apart, however, was just how deep he'd managed to get his fingers into the Meta-State."

Harry nodded. Although he'd been stationed in Auckland at the time, he knew all about Jack and Ethan exposing Director Harraway as a traitor, paid by Valadian to ensure the Meta-State looked the other way on his dealings.

"Which has got to be worrying for someone like Khun Sein, and his bosses," Harry mused. "Valadian paid Harraway money, but the others can't be sure he didn't pay in information as well."

"Exactly." Jack checked his computer again. Still nothing from Singapore. "I'm going to go see McIntosh and you can go to Tan and see if he can find out why Singapore's being quiet."

They trotted up the two flights to the tenth together, then parted ways as Jack turned towards the ITA director's office, and Harry headed for that of ETA.

"Make it fast," McIntosh said as Jack sat before her desk. "I have a meeting in five minutes."

Used to giving quick debriefs, he explained everything to Donna McIntosh, showed her the note and sat in quiet dread as she looked over the results of the cognitive model.

"This is not your best work," she murmured.

"I know. All the information is there, though."

"Just. And the note, I assume you got it from . . . a source you'd rather keep to yourself."

"Preferably, ma'am." His anger sparked again, but he tamped it down. McIntosh knew he was still in some sort of contact with Ethan Blade, but Jack wasn't sure if she knew exactly what that contact entailed and he wasn't going to reveal it now by losing his shit over this in front of her.

"And what does Unit Leader Sing make of it?"

Back on safer ground, Jack told her how there'd been no answer from Singapore and that Harry was chasing it up with Director Tan.

McIntosh called through to Tan's office, listened for half a minute, then hung up.

"Sing didn't clock in this morning and has been out of touch with her team for more than twenty-four hours. They've traced her to Changi Airport where she boarded a plane for Canberra." McIntosh paused, then said softly, "Her family is also missing."

CHAPTER TWO

Even with the evidence stacking up, the minister was reluctant to authorise a full operation. McIntosh gave Jack permission to head to Canberra while she and Tan worked on the politician. She couldn't provide much more than a helicopter and a basic field kit but promised she would do something about some support by the time he reached the country's capital.

Three hours after discovering Ethan's note, Jack set the Office chopper down on the tarmac of Canberra Airport. Airspace over central Canberra was restricted and Jack had no desire to alert any potential bad guys by buzzing them in the chopper. A decision he fully regretted when he and Harry hit the mid-afternoon traffic coming out of the airport.

"Shit!"

Jack slapped his palm against the steering wheel, teeth grinding about as hard as the brakes of the Nissan Patrol. The big car came to a juddering stop behind the micro-car-thing currently blocking their progress and sat at a standstill in the middle of the single lane leading onto the roundabout. The second roundabout of what seemed like a million between them and where they desperately needed to be.

"It's miniscule," he muttered darkly. "I bet we could drive right over it."

"Pretty sure you can't, boss," Harry said, half faux-amused, half you-seriously-can't. For some reason, he had developed serious doubts about Jack's driving skills. "We could turn back."

"No time," Jack growled.

The situation in front of them hadn't changed and behind them, it was only getting worse with more and more vehicles lining up, waiting, waiting, waiting for the idiot in front to grow some balls and actually *drive* that miserable little tin can some dickhead had decided was an actual car.

"Fuck this." He palmed the steering wheel into a furious turn left.

"I don't think that's going to work, either. You're too close."

"Don't care." Jack hit the accelerator, willing to take out the back end of the timid driver's car.

With a grinding *scraaaaape*, the Patrol pushed past the much smaller car, shoving it aside in its bid for freedom. When the front of the Patrol was clear, Jack slammed his foot down and the big car lurched forward. They jolted onto the grassy verge of the road and, tyres digging into the dirt, the Patrol powered toward the side road.

Thanks to the delay at the roundabout, traffic on the road Jack needed to get on was thick. It was the wrong time of day to be leaving Canberra's airport with any sort of haste. Too many people coming in on afternoon flights, and not one of the commuters looked willing to stop to let the Patrol back onto the road.

Ahead was a bigger roundabout and he needed to get onto the road and make a right turn, through two streams of traffic. Frustrated, Jack decided to just go for it. He was in one of the biggest cars available, with a powerful engine and few compunctions to not use either advantage.

As the Patrol flew up and over the slight rise onto the road and as other cars braked and swerved to avoid a collision, Jack momentarily wished he was back in the Ferrari. In such a car, the distance between him and his target would be negligible. When they thumped back down to the bitumen, rubber squealing as Jack rushed to dodge a slow-to-react commuter, he changed his mind. Not only did he appreciate the big tyres and suspension, but Ethan would probably put a ticket on his head for hurting another supercar.

An instant later, all thoughts of the man he'd left in his apartment that morning fled as they reached the next roundabout. Two lanes and neither of them looking like Jack could squeeze in somewhere anytime in the next twenty seconds. Abandoning all road rules he gunned the engine.

"Fuck!" Harry shouted as the Patrol ploughed right into the cross traffic.

It was chaos, but thankfully short-lived. They were across both lanes within seconds and bouncing, once more, off road. Jack angled across the middle of the roundabout, aiming for the exit he needed. The Patrol roared over flowerbeds and decorative grasses with equal prejudice, leaving a 4WD-wide swath of destruction behind them. By the time they got to the exit, most of the commuters had realised what was going on and traffic had come to a stop. Relatively safely, Jack arrowed them between the cars and onto Pialligo Avenue.

Finally free of the airport and with a mostly open road in front of him, Jack floored the accelerator. They drove for about a minute in complete silence, then Harry let out a soft "whoo" of relief. That was all though. Jack and Harry had already had the confrontation about Jack's tactics in an earlier mission. It was five months back and only two days after they'd met for the first time. Both of them had been covered in dust from a collapsed wall, trickles of blood and raw scrapes on exposed skin the only breaks in their grey coatings. Harry had nearly decked Jack and Jack had nearly let him. He'd gambled with their lives, and won, but it had been close.

"How convinced are we that the bad guys are at the ISO?" Harry asked.

"Pretty darn." Jack uncurled and curled his fingers around the steering wheel. "The International Security Office is an intelligence hub. They collect all the intel from the Office, ASIO and military intelligence. If Khun Sein wants to find out what we know about him and whatever larger organisation he's a part of, that's where Sein will have his people. Because he sure as shit won't be here himself," he added dryly.

Harry agreed with a sour grunt. "And if they're not there?"

"Then we keep looking," Jack said grimly. Somehow, one of their own had been compromised and now many, many more people were in danger. Jack wasn't going to stop until he'd hunted down those responsible. He barely slowed for the next roundabout, but only two of the Patrol's wheels lost contact with the road this time.

"Right. It's like Nemo said, just keep swimming."

Jack snorted. "It was Dory, you numpty, not Nemo."

There was a speculative silence for a moment, then Harry cracked up. "You know *Finding Nemo*?"

Scowling, Jack snapped, "Clearly you don't!" Which only made him laugh harder.

They turned onto Kings Avenue and started across Lake Burley Griffin. Ahead, central Canberra came into clear view.

The city was an odd dichotomy of country capital and pastoral town, forgoing the towering skyscrapers of Sydney and Melbourne in favour of parks and gardens and buildings that barely exceeded three stories in the central areas around Parliament House. As a planned city, it didn't have the hectic and chaotic aesthetic of the other capitals, which some people equated with a lack of personality. Sure, Sydney was the height of fashion and Melbourne was a cultural hub, but Canberra had the glory of being Australia's *coldest* capital city. It even beat Hobart, the most southern. Currently, the display on the dashboard indicated the outside temperature was eight degrees, which was going to bite when they had to get out of the car.

Jack had lived here when he was in Duntroon for officer training and hadn't minded the place. That, he suspected, had a lot to do with the fact he'd been settled in his personal life at the time. He was in the SAS, had a couple of successful missions to his name, had the respect of his peers and superiors. His father hadn't yet been diagnosed with early onset dementia and while he'd been single, and his sister only ever called to remind him he was just a glorified murderer, both of those things were so familiar they didn't bother him much.

"You really think they'll have a bomb with them?" Harry asked.

"It's the only logical reason they need Delta Subject. Implicate him as a lone wolf and when his body is found in the wreckage, blame is shifted to Indonesia and away from any Myanmar connection."

"Well, if there *is* a bomb, can you not shoot it this time?" He gestured at the surrounding scenery. "Canberra's already flat enough without you dropping walls on it."

Jack snorted and Harry grinned, pleased to have gotten the reaction from him.

"Look at it this way," Jack said, pointing out the temperature reading on the dash display. "If the bomb does go off, at least it'll warm the place up a bit."

Harry fought the snicker, but it got out. "That's terrible," he said when he could without chuckling.

He was right, but at the same time, not and for the first time in ages, Jack was struck by how young his partner was. Harry had severed four years with the police in Auckland, where his exemplary record had alerted an Office recruiter. Eighteen months later, he was Jack's second in Sydney and quickly proving himself to be one of the best assets the Office would have—after a couple years more experience. There were still green edges on the young man Jack had to knock off before he fulfilled his potential.

"It's part of the job," Jack said, gently serious. "Call it gallows humour, or detachment, or compartmentalisation. Whatever it is, it's necessary. If you can't keep some sort of barrier between you and what you have to do in order to get the job done successfully, then you won't last long in this game. Self-preservation isn't wrong."

After a long, silent moment where they left the bridge and Jack took the first exit off Kings Avenue, Harry sighed. "Yeah, I get that, but sometimes I wonder if . . . what if you get too detached?"

It was almost as if Jack was back in the desert, dangerously confused and reckless with his life in the presence of renowned assassin, Ethan Blade. After fifteen months undercover with Valadian's organisation, he'd been close to falling over the edge into a dark abyss. Clinging to the ragged remains of his morals, Jack had found his anchor in the unlikeliest of places—the very assassin who'd betrayed and lied to him.

Leaning on the filing cabinet drawer he'd shoved Ethan into earlier, Jack took a deep breath and answered. "That's just as bad. You have to find something, or someone, to keep coming back to. Girlfriend, boyfriend, family, a hobby you love. Anything to give you direction out of the dark."

Yet another roundabout had been successfully circumnavigated when Harry responded.

"Did I tell you my sister had the baby? A little girl. Well, not so little. She was nearly five kilos. Sally says the poor thing looks too much like her father."

Jack smiled. Not because he'd been eagerly awaiting news of Harry's niece, but because his partner had just found his anchor. "That's great. Have they named her?"

"Not yet. I'm barracking for Harriet, of course. They're leaning towards Moana, for *reasons*."

Any more family discussion was shelved as Jack turned down a side street and the ISO came into sight. Like most other structures in the area, it was a low, wide building: three stories of bland, government-approved façade surrounded by a neatly landscaped garden of native plants and discreet security measures.

Jack's cover for his position with the Office was that of a specialist security adviser for ISO, which meant he was supposedly responsible for the security of Australian dignitaries while they were abroad. He did occasionally show up to design a security plan and put together task groups so he was familiar with the ISO building and its security.

Nothing appeared unusual from what he could see. The drive, which looped around in front of the entrance, was clear of cars, giving an unrestricted view of the doors. The tall, darkened-glass panes were closed and unsigned. If you didn't already know it was the ISO, then nothing about its public façade gave it away.

"Looks quiet," Harry said.

"Yeah." Jack swung the Patrol into the parking lot of the museum across the road. "McIntosh will have the word out by now. We should have back-up . . . There."

In the corner of the partially filled carpark was a cluster of vehicles that all but screamed government—darkly coloured standard model 4WDs. A couple of plain-clothed people leaned against one of them, seemingly chatting, but as Jack pulled up next to them, they came alert, hands moving toward concealed weapons.

Jack braved the icy atmosphere and rolled his window down, his rarely used ISO ID already on show. "Jack Reardon, specialist security adviser. Initial on this case."

The woman came forward and, after doing a subtle double take at the colour of his skin, eyed his ID. As sad as it was, her reaction wasn't unique and Jack was used to it, if not totally accepting. Usually, when he presented himself under his cover as a government security agent, the other person showed a certain amount of scepticism, or outright challenged him.

Jack wondered how this woman would move forward. She was about his age, compact and capable looking. Wearing jeans, blue puffer jacket and practical sneakers, she could have been visiting the museum, but the cool, calculating gaze she levelled on Jack was all cop. Probably AFP and therefore had a high chance of being reasonable.

"You made the call about the bomb threat?" She already knew the answer.

Pretty sure he wasn't going to get handcuffed or shot, Jack opened the door and slid out. Their hasty departure from Sydney hadn't allowed for a wardrobe change so all Jack and Harry had were black ISO jackets borrowed from the chopper. As the dry, cold air hit his body, Jack zipped up, coincidently flashing the ISO logo on the sleeve.

"Got a tip off." He wasn't exactly lying. "It's part of an ongoing investigation. A small terrorist group got in behind us and made it into the ISO."

While he spoke, Harry got out and went to the back of the Patrol to get their gear. The second cop wandered over to watch.

"No alarms have been tripped," the woman observed.

How much to tell her? She hadn't yet identified herself, but Jack could understand that. Until she was sure of him, she wouldn't give too much away.

"I didn't think there would be." Jack clicked an image of the cop with his neural implant and sent it back to the Office for identification, then clicked one of her companion who was watching Harry unpack the MAV with keen interest. "It's a small, highly trained group. Our plan is to get in, take down the suspects and hopefully everyone will get home for dinner, none the wiser."

"If wishes were horses, maybe. If you're right, and there's a group of terrorists in there, then I doubt any of us will be home for dinner."

Implant *ping*ing, Jack gave an it-could-go-either-way shrug and checked the incoming message.

From the Office, it was an ID and overview of one Lieutenant Celia Watson, Australian Federal Police, exemplary record, and a half dozen high profile cases to her name. Lt Watson's friend was Senior Constable Grady Everett, nothing too outstanding on his file, if you discounted a ten-year service without any hiccups. Which Jack didn't. It meant the guy was competent and toed the line. McIntosh had apparently called for the best and, as usual, got it.

It made sense his director had sourced help from the AFP. Their HQ was just up the road. And if things went spectacularly wrong, Duntroon was a fifteen-minute scramble away.

"Is it just you and Everett, Lieutenant Watson?" Jack asked casually. "Or do you have other officers here?" He nodded to the three cars.

Watson gaped for a second, then searched for an earpiece on Jack's head. He didn't bother explaining. The implant had come gratis with his SAS career and, like his SAS service, was best kept a secret.

Still a little wary, Watson said, "We have a team of ten anti-terrorist officers and another on standby on Kings Avenue. Our orders were to be discreet."

Invisible was about as discreet as a person could get, but as Jack looked around, he realised why they were parked here. Not only was it off the street and not immediately visible to anyone in the building across the way—why Jack had decided to come in here in the first place—but they were parked close to a stand of trees between carpark and road. In the shadows Jack found the rest of the AFP team. They wore the standard black, armoured uniform and were positioned perfectly to take out Jack and Harry if they proved to require it.

Jack nodded in approval. "What else were you told?"

Lips pursed, Watson said, "That we'd be working under SSA Jack Reardon of the ISO." She put a little stress on his name, probably for brown-boys-don't-have-English-names reasons and followed it with a cool, "And to follow his lead without question. What does a security adviser know about running an anti-terror operation?"

"A few things. If at any time you think I'm not capable, don't hesitate to call someone. They can talk to my boss about it. Harry!"

Harry put down the case holding their large firearms and trotted over.

"Lieutenant, this is Harry McGill, my partner. You and he should have some language in common. He used to be a cop. Harry, this is Celia Watson, AFP. You'll liaise with her and Everett."

"Pleasure to meet you." Harry smiled brightly at Watson. As a field asset like Jack, Harry's cover was also with ISO as a domestic security officer, or in Jack's words, a bouncer. He slipped an earpiece on and handed one to Jack. "We're all synced up, boss. Home base is coming online. Queen's plugged in and getting the MAV ready for flight."

On the flight from Sydney, Harry had come up with their codes for this operation, much to Jack's consternation. Their Sydney-based and dedicated tech, Liz Alderton, was Queen, Harry was King and Jack was, well, Jack. Harry had grinned for five minutes straight when he'd explained it to him.

"MAV?" Watson asked.

"Micro air vehicle," Harry explained. "A drone. Come on over and I'll show you."

Expression clearly saying she understood when she was being distracted, Watson still went with Harry, her curiosity outweighing her probable distrust of Jack. At least it meant she might not make a huge fuss about his ethnicity.

Temporarily alone, Jack pretended to fiddle with his earpiece, while actually syncing his implant to the communication channel.

"Queen, this is Jack. Respond."

"Jack, this is Queen," Alderton said in his head. *"You're coming through clear."*

"Likewise. King, this is Jack, respond."

Harry answered and satisfied, Jack headed over to the back of their car. Harry had the MAV out of its box and was testing it while their AFP friends looked on eagerly. There was a laptop sitting open on the empty drone box, its screen filled with several windows, some showing data or building schematics while others waited patiently to receive video from the drone.

"The building is heat shielded so we're not going to get any thermal images of the interior," Alderton said, her voice coming from a small window in the laptop's upper right corner, showing her at her station in Sydney.

"As long as we can see anyone coming and going," Jack said. "How are doing on getting us feeds from building CCTV?"

Alderton screwed up her face. "Not great. We're still waiting on authorisation from above." Knowing there were AFP personnel present, the tech kept her words deliberately vague. "Apparently there's some dispute over the quality of the evidence."

Jack had expected the resistance. The politicians had to make sure their own arses were covered before giving the go-ahead. Still, he said,

"Let me see what I can find out," and headed away from the car and the AFP officers so he had some privacy to call McIntosh.

"Jack," she greeted him over the implant. *"Report."*

"Ma'am, we're on site and have made contact with the locals. Mobile station is up but until Queen gets the go-ahead to tap the CCTV, we're blind."

McIntosh snorted. *"The Big Boss is not going to cave easily. You didn't exactly give us definitive proof. You're lucky you got the chopper and the AFP."*

Expecting this, too, Jack asked, *"What do you need to convince the Big Boss?"*

"Visual confirmation."

"And how am I going to get that without the CCTV footage?"

As if he was right in front of her, Jack could all but see her warm blue eyes cool as she said, *"I'm sure you'll find a way, Jack. Don't disappoint me now."*

CHAPTER THREE

Jack found Harry standing with Watson and Everett. Now they'd been made, the rest of the AFP team weren't hiding as well as they had been, several dark shadows moving within the thin screen of trees.

"Any word on a go, boss?" Harry asked as Jack approached.

"Still waiting. I'm going to need a car and not something that screams government." Jack waved at the sparsely populated carpark around them. "Maybe something family orientated."

"Permission or forgiveness?" Harry asked, meaning did he ask for someone to volunteer their car, or just 'commandeer' one without bothering with the niceties.

"Permission," Jack decided. "Make it official. That way we can't be roasted if it goes tits up." If he could limit the height of the shit pile they might have to dig their way out of, all the better.

"Right." Harry dug his ISO ID out of a pocket and made a show of dusting it off before heading over to the museum to find a good citizen who wouldn't mind helping the state out in a time of need.

"What's your plan?" Watson asked suspiciously.

"To get a look at the inside of the building. Queen," he directed at the laptop screen, "did we get the MAV in the air?"

"She's up and about to get over the target. Footage coming up in three, two . . ." A window expanded on the screen and showed aerial images of the ISO building.

It was a stock standard façade—blond bricks, white trim, arched windows on the ground floor, rectangular ones on the first and second floors. The roof had a mild incline, but the inner side was flat and patrolled frequently. It overlooked a central courtyard, with sentry positions at each corner for external observation. No one currently manned the small towers; a very good sign. Jack didn't doubt the intruders would keep the patrol going for the sake of appearances, but unless they had a strong reason to suspect trouble, they wouldn't put anyone in the towers.

"Looks clear." Watson's scepticism came through without a hint of reticence. "Now what?"

"Now I get inside." Nothing Jack had seen had told him he was wrong and the sooner he got what McIntosh needed, the better. A silver Porsche Cayenne cruised up and pulled over. The driver's door opened and Harry slid out.

Jack grimaced. "A Porsche? Couldn't you find anything else?" He had a troubling history with Porsches, in that they didn't survive encountering him.

"Hey, the owner offered it up. He did specify that we'll have to pay for any damage to it. You aren't planning on crashing it through the front of the building, are you?"

Harry hadn't been in Sydney for the end of the Harraway situation, but Jack and Ethan driving a car right into the lobby of the building had become Office legend. Lewis, Jack's best friend and workmate, had taken great pleasure in introducing Harry to the Tao of Jack, as Lewis called his take on Jack's actions and philosophies. Harry had laughed a lot of it off, then he'd survived an explosion that A, should have killed him and B, shouldn't have happened in the first place. Afterwards, he'd begun to seriously question Jack about his motivations and plans.

"It's not part of the plan," he assured Harry as he handed over his shoulder rig and gun. Looking at the three people gathered around him, Jack dismissed Harry and Everett before settling on Watson. "Can I borrow your jacket?"

"Why?" the lieutenant asked warily.

Jack slid out of his thin ISO windcheater. "Because I can't go in their screaming I'm ISO, and a local would have warmer clothes."

Unable to argue that, Watson handed over her puffer jacket, taking the ISO one in return. Jack settled into the puffer jacket, feeling warm for the first time since he'd gotten out of the car. The sleeves were a little short and zipping it up would be a bit of a strain, but it was better than the other option.

"Thanks." Jack got into the Porsche. "I won't be long."

Leaving the carpark, he headed away from the ISO for a couple of blocks, then turned left, working his way around the general area so he came at it from a completely different direction. He slowed early, as if he was unsure of where he was going, then made a hesitant turn into the driveway. It curved around a small reflecting pool in the front lawn, widening before the steps leading up to the entrance. Jack pulled in, then moved the Cayenne forward so it wasn't blocking the steps, continuing the pretence of uncertainty.

He was in direct line of sight of the building cameras. Adding depth to his cover, he spent a minute going through the glove compartment, like he was trying to find something. Apart from learning that the owner of the Cayenne kept a stock of condoms in there, Jack didn't find anything he could use in the moment, so he slammed it shut and got out of the car.

Now the real fun began.

Patting down his pants pockets, Jack trotted around the car and up the steps. Head down, he pretended to be distracted by his futile pocket forage as he pushed through the front door.

The foyer was wide open, the floor polished parquetry, the ceiling high and surrounded by a balcony on the first floor, a convenient high ground for shooters. Opposite him was a set of French doors leading out onto a patio overlooking a central courtyard. The garden was winter-brown but lush with a subtle design of native flowers and decorative shrubs, and a central eucalyptus providing shade.

Taking it all in with a glance, Jack noted three subjects on the balcony and two in the courtyard, all dressed in ISO domestic security uniforms—black tactical clothing, armoured vest, weapons harness. Each of them carried an M4A5 carbine, sidearm and four grenades. At first blush, it all appeared normal, except he was pretty certain peak-caps and reflective shades hadn't been made part of the uniform since he'd last been here.

It was circumstantial evidence, but Jack hoped it would be enough to get the minister to start taking them seriously. Serious was good but convinced was what he was aiming for.

On the balcony, the faux-DSOs moved forward, not actually training their carbines on him, but not exactly not, either.

"Sir?"

Jack turned to the voice, as if he didn't already know where the front reception desk was. As if he hadn't already scoped the woman behind the desk. Mid-twenties, Caucasian, dressed in an official ISO grey blazer, long, brunette hair pulled back into a high pony tail. Everything about her appeared legit.

"Sir," she repeated, her tone calm now she had his attention. "I'm sorry but I'm going to have to ask you to leave. This isn't—"

"This is the Indian High Commission, right?" Jack headed for her, still patting down his pockets.

Raised Australian, Jack had nevertheless spent enough time in India with his mother's family to perfect a couple of different accents. The one he used now was light, definitely Indian but easily understandable to others.

"I'm sorry, ma'am, but I seem to have left my passport at home. I do have my driver's licence on me . . . somewhere. Sorry, I would lose my head if it wasn't secured to my shoulders, as my wife keeps telling me." He held out an arm and tugged at the sleeve of the puffer jacket. "I can't even pick up the right clothes . . ." He paused for a breath but didn't let the woman get a word in. "My visa is fine, ma'am, valid for another two years, but my boss says there's something wrong with it. Something about my work conditions. I was hoping someone could have a look at it for me. I need to know by close of business today or my boss is going to cut back my hours and I can't—"

"Sir!" She leaned forward, voice raised over his prattle. "I'm sorry, but—"

Close enough to read her name from her tag, Jack said, "Please, Marianne, ma'am, I know it's late, but this is very important." All the while he was looking around, as if seeking someone else to help him. His implant was recording everything he saw and anything he might miss in the moment could be found on reviewing the footage. "I can't lose any more hours. You have to—"

This time, Marianne slammed a fist on the desk between them. "This isn't the Indian High Commission!" There was a touch of panic in her voice now, a wild tint to her eyes. "I'm going to have to ask you to leave, sir. Now. Before I need to call security. Please."

The desperation in her last word was enough to convince Jack she *really* wanted him to leave. Combined with the fear in her expression, it was highly suggestive that something was very wrong in this building. While it only bolstered Jack's belief he was right, it probably wasn't enough to convince the minister, but either way, it was time to leave.

Jack held up his hands in surrender. "Yes, ma'am. I'll go. I'm sorry for my mistake. Please accept my apologies." He backed away from the desk, hoping like hell he made it out. Fingers crossed the imposters didn't want any random dead bodies.

Marianne nodded, relieved. "Thank you, sir. I hope you get your visa sorted."

Turning to leave, Jack saw one of the DSOs had come down from the balcony. He stood by the front door, ready to open it to let Jack leave, other hand resting on the stock of the carbine. It wasn't until Jack was only a couple of feet away he realised it wasn't a man. The bulky nature of the vest and harness hid her breasts and waist, but under the mirrored sunglasses, her jaw was finer and smoother than most men's.

She opened the door and gestured grandly for him to leave through it.

"Thank you, ma'am." Jack bobbed his head and fixed his sight on the floor. He didn't need her to be able to describe him well enough to anyone who might be interested in the lost Indian man.

The woman grinned. "No wukkas, mate."

Jack's blood ran cold. He knew the voice, knew the words. Knew just what sort of a person this woman was, and the last time Jack had seen her, she had been aiming a gun at him.

CHAPTER FOUR

It was her. Jack was certain of it. He'd kept in touch with the locals on the Gold Coast and they had never recovered a body from the Porsche crash. They were convinced the driver hadn't survived, but Jack had never accepted it. Until there was a body, nothing was certain.

Keeping his head down, Jack left. He'd recognised her, but it appeared she hadn't remembered him. Or perhaps he looked just like every other South Asian man to her. Either way, he made it down the stairs and back to the car without a bullet in his back. Once behind the wheel, he sat for a moment, to prove he wasn't rushing. When he'd judged sufficient time had passed, he started the car and pulled away.

Once again, he toured the streets in the general vicinity before heading back to the carpark where the others waited. Harry jogged over to meet him when he pulled into a park a little distant from the rest of them.

"Wow, not even a scratch." Harry gave him a thumbs up.

"I can drive a car without crashing it," Jack groused as he got out and handed over the keys.

"Statistics say otherwise, boss." He counted them off on his fingers. "The car through the front of the Office HQ. A *hot-pink* Ferrari on the GC. The Humvee in Singapore."

"Not my fault," Jack insisted. "That one was all you, McGill. You're the one who parked it there."

"Au contraire, you're the one who made big boom and bye-bye Humvee. And let's not forget this morning's little fender bender at the airport."

"What? That thing? Both cars were drivable afterward. It doesn't count."

"It does, because that one you actually did on purpose." Harry shook his head as they started back toward their 4WD. "Intent makes it much worse."

"So, when they find your body, whether or not I *intended* to strangle you would mean the difference between murder and manslaughter, right?"

"Exactly!" Harry gave him a big, goofy grin.

Jack ignored it, but when it didn't go away, he had to ask, "What's with this?" He gestured at Harry's stupid expression.

"You'd really strangle me?" He sounded positively hopeful.

"It's getting more and more likely," Jack muttered.

"I knew it! You do care about me. Strangling is a very intimate act, usually done in *crimes of passion*."

"You've discovered my deepest secret," Jack deadpanned. "I want you, Harry McGill. So bad."

"Yeah, you do." Harry laughed.

Jack knew he wasn't the easiest person to work with. He was stubborn and could be a bit moody and tended to take the path less travelled in search of an answer. If he didn't keep getting results, he was sure he'd have been quietly retired from the Office by now. But he did keep getting results, so he wasn't retired, and now he was working with Harry.

"Wait up a moment." Jack stopped them before they got too close to the others.

Turning serious, Harry asked, "What is it?"

Five months they'd been working together. Most of it closeted away in a tiny operations room in HQ, monitoring perhaps the most boring person on their watchlist ever. Jack wasn't a "people person" and generally found those who described themselves as such weren't either, but Harry had proven the exception to the rule. An admission Jack had grudgingly come to about a month into his relationship with the Kiwi. Something he'd also come to appreciate about him, as well. Which Jack hadn't ever said to him.

Likewise, Jack knew he'd dragged his feet on having *the* talk with Ethan. His excuses were getting thin—it had been too hectic at the end of their trip to the Gold Coast; he'd been too sick last time; he'd been waiting to see why Ethan had been acting so weird last night. And if this ISO situation wasn't cleared up tonight, he would probably miss another chance to tell Ethan just how he felt. Jack was here, freezing his nipples off and Ethan was in Sydney, maybe. That was, if he hadn't hightailed it out of the country after delivering his little message. Even if he was still in Australia, or even Sydney, Jack had every reason to think there was a bomb in the building across the road. A building he was planning to go back into very shortly. He shouldn't let *this* chance slip by him, either.

"Listen," he began, his voice low. "Um, I just wanted to say thanks."

Harry's expression turned wary. "Thanks for what?"

"For, uh, being a good second. I mean, a good partner. You're a good field asset and I really appreciate all the effort you put into the job."

Expression unchanged, Harry eyed him for a moment, then said, "You're serious."

Jack knew this had the potential to blow up in his face, so he just grunted and resumed walking. After a moment, Harry caught up to him.

"Thank you, Jack." His tone was serious. "That means a lot. I like working with you, too." A couple of seconds of silence, then, "When you're not trying to blow me up."

Resigned to the resumption of the status quo, Jack headed for their 4WD. "Where are our AFP friends?"

Harry nodded towards one of the black SUVs. "Conferencing with home base, I believe. The lieutenant isn't your greatest fan and I'm pretty sure she told me I should go home and get a job there." He scowled in her direction.

These were just some of the hurdles encountered when working for a covert, international agency.

"Let's keep playing nice for now," Jack said, then asked Alderton, "You got the footage?"

"Final filter has just finished," she said from her tiny window on the screen.

The images from Jack's implant weren't crash hot in real time. Taken directly from Jack's right eye and optic nerve, the raw footage was mostly un-viewable and had to go through a few filters to make it appear "correct." Which was why, while the Office preferred to keep

Jack's enhancement quiet, those who worked with him had to be told. It was a pain having a forty-five-second delay on getting a clear picture, but the benefit of not having to rely on an external camera that could be found in a physical search outweighed it.

"There's nothing vital until the last couple of minutes," Jack said. "I need a screenshot of a particular person."

"Who are we looking for?" Alderton sped up the playback.

"One of the fake DSOs, just as I'm leaving. That one." He pointed out as the screen showed the woman at the door. "Female, about five nine, sixty to sixty-five kilos. She's the assassin I encountered on the Gold Coast a couple of months back. Designated as Porsche on the JSL Auxiliary."

Ethan, who'd sat steady at number seven for years on the John Smith List, had dropped back in recent times. He was currently at position nine, thanks to no attributed kills in over a year. It didn't mean Ethan had been a saint during that time, just that he'd mixed up his MO enough they couldn't call a kill his with enough confidence, not even the Liechtenstein duchess. Jack was certain, but no one else was.

The auxiliary to the list were the names of potential assassins, those who hadn't yet had any kills confirmed. Jack had entered Porsche into it himself, when he hadn't been able to match the woman to any current listing.

"That's her," Jack said as the footage got to her opening the door for him. "Screenshot it and send it to the boss."

"On it," Alderton muttered.

"She didn't recognise you?" Harry asked Jack quietly.

"Doesn't appear to, but don't take it as gospel. I'm going to talk to the boss. Hopefully this will convince them it's real."

"Good luck," Harry said.

Leaning against the front of the Patrol, Jack called McIntosh.

"Jack, interesting footage. The Big Boss is reviewing it now. Anything to add?" McIntosh didn't waste time when lives were at risk.

His director didn't need him to point out all the small irregularities he'd seen on his recce. They were more than capable of picking up on the mistakes in the DSO uniforms and the clearly distressed nature of the admin assistant.

"Just the screen shot Queen sent, ma'am. It's the assassin from the GC incident. Porsche, on the JSL Auxiliary."

There was a small pause as McIntosh presumably studied the image. *"Are you certain?"*

"One hundred percent."

"Hmm. Okay, give me a moment."

Before Jack could protest, he was put on hold. Christ, he hated being put on hold while using his implant. Hold music was torture enough when it wasn't being piped directly into his head. Thankfully, it didn't last long.

"Jack, the Big Boss has given the full go-ahead," McIntosh said. *"You can call in the AFP backup and we're going to scramble an RRF from Duntroon. Give them thirty minutes to reach you. Queen will have CCTV access within ten minutes. You have command until the army gets there, then you'll advise the CO."*

Jack ground his teeth. While he appreciated the added punch of a rapid reaction force from Duntroon, he didn't want to give up control to the army. This was Jack and Harry's job. They'd done the hard yards for it and they deserved to run this op.

"I'd rather keep control."

"I wouldn't expect any different," she replied wryly. *"If only you had an ace up your sleeve."*

Jack's jaw dropped. When Harry had registered their codes for this op, Jack had grumbled about the ignominy of having his actual name as his code, but within minutes had added a fourth code to the op—Ace. Leaving the attribution open, Jack had given himself some room to manoeuvre if required. In his head, he knew who his Ace was, and with her last words, McIntosh had pretty much said she did as well.

Sometimes, Jack worried about how much his superiors knew about what happened behind his closed doors. Other times he could ignore the nagging concern. It was, after all, why he'd made his devil's agreement with Tan.

"Yes, ma'am," he repeated, just as dryly. *"I'll get straight on it."*

"Good luck, Jack." And she was gone.

Sighing, Jack pinched the bridge of his nose. He'd been planning on calling his "ace-up-the-sleeve" regardless, but at least now, with vague permission given, he wouldn't have to beg for forgiveness. Hopefully.

He opened the filing cabinet and, as he released his anger, called Ethan.

"*Jack,*" Ethan murmured, when he picked up. "*This is a surprise.*"

The dry British accent didn't help Jack's already strained patience. "*Is it?*" He thought the words with all the sarcasm he could.

"*Well, I had hoped to hear from you, but was far from certain. I trust you got my note.*"

"*Of course I bloody well got your note. Jesus, you still can't just be straightforward with me, can you?*"

"*Just as you were straightforward with me when you declared I wasn't allowed to interfere in your work ever again,*" Ethan returned, mildly.

Jack internalised a grimace. "*Yes, just like that. Exactly like that, but you could have just told me. That information blew this entire thing wide open. How long were you sitting on it?*"

There was an extended pause, and when he answered, Ethan's tone was serious. "*Not long at all. When I realised what it would mean for your job, I came here immediately to make sure you got it.*" Another pause, then softer, "*I hadn't meant to return to Australia for some time.*"

That admission kicked Jack in the guts. "*Why?*" God, he hated sounding so needy but he had to know.

"*That is perhaps a conversation for a more settled time, Jack. I can only assume you're in Canberra right now.*"

At least Ethan warned him about the sudden topic change. That was progress, of a sort. And Jack could understand it. Now wasn't the time to hash out why Ethan hadn't wanted to see him again so soon.

"*Yeah, across the road from the ISO. We've just been given the official go-ahead. I found something to convince the Big Boss this is a real threat.*" He took a deep breath, even though he wasn't speaking aloud. "*Which is why I called you. I think you should be here for this.*" At first, he wondered if Ethan would tease him about how it was Jack who'd said he couldn't ever get involved in his work, and he was ready to defend his backflip.

Instead, all Ethan said was, "*How soon would you like me there?*"

It took about ten seconds to realise it wasn't a sarcastic dig at Jack's change of mind. Five seconds after that he dissected the actual words and groaned.

"You're here, aren't you," he hissed aloud. "You're in fucking Canberra."

Ethan was totally unrepentant. *"I left Sydney this morning, after you went to work. I've been here since lunchtime."*

Crap. The moment he found the note he should have known this was inevitable. So much for being straightforward and expecting Ethan to play along.

"Please just tell me you're not in the museum." Jack got enough control back to keep quiet. Of course, if Ethan was that close, what was to stop him from actually being one of the black-clad AFP personnel? It was a disturbing enough thought Jack stepped away from the 4WD to check on the team.

"No. I'm about ten minutes away. I wanted to keep my distance, in case things didn't go according to plan and I needed to change my tactics."

"Yeah." Jack wasn't really listening.

The AFP team wasn't hiding anymore. Not even a little bit. They were advancing on Jack's 4WD in a fast but precise pattern, moving in flowing waves, three lots of three. Rifles up, ready, pointed right at Jack.

CHAPTER FIVE

Shit! What the fuck was this?

"Ethan," he sent silently, *"abort. Things just went TU here."*

"Jack—"

Jack ruthlessly cut him off and linked to his team's comms.

"King? Status?"

Nothing. Jack looked around for Watson and Everett. Not anywhere he could see right then. *"Queen?"* he tried.

Silence.

Fuck!

The closest AFP guys paused two cars away, weapons pointed at Jack.

"Hands up and don't move," one of them commanded.

"What's up, fellas?" Jack slowly raised his empty hands. "We're all on the same side, aren't we?"

"That's up to someone above my pay grade to say," the cop replied. "Right now, we've got orders to take you in."

"I'm sure there's been a mistake somewhere. I'm ISO."

"And the word from the ISO is they've never heard of you," Watson said, coming around from the back of the 4WD. Her piece was out, not quite pointed at Jack.

Following the lieutenant was Harry, hands on the back of his head, earpiece missing, and apologetic look in his eyes. Behind Harry was Everett, taser at the ready.

"Then they're lying to you," Jack said evenly. "You know there are terrorists in—"

"No, actually, I don't." Watson stopped just outside Jack's immediate reach. "I've only got your word on that and you're clearly—" The clack of the lieutenant's teeth as she cut off her words and the aborted gesture she made toward his face told Jack what she'd been going say.

"I'm clearly what?" His tone was low and cold. "Not white? A brown-skinned terrorist?"

Behind Watson, Harry winced. For her part, Watson flinched, then firmed up her convictions. Shoulders straightening, she shifted her gun to point at him.

"We've been in contact with the head of security in the ISO building," she said grimly. "They're under the impression the terrorists are out here, trying to get in."

Anger starting to boil up, Jack repressed all derisive reactions, except for a sour grimace. "And you believe an anonymous voice over the phone rather than the people in front of you with IDs?"

"I'm not saying I believe them over you." Watson's tone was very reasonable, obviously trying to smooth things over. "However, ID's can be faked and until I'm convinced, I'm going to need you to cooperate with us and surrender any weapons."

"This is bullshit," Harry muttered.

"Harry," Jack said warningly. Then in a tone matching Watson's, "You saw the footage from inside. You know they're imposters. There's a woman in there—"

"Wanted for a shooting incident on the Gold Coast," a new voice said from behind Jack.

A terrible sinking feeling in his guts, Jack turned slowly. "I wondered if you'd recognised me."

Porsche grinned at him. She was still in her fake DSO outfit and had five of her fellow imposters with her.

"Never forget a face as pretty as yours, babe." Looking past him, she said to Watson, "This is him. He's the one who made a scene on the Gold Coast, stole a very expensive car and drove another person into a river. They never did find the poor woman's body. We've been on the lookout for him for months."

"Lieutenant," Jack tried, even as two of the AFP guys came forward with plastic cuffs.

Watson watched grimly as Jack was turned around and shoved against the side of the car. "I'm just following orders, Reardon. It'll all get sorted out back at HQ."

Harry ended up beside him, both of them thoroughly searched and relieved of everything not actually sewn together, including Harry's docket from the coffee and six-inch Bowie knife, and Jack's unused earpiece. They lost their personal wallets and ISO IDs. Then they were secured with plastic cuffs.

"We'll take them from here." Porsche signalled her people to come forward. "Thanks for all your help, Lieutenant Watson. I'll make sure your name is front and centre on the report. You might even get a medal."

"Wait a minute. I was told the suspects would remain with the AFP." There was a glimmer of doubt in Watson's eyes now. While she had been fed wrong information and acted on it, she wasn't completely convinced.

"Sorry, Lieutenant." Porsche commanded her people to surround Jack and Harry. "This is an ISO matter now. If we need anything more, we'll be in touch. In the meantime, perhaps you could go reassure the good citizens that everything's okay and to not be alarmed."

Watson glared at the smirk in Porsche's tone, but after a quick glance at the gathering crowd of museum patrons, turned and issued orders for the AFP team to keep the spectators at bay.

Porsche took the moment and lead her own group and their prisoners away. As they were crossing the road, Jack's implant *ping*ed.

"Jack, report," McIntosh snapped.

Clearly she'd been alerted to something going haywire on site, probably Alderton either witnessing Harry being detained or losing contact.

"We've been made," he sent grimly. *"Porsche and her team of imposters have us. They managed to convince Watson we're the bad guys. King and I are restrained and being taken into the ISO HQ."*

There was a couple of seconds of silence, during which he got another *ping*. Probably Ethan trying to find out what was going on. He ignored it for now.

"We're calling back the second AFP team," his director announced. *"RRF still en route. ETA twenty minutes. Jack, was this intentional? Is this some mad plan to get inside the building?"*

Jack internalised a snort. *"Not intentional, ma'am. I wouldn't have included King if that were the case."* He would have needed Harry coordinating on the outside. *"Definitely going to make the best of it, though. Hold the RRF in reserve for now. Ace was told to abort but I doubt he'll hold back. I'll keep you informed as things progress."*

"Actually, you won't. The building's gone dark. The CCTV cameras are going offline even as we cycle through them, and they're actively blocking mobile signals. You won't be able to contact anyone while you're in there."

"Shit." The ISO HQ was getting ever closer. Jack had maybe a minute before he lost all touch with home base. *"Keep the RRF in reserve. We'll work the situation from the inside. If we need backup, I'll get a signal out somehow."*

"We'll be watching, Jack. Good luck."

"Thanks."

She was gone before he even finished the thought.

They'd reached the stairs to the entrance of the building and even though Ethan was *ping*ing at short intervals, Jack continued to ignore it. He needed to concentrate on what was going on directly around him. Then a message flashed into the implant.

To your left.

While the faux-DSOs opened the doors and channelled them inside, Jack glanced left. On King Edward Terrace, a sleek black car cruised by.

Victoria.

Goddamn Ethan. He'd been closer than he said. Yet Jack couldn't help but feel happy about that. And frankly, he shouldn't have expected any different. Ethan rarely did as he was told.

Then Jack was at the doors to the building. He pretended to stumble and while he leaned against the doorframe to supposedly get his balance back, he closed his eyes and went *sideways*. The overlay for his implant flashed up before his inner eye and he flicked the kill switch.

"Hurry up," one of the DSO snapped and pushed him the rest of the way.

Thankfully, he'd shut down the implant before whatever jamming the enemy was using could knock it out with a burst of pain across his temporal lobe.

Inside, nothing had changed, except that they were no longer keeping up the pretence of having someone on the reception desk. There were two more DSOs inside and they gave Jack and Harry another pat down.

"What's going to happen now?" Jack asked Porsche.

"Well, pet, right now all the internal cameras are being disabled. As are the thermal scanners. We weren't expecting to be discovered quite so fast, but we can adapt. Kudos, by the way, for getting here in record time."

"My pleasure." Jack frowned at the bad guy currently getting a bit too intimate. "What do you expect to find in there?"

The man grinned evilly. "I know how you James Bond wannabes get. Think you're smart, hiding a knife or something where you reckon no dude would go on another dude."

Harry snorted, but it was cut off as he too was subjected to the same search. "Dude!"

"And what happens with us?" Jack asked.

"*That* is under some debate, cutie," Porsche said. "I'm all for immediate gratification but the boss man isn't ready to rush into anything permanent. He's commitment shy. So, for now, we'll tuck you away somewhere nice and secure." She blew him a kiss. "Till next we meet, sweet thing."

Jack was roughly grabbed by his biceps and hauled away, Harry dragged along behind him.

"What was with all the endearments?" Harry asked as they were ushered past the reception desk and into a long hallway. "It was creepy."

"It's a distancing technique," Jack answered. "A name humanises the target, makes it harder to kill them."

Harry's "Oh" was low and drawn out. "That's a bit of downer, isn't it?"

"Just a bit."

Toward the far end of the corridor was a pair of bad guys standing sentinel outside of a door. When they reached it, the door was opened and Jack and Harry were shoved in. It was a safe room, one of many in the building. No windows, no electronic devices or camera coverage. Air circulation was through four tiny vents high in the walls. It was soundproof and shielded from external surveillance.

Nothing got in or out that didn't arrive or leave with whomever came and went through the only door. There was supposed to be a manual barricade on the inside of the door, but there were only gouges in the walls where it had been crowbarred off. Normally, there would be a table and chairs, for comfort during what could be long conferences or debriefings, but any potential weapons had been taken out as well, so three of the four prisoners were left to sit on the floor.

The fourth was Keri Sing.

Even though her arms were tied behind her back, Keri stood protectively over a man and a child, legs braced, expression angry. Her dead-straight black hair was tangled in its loosening ponytail and her once immaculate grey skirt-suit was rumpled and stained. She'd cast aside her low heels in favour of going barefoot.

Behind her, the Asian man on the floor was dressed in business casual. If he'd had a dark-blue jacket to match the pants, it wasn't in evidence now. They'd left him his black-rimmed glasses, but the smudged lenses didn't do much to dilute the simmering mix of anger and fear in his dark eyes. The little girl, dressed in a white blouse, blue skirt, white knee-high socks and tiny black Mary Janes, huddled on his lap, her thin arms locked desperately around his neck. Big, tear-filled, brown eyes stared at Jack, a lock of her black hair tucked between her trembling lips.

"Reardon." The slightest amount of tension left Keri's shoulders.

"Sing," he returned mildly as the door was shut behind him. "I'd like to say I'm surprised, but . . ." He shrugged, showing off his own bound hands.

Keri stiffened again. "They had people on my family," she snapped, taking a step forward. "I had to do what they wanted or they would have ki—" She visibly clenched her teeth from blurting the rest out in front of her husband and daughter.

Not that her husband didn't know what was hanging over their heads as well as Keri did, but hopefully the girl was too young to understand. The man was struggling with his ties, clearly wanting to hold his little girl. Christ, if he could, Jack would have cuddled her, as well. No kid should have to go through this.

"I get it," Jack said, tone soft. "I really do. When I worked out what was really going on this morning, and we couldn't get hold of you, we suspected something like this."

As if she was too tired to stay angry, Keri sagged, stepping to the side so she could sink down the wall and lean on her husband's shoulder. "Please tell me this is all part of your plan to get us out of here."

CHAPTER SIX

"**Y**eah, about that." Harry came to Jack's side. "I'd kinda like to hear the brilliant plan, too."

"Me too," Jack muttered.

"You mean you don't have a plan?"

"Why do I have to have the plan?"

"You always have the plan."

Jack gave Harry a withering glare; Harry just smiled in return. It wasn't quite his usual carefree smile, but it was close enough that it gave Jack some hope. If Harry could still grin, then things weren't so desperate. But he was right. They needed a plan.

On the floor, Keri had turned her body towards her husband, shielding her daughter as much as she could. The sight caught at Jack's heart, reminding him of his niece, Matilda. Even though he hadn't seen her in a long time, Jack had adored spending time with her. They'd play games, have tea parties and she'd once decided he was her rocket-ship to the moon. She'd be seventeen now but all he could think was what if little Tilly was here right now.

Wish you were here?

"Right," Jack grunted. "A plan."

He looked around the rather empty room for inspiration and his gaze landed on the final prisoner in the far corner. The guy had his knees pulled up to his chest, head buried in them. He was half turned away like a frightened animal. Like the rest of them, his hands were secured behind his back.

"Jack," Keri murmured. "He . . ."

Jack nodded in acknowledgment and went over to the young man and crouched. The poor kid was shivering despite the long-sleeved tee and jeans.

"Hasan? Hasan Darmadi?"

Slowly, the kid raised his head and blinked at Jack. He was barely twenty, with a slightly too narrow face, but with nice features accentuated by sharp cheek bones and big, soulful eyes. His skin was about the same shade as Jack's, his hair midnight black. There were small studs in his ears and one in his nose, with holes above and below his left eyebrow but no bar. The nose and brow piercing were new since Jack had last seen him. Well, seen him clearly. The hazy memory Jack had of the night in the club wasn't detailed enough to say either way.

"Or, should I say Dixie Normous." Jack smiled gently. "I missed your performance, but you looked great. I'm sure it was awesome."

Hasan's eyes got even bigger. "Really?" He shrugged. "It was okay. I forgot the words to the song and missed some steps."

"I'm sure the next one will be brilliant."

For a moment he looked hopeful, but then his shoulders slumped. "We won't get out of here."

"We will." If only Jack knew how. "When did they take you?"

"Um, three days ago? They kept me somewhere else but this morning we came here." Hasan glanced across the room at the Sings. "Then they came and she said . . ." Trailing off, he let out a shuddering breath. "She said . . ." Tears welled and, unable to carry on, Hasan tucked his face away again.

"It'll be fine. I promise." Goddamn. A pair of big, sad eyes and he was making stupid proclamations.

Standing again, Jack left Delta Subject alone and went back to Keri. Harry had managed to get his hands in front of his body and was unlacing his shoes.

"We need to talk," Jack said to Keri.

She nodded, whispered something in Malay to her husband, then got to her feet. "You're the field leader. How do we get out of this mess?"

Indicating Harry, Jack said, "We're working on it, but it would help to know *exactly* what's happening. I know some of it, but not all."

"What do you know?"

"I know that Delta Subject over there is about as far from a terrorist threat as anyone can get."

The entire time Jack had been tasked with keeping tabs on Delta Subject, he had felt there was something off about it. And not just because Director Tan had held their agreement over his head to get Jack to take the assignment. He shouldn't have waited so long to review his cognitive model. It had only supported what Jack had believed all along. Hasan wasn't in Sydney to pave the way for his uncle's radical ideas, or to lash out on his own; he was here to get away from a family that couldn't accept him for who he was—a young gay man with dreams of being a drag queen.

And by the expression in Keri's eyes, she was well aware Jack was right. "I know. I didn't at first, but when your reports began coming in, showing there was no risk with Delta Subject, I wanted to end the surveillance." With a quick, worried look at her family, she lowered her voice even more. "But then I started getting photos delivered to my home. Of Aiman at work and Millie at school. Of them at the park, in our home, shopping." Her shoulders shuddered.

Harry had his shoelace threaded through his cuffs and clenched between his teeth so it stretched taut. He sawed the plastic of the cuff up and down furiously. It was a slow process but one that would work, eventually.

"I couldn't go to my director. They were too close to my baby. I couldn't risk it," Keri continued, almost as if she expected Jack to admonish her for needing to protect her family.

Even if Jack had wanted to berate her for it, it would have been hypocritical. Hadn't he defied the Office for Ethan several times?

"It was Khun Sein, wasn't it," Jack prompted.

"I didn't know at first," Keri admitted. "It was just the photos at the start, then actual threats and commands. I tried to find out who it was, but an overt search would have signalled the team and my director that something was wrong. It wasn't until two days ago I found out it was Sein. That's when they took Aiman and Millie and said if I didn't follow them to Canberra, they would . . . kill Aiman, slowly, and take . . . take Millie for themselves." A couple of long, deep breaths to calm herself, and then she said, "So I came to Canberra. They got me just outside of the airport and here we are. And I still don't really know why."

Jack sighed. "I think I do. He was linked to the subject of one of my old jobs. The subject, and Sein, are part of a larger organisation. We're not sure what their goal is, but it requires a large number of trained soldiers and weapons—" Which Valadian had been working on. "—and undoubtedly was being funded in part by money made from drug production in the Golden Triangle. I guess Sein is here for information. About Valadian, or other members of the group. Or just to find out how much we know."

"And Delta Subject was being set up as the fall guy. Flag him as a terror suspect and when this place blows, and his body is found . . ."

Jack glanced at the huddled kid. "I'm just sorry I couldn't clear him before now."

"You did, though," Keri whispered. "I knew it, too, but I was the one who said you had to keep watching him, keep him a suspect."

"Under duress," Jack reasoned.

Harry's hands flew apart, the sawn through cuff dangling from one wrist. Grinning widely, he got up and came over to Jack. "Can't help but see you're still cuffed."

"Had a few slightly more important things to do," Jack replied dryly. Then with a little flourish, brought his freed hands around to show Harry the loosened cuffs dangling from one finger. "But I can multi-task."

Smirk vanishing, Harry grabbed the cuffs and studied them. "How the hell did you do that?"

"With this." Jack held up the pin he always kept tucked into the back of his waistband. While he'd been talking with Keri, he'd managed to pull it free of the material and insert it into the lock on one cuff. The thin metal was just enough to pull the teeth away from the roller lock. He'd then pulled the strap out of the lock, loosening the cuff.

"What the . . ." Harry took the pin and studied it, then the cuffs, quickly getting how it worked. Grumbling to himself, he freed Keri, then went to her husband.

Jack looked around the room again, searching for something that would help them get out. By the time Harry had everyone freed of their cuffs, Jack was trying to decide if he, Harry and Keri could battle their way through at least ten fake DSOs, an assassin and find whoever Khun Sein had sent to do his dirty work.

Before he could conceive of a working plan, the lock on the door clunked open. Hastily, everyone grabbed up their discarded cuffs and, hands behind their backs, pretended to still be restrained. Harry moved up beside Jack, between the door and the others.

The door opened and two of the DSOs came in, dragging a third man between them.

"Found this one trying to sneak in the back way." One of them sneered at Jack. "Figured he was one of yours. We decided to punish him for being dumb enough to get caught, just so you wouldn't have to." He grinned like it was the biggest ever joke.

The prisoner sagged between his captors, held up only by their grips on his upper arms. His head hung forward, lolling loosely on his shoulders, dark hair falling over his face. A drop of blood hit the floor under his head. He wore dark tactical clothing similar to the AFP special ops guys, and his weapons had been taken away. In fact, Jack thought the butt of the gun sticking out of the waistband of the DSO to the left was that of a Desert Eagle.

"Thanks," Jack muttered dryly. "You shouldn't have."

"Our pleasure," the DSO said as he and the other guy dropped their prisoner to the floor at Jack's feet.

"No, really," Jack said as the prick tossed him a cocky salute. "You *shouldn't* have."

Before the frown had even started to form on the mouthy DSO's face, Ethan was moving.

CHAPTER SEVEN

Rolling onto his back, Ethan scissored his legs, catching the prick's calves between his. A twist and the dickhead was on the floor, shouting in surprise, arms flailing.

Jack lunged for the second man, ploughing his shoulder into the quiet DSO's gut, lifting him off his feet and propelling him backwards into the wall beside the door. The man was so startled he didn't defend himself when Jack pulled back and punched him. Grabbing his shoulders, Jack slammed his knee into the DSO's groin, then, stepping back, brought the man's face down to meet his knee in another hard blow. Nose squashed, blood splattered across his face, the fake DSO crumpled to the floor. Jack spun to help Ethan.

It wasn't required. The other DSO was on his back, pinned down by Ethan straddling his chest, knees locking the man's arms to his sides. Ethan roughly pulled the man's head up by a fistful of hair, said, "You *really* shouldn't have," and slammed it back down. With a faint grunt, the man went limp. Calm as you please, Ethan fished his sunglasses out of the downed man's pocket and slipped them on.

Harry had charged past them both and was holding his own against the two door guards, but if it went on much longer, chances were one would get away and alert the rest of the enemy. Jack threw himself into the fight, diverting one of the DSOs and in short order, Harry's opponent was down, followed quickly by Jack's.

While Harry and Keri secured the imposters with their own cuffs, Jack motioned Ethan away from the others.

"Didn't I tell you to abort?" He tried for stern but missed wide, unable to deny the fact that Ethan's appearance was just what they'd needed. Unable, as well, to not be happy that Ethan hadn't fled the country at the first chance.

"And miss all this fun? Did you truly expect me to stay away?" The tone was light but had undertones of seriousness.

Suddenly aching to hold him, Jack shook his head. "No."

"Good." Ethan smiled, then winced and touched his nose gingerly. "That lug wasn't particularly effective with his 'punishment,' but he did manage to land that punch well."

Jack tilted Ethan's head back. "Is it broken?" His nose had stopped bleeding but would probably swell to a nice size.

"No, just a bit pummelled."

"Ah hem."

Jack looked over at Harry. "Yes?"

"Jack, that's Ethan Blade," Harry said carefully.

Keri snapped around to focus on Ethan as well, the name being rather well known to most people who worked in the Office.

Ignoring the "oh shit" expressions, Jack said, "Well spotted. King, meet Ace."

"Ace?" Harry's eyes darted over Ethan quickly, then back to Jack. After a moment, his sceptical expression changed into a furious frown. "He's the source, isn't he? I knew it! You two planned this all along!"

"Not exactly," Ethan murmured.

"Yes, he's the source, and no, we *didn't* plan this," Jack told Harry as he gave Ethan a withering look.

Ethan snorted, then sucked in a sharp breath, a hand hovering over his nose.

"Is he working for us?" Keri asked warily.

"No," Ethan said, as if she had asked him if he enjoyed having his nut-sack waxed.

"Sort of," Jack amended. "Subcontracting."

"Does this mean I'll get paid?" Ethan asked.

"We'll discuss that later. Did you get much of a look around before you were 'caught'?"

Ethan went to the DSOs who had brought him in and retrieved his two Desert Eagles, a Glock 17 and several knives. "I managed a quick recon. It appears as if the staff are all being held in rooms like this, on the inner side of the structure, all in this wing. For now, they seem secure enough. There are at least a dozen more armed soldiers like these."

Jack accepted an M4A5 carbine from Ethan, checking the mag swiftly.

"And the bomb?" Harry stepped up to take a weapon as well.

Ethan's eyebrows almost hit his hairline. "Bomb?"

"There has to be a bomb." Harry's tone was tinged with condescension. "Khun Sein will need to cover up why he was here, so a bomb to destroy evidence of what he was after, and a terror suspect to blame it on." He carefully didn't look at Hasan, but the kid wasn't dumb.

"It's me, isn't it. That's why I'm here," Hasan whispered. "That's why she said we were all going to die." His gaze flicked to Keri.

"Don't worry," Harry said to him. "We cleared you of anything suspicious. You're not going to die and so long as you keep out of trouble, you're not going to prison."

"We should move very soon." Ethan checked over his Eagles. "The others will miss these ones shortly."

"Right. With the jamming in place, the bad guys won't be able to communicate too quickly. If we move fast enough, we can take them by surprise." Jack turned to Keri. "Someone needs to check on the other hostages, make sure they're all okay and ready to evac if required."

"Why can't we start evacuating them now?" Keri asked.

"We don't want to alert the enemy too soon and, frankly, they're safer where they are. The less people in the corridors that we have to worry about, the better."

The unit leader accepted that with a nod, then along with Harry, lead her family and Hasan out of the room.

Once they were alone, Jack caught Ethan's arm and pulled him close.

"Crazy bastard," he murmured into his hair.

"Half right, Jack." Ethan pressed against him for a moment, then pulled away. "How angry are you with me?"

"Right now, not very. I do, however, reserve the right to chew you out for interfering again when we're all safe and away from here."

A little quirk of Ethan's lips. "I look forward to it." Seriously, he added, "You understand that I had to, don't you?"

Jack's anger spiked for a moment, giving voice to a little growl. "Yeah, I do, but I told you not to do this anymore and you agreed."

"I don't recall actually saying I wouldn't—"

"Ethan!"

With a visible effort, Ethan relaxed his shoulders. "You can ask me all you wish to not interfere with your job, Jack, but you *cannot* ask me to not care about you. If I know you're walking into a dangerous situation, I will not stand back and let you get hurt."

Jack swallowed to ease the sudden ache in his throat. "Yeah. I get that. I would do the same for you."

"Then is this argument over?"

Rubbing a hand over his face, Jack nodded. "I guess. Just, in future, don't play games like this, okay? If you have something that could help, just tell me."

Ethan sighed. "Jack, I would, but . . ."

Stomach sinking, Jack prompted. "But what?"

"But I fear if I openly offer you intelligence or my help, it will only give Director Tan more to hold over you than he already does. I'm the reason you made the agreement with him in the first place, Jack, and I don't wish to make it any worse." Ethan ducked his head.

Jack bit back a sigh. "I don't regret making that agreement. Be it McIntosh or Tan telling me where to go and what to do, it's all the same." For now. Jack would probably have something different to say if Tan decided he needed Jack in India. But even then, he wouldn't want to change the agreement. "If I wasn't here in this mess right now, I'd probably be in another one, and facing worse odds because you wouldn't be there."

Ethan lifted his face to look at Jack. "So, you're glad I'm interfering."

Mouth opening and closing a couple of times, Jack scrambled for something that would save him. Before he could find it, Ethan chuckled and, throwing one arm around Jack's neck, pulled him in for a lingering kiss on his cheek.

"It's all right, Jack. I understand."

"Glad one of us does."

Harry stood in the doorway, expression disbelieving. And horrified. Jack and Ethan sprang apart like a pair of teenagers caught together behind the toilet block at school.

Stomach falling to his knees, Jack took a step toward him, hand up in a soothing gesture. He didn't get a chance to say anything, though.

"The Sings and Hasan are secured and Keri's talking with the other hostages," Harry ground out, glaring at Jack and completely ignoring Ethan who'd moved further away and was meticulously checking his weapons with snappy, tight motions.

Great, Harry had sparked a compulsion. "King," Jack began.

"I think we really should get going." Harry barrelled right over the top of him. "Wait too long and the bad guys are going to get suspicious. I was hoping you were busy coming up with a plan, but I see that was wrong. Unless this," he waved between Jack and Ethan, "is the plan. Is it?"

Again, before Jack could open his mouth, he was cut off.

"Jack, I will scout this floor of the wing. I'll meet you at the bottom of the stairwell." Ethan jerked his weapons harness into precise alignment and, ignoring Harry, stalked out of the room.

"Jesus, King," Jack snapped when Ethan was gone. "What the fuck?"

Hands on hips, Harry shook his head slowly. "You don't get to 'what the fuck' me after what I just saw."

"You never had a problem with the gay before."

Harry spluttered for a moment, then burst out with, "I don't care about that. I do care that you're doing it with . . . with . . ."

"With?" Jack prompted with a growl.

"With a paid killer. He kills people for money!"

"So do we." It came out low and cold.

"That's different."

Almost laughing at the replay of an argument he and Ethan had had in the desert, Jack said, in a more modulated voice, "Not as different as you want to believe. Trust me, that's something you're going to have accept if you plan to make a career of this."

Harry turned away, hands raking back his hair. "It's just that . . . I mean working with him is fine, I guess. But, but . . . anything more is—"

"None of your business," Jack finished for him.

"Really? So this . . . thing hasn't ever *interfered* in your work?" Harry's tone was bitter. "Because, Jack, your work is *my* work, and therefore, it is *my* business. You're my partner!"

Christ! Harry had obviously been in the doorway for longer than Jack thought.

"You're my second, not my partner," he snapped, harsher than he'd intended.

And nothing else he'd ever said to Harry, including the jab that had nearly seen him punched, had left him with such an expression of betrayal.

"Fuck," Jack hissed. Before he could do any more damage, he said, "You're right. We need to keep going. Ace should be done with the recce by now." He picked up his M4A5 and two of the Glocks the enemy carried and when he faced Harry again, the betrayal was hidden behind a stony mask.

"Let's go," Harry muttered, accepting one of the Glocks before moving out.

It had finally happened. Someone from work had found out about him and Ethan. Specifically, that Jack's ongoing contact with the wanted assassin was much more than professional. His fear of this day had been a constant niggle in the back of his head. Jack could cover his arse with the agreement he had with Tan, but only so long as the shady bastard didn't backtrack on his part in it. Even then, he didn't think a verbal, "Keep Blade happy," would be enough to change Harry's perception of what he saw.

And it couldn't have happened at a better time.

Jack threw that unpleasant little aside in the filing cabinet and concentrated on the immediate. They had a job to do and he trusted Harry to get it done. The aftermath could wait.

They made their way along the hallway fast, covering each other, aware that Ethan had already been through. He was waiting at the door to the stairwell, Desert Eagle held to his side, ear pressed to the door, listening intently.

"There's movement on the stairs," he whispered when they reached him. "We'll have to fight our way upwards."

Jack grimaced. "Ace, you and King go first. I'll cover you to the landing."

Harry's lips tightened at the command. "And then?" he asked, tone cold.

"Wherever the bomb is, they'll have it guarded," Ethan said. "Which means it's not on this floor."

"We're pretty sure they're here for information and that means they'll want to cover their digital footprint," Jack said. "They'll need to make sure the servers are taken out in the explosion. The server room is on the first floor, at the rear of the building. When we get up there, our first job is to disarm the device. King, since you've had the most recent training, job's yours."

"Fine." The shuttered look Harry gave him held all sorts of accusations. "And what will you two do?"

"Find Porsche and whoever she's working for, and deal with them."

"Porsche?" Ethan asked.

"Yeah. Named her myself. The assassin who picked up the ticket on you at the Gold Coast."

Eyes going wide, Harry snapped, "*That's* what that was all about? *Him?* And you didn't tell me."

"Need to know, King."

"I think I *need*—"

"Gentlemen," Ethan interrupted. "Later, perhaps?"

Both of them agreed grudgingly.

"On three?" Ethan asked.

"On three." Jack grabbed the door handle. "One, two ..."

CHAPTER EIGHT

"**T**hree."

Jack pushed the door open and moved through, tracking high. The stairwell was narrow and tight and currently, they were hidden under the landing for the next floor. Slowly, Jack eased up the first couple of steps, back to the wall, Glock aimed upwards.

"Jerry?" The voice floated down from above. "That you?"

A dark-clad person leaned over the railing on the landing above.

"Sure," Jack replied and shot him. The body jerked back and dropped out of view. Instantly, there was shouting from the first floor and footsteps pounding, getting louder as they neared the stairwell.

Ethan slipped past Jack, taking the stairs up two at a time. Harry was right behind him. They'd just reached the midpoint landing, where the stairs switched back, when the first-floor door slammed open. Ethan shoved Harry down behind the meagre cover of the railing and fired at the enemy piling through the door. From his crouched position, Harry also opened fire. One eye on the ground-floor door, Jack jumped up a couple of steps and added his own fire to the mix.

On the mid-landing, Ethan had to duck behind Harry. He had both Eagles out and was firing from either side of Harry. Jack didn't envy the Kiwi the position. Two big, .50 cal handguns booming that close to his head had to be deafening.

The problem with the situation was that they were attacking the higher ground and the enemy were on their bellies, providing small targets without limiting their ability to return fire. The bad guys had all the advantages right then and the only thing Jack and the others were doing was wasting ammo.

Jack skipped back down into cover, tucked his handgun into his pants and swung the carbine around to the front. Taking a deep breath, he leaped up several stairs, brought the carbine up and unleashed it on full-automatic mode. The angle wasn't great, his field of fire worse than that of Ethan and Harry, but that wasn't Jack's intention.

The stairwell was totally made of brick and cement. The first-floor landing was a slab of cement a foot thick. Rapidly fired bullets tore into its upper edge, chipping away at the cement causing dust and tiny projectiles to explode in the air—right in the faces of the bad guys lying there. Return fire stopped almost instantly.

Ethan sprinting upwards and the moment he cleared the stairs, Jack stopped firing.

Boom. Boom. Pause. *Boom.*

In the ringing silence, Ethan called, "Landing clear."

A second later, more gun fire started up outside the stairwell and Ethan answered it as Jack and Harry hurried to join him. Ethan crouched with his back to the wall beside the open door, forces in the hallway keeping them pinned in the stairwell.

"I believe they're aware of our presence," Ethan said mildly.

"Appears so," Jack replied dryly. "Any ideas?"

"Oh, plenty. You wouldn't happen to have a grenade or another incendiary device on you?"

"Other pants."

"Well, that limits our options. Cover me?"

"Got nowhere else to be."

"Lovely. Wait for my signal."

Jack sent a spray of bullets into the hallway from an awkward angle. Then Ethan was gone, sprinting up the second flight to the third floor.

"What signal?" Harry asked as the enemy resumed firing.

"I'm sure we'll know it when it happens."

They kept trading useless shots with the bad guys. In the infrequent lulls, there was also gunfire above them, but only an occasional shot, which meant Ethan wasn't encountering too much resistance. The signal came when, from further away, more gunshots rang out. For a moment, the bad guys stopped firing at the stairwell.

Jack surged to his feet and took in the new hallway in a fast look. Four bad guys were entrenched in doorways about halfway along, two to each side. At the far end of the hallway, Ethan fired on the bad guys from the cover of an office doorway. Somehow, he'd flanked the enemy.

The enemy were scrambling for more cover and Jack added to the confusion. One poor guy actually came out into the hallway instead of back into the safety of the room. He went down, Jack uncertain if it was his or Ethan's bullet that got him.

Jack got Harry up to date on which rooms the last three bad guys were hiding in and they swiftly took them out. They headed for the server room. While Jack and Harry covered the hallway, Ethan picked the electronic lock, which consisted of bashing a hole in the wall beside it to expose the wiring. Grabbing a handful, he turned to Harry.

"This will only give us about three seconds before the backup kicks in. Get ready."

He nodded grimly and grabbed the doorhandle. "Just keep swimming."

Ethan quirked an eyebrow at him.

Harry grimaced. "Ready."

With a nod, Ethan turned his face away and jerked the wires out of the wall. Sparks flew, the indicator light on the lock went out and there was a faint *clunk*. Harry twisted the handle and pushed in the same moment. The door opened and he almost fell into the room.

Bang.

Harry cried out and fell to the side, pushing the door open even further. Jack whirled around, Glock at the ready, but Ethan was already moving. Eagle returning fire in one hand, he dragged Harry out of harm's way with the other. Jack grabbed the back of Ethan's collar and hauled them into cover faster.

"Well," Jack muttered when they were all relatively safe. "That's disappointing."

"I probably should have expected it." Ethan frowned as a bullet ripped through the doorframe a couple of centimetres from his shoulder.

"We all should have," Harry muttered grudgingly. He peered at the tear in his right shirt sleeve.

"How is it?" Jack asked.

"Just a scratch, barely bleeding."

"Ace, cover us." Jack didn't wait for Ethan's affirmative before tearing a strip off his own shirt to bind Harry's arm.

"It's fine." Despite his grumbling, Harry let Jack finish.

"It's the little ones you have to watch."

Harry grunted but it had a tone of acceptance, then groaned again in pain when Jack tied off the make-do bandage with a firm jerk.

Satisfied Harry was okay, Jack turned to Ethan. "Care to try your flanking move again?"

"I doubt I could. If they designed this place currently, there should only be the one entrance to the server room."

"Probably. Do you think these guys are fanatical enough to set the bomb off while still in there?"

Ethan snorted. "I highly doubt it. They're mercenaries, Jack, and I don't think they've worked out how to take the money with them."

"Did you get a look at the inside of the room?"

"Not a detailed one, no. I couldn't see the device, but there appears to only be two guards."

"Only two, huh?" Jack hefted his carbine. "Want some cover?"

Ethan smirked and re-holstered his guns. Taking out two knives, he flexed his wrists. "It would be appreciated."

"Aim high," Harry muttered, settling his own carbine into position. "You've already reached your shoot-the-bomb quota for the year."

A little spark of hope flared in Jack's chest. Perhaps he hadn't ruined his partnership with Harry after all if Harry could tease.

Jack moved so he was closer to the doorway, carbine out. Ethan crouched at his feet, knives tucked back along his forearms. Jack counted down silently. On three, he stuck the mussel of his carbine into the room and fired wildly. Return fire stopped quickly and the moment it did, Ethan rolled in. Jack kept up the barrage while Ethan sliced and stabbed his way through the bad guys.

"Clear!" he shouted a surprisingly short time later.

Harry went in and, picking his way over the bodies, searched the large room. "Found it. Right in the middle of the server towers."

"How does it look?" Jack asked as he kept watch at the door.

"Not good. I don't think I can disarm this. It's not something I'm familiar with."

Halfway out the door, Ethan paused. "Perhaps I could have a look."

Jack didn't even have to think about it. Personal problems meant nothing compared to a bomb. "Yeah, go."

Ethan turned, then stopped. "Before I do, I have something to tell you."

He sounded so serious Jack's stomach tightened in dread. Was this about why he hadn't wanted to return to Australia?

"I discovered Porsche's real name," Ethan said softly. "It's Sonia Bell."

Jack let out an explosive breath. "Is that all?"

Frowning, Ethan added, "I do have a full dossier but now is hardly the time. Trust me. Confront her with that and she'll falter."

"Okay. Thanks." He was relieved and, strangely, disappointed that's all Ethan had to tell him.

Ethan went into the server room and Harry reappeared. "Shall we do this thing?"

As they started back towards the stairs, Jack said, "If we're right about Sein wanting information, the best way to access it is through the senior director of operations. The SD's office is on the second floor, front of the building. That's where we're heading."

The second-floor landing wasn't manned, as the first-floor one had been, so Jack and Harry made their way up cautiously but without resistance. The hallway beyond the stairwell door was another story. Enemy fire opened up the moment Jack nudged the door open for a peek. They waited out the first barrage, which pretty much reduced the door to matchsticks, then they took turns covering while the other checked the situation.

"One, two doors up on the right," Harry muttered. "Two, three doors further up, one to each side. Two more at the far end, guarding the corner office. Couple more than your boyfriend said."

"He's not my boyfriend and two off is still pretty good. That's the SD's office," Jack said.

They waited while the enemy killed the fuck out of the walls.

"He looked like your boyfriend." Harry sprayed the hallway with bullets without looking.

While the bad guys were ducking behind their doors, Jack took a quick look. "Middle two have come forward. They're just behind the solo guy. And it's not that simple."

After a moment, Harry said, "What relationship is?"

Jack glanced at him and got a grimace in return. "Tell me about it. Cover me?"

Harry checked the magazine on his M4A5. "I got you."

While his partner distracted the bad guys, Jack ran for the first set of doors, feeling the deadly wind of several enemy bullets zip past him as he skidded into cover. He rolled and came up against the wall, flinching as the outer side of it was targeted. When Harry sent another barrage down the hall, Jack sneaked a look. In the micro-second between Harry pulling back and the bad guys coming forward, he darted out. In two long strides, he cut diagonally across the hall and threw himself bodily at the solo guy. They tumbled back into the room just as his fellows fired again. It was dirty and quick, but Jack broke the man's neck.

Jack had no sooner got to his feet, when he was hit from behind. Twisting as he fell, he got an arm around the man's neck. When they crashed down, Jack flipped them over, driving a knee into his groin. Shoving the bad guy's carbine away, Jack grabbed the Glock from its holster and pressed the business end under his chin. The man froze.

"No need for you to die." Jack took a couple of plastic cuffs from the guy's belt.

Outside, the gun fight continued, which meant Harry was still going strong. Smiling grimly, Jack rolled the bad guy to his belly and cuffed his hands behind his back. He was just tightening the cuffs around the man's ankles when a gun barrel was pressed to the back of his head.

Shit. One slipping past Harry was okay, but two? Two guns were still barking, so his partner wasn't down, at least.

"Hands behind your head," the bad guy growled.

Jack complied slowly. On the floor, the tied-up man chuckled.

"What are you waiting for?" Jack asked.

"Stark wants you," the man holding the gun on him said.

"Who's Stark?"

"You'll—"

Bang!

A dead weight landed on Jack's back. He tumbled forward, sandwiched between the bound guy and the hopefully dead one. A moment later, the body on top was hauled off.

"Fine time to be taking a nap," Harry said.

Jack shoved up to his knees, then his feet. "I was getting tired of doing all the work." He checked Harry over with a quick look, finding no blood. "Did you Butch Cassidy your way in here?"

"Huh?"

"Jesus, Harry, you're not that young. We're down to two bad guys?"

"And whoever's in the office."

Risking a glance out into the hallway, Jack was greeted by a quick spurt of gunfire. "Okay, I think I've got a plan."

CHAPTER NINE

Five minutes later, Jack leaned against the wall by the door and yelled, "Hey! Bad guys!"

After a couple of seconds, a voice replied. "What?"

Reversing his grip on his carbine, Jack held it out into the hall. "I'm all alone. I want to surrender."

Another moment presumably filled with hushed debate. Then, "The other bloke was in there with you."

"Dead," Jack groused, like he was pissed at both the enemy who'd killed his mate, and at his mate for getting killed. "I got no way out now, so I'd like to see if there's another option."

When no response came after half a minute or so, Jack added, "Apparently Stark wants me."

"Jeez, okay," was the exasperated reply. "Toss the rest of your weapons then come out, hands up."

Jack threw a couple of Glocks into the hallway and a random knife he'd found on one of the baddies. "I'm coming out now."

There was absolutely no guarantee they wouldn't just shoot him the moment he appeared. He was putting a lot of faith in one prick's comment, and his own ability to spot a fake-out and move fast. Hands up, fingers spread, he stepped out.

The last two bad guys were covering the hallway from the protection of two doorways just this side of the SD's office. In the office door, Porsche stood, not particularly caring she was presenting herself as an open target. She grinned at Jack.

"Hello, pretty," Porsche said. "I'd hoped you'd make it this far. Come on down, winner."

"The name's Jack," he said, matching her grin. Striding forward, he added, "Nice to meet you, Sonia Bell."

Porsche's eyes went wide, then snapped into narrowed slits. One of the mercenaries glanced over at her, uncertain.

"Trying your hand at being a mercenary now that you've failed at being an assassin?" Jack asked conversationally.

One of the men came out and patted Jack down. It was just as invasive as the first had been, though his hands did falter when Jack said "assassin."

Bell's surprised anger cleared into smugness. "Who says I failed?"

"For starters, Ethan Blade." Deemed clean, Jack was grabbed by his upper arms and pushed forward. "I'm sure he'd love to discuss your definition of failure with you."

"He knows it was nothing personal." Bell smiled again, thought it wasn't as cocky as usual. "It was just a job."

She wasn't convinced but she covered it with a brisk gesture at one of the bad guys to take Jack into the room.

The SD's office looked much like any other—crowded bookshelf to one side; a big desk in front of a wall with framed certificates and pictures; a couple of perfunctory chairs opposite the big, leather office chair; a coffee table and two more comfortable looking chairs along the wall with a window looking out over the interior courtyard.

The senior director, Philip Maynard, sat at his desk, two screens angled toward him, fingers poised on a keyboard. Two women sat in the chairs by the window: the admin assistant, Marianne, and another woman. They sat stiffly, hands on the armrests, watching Jack warily. Another merc stood watch over them, and a ghost from Jack's past stood behind Maynard.

Bell drew her sidearm and motioned to the merc watching the women. "Go check the other one, make sure he's dead."

The man nodded and headed out. Bell moved to stand beside Marianne, draping the arm holding the gun over the back of the admin assistant's chair. All she had to do was bend her wrist and she could shoot Marianne in the head. Bell smirked at Jack.

The ghost rested a hand casually on the back of Maynard's chair, as if they were friends, or workmates. Except that Maynard was sporting a sluggishly bleeding lip and red marks that would bloom into impressive bruises given time.

"Jack, was it?" the ghost asked.

Jack had done some despicable things while undercover in Samuel Valadian's organisation. He'd delivered beatings to those who annoyed Valadian, helped highjack arms shipments, broken into government buildings and stolen from military bases. He'd also executed a man who'd broken one of Valadian's few rules.

Link Rindone had been a murderer and rapist. Jack had hated the psychopathic cretin. But, shooting him between the eyes, while he'd been on his knees before Valadian had left Jack feeling sick and dirty. It had been his first step down the steep slope to madness.

He knew Rindone was dead, but his eyes told him otherwise. There was no way it could have been faked, and as he studied the man, he began to see slight differences. Both were blond, but Link's eyes had been brown and this man's were blue; Link had had a cleft in his chin this man was missing; and there had been an unmissable "creep" factor in Link that Jack didn't get from this man. He spoke with the same German accent as Link, so Jack guessed they were brothers or maybe cousins who happened to look extraordinarily alike.

Jack conceded with shrug. "That's me. And you are . . .?"

"Sorry. Please call me Stark." He leaned across the table, offering to shake.

Racking his memory for everything he'd learned about Link, Jack took the hand. Stark's grip was firm but not crippling, his palm dry. A man in control. He gave Jack a warm smile.

"A pleasure to meet you, at last." Stark let his hand go.

He was trying so hard for urbane politeness, Jack decided not to disappoint him. "Likewise. Apparently, you wanted to see me."

"I did. It's nothing big. You see, Bell told me all about her encounter with you on the Gold Coast and I simply wanted to see what sort of man would go to such lengths to keep a cold-blooded assassin alive." He dropped his gaze down Jack's body and back up again. When he met Jack's eyes, all the warmth had gone and he looked more like Link than ever. "Now I know."

Suppressing a shiver, Jack wondered how Stark fitted in to the ticket put on Ethan. As far as anyone knew, it had been bought by a Liechtenstein duchess, and since Ethan had killed her for it, she wasn't about to tell anyone why. Maybe this man knew.

"Yeah," Jack agreed coolly. "Now you know."

A merc appeared in the doorway. He had his cap pulled down and his sunglasses lowered so they rested on his chin. Bell raised an eyebrow at him.

"All clear," the man grunted and stepped back to take up position with the other bad guy guarding the office.

"Well, that seems final." Stark smiled. "And if I'm not wrong, we're just about done here, aren't we, Philip." It was a statement, not a question.

"Nearly there," Maynard said, voice tight, fingers back to tapping on the keyboard. "The last file you want is almost done. The one on—"

Stark cut him off with a casual slap, knocking the grey-haired director sharply to the side. Bell pushed the barrel of her gun into Marianne's head. The admin assistant's whimper of fear caught Maynard's attention, so when he straightened up, he got back to work without protest.

"Nice try, Philip," Stark said, conversationally.

Jack was about done with it all. It was time to finish this. "I'm curious about something."

"About?" Stark asked if they were passing a pleasant evening discussing the weather.

"I won't lie. I'd really like to know what information you're after here. I mean, it must have something to do with Samuel Valadian's defunct organisation. *That* part is obvious."

Apparently Stark didn't think it should be. His reaction was subtle—the tightening of his grip on the chair back, a narrowing of his eyes, a thinning of his lips—but Jack had been watching for it, so he knew he scored a hit.

Barrelling on, he said, "I certainly don't blame Khun Sein for wanting to know just how much information Valadian gave up about him before he died. I mean, he couldn't buy the level of protection he did with money alone, could he."

Stark huffed, but the sound wasn't as blasé as he probably wanted it to be. "I guess I shouldn't be surprised you worked it out. You figured out we were here, after all. I wonder, though, if you're aware of the bomb?" His free hand delved into a pocket and removed a remote trigger. "Oh, don't worry. This trigger works on a very different frequency than the jammer. Be assured it will work . . . if needed."

Whether or not Stark was lying about the trigger, one thing was clear—he didn't know that Jack and Harry had found the bomb, or that they'd been joined by Ethan. Hoping that Ethan had disarmed the bomb, Jack shrugged casually. "Yeah, I don't think you're going to blow us all up just yet."

"Really? Why not?"

"Because there's something else you're after. Something personal. I bet you're trying to find out who killed your psychopathic deadshit of a brother, aren't you, Landon Rindone?"

The reaction was instant. Rindone gaped, one hand falling from the back of Maynard's chair and the other clenching around the trigger. Bell jerked in shock but recovered lightning fast and switched targets to Jack. Just outside the door, the merc who'd reported the all clear whipped his carbine up and shot the other one, point blank through the head.

Jack leaped forward just as Bell fired. It was like someone had punched him in the side, but he had the momentum to catch Bell around the waist. They crashed into Marianne's chair, sending her flying as well. Bell fought dirty but Jack managed to grab one hand and pin it. He clamped his knees tight around her legs while she tried to drive the side of her hand into his throat.

Harry yelled, "Stand down! Stand the fuck down!" There was a crash and a man cried out. "Sir! Move!" Then, *bang!*

One of the women screamed but Jack was too focused on Bell to see which body it was that thumped to the floor behind him. Bell managed to get a leg over Jack's and, with a heave and twist, rolled them so she was on top. She punched him once, twice, then jammed her fingers into the wound on Jack's side. He jack-knifed in sudden, intense pain.

Bang!

Bell raised her fist for another blow, but a dark shape flashed overhead and the assassin was thrown off Jack. Marianne took another step forward, lifting the chair she'd used to hit Bell. Snarling, Bell rolled out of range and flipped to her feet. Without a backwards glance to see if her fellows needed help, she was out the door and running.

Jack came up into a ready crouch, ribs protesting the move sharply. He took in the situation in a glance. Marianne slowly set down the chair, gripping its back so hard her knuckles went white, her shoulders heaving as she dragged air into her shaking body. The other woman was pressed into the wall, wide-eyed but seemingly unharmed. Rindone was slumped across the desk, unmoving. Maynard stood over him, hands curled into fists, panting. He too appeared okay. Harry was . . .

"King?" Jack took a long stride to reach his partner.

The Kiwi was lying on the floor, carbine held in one hand, the glasses and cap of his borrowed disguise knocked askew. Jack's chest tightened as he went to his knees beside Harry, ignoring the pain in his side. "Harry!"

"I heard you the first time." Harry opened his eyes. "Just having a nap. I mean I did all the work here. Got the last two mercs *and* the main bad guy. I mean, I was lying on my back when I shot him. That's gotta be worth a medal right there."

Jack didn't know whether he should kick or hug him, so he settled for getting back to his feet and holding a hand out. "Dickhead," he said fondly, as he hoisted his partner upright.

"Aw." Harry grinned. "I think we just bonded."

"Great," Jack muttered. "BFFs forever."

"Best friends forever forever?"

Jack shook his head. "Let's go get the last bad guy."

"Lead the way."

Jack stopped long enough to snatch up a carbine from the dead merc and he and Harry followed Bell. She was just disappearing into the stairwell, so they sprinted after her, taking steps downward two and three at a time.

"Ace!" Jack shouted as the hit the first-floor landing. He wasn't certain Ethan would hear him, but he had to try. "Bell's on the run!"

Harry overtook Jack while he was yelling and was halfway down to the ground floor before Jack took the first step. Jack looked over his shoulder as he reached the mid-landing. Ethan hadn't shown up. It was going to be just Jack and Harry then. Which was fine because they were more than capable.

When Jack burst out of the stairwell on the ground floor, Harry was pelting along the hallway, well ahead of him. Bell was even further along and seconds away from the door to the foyer.

Jack skidded to a stop and swung his carbine up. "King! Drop!"

Harry tucked his shoulder and hit the floor in a controlled roll. Jack fired directly down the middle of the hallway. The door to the foyer was pocked with bullet holes, making Bell skid to a stop and drop.

"Stay down, Bell," Jack ordered.

She didn't and, just like on that mad chase on the Gold Coast, was desperate enough to take a risk. Bouncing to her feet, she threw herself at the door just as Jack shot again. The door burst open and she tumbled through, a spray of red and startled cry heralded a hit.

Harry sprang up and kept after her. Jack was right behind him. Harry crashed through the door to the foyer and a moment later, Jack followed. Bell was sprinting across the foyer's open expanse, not for the front doors where, hopefully, the RRF from Duntroon was waiting, but toward the doors to the inner courtyard.

Bang! Bang! One of the big glass doors leading to the courtyard shattered under the impact of the bullets, an instant before a dark shape dived through in a spray of glass. Ethan tumbled in a precise roll, coming up on his feet. Two big handguns came up, pointed unerringly at Bell. Almost as fast, Bell brought up her handgun.

In the same space of time, Harry reached the corner of the front desk. He grabbed its edge to pull himself around it in a tight turn. A fake DSO propelled himself up from his position in front of the desk. His arm swept up and around, the edge of the tactical knife he wielded scraping over the chest plate of the armour Harry had purloined.

All Jack knew was that his men—work and personal partners—were in deadly danger. But, just as with the terrorists in Singapore, Jack didn't think. Training kicked in and his emotional heart shut down. In a split second he'd assessed and decided. The carbine swung and he fired.

Bang!

Bang! Bang!

The DSO's head snapped backwards as the bullet from Jack's gun slammed through it. He crashed to the floor, silver knife spinning away, trailing red drops.

Bell tripped over the lowest step leading up to the courtyard doors, falling prey to the Eagles. She hit the steps hard, gun clattering out of her hand.

Ethan went down to one knee, both guns still trained on the other assassin who didn't move.

In front of Jack, Harry staggered.

"Harry?" Jack slung his carbine over his shoulder and grabbed for his partner.

"Jack?" Harry sounded dazed. "I think . . ." He lifted his hand to his neck and slowly pulled back the collar of his shirt. Blood pumped from a deep wound just over his collarbone.

"Fuck." Jack caught Harry before he fell. "Harry! Jesus." He got Harry down gently. "It's okay. You're going to be okay." Over his shoulder, "Ethan!" Then, to Harry, "Lie still, mate. Help's coming. Don't worry."

Dark blood was pooling under Harry's neck, pumping steadily from his torn jugular. Jack pressed his hands over it, but it kept pushing out between his fingers.

Harry, already startlingly pale, looked up at him, big brown eyes wide. "You look . . . worried."

"Nah. This is my bored face." He pressed harder, making Harry groan. "The girls are going to love it, Harry. They'll lap up the story and you'll have a tiny scar to prove it. Just hold on, okay."

"Liar." Harry's hand fluttered at Jack, landing on his arm, absolutely no strength in his grip. "You said, it's the little ones you have to . . ." His voice trailed off, eyes going glassy.

The blood wasn't slowing down and Jack didn't want to take even one hand away to find something else to use to put pressure on the wound. "Ethan!"

"Here." Ethan skidded down beside him. He had a wad of material ready, ripped from his black top. He pushed it over Jack's hands and one at a time, Jack slipped his hands out of the way. More blood pumped out a second before Ethan pressed down hard.

"Hold it," Jack snapped at Ethan. "I'm going for the RRF. They'll have a medic."

"Jack," Ethan began. "Stay. I'll get the—"

"They won't listen to you fast enough," Jack snapped at him. "It has to be me. Stay with him," he commanded and scrambled to his feet, ignoring the way Harry's hand slipped listlessly from his arm.

Jack raced for the front doors, praying the RRF was right outside.

In the mess that followed, Ethan disappeared. When Jack stopped long enough to think about it, he wasn't surprised. Even though his participation in the fracas had been sort of sanctioned by McIntosh, Ethan wasn't going to let himself be taken in by the Office again. For once, Jack was glad he was gone. There was too much else he had to deal with to worry about Ethan as well.

The RRF had cordoned off the ISO building and had bought in the fire department and ambulances. The instant they'd confirmed Jack's friendly status when he burst out of the building, they'd rushed in with their medics and, bare moments later, had Harry out and in an ambulance. Ten minutes after that, they were speeding away, lights and sirens going. The next time Jack heard anything, between giving a quick rundown of events to the RRF CO and having the bullet graze in his side tended, Harry was in theatre, his condition critical. His worry was diverted by seeing Lieutenant Watson detained for questioning regarding her decision to hand Jack and Harry over to the terrorists, but it was a momentary distraction only.

It was midnight and everyone, including the hostages, the fake DSOs that were still alive, and Jack, had been transported to Duntroon. Jack had just finished a slightly more thorough recitation of it all to several government types—a general, a couple of senators, a quiet ASIO guy—when he got more information on Harry.

They gave him a few moments alone. Numb, Jack called Ethan through the implant. He didn't answer, so Jack left a message.

I know why you couldn't stay. That's okay, but I need to see you. Soon. Please. I need you.

Jack waited, almost as if Ethan would answer, but really needing a moment to say one final thing.

Harry didn't make it.

(JULY)

CHAPTER ONE

It was nearly a month before the funeral took place. There was the investigation into the events at the ISO HQ, review meetings with the military, endless *discussions* with various government officials and a debrief session with the prime minister, as well. When everyone and their fucking uncle were convinced everything that could have been done *had* been done, and done as well as it could have been under the circumstances, they finally released Harry McGill's body.

Jack, Lewis and McIntosh travelled to Auckland for the funeral. It was a huge affair. Harry had been loved and well respected. There was an array of different people: a vastly extended family; friends from school and uni; his old cricket and footy teams; and, nearly every cop in the city, a veritable army of blue dress uniforms. It didn't matter Harry hadn't been a cop for two years. Or that he'd moved to Australia for a job no one in the crowd knew about. That was just who Harry was . . . who Harry *had been*.

Jack had never met any of Harry's family but he'd heard enough to recognise them. His mother, a tiny, sweet woman with a smile for everyone; his father a quiet giant of a man, a steady foundation for everyone around him; his younger sister, Sally, devastated and clinging to her husband, the newborn niece Harry hadn't even met not in evidence.

"Jack," Harry's mother said when he went to pay his respects. He hadn't even had to introduce himself. "You're exactly how Harry described you." She took his hand in both of her small ones, firm but soothing.

"As are you, ma'am."

"You get to call me Libby," she said and pulled him down and kissed his cheek. Then Libby held his face and touched her forehead to his, holding them together for an impossibly long moment. Jack hadn't cried but he nearly did right then, looking into her clear brown eyes, so like Harry's. So much like Harry's when he'd stared up at Jack, life bleeding away and Jack couldn't do a goddamned thing to stop it from happening.

"I'm sorry," he whispered.

"No." A hard edge came into Libby's voice as she tightened her hold on him. "You don't get to blame yourself. They told me what you did for my boy. You were there with him. You did everything you could. They told me that, Jack." Libby's lips quivered, then firmed up and fiercely she said, "They told me you killed the man who hurt my son. Thank you." She kissed his forehead, then let him straighten, reclaiming her hold on his hand.

Jack had barely cared when the initial hearings had cleared him of any misconduct during the whole thing. But hearing Libby's words, feeling the honesty behind them, soothed the sharp edges in his chest.

"He was a good man," Jack managed, throat tight. "One of the best I've ever worked with."

Libby beamed. "Of course he was. Now tell me the rest."

"Rest?"

"Yes! He could be an annoying little shit, too. I don't think you wouldn't have noticed that."

Jack smiled for the first time in weeks. "Ah, yeah. He could be a pain the arse, and I'm pretty sure he wasn't half as funny as he thought he was. But I wouldn't have wanted to work with anyone else. Without him there . . . that day, we wouldn't have got all the hostages out alive. They . . . *We* owe him everything."

Libby's bottom lip trembled, but she shored it up and gave him a sweet smile. "Thank you for that."

He had to move on before she broke him down completely. Jack kissed her cheek, gently extracted his hand and faced Harry's father.

"Sorry we couldn't meet under better circumstances," Stan murmured after introducing himself. As Libby had done, Stan held Jack's hand in both of his, swallowing it whole. "Thank you for being there for our son when he needed you."

"He would have done no less for me. For anyone."

"Always knew my boy would be a hero." He reached up and touched the medal pinned over his heart, a bronze medallion on a red ribbon. A Bravery Medal awarded posthumously to Harry and presented to his family the week before.

Jack could only nod, suddenly feeling wrung out and exhausted. He had nothing but admiration for the McGills, standing strong together in the face of not only their own grief, but that of half of Auckland as well. Jack's family hadn't coped with the loss of his mother, fracturing under the pressure.

Before Stan let him go, he said, "We wanted you to know that Sally named our granddaughter Moana Harriet, to honour her uncle."

There were no words, so Jack just nodded again, mute with raw pain.

By the time Jack was back in Sydney, he'd successfully stuffed it all in the lowest drawer of the filing cabinet and proclaimed himself ready for work. McIntosh put him on two weeks leave. Non-negotiable. Enforced.

Four days into his exile, Jack had just emerged from the shower after his morning routine of beating the shit out of a kick-bag in the building's gym, when someone knocked on his door. Towel around his waist, he checked the screen by the door. A courier fidgeted on the other side, a slender envelope in one hand, his PDA in the other. Jack had undergone mandatory counselling after the ISO incident and he knew his alert level and reaction instincts were still heightened. Part of why he was currently at home. So, he didn't go for one of the guns he had hidden around his apartment and opened the door.

"Jack Reardon?" the courier asked hopefully.

"Yeah."

"Letter for you." He held out the slim cardboard envelope printed with the courier company logo. "And just a signature here." The PDA was presented.

Jack signed and took the envelope, wondering what the fuck it was. He closed the door without acknowledging the courier's parting, "Have a good day."

Whatever it was, it could wait until he was dressed and had something other than bile in his belly. He tossed the envelope on the kitchen counter and marched to his bedroom. Before he even got there, he turned on his heel and went back to the kitchen and stared at the yellow rectangle for a good minute, daring it to be important. Satisfied it couldn't be, he went and got dressed. Glaring at the fucking intrusion to his supposedly peaceful time off, Jack made lunch and went and sat in front of the telly. He was determinedly working his way through the remaining episodes of *Strike Back*, ignoring the niggling reminder he was supposed to watch it with Ethan. Ethan wasn't here, didn't *want* to be here, so screw him.

Even before the opening credits were finished, Jack was back in the kitchen, fists planted on either side of the envelope.

It was stupid. Fucking stupid. He knew it was from Ethan. Knew this was the communication he'd begged for over a month ago. Had it arrived back then, he would have opened it, greedy for whatever Ethan could give him. Even a week ago, he'd have savoured the contents, knowing Ethan had heard him. Not now, though. Not after the funeral. Not after having gone through that without knowing Ethan was close by.

His eyes had been opened. It had been foolish to believe they could have something normal. Or even close to normal. Coming to rely on Ethan for anything more than randomised visits was insanity. This was all Jack's fault for thinking otherwise.

No. To be fair, part of it *was* Ethan's fault. His visits hadn't been for work. They'd been for Jack. Ethan had expended a lot of effort and time on sneaking into the country just to see Jack. He'd installed a security system in Jack's apartment so he would feel safe. He had set up a precedent for Jack's expectations for something more than sex. More than unwanted backup. So, it wasn't entirely Jack's fault for thinking Ethan might actually care enough to be there for him.

Maybe the contents of the envelope would tell him why Ethan didn't.

Jack ripped it open and tipped it up. Several pieces of paper fell out. One was a plane ticket, leaving Sydney for Hanoi, Vietnam, the flight booked for the next day. Another was a receipt for a local Hanoi service to drive him to somewhere called Cao Bằng, where, a note in

Ethan's precise hand writing said, he would be *met*. By whom, there was no indication.

That was it. A fourteen-hour journey with no hint as to what was at the other end. He could guess, but guessing with Ethan was never a smart move. The only thing that kept him from outright believing it was all a trap was the initials at the bottom of the note.

P StC.

Unless that little confession Ethan had given him about his real name—Paul St. Clair—at the homestead in the desert was another lie, Jack took it as a sign this was legit. That this was personal, not professional.

The question now was, did he go? Why the sudden switch up in procedure? Ethan had proven he was willing to come back into the country after a scramble. It had been a month since Canberra, so surely he could sneak back in now, if he wanted.

Or maybe it wasn't just about wanting to see Jack, for whatever reason.

Each and every visit over the past six months had been Ethan coming to Jack. Ethan taking all the risk of sneaking into the country, of finding Jack and being wherever Jack was. Perhaps he'd decided it was time Jack went to him for once. Maybe that's what he meant when he said he hadn't been going to visit for a while.

Jack was packing before he'd even made the conscious decision to go. Even as he stared at a half-filled bag, he knew he *would* go. He needed to find out what the fuck was going on. Did Ethan still want whatever they had going? Or did he just want to break it off in person? Even if it was a goddamn trap of some sort, Jack had to go. Didn't mean he had to spring the bloody thing, though.

Leaving behind the ticket Ethan had sent, Jack jumped on the first flight available out of Sydney, setting down in Ho Chi Min City ten hours later. The connecting flight to Hanoi didn't leave until the following morning, so he got a cheap room in a hotel near the airport and made sure he wasn't being followed. Clean of pursuit, Jack spent the night organising alternative transport to Cao Bằng.

It all went smoothly and at one p.m. the following day, Jack was standing on a dirt-strip airfield nestled in a shallow valley in the middle of northern Vietnam surrounded by lush green and melting in humid, thirty-plus degree heat. Sydney in winter wasn't something he missed terribly, but when his t-shirt was soaked with sweat after ten minutes in Cao Bằng he wasn't sure about this place, either. Over the tops of the surrounding hills, bruise-dark clouds gathered on the eastern horizon, saturating the air with sticky warmth so it felt like he was all but swimming through it. Behind him, the small cargo plane he'd hopped a ride on was busily being unpacked by the two-man crew, stacking crates up on the grassy edge of the landing strip. No one was here to collect it, but considering the airstrip wasn't on any map Jack had seen, he suspected it was smuggled goods, so hadn't expected a big welcoming committee. Wasn't quite sure that finding absolutely *no one* was so great, either, though.

This was what he got for ignoring Ethan's planned itinerary, but at least he was here on his terms. Here but not *summoned*.

Snorting at his own delusion, Jack hefted his bag to his shoulder and started down the only road—or rather, the only narrow, barely there pair of wheel ruts. The signal his implant was picking up was weak, but it was enough to give him a GPS location. He was only ten or so klicks north-east of Cao Bằng city itself.

While in Hanoi that morning, Jack had got his hands on a HK P8, a modified USP, so it was a familiar weight at the base of his spine. The jungle here wasn't exactly like that of the Chota Nagpur plateau in India, but like it enough that Jack was wary of attack, from all types of native wildlife.

He'd stopped to take a drink from a bottle of water when he heard a car or truck coming toward him, from the direction in which he was going. Jack moved off the track and into the trees. Crouching, he drew the gun and watched, implant on to catch anything he might miss in the moment. A late 1960s or early 1970s era Jeep, complete with camouflage-pattern paintwork, barrelled into view not long later. It belted along, engine growling smoothly, big tyres digging into the narrow path of the rough track, ploughing down plants unfortunate enough to have taken root between the shallow wheel ruts. Over the engine, music blared, too loud and too fast in passing for Jack to make it out. It was definitely pop, though, a bright, flouncy rhythm full of synthesised sounds and high-pitched voices. Not the choice of any smuggler Jack had had the misfortune of crossing paths with.

The Jeep was gone before Jack got a good look at the driver, so he replayed the recording from the implant. The slowed down footage showed the driver was a kid, twelve or thirteen at most, of Vietnamese descent. Skinny arms barely reached the steering wheel, equally thin legs having equal trouble reaching the pedals. How he managed it, Jack couldn't see, but somehow the little shit was driving well enough to not crash at the ludicrous speed he was going.

Maybe this was how the smugglers operated here. Send in the most unlikely perp and blame the misjudgements of youth if he was caught. Though, even as he stepped back out onto the track, another idea popped into Jack's head, so silly it had a chance of actually being right.

Sure enough, barely ten minutes later, the Jeep was coming back, its arrival announced by the music and roaring engine. This time, Jack stayed visible. The Jeep came to a dusty, screeching halt beside him.

"You Mr. Reed?" Leaning across the bench seat, the kid peered at Jack through locks of black hair. He was about as skinny as one of Jack's legs, wearing cut-off jeans and a Real-Madrid t-shirt with the sleeves torn off.

Jaidev Reed had been Jack's cover identity with Valadian's group. Ethan had known right from the start it wasn't his real name, but he had clearly remembered the alias.

"And you are?" Jack asked, partly fascinated, mostly wary. On one hand, this was classic Ethan. On the other . . . well, Jack was always wary of the other hand.

"Call me Tom." The kid grinned ear to ear. His teeth were brilliantly white but crooked as all hell. He held out a hand. "It is a pleasure to meet you, Mr. Reed." His accent was thick, but his pronunciation precise, like he'd been schooled in these exact sentences.

"Likewise, Tom." Jack took his hand, Tom's thin fingers barely getting around Jack's much broader palm. "I suppose you're my ride, huh."

Tom nodded enthusiastically. "Mr. Saint sent me."

Mr. Saint was presumably Ethan, which meant that he had somehow discovered Jack's alternate travel plans. Typical.

Jack tossed his bag into the back of the Jeep and climbed in. "This beast is yours?"

"Bought and paid for," Tom announced proudly. "Mr. Saint help with engine, but all mine. I take you on tour, Mr. Reed! Competitive prices, just ask."

An entrepreneurial little shit. Jack grinned. "Where did Mr. Saint find you?"

"In the phonebook. Under local knowledge," Tom said in that singsong, rehearsed cadence. "Let's get this show on the road."

Tom wasn't quite as sublime as Ethan in his ridiculously expensive Aston Martin, but impressive nonetheless. Seat cranked all the way forward, several cushions under his butt so he could see more than the dash and blocks strapped to the pedals so he could reach them, the kid looked cool and confident. He even took a pair of aviator sunglasses from a pocket and put them on with a grin.

As he started the engine, he said, "You came in that thing? You're braver than I thought," and hit the accelerator.

Jack cackled as they rocketed away.

CHAPTER TWO

They skirted the edge of Cao Bằng city and kept to the forested surroundings following dirt roads which curled around hills, dipped into valleys and passed by terraced slopes, through a tiny village chasing goats and skinny dogs out of their way with blasts of the horn, then along a bend of the river, trees on one side, brown water on the other. Locals waved at Tom as they belted past, rooster tails of dirt and stones kicking up behind the Jeep.

Tom turned off the main track and into the trees, followed another dirt road, taking the narrow corridor at speed. He sang along to an eclectic mix of music, though his words never quite matched the singer's. Sometimes, he'd stop singing and prattle at Jack in a mix of Vietnamese, which Jack didn't know, and movie quotes, some of which Jack did know. Not that Jack really needed to understand what the kid was saying. Tom wasn't expecting a two-way conversation: it was talking just to be talking, probably how he expected a tour guide to be. As such, he pointed out presumably interesting spots of trees as he hurtled them along a road that rose up into the mountains.

They passed into true jungle between one curving incline and the next. Trees dripping in thick foliage and strangling vines leaned in so close Jack could touch them as they went past. The air cooled and grew even thicker with moisture. The caws and squawks of birds could just be made out over the sound of the engine and the music.

It was strange and beautiful and as crazy as anything Jack could have expected when Ethan was involved.

Then Tom barrelled over a peak in the road and slammed on the brake with both feet.

Thrown forward, Jack caught himself on the dash and when his brain stopped reverberating, he saw nothing but dark, boiling sky in front of them.

"Holy shit." Another couple of feet and they would have been flying off the bloody mountain and describing a nice arc into the valley far, far below them.

"Whoa," Tom said, eyes wide. "Game over, man!"

Inching back in the seat to keep the weight away from the drop, Jack asked, "Did we take a wrong turn?"

But all Tom said was, "Tour over, Mr. Reed. Out!"

"What?" Jack demanded. "This is it?"

Tom nodded. "Mr. Saint said be here. You here. Out!"

Christ. Did he trust Ethan enough to get out of the only vehicle he'd seen in this remote, wild place? Shit, even if this turned into one big joke or trap, Jack had some of the best survival training in the world. And there was a road right here he could follow back to civilisation.

Jack got out and fetched his bag from the back. He was barely clear when Tom had the Jeep screaming backwards down the mountain, using only the rear vision mirror as a guide. If anyone had ever been taught to drive by Ethan Blade, there he went.

Half an hour later, Jack wondered just how long he should wait. Or even if he was supposed to. Or if he was even in the right place. As cute as he'd found Tom, he had to wonder if the little shit had actually known where he was going.

Jack was studying the abrupt end to the road—a jagged edge where part of the mountainside had washed away at some point in the recent past—when Ethan finally appeared. He stepped up beside Jack, dark glasses following Jack's line of sight to the distant river in the valley. Jack waited, to see if Ethan would make the first move, but as the silence stretched out, he knew he would cave first, so he just gave in.

"Ethan." He kept his voice neutral. The hurt still prickled under his ribs, but the edge of his anger had been taken off by the long journey and young Tom's driving. For a traitorous moment, his body wanted to turn to Ethan, to touch him, hold him, bury his face in his hair and breathe as if he'd been under water these past four weeks.

Then he remembered Harry's funeral.

"Hello, Jack." Ethan's voice was rough with some emotion he kept tamped down. "I wasn't certain you would be here."

For once, Jack thought he might actually have the upper hand. He was the one who'd come all this way, the one who could threaten to leave if things went bad. But even as he thought it, Jack was disgusted with himself. This wasn't a competition. He wasn't here to make Ethan feel bad. He was here to find out why he'd been silent in the wake of Jack's need. To find out just what the fuck Ethan Blade wanted from him.

Jack sighed, hands shoved in the front pockets of his jeans. "I wasn't sure I'd be here, either."

After a long moment, Ethan said, "I'm glad that you are."

The only response Jack had was a sour grunt.

Ethan turned to him. "Jack—"

"No. Don't 'Jack' me." The bitter tone was a surprise to Jack as well as Ethan, but all Jack cared about was answers. He was going to get them. "Where the fuck did you go? You disappeared when I ne—" He'd said the words back then, in grief and pain, but now, angry and confused, they stuck in his throat. "Christ. You didn't have to leave."

"I did, Jack." The barely hidden emotion was gone, his tone low and steady.

"No, you didn't. Your part in the job was sanctioned. No one was going to arrest you."

Jack finally had the strength to face him and, thankfully, found he could resist the usual allure. It was like the first days in the desert, when Jack had been wary about Ethan's intentions toward him. When the admittedly hot body meant less than the fact he'd taken out a small army mostly on his own.

Right now, all Jack could focus on was the memory of Mrs. McGill's face, smiling through her grief, as she assured Jack he hadn't failed her son. How, in that moment, he'd wanted, *needed*, someone to lean on and the only person he'd wanted to lean on in a very long time was thousands of miles away, doing fuck all to help anyone but himself.

As if seeing it in Jack's eyes, Ethan took a small step backwards. "Jack, I don't think this is the right place for this conversation."

Gesturing at the wilderness all around them, Jack asked, "What? It's not *secure* enough for you?" He regretted the words as soon as they were out. Using Ethan's issues against him was something Jack had never wanted to do. He didn't even have the excuse of burning up with a fever this time. Yet, he couldn't take the words back. Couldn't say he was sorry, because Ethan spoke before he could.

"It would be, except for the fact that if we don't get going now, we'll be caught out in that storm." He nodded toward the low, dark clouds inching ever closer. A nearly opaque curtain of rain blocked the far side of the valley from view.

And didn't that make Jack feel like a dickhead. He'd been staring at the approaching rain all this time, not even seeing it through his inner turmoil.

"Will we make it in time?" A little rain never hurt anyone, but that wasn't a "little rain." It was the sort of rain that could wash out mountain roads.

"We should, if we go now."

Jack hefted his bag to his shoulder and grudgingly followed Ethan into the trees. A short distance in, two horses waited. They stood close together, heads hooked over each other's necks. Both looked over when Ethan approached, murmuring to them in a soft tone. The grey untangled itself from the roan and turned to greet Ethan, lipping at his hip pocket.

"More?" Ethan scratched the horse's forehead. "Do you know how much trouble I'll be in if you're fat and lazy when I leave?" Still, he produced a couple of sugar cubes from his pocket and let the horse snuffle them up. "Do you ride, Jack?"

"I can," he admitted. "At least it's a horse this time, not a bloody camel."

The corner of Ethan's lips quirked up. "And you get your own mount, as well. This," he said, untying the grey's reins and mounting in a single, smooth motion, "is Smith. And the roan is Jones." Some of his tension had vanished, though that was probably the effect of the animals. He stroked Smith's neck and smiled at the way it tossed its head, transferring that smile to Jack as if he'd forgotten the sharp tones of moments before.

What a waste of a good head of steam. One smile and Jack was crumbling from the inside out.

After a brief negotiation with Jones, Jack had his bag secured and mounted. Ethan and Smith moved out, Jack and Jones trailing after.

The light dimmed dramatically the deeper into the trees they went, and the buzz of insects increased. Birds chittered around them and a soft breeze shushed through the lush greenery, doing nothing to help ease the heavy humidity. The horses' hooves thumped mutely on the springy ground covering, the creak of leather tack muffled by the thickness of the air.

There was a sense of reverence amongst the dense foliage. An undeniable presence of something larger than Jack, something more profound than one man and his tiny thoughts. The concentration of so much life, like the weight of a warm, breathing shroud, wrapped all around him, compressed him until there was no room for anything other than existing. For the first time in weeks he wasn't chasing the same thought around and around in his head: *Harry's dead and I couldn't save him.*

Its absence, after so long of infecting Jack's waking and sleeping mind, left him a little aimless. His anger with Ethan was patchy at best, and now with his guilt fading, he found himself thinking clearly about the current situation.

Right at the start of this doomed affair, Jack had wondered what he would get out of it. Ethan got the opportunity to enjoy something with someone he trusted that had been denied him for so long. And it hadn't been a hardship on Jack's part to give him that. He'd jumped head first into the chance to keep Ethan around in any capacity he could. Great sex made brilliant because the other man was someone he actually liked spending time with. It wasn't a mostly anonymous hook up with a guy picked up in a bar.

The problem was Jack had never thought—not allowed himself to think—that Ethan Blade would become an indelible part of his life. He'd known he wanted more than sex with Ethan for several months, but the absolute *need* for him had crystallised in that interview room at Duntroon, when they told him Harry hadn't made it. Before he'd even completely understood what that meant, he'd been looking for Ethan. Reaching for him.

And it had taken over four weeks for Ethan to reach back.

Encapsulated in the close environment of the jungle, the approach of the storm was muted. A very distant, muffled rumble of thunder every now and then, what might have been the drumming of heavy rain when the wind gusted enough to break through the trees. It got darker, even though Jack's implant informed him it was barely three p.m. So dark Ethan removed his glasses, tucking them into the front of his shirt.

Not long later, they broke out of the jungle into an open area. It wasn't much brighter out of the trees, the light grey and the air dense and warm with the coming weather.

They'd come around the mountain so that the plateau they emerged onto was facing east and unlike the other clearings they'd passed through, this one was manicured to a golf-course quality. There was even what appeared to be a vegetable patch, surrounded by a wood and chicken-wire fence under a shade cloth. Beyond that was a small paddock attached to a stable made of big bricks that had the slightly asymmetrical look of handmade about them, but the structure was finely crafted.

Hopefully, they wouldn't be bunking in the stable this time, because the dark building looming at the edge of the plateau was surely a house. It was made of the same expertly crude bricks as the stable and two storeys high with a sloping roof, lower on the side closest to Jack. It had a solid exterior with a few narrow windows covered in ornate grating cemented right into the bricks. The only door Jack could see was heavy, steel-reinforced and barely wide enough for him to pass through without scraping his shoulders.

Fortified was the word that jumped out at Jack. No one was breaking in there without some heavy assault equipment. Maybe this was one of Ethan's lairs.

Ethan directed them through stabling the animals. As he brushed Jones down, Jack found an odd calm in the long, sweeping strokes across the beast's back and sides. Jones almost purred at the attention.

When Jack looked up from his work, Ethan was leaning on the door to the stall, smiling at him like there was no argument hovering over them like a Sword of Damocles. Somehow, the distance between them vanished and Jack pressed against Ethan, palms dragging down the firm shapes of his arms. They didn't embrace, didn't hold hands, just leaned into each other and rested. Ethan tucked his head into Jack's shoulder, making small, contented sounds that settled into

Jack's chest like a smouldering coal, sending delicious licks of warmth lower, as well.

Unless Jack had lost all ability to read Ethan—or never had it in the first place—this was a good sign. Whatever had kept Ethan distant and silent for the past month wasn't due to a lack of *want* for Jack. The realisation settled the lingering wariness in Jack's heart. Whatever else was going on, they'd work through it, as they had before. He just had to remind Ethan, and himself, that questions still needed to be asked and answered.

"This doesn't mean we're okay," he whispered into Ethan's hair.

Shivering, Ethan replied, as quietly, "I know."

Neither of them moved.

God. Jack missed this. Not the physicality, though he had missed that too. It was more the *presence* of Ethan, the simple fact of him being there. They didn't have to be touching, didn't even need to be talking, but just knowing he was there if Jack decided he needed those things had been comforting.

Which was why Ethan's silence had hurt so much.

E than moved first, lifting his head to angle his sunglasses at Jack's face. "We should get inside before the rain reaches the plateau."

Jack grunted agreement and they peeled apart. Ethan picked up Jack's bag and walked out. Giving himself a self-indulgent ten seconds to let Ethan's jeans-clad arse hold his attention, Jack closed the stall gate and followed him.

Ethan was right about the rain. The sky was darker and lower, the air heavier, and the sound of the approaching rain pummelling the jungle was impressively loud. Jack huddled under the eaves on the house while Ethan unlocked the door. When the sky finally succumbed to the pressure, a Biblical scale torrent of water fell in big, fat drops that hit Jack's back like mini grenades.

The door opened and they entered into a dim space that felt vast. Jack peered into the shadows, making out the vague shapes of furniture in an open-plan room that seemed to span the entire length of the house. Ethan locked the door and turned on the lights.

"Holy shit," Jack whispered.

"Take a look around. I'll stow your gear and get some drinks. Is beer all right?"

Captivated by the sight before him, Jack muttered, "Sure."

While Ethan walked away, Jack gaped. The room did indeed take up the entire width and breadth of the house, the walls behind him and at either end were the undressed bricks of the outer façade, a dark, greyish-brown shade in the glow of the lights. Canvases of landscapes crafted with rough, broad strokes that nevertheless effortlessly portrayed beaches, forests and deserts decorated the three walls. The fourth wall, in front of Jack, was an unadorned dull grey.

A large fireplace was embedded in the wall to Jack's right, surrounded by a herd of plush leather couches, wingback chairs and coffee tables. The floor, bare boards polished to a high sheen, was covered in several large, thick rugs. There was an open space of bare floor boards between a baby grand and a dining table stained a deep, dark red, big enough to seat eight in comfort. At the other end of the open-plan was a generously sized kitchen. All surfaces were glossy granite with flecks of quartz, the cabinets the same wood as the dining table, the appliances stainless steel with a hammered finish.

Beside the kitchen was a cosy nook that could best be described as a library. Bookshelves lined the wall and there were two ridiculously large, comfy looking couches facing each other, a coffee table in between them.

Between kitchen and library was a staircase Ethan was currently descending. It had no railings but was wide enough to give an illusion of safety. It rose up to a loft that covered a third of the length of the house, hanging under a ceiling of exposed beams. Like the staircase, it had no railings around it. From his angle, Jack couldn't see anything up there, but judging by the lack of his bag over Ethan's shoulder, he guessed bedroom and bathroom.

"Do you like it?" Ethan asked, going into the kitchen.

Jack forced a nonchalant shrug. "A safety officer's nightmare, but it's got a bit of style."

"Hmm, just a bit, yes. How about now?" He picked up a remote on the kitchen counter and pressed a button.

With a soft hum, the plain wall on the far side of the house began to move upwards. Not a wall but a series of roller-shields that retracted to expose a long, floor-to-ceiling window.

Jack strode across the room to the window. There was a balcony, unsurprisingly without a railing, but big enough to host a dozen people without fear of falling off. Currently, it was home to a pair of well-padded deckchairs and a glass-topped table between them, protected by a waterproof sail. The light outside was dimmer than that inside, but even through the shifting curtains of rain, he could vaguely make out the view. The river valley Tom had driven them through stretched out far below, more mountains in the far distance. Without the rain and cloud cover, the sight would be glorious. Even with it,

Jack was entranced. He hadn't realised just how high they'd come. He felt like he could have stood on the edge of the balcony and touched the clouds.

"We're completely alone," he said wonderingly.

"This is why I wanted you here," Ethan said softly as he came up beside him. "There's no one else on this mountain with us. No Office, no jobs, no one but each other. So we can sort things out."

"What about Tom?"

"He won't come back until the end of the week when he brings supplies." Ethan smiled fondly. "I'm glad he got to practice his tour on you."

The pride in Ethan's tone unsettled Jack's belly. It wasn't exactly jealousy but the thought of Ethan spending time with the kid sparked his anger.

Turning away from the view, Jack leaned a shoulder against the glass and crossed his arms. "He's one of yours, I'm guessing."

"One my what?"

"I don't know. Protégé? You taught him to drive."

"Not so much *to* drive, but rather refined his existing knowledge."

"And you did up his Jeep for him."

The tone of Jack's voice finally had an effect on Ethan. Shoulders stiffening, he turned away and headed back to the kitchen. "Was I not supposed to help a young man trying to better his lot in life, Jack? Or are we back to you believing I'm nothing more than a cold-hearted monster?"

After a moment, Jack followed him. He was ready for a fight but didn't particularly want to start it off by shouting across a big room to be heard over the solid drumming on the roof. The shouting could be worked up to.

"Maybe." Jack kept his voice even. "What else am I supposed to think? You said you cared for me, yet when I needed you, you couldn't even be bothered getting in touch. Instead, you pissed off, like you always do. How do you expect me to feel knowing you were here all this time, messing around with an old car? Though it *is* nice to finally know just where on your scale of importance I actually fit."

Ethan didn't answer, just went about filling a kettle and setting it on the stove top. From the freezer he took a frosted glass and a beer from the fridge. Pouring it expertly, he slid the drink across to Jack.

"If you honestly believe that, Jack, then I'm surprised you're here."

Just because he was right didn't mean Jack had to agree. He took a sip of beer, instead. Not a brand he was familiar with, it went down well enough all the same and the glass was half empty when he set it down. The cold weight in his belly anchored him in place and he pulled out a barstool and sat.

"Can you just tell me something," he said into the silence.

"What would you like to know?"

Everything, but Jack said, "Something true."

Ethan took a deep breath, held it, then let it out in a long sigh. "I haven't been here the entire time. I arrived two days ago."

"And you know Tom from . . .?"

"Previous stays. This isn't one of my places but I do feel secure here. Before the road was washed out last month, Tom used to bring supplies up to the house. That's when I helped him with his Jeep."

Jack nodded, swallowed some more beer, then said, "And when you left Canberra, you went . . .?"

Ethan's patient expression lasted until the kettle whistled and he turned to tend it. "Initially, to several other places."

"Ethan." He put some warning in the name.

"Plausible deniability, Jack," Ethan replied with the same tone. Quickly assembling his tea, he turned back and set a teapot on the countertop to steep. "Eventually, I landed in Kuala Lumpur. I have a safe place there and . . . and it wasn't so far from you."

Unable to look at the dark planes of his glasses, Jack focused on tracing random lines through the condensation on his glass. "Far enough. Especially when you could have stayed."

"Jack, you know . . ." Another deep breath. "You know I trust you, but the Office . . ." Jack looked up to see Ethan shaking his head in quiet but firm denial.

"Okay." Jack actually agreed with that one. "You could have called, though."

Rocking the teapot gently, Ethan murmured, "I could have. I wanted to."

Christ. Pulling hens teeth would be easier. "But?"

Ethan poured his tea and took a sip, setting the cup down with a gentle click of ceramic on stone. "Partly, I didn't know what to say.

I have no experience in offering such comfort. I knew you were hurting and I wanted to be there, but I didn't, and *don't*, know how to be what you needed." He picked up his tea and took several gulps.

Swallowing the urge to do a few incredibly stupid things, Jack chased it with most of the rest of his beer. He still needed answers. "And the other part?" he prompted.

To which Ethan replied by topping up his tea and taking a series of determined sips.

Jack waited him out. Normally, Ethan was the one with the endless patience, but this time Jack felt like the calm, rational one. Ethan, however, all but shouted his frustration by fastidiously aligning the teapot so it was perpendicular to the edge of the counter. By turning his cup three times clockwise before taking another drink. When he reached across to move Jack's glass to make the third point of an equilateral triangle, he finally seemed to realise what he was doing and, leaving the glass where it was, curled his hands into fists and pressed them into the countertop.

"The other part was," he eventually continued, "that I wished to know if you really needed me, or if I was just convenient."

Jack grimaced. "You, Ethan Blade, are anything but convenient."

"Poor choice of words."

"Clearly." The light was dim enough, so Jack leaned over and removed Ethan's glasses. "Just spit it out."

Blinking in, what was for him, the sudden brightness, Ethan nodded. "I've been coming to you for the past six months, and that was my choice. I have more freedom of movement than you do."

Jack snorted.

"*Relatively*," Ethan amended wryly. "I know I make it impossible for you to find me if I don't wish to be found."

"That's some high opinion you've got of yourself," Jack grumbled.

Eyebrow arching over one wide, white eye, Ethan merely said, "I never expected you to travel to me, but that didn't stop me from wondering all the same if you would actually do it given the chance. And the previous couple of visits didn't exactly prove I meant a great deal to you."

Jack sat back on the stool, stomach tightening in surprise. "How the hell did you get that idea?" The last several visits were the ones where Jack had started to admit just how *much* Ethan had come to mean in his life. The fact Ethan thought otherwise kicked him in the guts. "Is that why you said you weren't going to come back?"

Shoulders slumped, Ethan nodded.

"Christ." The anger he'd thought gone for good back with a vengeance. "Explain this to me. Tell me exactly how I don't care about you. Show me how little you actually mean to me, please, because I'm having a fuck load of trouble picturing it. No wait, let me try. Um, was it because I went to the Gold Coast with *you*, so *you* could do something *you* really wanted to do but that I had no real interest in? Was that it?"

"Yes, Jack, it was. Driving is the one other passion I have, and I wanted to share it with you, and you kept talking about leaving to go look at other men." Ethan's tone was about as cold as his white eyes. Why Jack had thought taking off his glasses would make anything better was beyond him.

"I didn't, though," Jack ground out.

"You took the policeman's number."

Guilt made Jack's words sharper. "You let Brendon touch you."

Ethan calmly picked up the teapot and his cup and turned away, going to the sink.

Jack was suddenly transported back to the Great Sandy Desert, when he was learning all about Ethan's quirks. When he'd pushed and pushed just to get something other than an exquisitely controlled response. It had worked then, and he'd survived.

"Did you ever fuck him? Or maybe Vicky?"

The mixer tap was snapped on a bit harder than necessary. "I told you then, no, to both."

"And I told *you*, that the policeman was nothing. Harmless flirting, on his part. I didn't encourage it. Just like I told you there had been no one else for ages before that."

"Actually, you didn't tell me that then, Jack." Ethan washed the teapot, movements precise and snappy. "You waited until you were delirious with fever to trot that one out."

"And that makes it any less true?"

"It does lend it a certain incredulity. You aren't exactly in control when you're sick, Jack. You tend to say, and do, inappropriate things."

"Holy fucking shit. I can't believe you're holding the *flu* against me."

"I'm not holding that against you, Jack. It wasn't your fault you got sick, just as you can't be blamed for what you do or say while compromised. It did, however, open my eyes to certain aspects I'd previously missed."

Jack gaped at him. "Really? What sort of *certain aspects*?" He exaggerated a British accent on the last words.

Clean pot and cup were set to drain on the sink and, drying his hands on a small towel, Ethan faced Jack. "Perhaps this isn't the time to discuss it. You've been travelling most of the—"

"Fuck that. We're talking now. I think we're actually getting somewhere."

Ethan quirked another eyebrow at him, lips pressed into a thin line.

"Seriously. I mean I don't remember much from that visit, but I do know I apologised for a lot of shit I'm not even sure I did, so fill me in. What the fuck did I do that hurt you so bad?"

Shaking his head, Ethan walked out of the kitchen. "Forget I mentioned it. It was stupid, anyway."

"Stupid or not, it meant something to you." Jack slid off the stool and followed him to the middle of the open space between dining table and piano. "Just fucking tell me what I did." Too late, he wondered if Ethan had picked this spot so he wouldn't break anything when he took Jack down.

"It's not what you did, Jack, but what you didn't do."

One of the clear memories Jack had of that time sprang out at him. Something he hadn't been able to do, even after pretty much promising he would. Heat flooded his neck and cheeks. "Is this about the blowjob?"

Ethan frowned. "Pardon?"

"You know, when I got you all primed, but couldn't . . . deliver."

The pound of the rain was the only noise for a very long time.

"No, Jack," he said, barely audible over the rain. "That wasn't it."

Not exactly feeling the relief, because what the fuck else had there been, Jack asked, "What then?"

Ethan sighed. "You tend to talk, a *lot*, when you're very sick. You carry out these one-sided conversations with people who aren't there."

"Yeah, I do the same when waking up from anaesthetic." Jack ran a hand over his face in resignation. "I said something, didn't I?"

"No, as I said, it was something you didn't do. In your ramblings, you mentioned everyone who was important in your life. Your father and sister, your directors at work. Hamish and Ian, whom, from context, I presume were past boyfriends." With a sad smile, he added, "And Harry."

Christ. Jack got it now. About to open his mouth to defend himself, he stopped when Ethan's expression changed to a slightly puzzled frown.

"You even mentioned Scott and Stonebridge from *Strike Back*, but that was different from the others."

"I should fucking hope so." Jack felt like he was fifteen and Meera had found links to gay porn on his computer. "You're pissed that I didn't talk about you."

Cheeks pinking up as they did when forced to talk about sex, Ethan ducked his head. "I told you it was stupid."

"Yeah, well you did say that." Jack wasn't sure what to make of it. He could sort of see why it would have twisted Ethan up in knots, but at the same time, couldn't. It felt a little bit . . . silly. Juvenile, even. But given the fact this was Ethan's first attempt at a relationship outside of his job, and with the preceding slights from the Gold Coast trip, perhaps it wasn't so unbelievable. In that context, everything else became clearer as well.

"So, this is what you do to find out for sure?" Jack gestured at the house around them. "Let me know where you are and see if I come running?"

"When the ticket I sent you wasn't used, I believed you weren't coming."

"Then why send Tom to pick me up?"

"A last desperate grab at—oh!"

Jack had closed the distance between them and, arms around his waist, pulled Ethan to his chest with a bit more force than necessary. He didn't let go or apologise, however, just held on until, after a startled half minute, Ethan embraced him back.

CHAPTER FOUR

As in the stable, they remained like that for a long time. Not moving, but at least holding each other this time. Jack could feel Ethan's heart beating a mile a minute, much as his own was. Yet simply having Ethan so close eased Jack's heart back into a normal rhythm. Ethan's followed suit.

"Crazy bastard," Jack whispered.

Ethan huffed. "Half right, Jack."

"Really?"

Arms tightening for a moment, Ethan said, "If I'm crazy it's because you drove me to it."

Jack chuckled and, reluctantly, pulled back enough to look into Ethan's unfathomable eyes. "You have to stop doing this."

"Doing what?"

"Testing me."

"I don't—"

Stopping the protest with a finger against Ethan's lips, Jack said, "You *do*. You did it in the desert, and at the Office. And again, now. The desert I can understand, but the others? You have to start trusting me."

"I do—"

"If you're unsure of something, or just want to know something, then *ask*. If I lie to you, *then* concoct one of your elaborate scenarios to find out the truth."

Under his pressing finger, Ethan smiled.

"Is that agreement?"

Ethan nodded.

"Good. I'm holding you to it." Jack dragged his finger over the lovely shape of Ethan's lips, then along his jaw to his hairline. Running his fingers through Ethan's hair, Jack was relieved when Ethan simultaneously pushed into the touch and melted against him. "Jesus, Ethan, you couldn't have picked a worse time for your little test."

"I don't exactly have a good track record for straight thinking where you're concerned." He cupped Jack's face in both hands and drew him close enough to kiss. Instead, he whispered, "I am truly sorry about Harry. I know he was a good soldier and an even better man, because you wouldn't have picked him otherwise."

Throat closing up, Jack shook his head in the confines of Ethan's firm hold. "I did pick him. I put him in the position to get killed."

"It was the risk *he* took, Jack. Harry knew the job and he was there with you, all the way."

He'd heard it so many times over the past four weeks, but something about the accent, the low timbre, the touch, was different, but not quite enough.

"I know, but I can't help thinking I should have left him with the bomb. Taken you to confront Porsche and Stark. Maybe he wouldn't have died."

One of Ethan's hands slipped to the back of his neck and gripped him gently. "Jack, you can't get caught up second guessing yourself. You made the best decision you could in the circumstances. There was no plan in the world that would have prevented pure happenstance. It was simply a bad situation, no matter how you look at it." He forced Jack to look into his eyes. His expressionless, flat eyes. "It could have just as easily been me, Jack."

Jack shook his head mutely.

"Yes, it could have." Ethan's fingers tightened on Jack's skin as he frowned. His next words were husky with pain. "It could have been you." He kissed Jack's jaw, his temple, his forehead, back to his jaw. Cheek to cheek, he murmured soft, soothing words into Jack's ear.

Jack collapsed around him, all of the fragile scaffolding holding him up since Harry's death broken away. He clung to Ethan, listened desperately not to the words, but the tone, the meaning, the intent—the support. Somewhere in the mix, he cried.

An uncertain amount of time later, Jack realised they were moving. Swaying gently, occasionally shuffling in a small circle. It was quiet but for the now placid drumming of the rain on the roof. Ethan had stopped talking and just held him, guiding their aimless steps. Not dancing. Just moving together.

"This," Jack whispered.

"Hmm?" Ethan sounded almost sleepy.

"This is what you do to comfort me. This is what I need from you."

After a long silence where they made another slow circle, Ethan said, "Oh. Well, this I can do."

Jack chuckled, surprising himself. "Good to know."

As much he would have liked to keep doing what they were doing, Jack felt a little self-conscious now he'd acknowledged it. His extraction wasn't as smooth as he would have liked but Ethan let him put a bit of space between them, though he kept his hand on the side of Jack's neck, thumb stroking his jaw.

"I *am* sorry for leaving you, Jack," he said. "And for Harry."

"Thanks. I think, given a chance, he would have liked you."

Ethan shook his head firmly. "No, he wouldn't have."

Jack considered it for a moment, then smiled. "Yeah, he wouldn't have."

They stood for a moment longer, gazes locked, then Jack's stomach rumbled.

Ethan chuckled. "It's a trifle early, but I'll get dinner going if you want to wash up." He pointed out a door all but hidden behind a big walk-in pantry.

Through the door, Jack found a tiny room with a toilet and sink. He peed, washed his hands and splashed a bit of cool water on his face. Wiping away the dried tears, Jack eyed himself in the small mirror. He looked tired. Bloodshot eyes, shoulders slumped, hair carelessly rumpled. Tired but, for the first time in weeks, content. Grief and guilt still curled through his guts, and would for a long time yet, but at least the sharp edges had been dulled.

Despite his constant assurances he wasn't a good cook Ethan turned out a very edible pan-seared barramundi and noodle salad for dinner. After Jack did the dishes, they settled onto a couch that faced the huge window and killed a bottle of sav blanc while watching the rain. In bare words, Jack told Ethan about the inquest after the ISO job.

"I don't know exactly what he said, but Tan covered your part in it." Jack swirled the last couple of mouthfuls of wine around his glass. "After that, they stopped bugging me about it, thankfully."

"Hmm, I guess Director Tan has his uses."

"Yeah. Hate to admit it, but I was grateful. I was starting to run out of excuses for why you would help us."

Ethan sipped at his wine, then said, "You could have said an anonymous third party had paid me to do it."

Letting his head drop back, Jack stared at the exposed rafters. "I know you think we're as hopeless as toddlers in a dark room, but we can and do find out stuff other people wish to keep secret. If I'd said you'd been hired on by someone else, they would have discovered it wasn't true." With a pained grimaced, he clarified with, "Eventually."

"Maybe, maybe not," Ethan said, smirk evident in his tone if not on his face.

"Really? Um, okay. Lichtenstein."

Ethan snorted. "I wasn't even trying for subtly."

Jack put a mark on his imaginary scoreboard. "Just between us, why did she buy a ticket on you?" What he really wanted to know was what Ethan's note—*This is what revenge looks like – EB13*—meant, but that felt like pushing it. An instinct proved correct with Ethan's answer.

"An old slight that means nothing now," Ethan said, softly but with a finality about it.

Curiosity not even mildly appeased, Jack knew not to pursue it. Instead, he steered the conversation to something safe.

"Any new cars in the harem?"

"Harem?"

"Look me in the eyes and tell me it's not a harem," Jack challenged mockingly.

Which Ethan couldn't without laughing and things just devolved from that point on. Fifteen minutes after that, Jack finally had Ethan where he wanted him. On his back on the couch, shirt half unbuttoned and gasping as Jack hit all his sensitive spots between neck and navel.

"Jack." Ethan fisted his hand in Jack's hair and hauled his head up. "Wait, please."

"Yeah, okay." Jack took a moment to catch his breath. "We should take this to bed."

"Hmm, yes, but perhaps first, a shower. You smell of aeroplane and horse."

Levering himself up, Jack took a sniff of his own armpit. "True. Join me? You're no bouquet either."

Ethan chuckled. "You go on up, Jack. I'll join you once I've locked up down here."

"Really?" Jack looked around as he stood. "What's left to lock?" There was precisely one door into and out of the fortress, and Ethan had locked it when they first arrived.

A socked foot landed on Jack's hip and pushed him away. "Go wash. I'll be along shortly."

"Fine. Just remember where we left off."

Ethan's throaty "I will" followed him as he trotted up the stairs.

The loft was nothing surprising, given the rest of the house. A big bed with a carved mahogany headboard and hand-painted silk spread. It sat in the centre of the space but there was enough room left to have a pair of plush chairs by the window, a wardrobe against the brick wall and a fairly generous bathroom with a tub/shower combo, toilet and freestanding basin. There was another of the landscapes on the wall behind the bed, a beach at sunset, judging by the use of flaming orange, glowing red, and golden yellow.

Jack found his gear stowed in the wardrobe and after going through it for a minute, he realised he didn't need any of it. Stripping right there, he went into the bathroom and stepped into the shower. He faffed around for a while, waiting for Ethan to join him and wanting to keep the fun stuff for then, but eventually he started washing. When that was done, he lingered under the warm water, still waiting. Finally, he turned off the water and got out. Towel wrapped around his waist, he wandered out and peered over the edge of the loft.

Contrary to his promise to be along shortly, Ethan stood at the window, staring out into the dark night. Arms crossed, he was perfectly still. Jack could sympathise. They'd talked through some pretty heavy stuff and even Jack was feeling a bit uppity. Jack's method of dealing was physical—punching or sex. Ethan's was to think and think and if he couldn't see an escape route, then he'd make one. As Jack watched, Ethan seemed to come to a conclusion. Slowly, he turned and walked to the kitchen, picked up the remote and, with a soft clank and whir, the shield gently dropped over the window. Taking that as a good sign, Jack dropped the towel and draped himself decoratively across the bed.

When he woke up, his implant informed him it was 0452 the next morning. The wine and travel had taken its toll and he'd slept deeply, feeling refreshed as he stretched. Under a cotton sheet, his feet encountered solid muscle and sparse, curling hairs; Ethan's calf, ending in his socked foot, lying close to Jack's legs.

The house was dark. The sort of dark that could only be found in rural areas, where light pollution wasn't a thing and the sun hadn't yet risen. So, Jack explored by touch, finding Ethan properly asleep and unresponsive to his touches.

Jack pressed his face into Ethan's shoulder. He'd showered the night before, as well, no longer smelling of animal but clean and warm skin. Jack breathed in deep, filling his senses. After a long time during which Ethan didn't move, Jack kissed his collarbone then rolled away. As much as it might be nice to wake Ethan up with a blowjob, Jack decided against it. Ethan had avoided sex the night before, so it wouldn't be right to surprise it on him now.

Working by feel and memory, Jack got out of the bed and found his gear in the wardrobe. He was used to dressing in the dark from years of surprise night drills in the army. In shorts and shirt, with a tiny torch he packed for just these sorts of situations, he went downstairs. The torch's narrow but bright beam guided him to the kitchen and the small coffee machine he'd spied the evening before. It was fresh out of the box, the instruction manual on the counter beside it, along with a sampler of different flavoured pods. While the least-offensive-flavoured pod was chuffing away in the machine, Jack studied the remote Ethan had used to open and close the window shield. After a second's hesitation, he hit the button labelled 'door'. At the far end of the house, a narrow section of the shield retracted upward. Coffee mug in hand, Jack went over and found a door cut into the glass. It must have unlocked when the shield went up because Jack could push right through.

The air outside was crisp and cool, carrying a hint of moisture from the wet night that promised to turn into uncomfortable humidity when the sun got to blazing. A faint glow on the eastern horizon heralded dawn and Jack settled onto one of the deckchairs to watch. It was stupidly relaxing, lying back on the soft cushions, sipping a smooth blend and watching the world slowly resolve itself out of the shadows. First in shades of grey, then in slow revelations of green, brown and blue. An invisible hand painted broad strokes of pink, purple and gold on the horizon like one of the paintings inside. There were no sounds other than the gentle sway of the leaves, the first whistles and caws of birds and the fading chatter of night's insects. No human voices, no traffic, no dogs barking. It was breathtaking and peaceful, and the very last measure of tension seeped out of Jack and vanished into the cool air.

"Good morning, Jack," Ethan said softly.

Jack twisted his neck enough to watch Ethan approach. He carried a cup of steaming tea and wore only a pair of loose, grey pants, his sunglasses hooked over the elastic waistband. His hair was still sleep tousled, inviting fingers to run through the disarrayed locks.

Unable to help a sappy smile, Jack managed a distracted, "Hey."

Ethan sat on the other chair. "I trust you slept well."

"Incredibly. Sorry."

"Whatever for?"

"For falling asleep before you got to bed." Jack eyed him for a response, hoping to find out why Ethan hadn't wanted to fuck the night before.

"It's perfectly fine." Ethan put down his cup and stretched, back arching up off the deckchair, legs flexing. The soft touch of dawn's light slid over his toned abdomen, catching in the dips, gilding the planes. "You needed the sleep, Jack."

Jack's dick awoke with a spasm of appreciation. "Apparently." He took a slurp of coffee to give himself an excuse to swallow.

"Is the coffee satisfactory?" His hips wiggled, searching for a more comfortable position.

"Coffee's good." It could have been mud, for all that he tasted it.

Ethan made an appreciative sound. Whether it was for Jack's response or because he was smoothing down the material of his pants to the point of outlining his semi-hard dick was a mystery. Whatever had held Ethan back last night didn't seem to be a problem now.

"I'm pleased," Ethan said. "I worry because I'm not a coffee aficionado and as such I'm never quite sure—"

"The coffee's good," Jack interrupted, tone as firm as his dick was getting. "I was in the army for nine years. You don't have to worry about offending my coffee tastes, trust me."

Ethan looked over, eyes wide. His innocent expression was, however, belied by the way his hand rubbed over his lower abs, just above the waistband of his pants.

"Jesus, Ethan." Jack stood and stepped around the small table between them. "Didn't we talk about this before? If you want to fuck, just say so. Legs up."

"Jack, I—"

"No. Do you, or don't you?"

CHAPTER FIVE

After a silent moment, Ethan lifted his legs off the deckchair. With a thankful moan, Jack straddled the chair facing Ethan and sat. He scooted up close, until their groins were almost touching, then lowered Ethan's legs on either side of his hips. Dragging his hands up the cotton covered thighs, Jack leaned forward and nuzzled into Ethan's neck.

"You had me worried," he said against the warm, soft skin.

Legs wrapping around Jack's waist, hands sliding over his shoulders, Ethan said, "I did?"

"Yeah. When you didn't join me in the shower and waited until I'd fallen asleep before coming to bed." Jack kissed a fervent line down one side of Ethan's neck, across his clavicles and up the other side.

Ethan's fingers pressed into Jack's scalp. "I didn't mean to upset you, Jack. I just . . . ngh . . . just wanted . . . to talk . . . to you about . . ." He trailed off into a series of nonsensical sounds that arrowed straight into Jack's gut.

Dizzy with need, Jack chased the idea of Ethan wanting to talk about . . . something . . . for a brief moment only, because with a determined grunt, Ethan shifted forward, bringing his arse right into Jack's lap.

"Jack," Ethan moaned, then attacked him.

He'd missed this. The way Ethan's lips and tongue and teeth could set his skin afire with the barest of effort. The soft noises he made as he tasted and touched. His fingers curling through Jack's hair, positioning his head so he could kiss the sensitive flesh under Jack's jaw. The rock of his hips against Jack's, the coil and stretch of his thighs as he moved over him.

God. The things this man caused to happen in Jack's chest were unbelievable. Burning, aching, tightness, pressure. Coursing down into his guts, into his balls and straining dick. The sensations lit him on fire. It was all too much and not enough.

Jack wrapped his arms around Ethan and lifted them both up. Ethan gasped, his holds with hands and legs tightening.

"Jack?"

"Grab the cushion off the chair," Jack commanded.

One arm locked around Jack's shoulders, Ethan leaned back and unhooked the long cushion from the deckchair and between them, they got it off and onto the polished timber of the deck itself. The moment it was down, Jack sank into a crouch, thighs burning but negligible when compared to the aching need spearing his chest. Lowering Ethan to his back on the cushion and coming down on top of him, it was all Jack could do to keep from saying silly, dangerous things. He distracted himself by dragging his hips back and forth over Ethan's, their solid dicks clashing and rubbing through layers of material that both enhanced and frustrated. Ethan clenched his fingers into Jack's hair, head dropping back as he moaned long and loud, the sound as primal and natural as the wilderness around them.

Propped up on an elbow, Jack skimmed his other hand down Ethan's side, tracing his ribs, the jut of his exposed hip bone, across his shivering abdominals, up to his pecs to tease his nipples. Jack was caught by the contrast between their skin. The stark delineation of his darker tone against Ethan's paleness, even as it flushed hotly with blood in the wake of Jack's hand. It was nearly enough to make him blow then and there, but when Ethan put his own hand over Jack's, sliding his fingers between Jack's—brown, white, brown, white, brown, white—the pressure moved from his dick to his chest.

Then they curled their fingers down together, unconsciously sharing the same desire for closeness, for unity, and Jack's chest grenade went off. It didn't scare him this time. Didn't start an internal battle between running away and making the one gesture he hadn't made in so many years. This time he just basked in the glow, revelled in the heat spreading through his body, smiled at how it pulled him closer to Ethan.

While Jack licked a delicious path around and over Ethan's pecs, Ethan scrabbled at his shirt, pulling it up so he could get his hands on Jack's skin.

"I could take it off," Jack offered.

"You could." Ethan arched under him, pushing the bared skin of their bellies together. "Or you could keep talking about it and wasting time."

Jack snorted and sat back on his heels. "Got somewhere else to be, huh?"

Sitting up, Ethan pulled and pushed until Jack's shirt was off. "I may have other things planned." Once that was done, he fell back and lifted his legs up, knees slightly bent. "Get me naked, Jack."

"Fuck, yeah."

Ethan laughed at Jack's hasty, clumsy removal of his pants, laughed harder when Jack accidentally rolled off their improvised bed to the deck while escaping his shorts.

"You bring the gear?" Jack ignored Ethan's chuckles as he climbed back on.

Amusement dying, Ethan stilled in the act of wrapping his legs around Jack's thighs.

Sinking sensation in his stomach, Jack moaned. "You forgot?"

"No." Ethan pointed to his discarded pants.

Jack grabbed them and fussed about until he found a lumpy pocket. "Thank God. All my stuff's upstairs and I'm not carrying you up those stairs, no matter how fucking hot you look . . ."

Ethan squirmed, cheeks flushing redder than his dick. After a silent moment, he prompted, "Jack? Are you all right?"

Jack looked at what he'd fetched out of Ethan's pants' pocket, then at Ethan, then back at the objects. There were two of them. Correct number. Incorrect composition. One, which Jack could accept at face value, was a sachet of lube. The other was a folded piece of paper.

"Um . . ."

"That's what I wished to talk to you about," Ethan said softly. "Last night, but I lost my nerve. It's not my name, or any of the names you know I use, but I can assure you, Jack, that the results are mine."

Sitting back, Jack dropped the sachet onto Ethan's belly and unfolded the paper. The logo of an Australian based pathology company was at the top of the sheet and under it, the name of the patient, Jason Strachan. Then a series of tests, all negative. It was the date, however, that stood out for Jack.

"You had this done two months ago."

"Yes." He seemed about to leave it at that, then continued with a rueful smile. "After the Gold Coast, I thought perhaps you needed a sign that I was . . . committed to what we had. I had planned to tell you during the next visit, but you were sick and . . . well."

Jack closed his eyes. He needed a moment to process it all. A moment where he wasn't distracted by Ethan's naked body and his earnestly hopeful expression. Christ. Just when he thought he had a handle on everything, Ethan went and tipped him over again. Finding no answers in the dark, he opened his eyes. Ethan was struggling to maintain his optimism. His dick had given it up for a lost cause already and frankly, Jack's wasn't in any better state right then, either. However, his chest still kindled a warmth left over from the grenade explosion and it didn't seem to be fading. In fact, it only got hotter the more he looked at Ethan, the more the idea of what he was proposing sank in.

Very carefully, Jack folded the results up and tucked them back where he'd found them. "You did it again."

"Did what?"

"Concocted a plan rather than just talk."

Ethan let his head drop back so he could stare at the leaf-littered sail above them. "I know, Jack." He sounded defeated.

Jack casually picked up the lube sachet and flicked it a couple of times, like he was preparing to open it. The sound of the foil snapping made Ethan look at him, eyebrows raised, lips parted on a silent question.

Grinning, Jack dropped down until he was lying on Ethan again. "You're just lucky I'm fully on board with this plan."

Tentatively, Ethan raised his knees to cradle Jack's hips. "You are?"

"Yeah, I am." Jack kissed his neck, his Adam's Apple, his shoulder. "I got tested after Canberra, after Harry . . . after I got blood all over me. I'm clean. And, just to be perfectly clear, there's been no one else for nearly six months. And I always used a condom."

Ethan nodded, as if he didn't trust himself to speak.

Jack believed he knew the answer but asked anyway. "Have you been with anyone else lately?"

"There's only been you, Jack." Ethan ran his fingertips lightly across Jack's jaw and lips. "Only you since we parted at the homestead."

Nineteen months, twelve of which Ethan hadn't been with him. It meant Ethan hadn't been fucking his way through jobs in between, which was more important to Jack than he thought it should be. He kept his trap shut and distracted it by kissing his way down Ethan's chest.

Ethan arched his back, pushing into the kisses with his whole body. He breathed Jack's name, then gasped it when Jack forwent further teasing and wrapped his lips around Ethan's dick. Only semi-hard, it took maybe three sucks to go full on stone-monolith and Ethan was moaning and clutching at Jack's shoulders after two more. Jack's dick was a steel rod pushed up into his belly by the deckchair cushion. He humped the waterproof material until the rough surface threatened to get him off. But as neither of them blowing like that was part of his plan, Jack pulled off Ethan with a sucking pop.

He couldn't resist any longer. Finding the sachet, he tore it open and squeezed a bit of lube onto his fingers. Ethan watched avidly, and Jack was grateful it still wasn't too bright for him to need his sunglasses. Jack really wanted to see his eyes. They weren't strange to him anymore. They were simply Ethan's eyes and Jack needed to know they were watching him as much as he was watching Ethan.

Sliding his hand under Ethan's balls, Jack slowly, teasingly, worked a slick finger inside him. Ethan hummed approval, shifting his hips for a better angle. Jack feasted on his neck and jaw, his ears and his chin, hearing and feeling the delighted rumblings coming from Ethan's throat. Ethan rushed Jack through the second and third fingers and when Jack sat back on his heels to squeeze more lube onto the head of his dick, Ethan shifted restlessly, rubbing his socked feet along Jack's thighs.

"Jack." The tone was plaintive yet commanding.

Chuckling, Jack spread the lube with a couple of firm strokes. "Patience, Blade. It's a virtue."

"Jack." More command and threat this time.

Balanced on one hand, Jack loomed over Ethan, still holding his own dick. "Just making sure you really want this."

Ethan ran his fingers across Jack's chest. "I do, Jack. Very much."

"Yeah?" Jack transferred his hand to Ethan's dick, smearing lube up and down its length. "Or we could do it the other way . . ."

He gently stroked Ethan as he waited for the reply. He'd left it up to Ethan to say he wanted to top, but the fact they were about to do something new to them had him wondering if another might be just as inviting.

Eyes widening, Ethan stared up at Jack, lips parted in surprise. His dick stayed plump and hard in Jack's hand, so the idea wasn't a total turn off, but he didn't immediately jump all over the opportunity. Instead, he locked his ankles together behind Jack's back and pulled him down until they were pressed tight.

Nuzzling into Jack' neck, Ethan said, "Maybe later. Jack, please. I need this." He nipped at the corner of Jack's jaw. "I need you."

"Fuck." Jack nodded against Ethan's shoulder. It could wait. Anything else except this right now could wait.

Jack had to bite his lips as he pressed slowly into the heat of Ethan's body, needing a distraction from the overwhelming awareness of having nothing between them. He'd forgotten the rawness of the sensation, the intimacy of the complete connection. Everything felt so much warmer and closer and deeper and . . . just *more*. It wasn't only physical, although Ethan's legs felt like they were clamped impossibly tight to his hips, his fingers dug into the muscles of Jack's back, and the heat rolling between their rocking bodies almost steamed in the damp atmosphere. The trust between them was stronger, the passion hotter, the honesty deeper.

Unlike the last time, the slow, deliberate pace Jack set appeared to be what Ethan wanted as well. He moved with Jack, nodding frantically, unable to voice his agreement. One hand slid down Jack's back and splayed over his tailbone, feeling Jack's spine flex. The other cupped Jack's cheek, his thumb running over his lips. Ethan's gaze locked onto Jack's, wide and dazed, only breaking the link when he closed his eyes and moaned huskily.

At the sight of those long, thick lashes sitting on flushed cheeks and the inviting O of his wet lips, the urge to throw caution to the wind surged. Christ. Jack was so close to losing his last grip on sanity. And maybe he should. Maybe it was time he stopped denying it and just admit what he was feeling. It was getting harder and harder to shove that one fact aside.

He wanted to *kiss* Ethan Blade.

Not his neck or cheek or abs or dick, but his mouth. His soft, full lips that gave shape to his British accent, to his wry humour, to his excited prattle about getting a new fuel-injection system for the Lamborghini. His mouth which smiled at Jack, gaped when Jack did something unexpected, or pursed in disapproval. The mouth that had whispered support and comfort in Jack's ear the day before. Jack wanted to kiss Ethan and offer up everything that meant to him.

Jack closed the last miniscule distance between them. Bodies pressed close, noses brushing, he felt Ethan's panted breaths on his own lips, drew his air in and breathed his own into Ethan.

Ethan's eyes flashed open and the instant their gazes snapped together, his whole body shook in reaction to what he saw in Jack's eyes.

Feeling Ethan respond so viscerally shocked Jack out of the moment. The urge was still there, pressing insistently on his throat and temples and heart, but something held him back. Jack tucked his face into Ethan's neck instead.

"Jack," Ethan breathed, hand on the back of his head, holding him gently. "Please."

The plea could have been for the missed kiss, but Ethan followed it with an urgent buck of his hips, heels pushing into Jack's thighs. His whole body clamped around Jack in desperation.

"Yeah," Jack agreed, the word muffled in Ethan's warm skin.

Still pressed so tight together the shape of Ethan's hard dick was imprinted on Jack's belly, he began to increase the tempo of his thrusts. He wasn't going to last long, not with the added intensity of being bare inside Ethan. The speed and pressure only seemed to make him more sensitive to every nuance in Ethan's body, each little motion and ripple feeding back into Jack tenfold. Ethan, too, seemed overcome by the raw force of it. His hands gripped at any part of Jack he could reach, his legs curling and flexing, chest heaving as he fought for air around totally involuntary moans and gasps.

Stimulated by the friction between them, Ethan came. His dick pulsed and pulsed, heat slicking the glide of their bellies as his body convulsed around Jack, intensifying the already mind-bending connection.

"Ethan," Jack groaned as his body went wild, fucking without guidance from anything other than primitive, driving compulsion.

"Yes, yes, Jack." Ethan pulled Jack even closer to his quaking body. "Please. I need you. Now."

Jack came. Vision and hearing both went white-out. Touch didn't. Even as he shuddered through a powerful release, Jack still felt every inch of Ethan against his skin. Still felt the strength of the arms around him, the heat of the body cradling him, the softness of the lips pressing over and over to his neck, his temple, his cheek.

Still felt the gunshot force of his need to kiss Ethan.

CHAPTER SIX

Breakfast was, by necessity, rather late, which meant Ethan pestered Jack through showering and dressing before ushering him out the door with as much haste as Jack could muster. Horses saddled, they set out into a warming day, Ethan and Smith in the lead, Jack and Jones trailing.

Ethan kept their destination a secret, promising with a smirk that Jack would enjoy it. Jack grumbled because Ethan expected it and after an hour of not getting answers, the grumbling was no longer just for show. The disgruntlement faded, however, when they reached Ethan's mystery spot.

Lush grass dotted with bright wild flowers carpeted the ground of the clearing. On the far side, a cliff face of dark rock was partially occluded by a sugary curtain of water falling into a nearly perfectly round pool. Under the blue sky visible through a break in the canopy, the water shimmered. The air was cool and free of the mugginess within the jungle.

"Well?" Ethan asked smugly as they dismounted.

Trying to regain some poise, Jack shrugged. "Yeah, it's okay."

Which didn't fool Ethan. Chuckling, he stepped up to Jack, arms slipping around his waist. "Just okay?"

Jack resisted, but it was a pointless effort. He ran his hands through Ethan's hair, wanting and getting the unconscious response of Ethan pushing into the touch.

"Perfect," he whispered.

Still keeping contact between his hair and Jack's hands, Ethan tilted his head quizzically. "Pardon?"

"It's perfect. The waterfall, the pool, everything."

"Good. The weather forecast said there shouldn't be any rain today, so we can spend a couple of hours here before heading back."

Jack made a show of looking around confusedly. "Gosh, what *are* we going to do for a couple of hours?"

Stepping back, Ethan thumped him gently in the belly, but laughed as he did so.

It was an entirely enjoyable couple of hours they spent at the waterfall. Swimming and wrestling in the water, rutting together under the spray coming off the cliff face, dozing side by side in the hot sun, sharing their packed lunch with the horses. All of it so peaceful and relaxing Jack fell asleep after lunch, lying on his belly on the grass.

When he woke, Ethan was lying beside him, his fingers tracing the tattoo on his left shoulderblade. Of all the men Jack had been with since he got the tattoo, Ethan was the only one he didn't mind touching it.

"Do you know Plutarch?"

The soft question roused Jack fully. "Um. Not personally, I don't think. He's some ancient Greek guy, right?"

Ethan snorted. "Yes, some ancient Greek guy. He wrote *Lives of the Noble Greeks and Romans*." He leaned over and pressed a kiss of the top of Jack's tattoo. "He had some rather interesting things to say about scars."

Jack lifted his head to peer at him. "Scars?"

The ever-present sunglasses hid Ethan's eyes, but the rest of his expression was pensive. He didn't look at Jack's face, but instead kept touching the black and silver shadings of the tattoo of the Saint Thomas Cross. "Mm. He said scars were the inscribed images of excellence and manly virtue. They described a life well lived, showing how a man had fought for the things he wanted, and was still alive afterward."

"Manly virtue? That's a bit sexist," Jack mused, even as he wondered at Ethan's point. He'd learned to just let Ethan talk, knowing he tended to sneak up on the actual topic from odd angles.

"I suppose." Ethan stroked his hand down Jack's spine and back up. "He was an ancient Greek guy, after all."

Just when Jack thought that was the end of the odd little discussion, Ethan added, "Tattoos are modern scars. They've come to mean the same thing. They describe our lives, marking those moments when we experienced something profound, and survived."

A rush of relief mixed with pain flooded through Jack. Relief because Ethan knew exactly what the tattoo meant to him. That it wasn't just a reminder of his mother, of her life and her faith, but that it was a turning point. A marker for when Jack's life changed more profoundly than even the loss of a parent could cause. All in one day, he got the tattoo and joined the army. Both actions for his mother, but both becoming entities on their own, apart from her memory. And pain because there was a reason the tattoo was on his back, where he couldn't see it himself.

After a long moment forcing the ache out of his chest, Jack smirked at Ethan. "What's this 'our,' pretty boy? You don't have any tats."

Of course, he couldn't fool Ethan. The annoyingly perceptive bastard simply pushed close and rested his cheek against Jack's, his strong fingers splayed across the tattoo, as if he could sooth the old pain with the warmth of his touch.

"No," he whispered. "I don't."

Quite apart from the fact tattoos were easily identifiable marks, Ethan didn't need them to describe his life.

He had the scars to do that.

After another swim, they packed up their gear and returned to the house. Jack didn't have a stable-boy kink, yet as they brushed down the horses, he couldn't take his gaze off Ethan. He watched the smooth ripple of muscles as he stroked the curry comb along Smith's sleek flank and was captivated by the flex and stretch of his arms and the firm shape of his thighs as he crouched to check the horse's legs. Jack supposed he could have waited until they were inside the house, but the moment the gates were closed on the stalls, he grabbed Ethan and pushed him back against the wall.

"Jack?" Ethan managed, then let out a low, rumbling growl as Jack sank into a crouch and unfastened his pants.

"Just this," Jack murmured, freeing Ethan's dick and giving it a long, hard lick. "For a bit."

"For a bit" proved true. Jack was too lost in his desire to draw it out. He took Ethan fast and almost brutally, needing the hot, messy end, needing the sounds and sensation of Ethan falling apart all around him. Ethan came fast, hands fisted in Jack's hair, incoherent sounds tumbling from his lips. His own hard dick in hand, Jack took half a minute longer, face pressed to Ethan's thigh as he strove for his orgasm, muffling his deep groan in denim when it rolled over him.

Sated, they staggered into the house, cleaned up and while Ethan lounged on a stool at the kitchen counter, Jack made butter chicken. It was the one recipe he'd bothered to learn from his mother, mostly because cooking was a turn on to some guys, and everyone loved butter chicken. Ethan was no exception, devotedly watching Jack as he worked, touching him whenever he got close enough, then devouring two servings.

Having cooked, Jack lay on one of the couches in the library area while Ethan washed the dishes. It was his turn to ogle.

"Any more surprises?" He tilted his head to keep an eye on Ethan's arse as he bent to fill the dishwasher.

"Nothing like today. Do you feel like a hike?"

Rubbing his full belly, Jack grunted a negative.

"Not now." Ethan threw a wadded-up tea towel at him. "Tomorrow. The forecast is a bit doubtful, but if it's clear, we could go."

"A hike," Jack grumbled. Nine years of army service kind of destroyed any pleasure to be had hiking. "Do I have to do it with twenty kilos of gear?"

Ethan sauntered over and picked up the tea towel Jack had left on his stomach. "Not unless you wish to."

Snagging the end of the damp material, Jack tugged on it. "Not particularly."

"So?" Ethan responded to the tug with one of his own. "There's a nice trail that goes further up the mountain. I haven't done it before, but the owner of the house says the view at the end is spectacular."

"Yeah?" Jack hauled down harder, making Ethan lean back to keep from being pulled over. "Not sure it really compares to the current view."

Smirking, Ethan asked, "How do you know that? You haven't seen the other one yet."

"No, but I'm very partial to this one." And he gave up playing, twisting his hand in the tea towel and yanking Ethan down on top of him.

Ethan landed with a surprised grunt, bracing himself on the leather couch so he didn't crush Jack. He squirmed into a better position and his eyebrows shot up. Another wiggle of his hips confirmed it and he shook his head. "Again, Jack?"

"Must be the altitude."

Of course, it was raining when they got up in the morning. The hike was put aside for a lazy day indoors. There was no TV but Ethan cued up a couple of episodes of *Strike Back* for them on a laptop. They sat side by side on a couch, sharing a packet of popcorn, the computer on the coffee table before them. At the end of the second episode, Ethan shut the laptop, turned and slung a leg over Jack, settling onto his lap. They'd messed around a little bit in bed that morning, neither of them getting off, just enjoying the physical closeness. After the day before, Jack wasn't sure he could actually get hard enough to satisfy either of them.

Ethan, however, didn't seem to be having naughty thoughts. He sat back on Jack's thighs and absently started massaging his shoulders, his strong fingers working already relaxed muscles into melted goo. Most of the shields were lowered, leaving only the one at the far end of the house open, to let in a bit of natural light, which was nevertheless dimmed by the rain. Ethan had put aside his glasses, leaving Jack ample opportunity to study his long, thick lashes. And to wonder if that suggestion of blue in the white of his irises was really there, or just in Jack's imagination.

"Jack, may I ask you something?"

"Is that what this is? Butter me up so I'll answer your questions?"

Ethan smirked. "It appears you have me all puzzled out, Mr. Reardon."

"Not by half, you crazy bastard. Ask away."

Fingers digging in a bit harder, Ethan was silent for a couple of moments, then asked, "Now that we've stopped using condoms, are we . . . committed?"

All of Ethan's work on Jack's shoulders reversed itself in an instant. Tensing up, Jack bit back a curse. He should have been expecting this. The *talk*. In all reality, they should have had it yesterday morning, before sex. Perhaps they had both been thinking that asking and agreeing had been a convenient short cut. One Ethan was now seconding guessing?

Reflexively, Jack grabbed Ethan's hips and pulled him a little closer, keeping hold of him, not wanting him to get away. Not resisting, Ethan slid his arms around Jack's neck and leaned against his chest.

"Does this mean yes?"

Jack hugged him tightly and suddenly the barriers were down. All the hard blocks in his head and throat and heart that had kept these words unspoken were gone, as if they'd never been. "It means yes. It means I've been in this thing whole heartedly since March. It means you're it for me." There were no sharp edges to the words, nothing that hurt or cut him on the way out. They were smooth and easy and soothing. The relief washed away the tension.

Against him, Ethan relaxed and nuzzled his face into the side of Jack's neck. "Good."

Jack chuckled. "Good? That's all you got for me?"

Ethan lifted his head to look at him. "Do you need more?" he asked softly, almost sadly. "Do you need to hear me say I've been *in this thing* for much longer? That I've been waiting for you, hoping, *wishing* you'd catch up. Or that I've been constantly wondering if I was being naïve and stupid to even think you might want to be with me as more than just casual . . . as occasional . . ." His cheeks pinked up, but he bravely kept his gaze locked on Jack as he finished with, "As fuck-buddies."

Jack wanted to say no, he didn't need to hear those things because he already knew. Because hearing it aloud would force him to confront just how shitty he'd been over the past six months. Those couple of nights he'd spent with another man had been nothing. A fun but meaningless distraction between visits with Ethan. Before he'd realised that Ethan had lied—again—about them hooking up when they *happened* to be in the same place at the same time. Like everything else he did, Ethan had meticulously planned every meeting, and had kept doing it despite the fact Jack usually messed them up one way or another.

He meant to say "no" but what came out was "I'm sorry."

After a long moment, Ethan nodded, though the apology didn't seem to make him any happier.

"Ethan?" Jack cupped his face gently. "What's wrong?"

"Me." With that, Ethan scrambled off Jack's lap and all but ran to the kitchen. "Do you feel like leftover butter chicken for lunch? We should probably finish it off sooner rather than later. Perhaps on toast. Don't you say leftovers are always better on toast?"

Feeling like he'd been buffeted by a strong wind, or perhaps the speed of Ethan's retreat, Jack sat for a nonplussed moment before saying, "Yeah, always better on toast." Then he got up and followed him. "What do you mean, you're wrong? You're right, as usual. I've been a complete wanker about everything. And I mean it, Ethan. I *am* sorry."

"I know, Jack, and thank you. One or two pieces of toast?" He kept his back turned, fussing with the bread and container of leftovers.

His tone was normal, but the way he moved with sharp, precise motions kept Jack on the far side of the counter. This was one of those moments where he wasn't sure if proximity would end in a hug, or a punch. Something had triggered Ethan's compulsion. Something Jack had said or done.

"Ethan, what—"

"Jack." There was a snap to the word this time, his body tensing and going still.

Jack froze along with him, waiting to see what he would do. After a minute, Ethan turned on his heel and walked out of the kitchen, heading for the door.

"Where are you going?" Jack fought to keep the worry out of his voice.

"To check the horses."

"Need a hand?"

"No, thank you. Best only one of us gets wet." At the door, he unlocked it, then paused. "Jack?"

"Yeah?"

Ethan took several deep breaths. "It will be all right. I just need some space."

Hoping like hell that was all he needed, Jack said, "Okay."

The door opened, letting in the unfiltered pounding of the rain, and just as quickly was cut off as Ethan slipped out.

CHAPTER SEVEN

Ethan was gone for the better part of two hours. Jack explored the house, finding nothing that told him who the owner was, apart from the paintings and the piano. Whosever place this was, Jack guessed they painted, played the piano and generally didn't want the world to intrude on them.

Replace the painting with cars and the piano with reading, and it felt a lot like Ethan, actually.

Jack eventually fed his rumbly stomach, though the butter chicken tasted a bit bland. Perhaps it was the toast, or the lack of company.

The rain had let up by the time Ethan came back in. Finding the towel Jack had left by the door for him, he dried off as well as he could before going upstairs. The shower ran while Jack heated up the last of the leftovers and a plate was waiting for Ethan when he came back down. He stalled at the sight of the food, then sat down to eat. When he was done, Jack leaned across the counter for the plate.

"Jack." Ethan's fingers brushed his hand. "Thank you."

Jack lingered for a moment, soaking up the small contact, then took the plate to the sink. "Are the horses okay?"

"They're fine. Jones is a little grumpy at not being allowed into the yard, but he'll get over it."

"And Smith?"

Ethan snorted. "He's a lazy sod, that one. Doesn't particularly care so long as he has his food."

Desperately wanting to ask how Ethan was, as well, Jack stayed on the topic of the horses. The more Ethan talked about them, the less distant he was. Then Jack prompted him to talk about his cars, and actually paid close attention this time, so he'd be able to ask informed questions and keep the conversation going. The more Ethan relaxed and came back to him, the better Jack felt. By evening, they were talking easily again, even laughing as Ethan read a particularly exciting passage from his latest action book. He even started touching Jack again after dinner.

In bed, Ethan tugged Jack's pants off and then his own, making his intentions clear. It was a hands-on-the-headboard fuck and excruciatingly glorious. Jack, who hadn't thought he could come again after the previous day's efforts, tumbled over first, and very nearly went a second time when Ethan crawled up his body, bringing his hard dick into range of Jack's mouth.

They slept deeply, wound together.

It rained intermittently the next day and the hike was put off again. Jack helped Ethan see to the hoses and they both ended up soaked when Jones made a bolt for the relative freedom of the yard and refused to go back into his stall. Eventually, Ethan corralled the horse and got him stabled again. Once they were all dry, Jack retreated to a couch with one of Ethan's books. He barely made it through the first chapter before his eyelids were drooping.

He was woken up by gentle piano music that slowly resolved into the same thirty seconds or so played over and over, slightly different each time. Even as he recognised it as Für Elise, a wrong note was hit, and Ethan muttered, "Blast it," and started over.

Hauling himself off the couch, Jack wandered over as Ethan repeated the snippet again. "I didn't know you could play."

Ethan spared him a pained expression. "Clearly, I can't."

Jack sat beside him on the stool. "You're doing better than I ever did."

Fingers tumbling across the keys, Ethan quirked an enquiring eyebrow at him.

"Dad plays." Jack sighed. "*Played*. He tried to teach me, but I was never that good. Or cared enough to practice. Meera did. She got all the artistic talent in our family."

"Then we're a pair. I don't have the aptitude for it, either. Not like some of—some others."

Wondering what Ethan had stopped himself from saying, Jack pointed toward the painting on the wall opposite them. "Do you paint, then?"

"I've never tried. Nor had a desire to."

Jack grunted. "So, I guess this really *isn't* one of your places."

That rogue corner of Ethan's mouth turned up, then went down with Jack's next words.

"It belongs to one of your associates. The woman I met in Sydney."

The clues had been lining up since the day before and Jack was pretty sure his conclusion was correct. For a moment, Jack though Ethan was going to run again, but although his shoulders stiffened, he didn't leave. He did, however, start tinkling once more. The same opening to Für Elise but there was a slight dissonance in the tune now.

"Vietnam's not that far from Australia she couldn't come over to help you in a pinch. The predominant colours in the paintings here are the same as the dress she wore that day. She's met me and, granted, didn't like me, but I know you wouldn't betray an associate by bringing someone they knew nothing about to one of their lairs."

The music cut off. "Jack—"

"It's okay. I'm not going to betray her, either." Jack nudged him gently. "You should know that about me by now."

Ethan stared at him for a moment, then nodded. When he started playing, the notes came easier, smoother, and he shifted so their thighs were pressed together.

The following day dawned clear and the weather forecast promised no rain, so the hike happened. It wasn't as bad as Jack feared. His pack was substantially less than twenty kilos, the terrain not overly steep for most of the way, and while it was warm and humid it wasn't hot or oppressive. When they arrived, the two hours of hiking was worth the incredibly spectacular and panoramic expanse of Cao Bằng spread out before them.

So much green, so many *different* greens draped over horizon to horizon rolling hills, cut through with the snaking brown of the river.

Puffy white clouds drifted above it all in a sky of cobalt blue, the sun burning bright and warm. They'd come around to the north face of their mountain and there was absolutely no sign of human habitation. Just pure, perfect nature.

Jack put his pack down and walked to the edge of the small plateau. It ended in an abrupt drop-off and a long, dizzying distance to the canopy of trees far below. Jack drank in the glorious view and felt a sense of déjà vu. He'd never been to Vietnam before, and while he had been to some breathtaking locations, nothing in his memory quite fit this beauty.

The similarity came to him when Ethan stepped up beside him. This was like the desert. Open and vast, it was enough space to get lost in, or to lose himself in. As he stood there, taking in the absolute emptiness of the air, the unhindered view of the sky, the distance of the mountains, Jack felt his worries ease. As if the world had to equilibrate and some of his pain was being absorbed into the openness. Harry would be with him forever, but being here, he thought he would be able to live with him in peace.

"Do you like it?" Ethan asked quietly.

Not yet able to talk, Jack just nodded. He slung an arm around Ethan's shoulders and pulled him close.

When Jack was ready, they retreated up the plateau and shared a light lunch. Afterward, they explored a little around the plateau, messed around trying to sneak up on each other and inevitably ended up naked in a warm, soft cocoon of ferns between two fallen trees. Picking each other clean of vegetative detritus, they dressed and headed back to the plateau. Ethan scrounged through his pack and pulled out a paperback. He settled against a tree trunk to read while Jack went back to contemplating the view.

There'd been another moment in the ferns when he'd nearly kissed Ethan. They hadn't even done much by that stage, just stripped and tumbled together into the greenery. A fern frond had ended up stuck somewhere delicate on Ethan's body and his battle to get it free had left Jack in stitches. Holding the mangled frond high in triumph, Ethan had looked so silly and beautiful the grenade in Jack's chest had damn near blown out his ribs. Jack would have kissed him then, he knew it, except Ethan had thrown himself on Jack and begun a slow, delicious roll of his hips that wiped Jack's head clear of every voluntary thought.

He looked over his shoulder at his man, absorbed in his book, his free hand idly flipping a knife, point to handle, handle to point, and wondered why he hadn't kissed him already. Jack was almost positive he wanted to, and even if he wasn't ready right then, he knew he would be soon. Possibly very soon. He just needed something . . . more. Though just what that "more" was, he had no idea.

Still perplexed, Jack joined Ethan and pestered him into reading aloud. As per usual, Jack dozed off to the soothing sound of Ethan's voice, content with his head nestled on a firm thigh and fingers curling through his hair.

Ethan nudged Jack awake a while later. Dark clouds had begun to gather behind the distant mountains, so they packed up their gear and headed back down the trail. The rain was obviously moving in fast because the already dim light within the trees grew darker as they went. By the time they'd come back around to the eastern slope, the light was so low Ethan took his glasses off.

They'd just descended the final steep passage, about half an hour out from the house, when Ethan stopped. His fist came up in a silent signal instantly recognisable. Jack froze and came on alert. Jack hadn't heard anything unusual but he didn't doubt Ethan's skills or senses, either. Very slowly, he sank into a crouch and retrieved the P8 from his waistband. A couple of feet in front, Ethan stood as still as the tree trunks around them.

A prickle of awareness slithered down Jack's spine a moment before he heard the noise. Voices. Soft and unintelligible, but definitely there.

Jack eased off the safety on the P8, then cocked his head, trying to work out which direction the voices were coming from. Tension coiled in his guts, that pre-game unease he'd learned to trust long ago.

Excruciatingly slow, Ethan lifted one foot and stepped back, putting it down with precise care, completely silent on the rotting detritus of the jungle floor. Another step and he sank down beside Jack. Twisting, he brought his mouth right to Jack's ear.

"Your two o'clock," he whispered, barely any sound to the words. "About fifty yards."

It took a while in the gloom and close vegetation, but Jack found them. Two men, downhill from their position. The trail he and Ethan were on switched back just up ahead and the men were probably on the lower part of the trail. He couldn't make out too many details, but the shape of them was unmistakable. The bulk of body armour and the distinctive barrels of assault rifles. They certainly weren't hikers who'd taken a wrong turn.

"Your eleven o'clock. Forty yards."

Jack found the second pair of men quicker this time. All four were focused away from Jack and Ethan, which gave them some breathing room. Keeping the downhill pair in sight, while Ethan watched those uphill, Jack carefully slipped out of his pack. He pulled a spare mag for the P8 and tucked it into a pocket on his pants. Ethan, likewise, freed himself of his pack and produced his two Desert Eagles. If they had to fight, it was going to sound like they were firing cannons up here.

Leaning in to Ethan, Jack asked, "Military?"

Ethan frowned, as if wondering if that made any difference, but studied the strangers for a long moment. He shook his head. "Mercs."

Jack had run into some highly effective mercenaries in his time, including those in Valadian's compound, but they were often just groups of disgruntled men with violent tendencies. Depending on who was paying for them, of course. Considering Ethan's life, who the fuck knew what sort of nutcase may have sent this lot.

Catching Jack's attention, Ethan laid out his plan with his hands. Even before he'd finished, Jack pushed his hands aside and leaned in to whisper in his ear.

"Need to find out why they're here. Who sent them."

Ethan shook his head firmly. "They're too close to the house as it is. I can't let it be compromised."

He'd been willing to give up his lair in Sydney for his madcap plan but, Jack reminded himself, this place wasn't Ethan's.

"They might already be at the house," he reasoned.

And just like that, the warm, approachable man was gone. Ethan Blade was in his place. "I know." Ethan feeling threatened wasn't conducive to negotiation.

"I'll only need ten minutes to find out why they're here," Jack whispered back. "That's all."

Nothing altered in Ethan's outward posture, but there was a subtle change to the way he looked at Jack in the wake of his words. It might just have been a trick of the gloomy light, but something in his white eyes softened. Not much, and Jack may have been seeing things, but he was pretty sure of it. With a stiff nod, Ethan agreed.

All of his personal revelations to the side, Jack realised Ethan had had one of his own. No matter how still Ethan went, how closed-down his expression was, how cold his heart got in the moment, he wouldn't turn on Jack. That last tiny measure of alarm Jack usually felt when Ethan went into killer-mode vanished. The target Ethan had once seen when he looked at Jack was gone.

CHAPTER EIGHT

Returning to hand signals, they worked out their revised plan. Ethan tried to hand over an Eagle, but Jack refused, patting the P8 contentedly. Shaking his head in silent exasperation, Ethan forced a tactical knife on him instead, revealing a second one tucked away in his boot. Taking the knife to keep the peace, Jack slid it through his belt.

Before they moved, Ethan griped the back of Jack's neck and pressed their foreheads together. His gaze locked onto Jack's for a full ten seconds, intent and grim, then he was gone, slithering off the track and into the thicker foliage without a sound.

Jack lost sight of him within seconds. He listened keenly, both to try to catch a hint of Ethan moving and to make sure there wasn't a change in the noises from their quarry. Negative for both, Jack eased away in the opposite direction.

It took nearly five minutes to move close enough to hear the pair of mercs clearly. The men showed no signs that they heard him, both of them more concerned with whatever it was they were discussing. Heads dipped toward each other, they were talking in soft voices in a language he didn't fucking understand.

Shit. He was going to have to get closer, which increased the chances of being discovered exponentially.

Jack crept around a wide tree trunk and, placing his feet with exceptional care, moved. The men would pause every now and then in their conversation, heads tilting as if listening to something. Freezing in the pauses, it took another couple of minutes to get close enough to use the implant. With a directed thought, he turned on the audio recording. Conveniently, the mercs found something interesting to chat about and Jack got a solid minute of recording before flicking it off and putting some distance between them.

Back to a tree trunk, a safe distance away, Jack slipped *sideways*, and the implant overlay appeared behind his eyelids. Opening one of his favourite apps, he translated the recording. The original language was Burmese and the translation was about sixty percent gibberish, probably due to the quality of the recording, but several words and phrases leaped out at Jack.

. . . who killed Rindone . . . Khun Sein . . . that Indian *bastard . . .*

Fuck. It wasn't Ethan they were after. It was Jack. Even bigger fuck, he was the reason Ethan's associate's safe place was about to become a warzone.

Before Jack could even contemplate what that meant, his ten minutes was up.

Boom! Boom!

The unmistakable thunder of the Eagles had Jack's two mercs spinning, looking for the danger, then diving into the cover on either side of the track. Another crack of a firearm reverberated through the trees followed by a wild yell in Burmese.

Jack had one clear shot, so he took it. The light was shit and the presence of armour meant small, inconvenient target points if he wanted to kill. His bullet took the mercenary through the neck and he collapsed without uttering a sound. The gunshot sent the second man rolling even deeper into the ground cover. Uphill, Ethan and at least one other merc were exchanging shots, both of them on the move as they fired.

Sending a shot in the direction of the other merc, Jack leaped across the open space of the track and back into the thicker vegetation. He had to conserve ammo, limited by the fact he only had two mags, fifteen rounds each, and he had no clue as to how many bad guys there were. The latter part of the problem seemed like it was going to be solved pretty quickly, though. Thanks to the open gunfire, whoever else was out there was most likely already on their way.

Jack slowed right back down to a cautious creep, hunting for any sign of his quarry. The man couldn't have gone far. Slinking through the undergrowth, he scanned constantly, senses on high alert. Of course, unwanted memories started flashing at the edges of his concentration.

The nightmare running battle in Chota Nagpur, his team unravelling around him as the insurgents hunted them down, scattered them into smaller and smaller groups, picked them off one by one. Watching men he'd known for years run right into a wall of bullets, or step on a trigger and be impaled on a rack of stakes. Stealing clothes from one of the dead enemy and pretending to hold two of his fellow SAS soldiers prisoner just so they could get past the perimeter and run for their lives. The relief of reaching the extraction point and hauling Nigel and Lionel onto the waiting chopper. The utter defeat when Lionel died right there, in his arms, just as they were safe for the first time in days.

Shaking those memories away, Jack prowled through this new, different, oh so similar, jungle and determined to be the hunter this time, not the prey.

They caught sight of each other at the same moment. Jack fired and instantly rolled away, the merc's bullet cracking into a tree behind him. Coming up on one knee, Jack sent another shot in the same general direction, looking for movement. Seeing a sharp motion of the merc flinging himself sideways, Jack fired again and shifted his own position.

His foot hit a slippery patch of leaves and went out from under him. Jack tumbled downhill, automatically tucking into the roll. A couple of rotations and he fetched up against a solid trunk. He came up on one knee and braced against the tree. Spying a short, half-rotten log, Jack kicked at it, uncaring of the noise he made. Two hard impacts dislodged it and a third sent it crashing down the slope.

Believing Jack was still tumbling, the merc popped up and tracked the sound with his rifle. Jack fired and the man jerked back, rifle flying out of his hands. The second bullet hit his body armour, pushing him the rest of the way over. Jack sprang to his feet and crashed through the clinging plants toward the merc. Down but clearly not dead, the bad guy pulled a handgun and, yelling wildly, began emptying its magazine in Jack's direction. Spinning behind a wide trunk, Jack returned fire with single rounds, just to keep the man pinned down until the merc ran out of ammo. The deadman's click came seconds later and Jack rushed him.

The merc had scrambled back to his feet and was turning to run when Jack caught him. Launching into a flying tackle, he caught the merc around his waist and they hit the ground hard. The merc cried out, obviously hurt, but he fought. Not well enough, but he tried.

The short, dirty fracas ended with Jack on his back, calves locked around the man's neck, strangling him even as he kept punching and kicking. Jack twisted his legs and clamped down harder on the man's neck. Eyes bulging, the merc panicked, reaching up to pry at Jack's feet, trying to find some leverage to pull himself free. Jack found the knife Ethan had given him and rammed it into the merc's armpit, aimed into his chest. The black, seven-inch blade found something important in there, the man's struggles weakening almost immediately. Barely half a minute later, he was hanging dead in the tangle of Jack's legs.

Pushing the body aside, Jack rolled in the other direction, coming up into a low crouch. Barely even giving the dead guy a second look, Jack wrenched the knife free and gathered up his P8 and the merc's fallen rifle. P8 in his waistband, knife hastily cleaned and slid into his boot, Jack settled the rifle into place, quickly giving it a once over. It was an AKM, well used but not well cared for. The 30-round magazine was close to empty, so Jack scavenged two more mags off the body and tucked them into the pockets on his pants.

Around him, the jungle had returned to an eerie quiet. The wildlife had been scared off by the firefight and all Jack could hear was the wind through the leaves. Thankfully, the rain hadn't reached them yet. Wondering what the hell had happened with Ethan, Jack set out.

He moved quicker now, going for a balance between speed and noise. Heading back uphill, Jack aimed for where the other mercs had been. He found a dead merc first. Single gunshot to the face. Jack moved on, following the direction he thought the running gunfight had gone—towards the house. He found the second man about two hundred yards along, throat cut and stripped of his rifle and mags.

Five minutes later, he spotted movement. Stilling, he tracked the dark shape moving through the trees. In the gloom Jack could make out a rifle slung across the man's back and a long-bladed knife in one hand. The man moved quietly, focused on something further away. Jack tracked ahead of him and found a shadowed shape that looked like a man crouched in the cover of a large fern. Back to them, the man was perfectly still, a rifle held to his shoulder, barrel hidden in the ferns. Jack wasn't certain, but he thought the crouched man's shirt was Ethan's dark-blue flannel. Which meant the first man was Jack's target.

Finding the merc, Jack settled his sight on him and followed his slow progress, waiting for the perfect opportunity. The AKM was unfamiliar and he had no idea how it fired, so he needed the best chance he could if he was going to keep the bad guy from reaching Ethan's position.

"Come on," he mouthed, wanting the shot, wanting Ethan to finally realise he had a stalker and move. Between them, they could catch this guy no worries, but right now, it was entirely up to Jack and his options for a good shot weren't getting much better the longer he waited. Fuck it. He resettled the rifle and pulled in a slow breath, finger starting to pull on the trigger.

A dark shape dropped out of the branches and landed on the creeping merc. He went down with a startled grunt, trying to roll free of the sudden weight, but his attacker clung on like a leech and they both crashed through the undergrowth.

"Shit." Jack raced forward, slinging the rifle, and pulling the P8.

He lost sight of the combatants, seeing only violently rustling foliage as they grunted and shouted. Then it all stopped as quickly as it had started. Everything went quiet and still. Jack skidded to a stop, P8 up and aimed. He waited for movement or sound and got neither.

Jack risked a hissed, "Saint?"

"All clear, Jack." Slowly, Ethan rose out of the undergrowth, bloody knife in one hand.

"Christ." Jack lowered his gun and stepped up to him. "You good?" He looked him over as he asked.

Ethan was shirtless and covered in dirt to camouflage his pale skin. There was blood on his chest and neck, but as there were no gushing wounds, Jack decided it wasn't Ethan's.

"I'm fine. You?"

"Yeah, good. How many have you found?"

Taking the AKM from the dead guy, Ethan said, "Four so far." He headed toward his decoy.

"I got the two I went after, haven't seen any others."

Ethan swiftly removed his shirt from the body he'd propped up and slung it back on. Doing up only a couple of buttons, he retrieved the rifle as well. "There are four more. This gentleman was kind enough to tell me that before he expired."

Eyebrow cocking, Jack asked, "You speak Burmese?"

"No, Jack. He spoke very poor Mandarin, which I do speak." He gave Jack a direct look. "They're here for you, I'm afraid. Sent by—"

"Khun Sein," Jack finished for him. "Yeah, I got that bit. Sorry. I really thought no one had followed me."

"They may just as easily have followed me." Ethan moved out. Like Jack had, he went quietly but not silently.

"Do you really think so?" Jack kept his voice low.

Ethan carefully picked out a path through the jungle, still heading toward the house, rifle tracking to their south. "No plan is ever fool proof, Jack. Shall we finish this?"

Jack grunted the affirmative and followed him.

CHAPTER NINE

In the next twenty minutes, while the light got lower and the air got thicker with the coming weather, they found and eliminated two more mercs. One went down silently to a thrown knife. The other made a run for it, Jack taking him out with a sweep of automatic fire from the AKM, which alerted the remaining two to their position.

They clashed about three hundred metres from the house, the mercs caught between them and their destination. The action devolved into a pitched firefight, Jack and Ethan covering each other as they tried to circle around the remaining enemy.

Things were going nowhere fast and only working to deplete their limited store of ammo. Down to his last mag for the AKM, Jack had resorted to single shots, waiting for a chance to at least wound, if not outright kill. Ethan, too, played conservative with his weapons, but he depleted one rifle quickly, dropping it and pulling up the second one.

"We have to get around them." Jack pressed his back to a tree as the bad guys unloaded on the poor thing.

"Agreed." Ethan, about ten feet away and similarly positioned, risked a look at the mercs. Then he made a series of gestures at Jack, who nodded and, on the go signal, rolled around and unleashed the last of his mag on full automatic.

Leaves and bark sprayed in a wild cyclone as bullets tore through the vegetation. All opposing gunfire ceased. Ethan tossed his remaining rifle towards Jack so it thumped down at his feet. Then, knife between his teeth, Ethan scaled the tree he was hiding behind and vanished into the low hanging canopy.

Knowing he was about to run dry, Jack crouched and scooped up the second rifle. Stock tucked under his left arm, he started firing it the moment his own clicked on empty. Hitting something was secondary to distracting the bad guys right then. He did grin when one of them cried out in pain, though.

Of course, the ammo ran out remarkably fast and the moment it did, Jack dived back into cover. He rolled and came up with the P8 even as the bad guys, after a couple of seconds to realise Jack was done, opened fire again. When he didn't return it even with single shots, they got cocky.

First one, then the other moved out of cover, prepared to advance on their enemy.

Boom!

The second merc, slightly behind his fellow, was thrown back to the ground, the .50 cal bullet ploughing down through the neck hole of his armour, fired from where Ethan perched in the treetops.

Jack spun into the open and fired at the last, stunned merc. Most of the bullets ricocheted off his armour, but one went through his shoulder, twisting him around and tossing the rifle from his grip. Still alive, he crashed to his knees, useless right arm hanging by his side. Even as Jack advanced on him, P8 trained on his face, the man scrabbled for another weapon, coming up with a handgun. The barrel swung up toward Jack, the merc yelling at him in a torrent of Burmese.

"Drop the gun," Jack shouted back. "Drop it!" He wanted a live prisoner, someone who could tell them exactly what the hell was going on here. Besides, he was down to a single bullet and didn't want to waste it.

The man didn't understand or didn't care, and he fired. Prepared for it, Jack dropped and rolled. The merc's bullet ripped through the air Jack had just vacated.

"Fucking drop it," Jack commanded, moving into a crouch, gun trained on the merc.

Again, he refused. Again, he aimed at Jack and—

Jack was thrown sideways, crashing into the undergrowth. Having pushed Jack aside, Ethan charged right towards the gun. The merc yelled wildly and fired but Ethan dove to the ground, rolling over his shoulder. He came up on one knee right in front of the injured man, arm sweeping to knock the weapon aside.

Even with the gunshot wound, the merc was good. He rolled with the blow, bringing his knee up into Ethan's unprotected side. Both men tumbled over, the merc landing on top and throwing punches with his good arm into Ethan's ribs.

Jack scrambled back to his feet, P8 with its final bullet trained on the fight. Ethan caught the merc's arm and, holding it aside, punched the man right in his wound. The merc screamed and Ethan rolled, knocking him off.

With the combatants separated, Jack advanced, weapon trained on the downed merc. The man twisted, foot scything towards Jack's legs. Jack leaped backwards and, given some space, the merc sprang to his feet. Ethan swept back in with a flying kick at his stomach. The merc stumbled backwards and Ethan followed with another kick and a flurry of punches and jabs. Between attempts to return blows, the merc pulled a long-bladed knife and, staggering from the assault, made a clumsy thrust at Ethan.

Dead-eyed and detached, Ethan calmly dodged the knife and caught the man's arm. With an upward blow from his other hand, Ethan broke the merc's wrist. The knife went flying. Ethan deftly snatched it out of mid-air, spun the handle to fit into his palm, and plunged the blade into the merc's neck.

Another person burst out of the dense foliage, all clumsy legs and flailing arms.

Without pause, Ethan twisted, bloody knife tearing free of the dead man, blade arcing for the neck of the surprised intruder.

"Ethan!"

Jack launched himself at the assassin. He was too late, though. The knife sliced, its point cutting across a hastily raised arm. A second later, Jack caught Ethan around his thighs and took him down. With a terrified wail, Tom staggered back, falling over his own feet and crashing to the ground.

Ethan fought Jack's hold. He was silent as he twisted and kicked. The brief glimpses Jack got of his face showed a deadly mask, cold and distant. He was so far gone Jack saw nothing of the man he'd been with that afternoon. Yet there was no hesitation when he crawled up Ethan's body, fighting against fist and knife.

"Ethan, it's me."

Instantly, Ethan stopped struggling. He didn't drop the knife or give up completely. Body still tense, he focused on Jack.

"It's okay," Jack said. "It's only Tom."

Nothing changed in Ethan's expression, as if everything else was still a threat, no matter what Jack said.

Jack got off him, confident despite the expression, and went to where Tom had fallen. The poor kid was curled up in a ball, arms wrapped around his head. The cut was bleeding freely. God, he was fucking lucky he got his arm up in time. Otherwise the knife would have cut right across his...

...Harry pulled back the collar of his shirt. Blood pumped from a deep wound just over his collarbone...

...throat.

"Fuck," Jack hissed. "Fuck, fuck, fuck." Frantically, he pulled off his shirt and pressed it to the cut on Tom's arm. It wasn't that bad, but he couldn't help himself. He had to stop the bleeding. Had to make sure Harry . . . *Tom* was okay. The boy whimpered and tried to curl up even tighter.

"Hey, Tom." Jack kept his voice calm even as his heart racketed around under his ribs. He wasn't going to lose anyone else. "It's Mr. Reed. Remember me? I'm not going to hurt you. Come on, sit up for me."

It took some coaxing, but eventually Tom unrolled enough for Jack to sit him up and get the shirt wrapped around his arm properly. Tom quivered the entire time, chin ducked to his chest, eyes squeezed shut. He was absolutely terrified, his cheeks streaked with new and dried tears, his pants damp from a loosened bladder. His clothes were different from the day Jack met him, thankfully, so he hadn't been with the mercs since then.

With the desperate need to make sure Tom was okay appeased, Jack stood. Ethan was gone, hopefully not too far and not too lost in his head to abandon Jack and Tom in the jungle.

Jack got Tom to his feet and keeping the boy close to his side, went in search of Ethan. He found him not long later, standing in a small clearing, fastidiously checking the Eagles. Head bowed over his quick, skilled hands, he nevertheless noted Jack and Tom's arrival.

"We should be clear to the house," he said, tone cold. "I'll take point."

Tom trembled, his eyes wide with shock as he watched Ethan walk away. Jack's heart, tight with the anticipation of emotions he knew would catch him when they were safe, clenched even further. Already scared witless, Tom had probably rushed towards someone he saw as safety. A friend. A mentor. Only to have that person come within inches of killing him.

"It's okay," Jack assured him. "He won't hurt you. It was just a mistake. Come on."

Tom didn't say a word all the way back to the house. Neither did Ethan. Jack was just grateful they moved fast and didn't encounter anymore opposition.

The rain hit just as they came into the clearing around the house. The horses, left in the yard for the day, were skittish. They didn't know if it was from the storm or intruders, so Jack and Tom kept to the trees while Ethan scouted ahead. Fifteen minutes later, he waved them out of cover and led them to the house.

Unlocking the door, he motioned Jack and Tom inside. "I'll get the horses settled."

Jack agreed and guided the wilting boy inside. Tom was shivering from shock and the rain, his eyes glazed and head hanging. Jack got him in the shower, warm water washing over his listless body, while Jack found something for him to wear. Warmed up and dressed in a pair of Ethan's shorts held up by a hastily adjusted belt, Jack carefully cleaned Tom's arm, gently probing for what had happened with the mercs. In broken English, Tom explained that the strangers had come looking for someone who knew where the hidden house was. Locals had sent them to Tom. Loyal to his friend, Mr. Saint, the boy had refused, but he was a kid against ten mercenaries, and they forced him along. The washed-out road had stopped them going directly to the house, and because Tom didn't know how to get there, otherwise, the bastards started searching on foot, dragging the boy along with them as a hostage.

Leaving Tom tucked up in the big bed, Jack went back downstairs. Ethan had come in and was making up one of the couches with sheets and spare pillows.

"Are we secure?" Jack asked, wary of getting too close. Ethan still had his killer-mask in place, his movements short and sharp.

"Yes. Even if there are more of them, we're safe in here." He finished with the sheets and stepped back. "For you. I'll take the watch." Turning on his heel, he stalked to the dining table and turned a chair out. There was already an arsenal laid out on the table top.

Ignoring the couch, Jack followed him. "I think we're good for now, at least." He told him Tom's story.

Ethan nodded once and settled in for his watch.

The rain had washed some of the camouflaging dirt off and Ethan must have attempted to clean more away in the stable. A few smudges remained around the corners of his jaw, the side of neck and across the exposed portion of his chest. Jack dampened a washcloth in the downstairs toilet sink and held it out for him.

Ethan stared at it for a moment, then put down the Eagle and took it. While he wiped at the last of the dirt, Jack set the kettle on the stovetop and the coffee maker to humming. His hands shook a little bit as he set the mugs on the granite countertop, the withdrawal of the adrenaline leaving him in that weird limbo between excitement and collapse. Opening the cutlery drawer, his heart thumped at the sight of the knives, images of other knives sweeping over soft flesh swamping him for a second.

"Jack?"

Blinking, Jack focused on the drawer he'd involuntarily slammed shut. "Shit." He leaned on the counter, waiting for his heart to settle.

"Jack?" Ethan came up beside him. The Eagle was back in his hand, but the other was free and raised towards him, as if he wanted to touch but wasn't sure.

Feeling exactly the same way, Jack turned back to making the drinks. "It's okay. I'm fine."

After a moment, Ethan tucked the gun into the back of his pants and fetched the milk. In silence, they finished preparing their drinks and returned to the dining table. Jack surveyed the gathered arsenal—which included an RPG-7 launcher complete with PG-7VR warhead—and found a box of ammo suitable for the P8. Falling back into something he knew so well it numbed his thoughts, he fed bullets into the gun's mags. Once that was done, he checked over a couple of carbines.

"Will Tom be all right?"

The quiet words stalled Jack's part-curious, part-wary reach for the shoulder-mounted RPG launcher. Ethan focused on cleaning one of the Eagles, the other lying whole and ready, close by his hand. He hadn't put his glasses back on and at this angle, all Jack saw of his eyes were fans of black lashes against his pale cheeks.

"Yeah," Jack answered, just as softly. "The cut will heal fine, as long as it doesn't get infected."

Ethan nodded, but said, "I meant, is he going to be all right after being taken hostage and . . . hurt by me."

"It was an accident. He knows that."

Motions snappy and curt, Ethan shook his head in mute denial.

"Ethan, it's not your fault. It was a bad situation. Tom shouldn't have rushed out like that. As much as we all wish it wasn't, friendly fire is a thing we have to deal with."

Ethan flinched. For the barest second, he touched fingertips to the scar on his chest, an exit wound from a bullet fired at his back. Silently screaming for an explanation, Jack just filed it away with all the other things he knew Ethan wasn't ready to tell him.

"It was a mistake," Jack continued calmly. "That's all."

Lips firming into a tight line, Ethan nodded. He concentrated on running a cleaning brush down the barrel of the Eagle. They worked quietly for a while, sipping drinks quickly going cold, listening keenly to the rain beating on the roof, alert for any sound that would indicate they weren't alone on the mountain.

"It wasn't," Ethan murmured, clicking the Eagle back together. "I knew exactly what I was doing. We were under attack and that's what I do. Eliminate threats. It's all I know how to do."

Jack stared at him. He wanted to say, "It's not," and "Don't be stupid," and "You're so much more than that," but in that moment, he finally understood what he wanted from Ethan, what he *needed* in order to move forward with him. So instead, what popped out was, "Live with me."

CHAPTER TEN

E than froze, then slowly looked up to meet his gaze. "Pardon?"

Just as shocked, Jack swallowed hard and repeated, "Live with me." Saying it intentionally only solidified it in his heart. "Move into my place. Don't just come for a visit. Come forever."

White eyes bored into him for a moment longer, then Ethan shoved away from the table, grabbed up the half-empty mugs and went into the kitchen. Tired of tiptoeing around Ethan's issues, Jack followed. In the narrow space, Ethan tried to evade him, but was quickly caught against the solid front of the fridge. A full body press to stop him from getting leverage, arms held tight to his sides.

"Don't," Ethan ground out, struggling against Jack's weight.

"Don't what?" Jack tried hard to not get angry. "You told me not that long ago I couldn't ask you to not care for me. Well, Ethan, this is me caring for you. A lot. So much so I can't keep doing what we've been doing all these months. This stop and start thing we have isn't a relationship. I don't want to be constantly wondering if you're ever coming back when you leave. I don't want to only see you for a couple of days every now and then. I want more. I need more."

"Why?" It came out as a hiss. "I don't understand why you would want *me* that close to you." He redoubled his efforts to get free.

Rather than have Ethan hurt himself, Jack let him go. Ethan rocketed away and was halfway across the house before he stopped. At least he was still inside this time, standing next to the piano, shoulders stiff, hands clenched at his sides. Head bowed, chest hitching as he struggled to breathe, or to not scream, and completely weapon-less. For the first time, Ethan Blade looked vulnerable.

Recalling Ethan say "Me," when Jack asked him what was wrong, and how pursuing the subject had sent Ethan into a full retreat, Jack went as far as the table. He wanted to be closer but feared pushing him further away.

"You know why I want you with me," he said evenly. "All those reasons I gave you right at the start of our little agreement, plus everything that's happened since then. Including today. It's because I trust you and I think I—"

Ethan cut him off with a sharp gesture. "Tom trusted me, and I hurt him, Jack."

"Jesus, Ethan. He trusts you still. Tom knows you didn't mean to hurt him. That it was a—"

"It wasn't a mistake." His voice rose to drown out Jack's. "I had a knife and I meant to kill. I would have if you hadn't stopped—"

"We all have knives." Anger bubbling up again, Jack shouted over him. "All of us! That's all any of us are. We're just a bunch of knives waiting to cut anyone who gets too close. Our insecurities. Our weaknesses, prejudices, arrogance. Everything that makes us who we are is a knife you can use to hurt someone else. God fucking knows I've hurt everyone around me. Family, friends, lovers. You. And they've hurt me. Stabbed me in the fucking heart." His voice broke on the last word and he realised how loud he'd been. Realised he had tears building. Taking a deep breath, he wiped them away with the back of one hand. "But that's what being close to someone means. You accept the risk of being hurt, of causing the pain. And you learn together how not to hurt each other. *That* is why I want you with me. Because I know you don't want to hurt me. Or Tom. Or anyone else."

Ethan grunted sourly.

"Yeah, okay," Jack agreed, anger conceding to wry sarcasm. "Anyone who doesn't deserve it."

Eyes closing, Ethan tipped his head back and took several deep breaths. "Jack, I understand what you're saying, but I don't—"

"Mr. Saint!"

They both spun to see Tom clattering down the stairs from the loft. He was in a flat panic, eyes wide, arms flailing. He missed the bottom step and crashed heavily to the floor. Before Jack got more than two steps towards him, he was up and lunging for the kitchen counter. And the shield remote.

"Mr. Saint," he gasped as the shields clanked and started rising. "They're here!"

In the seconds it took Jack to turn back to the window, he heard it. The pounding of the rain on the roof had morphed into an all too familiar thumping. Caught up in the argument, he had failed to notice the changes outside the house. Ethan was just as surprised, gaping at the view through the huge window.

Perfectly framed against the grey clouds, a black chopper swept past their position. It was an old Huey fitted with side-mounted guns. This wasn't a sightseeing tour. It had to be Khun Sein, looking for his mercenaries or just making sure the job was done.

Tom sprinted right past Jack and threw himself at Ethan's back. Arms around his waist, Tom tucked his face into Ethan's spine as if the man could protect him from anything.

Including an aerial assault.

"Get the shields down," Ethan shouted as the chopper swung around and hovered right outside the window.

All of Jack's lingering anger crystallised in an instant. All the pain he'd seen, that he'd *felt*, in Ethan over hurting Tom, over believing he wasn't good enough for Jack, that he wasn't a good person, honed his anger into a single point. A point he focused on the bastards responsible for the most immediate hurt.

As the chopper settled into position, Jack grabbed the RPG-7 launcher, slammed the warhead home and lifted it to his shoulder.

The guns on the sides of the chopper spat bullets and Ethan twisted, taking Tom to the floor, covering him with his own body. Glass crazing with repeated impacts, Jack aimed and, as the window shattered inwards, pressed the firing trigger. The small warhead whooshed through the house, out over the balcony and right into the nose of the chopper.

The explosion blew the last shards of glass out of the wall, superheated air rolling into the house. Jack dropped the launcher and hit the deck.

Silence came fast and eerily. Slowly, Jack uncovered his head and peered out. The airspace in front of the house was clear of the enemy. Just clouds and a thin trail of smoke curling upwards, quickly getting lost in the grey sky.

"Jack?"

"I'm good. You?"

Ethan stood, a shower of glass falling from his back. He nodded at Jack as he helped Tom to his feet. Swiftly, Ethan searched the boy for injuries. Tom swayed, and Ethan caught his shoulders, holding him steady. He spoke in soft Vietnamese. Big eyes focused on Ethan, Tom nodded bravely.

Not wanting anymore surprises, Jack found the remote—blown into the kitchen sink by the blast—and closed the shields. That done, he took stock of himself. Nothing serious, or even bigger than some small cuts from flying glass, and his hands weren't trembling too bad. Ethan approached, Tom trailing close behind. Wordlessly, Jack checked Ethan over thoroughly and finding no more than a few abrasions, pulled him into a hard embrace.

Ethan didn't hesitate. His arms closed around Jack with equal strength, his face smashing into Jack's shoulder.

After a long, soothing moment, Jack felt a tug on his shirt. Opening his eyes, he found Tom frowning up at him. Very seriously, Tom admonished him in Vietnamese, smacking his arm to emphasise his point, whatever it was. Against his neck, Ethan chuckled, the sound a little hysterical.

"What did he say?" Jack demanded.

Lifting his head, Ethan's smile was shy. "He wants to know why you aren't kissing me."

Blushing fiercely, Jack floundered. Tom rolled his eyes, gave him another smack, and stalked away.

Tom fell into an exhausted sleep not long later and Ethan tucked him into the unused couch-bed. Neither he nor Jack slept during the rest of the night. They tidied up as best they could, and Jack had to spend a couple of hours talking to Director Tan, reporting the hostile activity within his proximity. Tan didn't indicate his personal feelings on the events, just drily commented on the situation with Khun Sein—it had been his chopper and from the intelligence they'd gathered over the past day, the drug lord had been on board—and instructed Jack to leave the immediate area as quickly as possible and let the chips fall as they may.

"It'll be interesting," was all he said, when Jack asked Tan why.

Ethan agreed with Tan about Jack leaving.

"There's a smoking hulk sitting in the valley below us and ten bodies out in that jungle." Jack followed Ethan upstairs. "You can't take care of that on your own."

"I won't have to." Ethan opened the wardrobe and began removing Jack's gear.

Not wanting to argue so soon after making up, Jack took a moment to modulate his response. "Your *associates*?"

"Yes."

"Like the one who owns this place and knew we were here?" Jack threw himself onto the bed, quite ready to sulk.

Ethan stopped folding Jack's clothes and sat down beside him. "It wasn't her, Jack. She would never . . . hurt me like that."

Jack pulled him down so they were lying together, Ethan's head on his chest. "Tan thinks it was the smugglers I hitched a ride here with. I was careful, but you never know."

Ethan sighed. "Either way, I'm going to have a lot of explaining to do. Oh, blast!" He shot out of Jack's hold and off the bed. "The horses!"

Smiling at his hastily disappearing back, Jack got up and finished packing, resigned to the fact he had to leave. Ethan and Tan were right. If he stayed, his presence would only complicate matters.

The horses were jittery but otherwise okay and when dawn came, they saddled them and headed out. Tom rode double with Jack and Ethan lead the way, Eagle's at the ready, guiding Smith with his knees. The journey to the road was uneventful and they found Tom's Jeep where he'd left it near the washout. Alongside it was another 4WD which had carried the mercs who hadn't fit in the Jeep. Ethan gave the Jeep a complete going over before pronouncing it secure. Tom insisted on giving it another check, though.

"He'll be okay," Jack assured Ethan as they watched over the boy. "I'll make sure he gets home. And I've asked Tan to have one of our people check on him, see if he needs help dealing with any of it."

"Thank you, Jack." There was still pain in his voice, but there was acceptance as well.

Wanting to hold him but knowing it wouldn't be allowed while they weren't one hundred percent secure, Jack settled for saying, "You'll be okay, too, you know. You're a good man, Ethan. You wouldn't care about Tom the way you do if you weren't. Or me."

Once again hidden behind his sunglasses, Ethan nodded. Then he was hugging Jack.

Startled, it took Jack a moment to respond, but he did, pulling him close and feeling the urge to do silly things again.

"Yes," Ethan whispered.

"Yes, what? Yes, you'll be okay? Yes, you care for me?"

Ethan huffed. "Yes to all that. And yes, I'll come to Sydney. Not for a visit, but for good."

Jack's chest grenade went off with a deafening boom. He hadn't forgotten his impulsive offer, but he hadn't mentioned it again for fear of scaring Ethan away. Arms tightening, he managed, "When?"

Laugh muffled in Jack's neck, Ethan said, "When I've finished cleaning up here."

"I need a definite time frame, Blade. Have to know when to get the place clean."

Ethan pulled back enough to look at him and smiled. "I don't know yet. A couple of weeks, perhaps a month." The smile melted into a serious expression. "I don't think we should be in contact during that time. I have to find out what happened here and it may be best for all concerned if it appears we're not together."

As much as he wanted to protest, Jack agreed. "So, I'm just going to come home from work one day and find you in my apartment? Maybe wearing a ribbon?"

Cheeks flaming, Ethan hid his face against Jack's shoulder.

"Mr. Saint! Mr. Reed!" Tom tapped the steering wheel impatiently. "No time for hanky-panky. Let's go!"

Sighing, Jack grumbled, "I better go before he leaves me here."

Ethan smiled. "See you soon."

"I better."

ACKNOWLEDGEMENTS

And so this little story arc comes to an end. Jack and Ethan will be back in two more novels as action-packed and intriguing as the first. I have, however, loved taking this slight detour on their journey to get to know them better and to see how they work through their differences to end up as they have.

I have to thank the usual suspects, Allison Temple, Erin McLellan and Layla Reyne. You are all invaluable and please don't get tired of me too soon!

And you, dear reader, a massive and heartfelt thank you for sticking around while I got my act together. My deepest wish is that you get as much enjoyment from these stories as I got writing them.

ALSO BY L.J. HAYWARD

DEATH AND THE DEVIL

Where Death Meets the Devil – Jack Reardon, former SAS soldier and current Australian Meta-State asset, has seen some messy battles. But "messy" takes on a whole new meaning when he finds himself tied to a chair in a torture shack, his cover blown wide open, all thanks to notorious killer-for-hire Ethan Blade.

Why the Devil Stalks Death – Jack Reardon uncovers secrets for a living, and the Meta-State spy is pretty good at it. Or rather he thought so until he met Ethan Blade—assassin, warrior, enigma. The unlikely pair have decided to give living together a shot, but Jack's not entirely certain what he's gotten himself into—or exactly who he's in it with.

When Death Frees the Devil – Ethan is finally free. He's left the Cabal behind and embraced a civilian life with Jack, the man he loves. The only problem is that the Cabal isn't willing to let him go. A call in the middle of the night and a threat to Jack's family, and Ethan is back in the game. The only way out is to take on the organization that spent years warping his life.

NIGHT CALL

Blood Work – Matt Hawkins kills monsters for a living. Slay and pay. Werewolves, trolls, the occasional ghoul that gets a bit too big for its grave; but basically, whatever nasty critter crosses his path. Mostly, he kills vampires. While he's made something of a living out of it, he doesn't even need the promise of cash to take down a vampire. Sure, it's a nice bonus, but vampires are his personal crusade.

Demon Dei – It's been six months since the harrowing conclusion of *Blood Work* and Matt's waiting for the fiery repercussions. And waiting. And waiting. Even if no Big Bad wants revenge, shouldn't he be in hot demand? Like the lawyer who wins the unwinnable case. Or the mechanic who works out what that clunking noise is in your car. Instead, Matt finds himself struggling to maintain his career as the Night Caller. But things are about to get nasty in a big, big way.

Here Be Dragons – (short story) Sunday. Day of Rest. To anyone *not* Matt Hawkins, vampire-slayer extraordinaire, that is. A short story set in the world of Night Call, between the novels *Demon Dei* and *Rock Paper Sorcery*.

Rock Paper Sorcery – Vanquishing vampire Primals and defeating Demon Lords is one thing. They're dangerous in an obvious, tooth and claw way. But when a sorcerer comes to town chasing a murderous rogue, Matt Hawkins is faced with something he doesn't know how to deal with—competition as the city's resident badarse supernatural warrior.

ABOUT THE AUTHOR

L.J. Hayward has been telling stories for most of her life, a good deal of them of the tall variety. She loves reading but doesn't seem to have enough time between wanting to be a more disciplined writer, being the actual erratic writer she is, and working for dollars in a dungeon laboratory. She also lives on the Gold Coast in Queensland, but rarely sees a beach and can't surf, though she thinks living on a houseboat might be fun. At least then she'd have an excuse to get a cat.

Visit L.J. at her website, ljhayward.com; on Twitter, @ljhayward; or on Goodreads, goodreads.com/L.J.Hayward.